DEADLY INTENT

Lynda La Plante

SIMON & SCHUSTER

London • New York • Toronto • Sydney

First published in Great Britain by Simon & Schuster UK Ltd, 2008
A CBS COMPANY

Copyright © Lynda La Plante, 2008

1 3 5 7 9 10 8 6 4 2

Simon & Schuster UK Ltd
222 Gray's Inn Road
London WC1X 8HB

www.simonsays.co.uk

Simon & Schuster Australia
Sydney

A CIP catalogue record for this book is
available from the British Library

Hardback ISBN: 978-0-7432-9574-1
Trade Paperback ISBN: 978-0-7432-9575-8

Typeset by Rowland Phototypesetting Ltd, Bury St Edmunds, Suffolk
Printed and bound in Great Britain by CPI Mackays, Chatham, Kent

This book is dedicated to a
talented director and dear
friend, Ferdie Fairfax, who
will be sadly missed and
always remembered.

Acknowledgements

My gratitude to all those who gave their valuable time to help me with research on *Deadly Intent*.

With special thanks to Kara Manley and my committed team at La Plante Productions: Liz Thorburn, Richard Dobbs, Noel Farragher and especially Cass Sutherland and Nicole Muldowney for their invaluable assistance and advice. Thanks also to Stephen Ross, Andrew Bennett-Smith and Marko Lens.

To my literary agent Gill Coleridge and all at Rogers, Coleridge & White, I give huge thanks; they are a constant encouragement to me. To my publishers Ian Chapman and Suzanne Baboneau and to everyone at Simon & Schuster, especially Nigel Stoneman. I am very happy to be working with such a terrific company.

Chapter One

Monterrey, Mexico is not to be confused with Monterey, California. This Monterrey is a border town whose main industry and source of employment is a massive tile factory. Monterrey is where Dr Manuel Mendosa has his small surgical clinic. His father had also been a surgeon, attached to the American army in Vietnam. He always maintained that his finest work had been done during the war, as he was able to finesse his reconstructive surgical abilities on the burned and disfigured soldiers. His only son, Manuel, followed in his footsteps and became a qualified plastic surgeon. He had, under his father's watchful eye, opened a practice in Mexico City. After his father's death, Manuel had become addicted to drugs and sunk into debt. Accused of malpractice, he had gone into hiding. Manuel had then been coerced into operating on a known felon, altering the man's features to enable him to escape imprisonment.

Now, known in the underworld for his prowess, he was forced into performing many similar surgical operations. He was paid highly for his skill and silence, but he was nevertheless trapped and in constant fear for his life, should he ever refuse a request.

When Manuel received a call from a Mr Smith, he

knew this was yet another 'operation' requiring his skill as a surgeon. He knew, too, that his life would depend upon his silence.

Mr Smith was not American but English, and his arrival at the clinic, although expected, was met with trepidation. The patient was so tall he had to stoop to enter the small reception room. He was well-dressed in a cream-coloured suit and a white T-shirt. He carried a thin leather briefcase.

If Manuel felt trepidation, so did his new client. Miles from anywhere in the border town, he had arranged the meeting on word of mouth, hearing that Manuel was a genius. He had not expected to confront one of the most handsome men he had ever seen. Manuel was slender with beautiful artistic hands, dark hair swept back from a high forehead, every feature of his face chiselled, teeth white and gleaming. His pale blue cotton shirt with its priest collar, almost like a surgeon's short gown, was obviously handmade. The colour made his wide, clear eyes even bluer, like azure.

He was sitting expectantly as Mr Smith entered.

'Good morning,' the Englishman said.

'You needed to see me?' Manuel said quietly, in fluent English.

'Yes. That is correct.'

'You were recommended?'

'Yes. By . . .'

The Englishman said two names that sent chills down Manuel's stiff spine. He knew who they were – men he could not refuse.

'I will pay you in dollars.'

Manuel nodded and watched as the big man sat uncomfortably on one of the hard chairs in the reception area. He had no receptionist and no nurses. Only one person assisted him in his operations – an elderly Mexican, Enrico, who had worked alongside his father.

'I will need to take some particulars and discuss exactly what is required.'

'Obviously.'

Manuel liked his deep resonant voice, the way he appeared respectful. And yet there was a domineering confidence about him.

'Firstly, may I ask your age?'

'Sixty.'

Manuel leaned forward and picked up a clipboard from the coffee table.

'Do you suffer from high blood pressure?'

'Slightly.'

'Have you had any recent operations?'

'No.'

'Do you have any heart problems?'

'No.'

'Do you have any allergies?'

'No.'

'No allergic reactions to antibiotics?'

'None.'

Manuel used a slim silver pen to write on his clipboard.

'Have you any blood disorders?'

'No.'

'Do you have transport?'

'Yes.'

'Somewhere to recover after surgery?'

'Yes.'

Manuel replaced the board onto the coffee-table.

'Now I need to discuss the exact surgical requirements and modifications you would like me to achieve.'

Mr Smith had started to sweat in the overheated reception; it was eighty degrees outside and there was no air-conditioning in the room. Compared to Manuel, he felt overweight and clumsy.

'I need to look younger.'

Manuel nodded, watching as Mr Smith removed from his pocket a large envelope. He took out a thin folded piece of paper.

'Let me start with the liposuction. I want you to remove the excess fat from my stomach, armpits and chest area, and I want my buttocks lifted, so they are tighter and stronger. I'll leave it up to you whether implants are required.'

Manuel nodded. That part of the procedure was simple.

'I will also want my hands looked at, get rid of the age spots, get my fingerprints lasered.'

Manuel nodded and then leaned forward to pick up his clipboard again. He turned over the top page and started jotting down notes.

'How tall are you?' he asked.

'Six feet three and a half.'

'Your weight?'

'Nineteen and a half stone.'

Manuel tapped the silver pen against his perfect teeth as he calculated what the weight was in kilos. Mr Smith watched him, struck again by his handsomeness. He wondered if he was homosexual. Manuel wore no wedding ring, no jewellery of any kind, not even a wristwatch, and he seemed to remain cool, not perspiring at all in the oppressive heat.

'You want me to continue?'

'Yes.'

'Right. I want a new face. Nose, cheek implants, maybe even a little chin enhancement, and I want the mole on my right cheek removed.'

Manuel looked up and stared hard as Mr Smith concentrated on the notepaper. He could see there were some drawings on it. Mr Smith was showing his age. His grey hair, worn in a ponytail, was thinning, he had a hooked nose. His face had slight jowls and was heavily lined, as if he had spent many years in the sun. His lips were thin and his teeth stained yellowish from smoking. His eyes were dark brown and lined at the corners with hooded lids. Yet he was still what one would describe as handsome – or had been at one time.

'May I see that?' Manuel asked, with his hand out-stretched.

Mr Smith passed over the single sheet of paper. Manuel studied it for a considerable time. There were a number of drawings and indications of what plastic surgery was wanted.

'This is very extensive and invasive surgery, Mr Smith.'

'I'm aware of that.'

'When do you want to begin?'

'After this meeting.'

Manuel continued making his own notes. It was just after ten o'clock in the morning.

'I also want it all done in one session.'

'That will be impossible. The liposuction alone will take considerable time and it will be painful, requiring a few days to settle before the bandages can be removed. You will also need to wear elastic surgical bandages to maintain the tightness of the skin.'

'Yes, I know.'

'So may I suggest we start with the less invasive surgery

and then judge how soon you would be fit enough to begin everything else?'

'No. I want everything done as soon as possible. I've brought with me the required amount of Fentanyl in preference to any other anaesthetic. Are you familiar with this type of—?'

Manuel interrupted him. 'I'm aware of the use of Fentanyl for emergency surgery and that it is now quite commonly used in many hospitals as a fast means of pain blockage. I know how quickly, unlike most anaesthetics, it leaves the system. But it's a very potent opiate that can create respiratory depression if over-subscribed. It can be used as an intravenous anaesthetic, but I've never employed it.'

'I will determine how much I need.'

'That is a great risk, Mr Smith, and one I am not prepared to take. You will require a general anaesthetic, but it is up to you if you wish to use the Fentanyl as a means of pain relief.'

Manuel put his silver pen back into the breast pocket of his shirt. He hoped his request for a general anaesthetic would make his client change his mind. It didn't.

'Very well. If that's what you advise.'

'Have you eaten anything today?'

'No, not since midnight.'

Manuel leaned over to a pocket built into the side of the chair.

'I will need to call my assistant,' he said.

Mr Smith noticed for the first time that Manuel was sitting in a wheelchair and it freaked him.

'Is that a wheelchair?'

Manuel glanced towards him as he dialled. 'One of my own designs – very light and battery controlled.'

'You're a cripple?'

Manuel gave a strange half-smile. 'Does it worry you? I do not operate with my feet, but if it concerns you . . .'

'What's the matter with you?'

Manuel had dialled a number on his mobile phone, but he didn't connect the call.

'I was addicted to crack cocaine. My spine was injured in a fall.'

'Are you still an addict?'

'I will be for the rest of my life, but I am no longer a user. I've been clean for four years.' He held the phone up. 'Have you changed your mind?'

Mr Smith hesitated and then gave a curt shake of his head.

'Make the call,' he said.

Manuel wished he had walked out, but his client was obviously satisfied, so he called Enrico to come to the surgery.

In contrast to the reception room, the adjoining operating theatre was cold. Mr Smith felt every hair on his body tingle. He was instructed to use a small shower room to scrub his body clean with the disinfectant provided.

Then Manuel introduced Enrico, who led Mr Smith to the table. He had already prepared a row of needles and the vials of Fentanyl. He checked the client's heart rate and blood pressure, which he noted was high – 180 over 120. He prepared a vein catheter for Mr Smith's right hand and found a vein easily, attaching it for the anaesthetic to be given. An aspirator machine stood ready for the liposuction; large packs of gauze and two big bottles of Xylocaine and adrenalin, plus dark bottles

7

of iodine were at hand. Different rubber tubes were ready to connect to the cannula tubes, to attach to the liposuction machine. Next, Enrico opened Mr Smith's gown and, using a paintbrush, painted three quadrants, centre of his stomach and to both sides.

He checked that there was an oxygen mask ready and a resuscitation machine in full working order. He attached a small clip onto Mr Smith's index finger, which led to a machine to enable them to read the heartbeat. All of this was completed in total silence.

Enrico then went to assist Manuel to scrub up in a large sink. Manuel let him scrub both his hands with alcohol gel and wheel him to the trolley so he could open the paper-wrapped gloves.

'Do you wish to inject yourself?' Manuel asked his client. It took a while for Mr Smith to measure the exact amount before clenching his left fist and then watching as Enrico adeptly found a strong vein and injected him. It was very fast; Mr Smith just had time to lie back before he felt the warmth spreading throughout his body.

'You can get started,' he said, his voice slurred.

He eventually became used to the hideous sound of the suction pump working. The incisions for the cannula tubes pressed deeply and painfully into the fat. Enrico used his foot to keep the pump working as the fat drained into two big vats. It took three and a half hours. At one point Manuel was concerned: Mr Smith's pulse-rate was at 98. He used the oxygen mask and waited for the pulse to return to normal.

Manuel worked quickly, inserting the tubes and pumping out the fatty tissue. For him, it was a tedious, long drawn-out procedure. He sat making drawings for the facial work he was asked to complete. Twice during the liposuction Enrico gestured for Manuel to double-check their patient; he also needed his help to turn the big man over to take the fat from his buttocks. Manuel, for all his incapacity, was very strong in the upper part of his body, and together they had been able to move him.

One of the most strenuous parts of the suction process was drawing on the tight elastic bandages to make sure the body parts, where the fat had been removed, were held in place. The gauze was wrapped around first, then the bandages, then an elastic corset eased over the belly and chest. In truth the wrapping this time was perhaps too tight, but Mr Smith was a very big man and Manuel reckoned he was so macho, he would be able to deal with the constrictions and the painful bruising he was going to feel. They had removed an astonishing two and half litres of body fat. The next process was to tighten his buttocks. A banana-shaped incision was to be made across each cheek. Manuel calculated that he would spend at least an hour and a half on each, due to the number of internal stitches required layer by layer. The first general anaesthetic was administered.

Whatever pain he felt, three hours later Mr Smith sat up asking for water. He drank thirstily before resting back and closing his eyes. His entire body felt as if it had been run over by a ten-ton truck. The pain was making his head throb; it was excruciating and he could find no comfort, even lying on his side.

'How long do you need before you work on my face?' he asked hoarsely.

Manuel leaned close to him, checking his pulse.

'I really cannot begin any more surgery. I suggest you

9

rest for two days. Then we will be able to remove these bandages so you will be more comfortable.'

'I don't have that amount of time. I want it done today.'

'I have to refuse. Your blood pressure was very high and you will need to have a second general anaesthetic. It will be impossible to operate using only Fentanyl.'

'You get another ten thousand dollars if you continue.'

'It is too much of a risk. The work will take at the very least three hours. I have to virtually lift your entire face off and . . .'

'Just do it.'

'I advise you to rest at least for tonight and return tomorrow.'

'*Do it!*' the man hissed. He needed to be awake, to make sure he did not overdose on the Fentanyl. He trusted no one but himself to measure it. The pain dulled by the Fentanyl, he closed his eyes.

Enrico was silent, as usual, as he cleaned up and removed the bloody gauze pads. He was surprised when Manuel asked if he could remain all night at the surgery. He gave a small nod of his head and continued clearing up.

When Manuel returned to the table, Mr Smith was already lying motionless, his eyes closed.

'He is mad,' Enrico whispered.

'For Jesus' sake, don't let him die on us. And make me some strong black coffee.' Manuel raised his electric wheelchair to its maximum height. He would now be able to work from above the sleeping man's head and move easily around to the left and right of the table.

Using a black marker pen to draw the lines on Mr

Smith's face where he wished to cut, Manuel lifted both eyebrows up and took a section from the brow. He marked the upper and lower lids and made a line around both ears for an auricular incision. He then marked the lips to augment with silicone and put dotted marks between the eyes for Botox.

As he worked, he drank two small cups of thick black coffee, with heaped spoonfuls of sugar. His patient remained oblivious, eyes closed and sleeping.

Enrico prepared the prosthetic implants for the cheeks and chin, and when Manuel was ready, he administered the second general anaesthetic. It was, by now, almost six o'clock and cooler outside, but as always Manuel maintained a very low temperature in the operating room. They both went through the same procedure of scrubbing up, and now that the anaesthetic had kicked in, work began.

The first incision was to the eyebrows. Manuel removed a slice, like a small section of orange, drawing the skin upwards, and stretching out the lines in the forehead. This took a lot of pulling and stretching before he was satisfied. Then he cut a long line from behind the ear, continuing down to the chin. He drew up the scraggy skin of the neck, again removing a slice like another section of orange, so he could restitch and pull tightly back towards the lobes of the ears. He also implanted a small section of what looked and almost felt like a sponge. He inserted a piece into the lower chin, then used a thin flattening spatula to ease up two more sections to rest over each of the cheekbones, working with the finest suture scissors. He removed the mole from Mr Smith's right cheek and gave two neat stitches, before he began work on his nose.

Twice, Manuel became concerned as his patient's pulse shot up; his heart-rate was worrying too and it was a while before he felt he could continue. Enrico gave Mr Smith more oxygen until they were both satisfied that his pulse-rate was not life-threatening.

The bridge of the nose had a scar; his nose must have been broken at one time. Manuel broke it again and began reshaping and cutting around the nostrils. He was tired; it had been concentrated work and Enrico kept wiping his brow with an iced cloth.

'Only eyelids to go now,' he murmured.

The two men worked well together, Manuel checking his drawings and the ink markings he had made to Mr Smith's face. He didn't want to take too much from the eyelids, and as he was doing both top and bottom, it was imperative he took only his exact measurements. He couldn't remove the age lines from around the eyes completely, nor the two lines from the nostrils down to the lips, known as puppet lines. These he injected with Botox and collagen, and then at last it was down to the bandages.

Mr Smith did not regain consciousness until his head was tightly bandaged. He resembled something out of an old-fashioned horror movie. Only his puffy, bloodshot eyes and his swollen lips could be seen. He could not dress himself, as his hands had been operated on and laser treatment carried out on his fingertips. Enrico had to ease him into an old wheelchair to take him out into the reception.

Mr Smith was hardly holding it together due to the waves of pain that swept over his entire body. There seemed not an inch of him that didn't scream out. He said hardly a word, as Enrico wheeled him out into the early evening sun; he had been in surgery for over ten hours. A white, four-door Mercedes with tinted windows was parked outside. The driver had been waiting all day; his face was sweaty and his cheap black suit wrinkled and creased. His dark greasy hair was combed back and hung in a wave at his collar.

Enrico and the driver helped Mr Smith into the back seat. He let out soft moans of pain, but he didn't speak, just lay on his side, his legs curled up.

Manuel watched the Mercedes drawing away. He had learned over the years never to ask questions or get into even the briefest conversation with the drivers. It would be two days before he could check on the liposuction treatment and a further five days to examine and remove stitches. It would therefore be seven days before he was paid.

'Mr Smith' was hurried through the lobby of the Santa Cruz Hotel in the wheelchair. He was occupying the so-called penthouse suite. He found it difficult to even sit on the bed and he hadn't the strength to take off his clothes. He finally managed to ease himself down, thankful for the soft pillows.

The driver left the hotel with instructions to collect him in seven days.

Mr Smith remained lying on the bed for twenty-four hours, before he managed to undress. Beside the bed were an array of bottles of water, vitamins and antibiotics, and a large amount of arnica tablets. He consumed them in handfuls, as they helped the bruising, but ate nothing else, just drank bottle after bottle of the water and only moved to go to the bathroom. He was in constant pain and found it difficult to find a single position to lie in that didn't make him feel as if his body was on fire. Not only did the elastic bandages around his body feel too tight, but the dressings on his scalp and face were so uncomfortable that he found it difficult to breathe. His head throbbed. The discomfort didn't ease for forty-eight hours and he had, once again, injected himself with Fentanyl.

Manuel and Enrico entered the hotel suite to find Mr Smith lying on the bed with a towel wrapped loosely around him. Manuel watched as Enrico removed the wrappings from his body. The bandages were very bloody, as there had been some leakage. The torso was black from the bruises and yet the small incisions made for the tubes were healing well. Manuel placed small strips of Elastoplast over the incisions and then waited as Enrico cleaned up the bloody bandages and gauze. He unwrapped the bandages from around Mr Smith's head, checked his stitches were healing and instructed Enrico to rebandage.

'You are healing very well, Mr Smith.'

'My arse feels like I got some rabid animal chewing on it!'

Neither Manuel nor Enrico showed they were amused; they left as quickly as possible.

On the fourth day, Mr Smith got up and walked around the suite. It was painful but he forced himself to move. He still did not eat but sent down for more water, lemons and honey, and continued to use his Fentanyl stash to give him relief and help him sleep.

By day seven he was feeling stronger. Fully dressed, he walked down through the hotel reception to meet his driver.

Manuel was waiting at the surgery. He could see that his patient was making a remarkable recovery and could walk unaided from the car. They went straight into the operating room; Enrico had already prepared a tray with disinfectant swabs and needle-sharp scissors. There were still extensive black bruises almost covering the patient's entire torso. However, the small incisions were healing well, and Enrico cleaned them and replaced the small round plasters. Manuel then asked his client to sit in a chair beneath a strong lamp, and he personally unwound the head bandages. The fine, delicate stitches were snipped one by one and Mr Smith could hear a faint sound as each was placed into a stainless steel bowl. Once the last area of plaster across the nose had been removed, Manuel leaned close to inspect his work.

'Good, very good.'

Mr Smith examined himself in a mirror. His face was puffy and the scars were still red, but none were infected, and within hours the narrow bridge of his nose would broaden. His thinning hair was dirty and the ponytail was caked in blood. He had not had a total browlift because of his receding hair; hair plugs would have made the skin too stretched and raw.

'How soon can I get plugs done for a hairline?' he asked Manuel.

'In a couple of weeks, I would suggest.'

'What about the teeth? I can begin a series of dental implants, can't I?'

'Yes, of course.'

Manuel was astonished that his patient gave no re-action to his finished work. It was, even by his standards, a superb transformation. The man hardly resembled himself, yet he seemed intent only on leaving as quickly

15

as possible. Manuel was paid twenty-five thousand dollars in used notes, packed into a large brown envelope. Smiling, Mr Smith passed over a second envelope containing the extra ten thousand dollars.

Manuel placed the money into the pocket of his wheelchair without counting it. Then Mr Smith surprised him. He was about to click shut the briefcase when he hesitated and removed a small square box which he passed over to Manuel.

'A little extra gift,' he said. 'Enjoy . . .'

He strolled out, albeit stiffly because the liposuction still made it uncomfortable to walk. His suit hung as if too large and he placed a cream cotton cap on his head to cover his scalp and donned a pair of dark sunglasses.

Back in his hotel room, Mr Smith spent almost an hour staring at his reflection in the dressing-table mirror. It was an amazing transformation: his chin and neck were taut and the cheek implants made his face look chiselled. His lips were still puffy but his nose was looking much better. Before, he had had an aquiline, almost hooked, nose; now it was small but perfectly straight.

After a much-needed shower, he looked again at his reflection. Gone was the beginning of a paunch and he had regained a muscular slenderness. In fact, he had dropped at least fifteen years; by the time he had his hair transplants and new teeth, he reckoned he would look no more than late forties or early fifties.

Enrico had returned home to his family. As ever, Manuel had been very generous, but he was concerned. The box had contained four vials of Fentanyl and when he had tried to take it, Manuel had snapped at him to leave it in the fridge. Fentanyl was unobtainable in Mexico and he feared that the young man, although clean for four years, might be tempted.

Mr Smith flew to Los Angeles and from there on to Brazil for the rest of his makeover. Although he was still feeling some twinges of pain, the worst of it was over. He did as Manuel instructed and waited another six weeks before he had a full transplant of hair, not grey, but dark brown, combed back from his forehead and cut into a shorter style. Now it was just below his collar, exactly as Manuel had worn his.

Lastly, he had a three-week session with a dental surgeon who implanted six back teeth and gave him what they termed in Hollywood 'the smile' makeover. By this time he had begun to work out, not too strenuously, but he wanted to retain his slenderness.

The entire 'operation' had taken almost three months and he was finally ready to return to England. Money was running out and he was about to make one of the biggest deals of his life. His luxurious life had been disrupted by a disastrous turn of events in the German and American money markets, leaving him on the verge of bankruptcy. Never one to dwell on misfortune, however, he was certain that he could – and would – once again return to the lifestyle he had grown accustomed to. With his new image, he was confident that he could remain undetected until his deals had been organised.

Leaving Brazil, he flew to Spain to arrange finances for a boat he had ordered to be brought into Puerto Banus. Money by now was a major problem; he had to get financed and fast, and it had to be cash. But he remained assured that he would be able to accomplish his deal. However, dealing with drug cartels from Columbia, he could not afford to make any mistakes.

One mistake would obviously have been his connection to Manuel, but as a man who had been around drugs and addicts for many years, he was sure that temptation would rid him of any risk from that quarter. He was correct. Enrico, not having heard from Manuel for over a week, went to the clinic. He knew by the accumulation of black flies in the overheated reception room that what he had feared had happened.

Due to the low temperature in the operating theatre, Manuel's body was not too decomposed. The still-handsome man sat in his chair, his dead eyes staring, as if at the open box of Fentanyl resting on his lap. He had used only one vial but that had been more than enough to stop his heart.

Mr Smith made arrangements to return to England. He doubted that he would have problems entering the UK and he was looking forward to 'going home' once more. He was also confident that, using one or other of his many passports, he would not be recognised, even by his own mother.

Chapter Two

Detective Inspector Anna Travis's relationship with James Langton was long over. Since she had last seen him, she had been assigned two other investigations. She had read about his promotion to Chief Superintendent and so knew that he was overseeing all the Murder Squad teams. She also knew that her most recent cases would have come her way on Langton's recommendation. Anna had been nervous about confronting him again, but neither investigation had created much media attention and Langton had not even made an appearance.

The small flat, however, which had been hers before he moved in, retained his strong presence. To get him out of her system completely, she knew she should find another place to live. She put the flat up for sale and, in a matter of weeks, had received a cash offer – which meant she had to hurry to find herself a new home.

It was a depressing experience. One apartment after the other was nowhere near as pleasant, or as well-maintained, as the one she was selling. Finally, she found what she wanted: a top-floor maisonette, part of a new development close to Tower Bridge, overlooking the Thames, it had one spacious bedroom with bathroom ensuite, an open-plan living room with kitchen and dining space, and views of the river from wraparound windows. A balcony ran the width of the main room, with space enough for a small table and two chairs. There were only seven other apartments below hers, then underground garage parking, with a lift to all floors. The security of the building was a major plus.

Anna spent several sleepless nights wondering whether she should take on the apartment, knowing it would be a stretch, with her salary, to manage the high mortgage payments. It was during one of these nights, sipping a glass of warm whiskey, that she realised how few friends she had. She could think of no one whom she could take to see the apartment. She was feeling lonely; the ghost of Langton kept resurfacing. He lived not too far away from her, in Kilburn. This move would be a clean break: no chance of running into him or his ex-wife. Anna took leave for two weeks to accommodate the sale and the move.

In the heat of the moment, Anna opened an account at John Lewis on Oxford Street and ordered new bedlinen as well as new blinds and rugs, as the floors were all stripped pine. She even went crazy and bought a massive plasma-screen TV. She coordinated all the removal crates, tagging and bagging everything as if it was a massive forensic exercise. On the day of the move, she was up at eight, what small items she could ferry in her Mini stacked up and ready to go.

Later, standing in front of her new windows, over-looking the river, surrounded by her unpacked belongings, Anna broke down. She didn't understand why she couldn't stop crying; all the upheaval of the past few weeks was over. Was it exhaustion or the fact that, if she wasn't careful, she could run into serious debt? Or was it because she felt just as lonely as before?

With a huge effort, she pushed herself into unloading her china and glass and finding homes for it in the sparkling new cupboards. She worked hour upon hour, determined to get everything unpacked and in position before she went back to work. Late that evening, she flopped down in a state of exhaustion on the new bed. The bubble wrap was still on the mattress, but she was too tired to take it off. She just wrapped her duvet round herself and crashed out.

A couple of hours later, she was woken by a loud foghorn and shot up in a panic. No one had mentioned that the river boats were similar to street traffic. Anna stood in her pyjamas, staring down at the dark river below, watching the lit-up boats passing back and forth. Mist hung like a grey cloud just above the water. She took a deep breath: it was a view worth taking in. Suddenly, she knew she had done the right thing. This was going to be a very special place to live.

At eight the next morning, Anna got back into her jeans and an old sweater, intending to have another bout of unpacking and settling in. She went down to the garage and was impressed by the array of expensive cars there: a Porsche, a Ferrari, two Range Rovers and a Lexus. Each tenant had their own allocated parking space and security key to enter and exit the garage. She decided that, when she was settled, she would call in on her neighbours below and introduce herself. In the meantime, she needed groceries. Unlike Maida Vale, where she had lived before, there were no small shops nearby, so Anna drove round, looking for the nearest shopping parade. She didn't find one, but saw a Starbucks open, so pulled up and parked.

Standing in line, Anna was irritated with herself: she should have asked the estate agent about shopping amenities. She would just have to find a supermarket later that day, and stock up. Armed with cappuccino and muffins, she returned to her car, only to find a traffic warden putting a ticket on the windscreen. She couldn't believe it; thank God the flat had its own car park. She swore. As she put the key into the ignition, her mobile rang.

'Travis,' she snapped, switching it onto speaker.

She listened as she drove home. They hadn't spared her a day over her two weeks' allocated leave before putting her on to a new case.

Back in the apartment, everywhere she looked were unpacked boxes; she would have to contact security to let in the various deliveries. By the time she had made these arrangements, and given her keys to Mr Burk, the belligerent security manager, she knew she was going to be at least an hour late for work.

Then she had problems with the garage gates. No matter how many times she pressed 'open', they remained firmly closed. She was about to ring the emergency buzzer when a handsome young man in a pinstriped suit appeared.

'Jesus Christ, don't tell me they're stuck again,' he said. He passed Anna and pressed the emergency buzzer. 'This is every other bloody morning.'

Anna gave a small smile. 'I'm Anna Travis; I've just moved in to the top-floor flat.'

He glanced towards her. 'James Fullford. I'm in 2B.' He turned back to the garage doors, hands on hips, and pressed the buzzer again.

A side door opened and Mr Burk appeared.

'They're stuck!' Fullford said angrily.

Burk — ex-Navy, with a barrel chest and short legs — gave a curt nod and crossed to the gates. He used a set of keys to open the gate manually, then reprogrammed the electric codes.

'How many times a week do you have to do that?' Fullford was still livid.

'They're new,' was all Burk said.

Fullford revved up his Porsche and drove out. Anna followed, realising this was something else that she should have checked out. She gave a small nod of thanks as she passed.

Anna arrived at the location in Chalk Farm almost an hour and a half after she had said she would be there. She knew little about the new case, bar the fact it was a shooting; a Murder Squad team were gathering at the site. She had also neglected to ask who was heading up the enquiry. It was extraordinary. After only a small amount of time out, her brain had stopped functioning. But she could see by the array of patrol cars, ambulances and uniformed officers cordoning off the area that she had the right place.

She parked as close as possible and showed her ID to a uniformed officer who directed her towards a block of graffiti-covered council flats, a section of which had been boarded up. Outside one of the flats, on the second floor, were numerous forensic officers in their white suits and masks, none of whom she recognised. She made her way up the stinking stone steps. Keeping her ID held up, she continued towards number 19.

The front door and the window beside it had been fortified, with heavy wooded slats nailed across them.

Anna presumed, by the look of the place, that drug dealers had taken it over. At the open front door, she looked into a squalid hallway: it was filthy, littered with broken bottles and discarded junk-food boxes. The big room off the hall, where all the action was taking place, was lit by arc lamps; cables were being dragged along the corridor by forensic officers.

Just as Anna reached the front door, DCI Carol Cunningham stepped out, pulling off rubber gloves. She was tall, broad-shouldered and dressed in a dark trouser suit with a white shirt. Her hair was almost a crew cut, and she had dark brown eyes, set in a square face, with a strong jawline. She wore no make-up. 'You DI Anna Travis?'

Anna was surprised by her voice; it was cultured and quite soft. 'Yes.'

'I'm DCI Cunningham, heading up this enquiry.'

'I'm sorry it took so long for me to get here, Ma'am.'

'So am I.'

'It's just that I have recently moved house, and—'

'Don't want to hear it. I'd like you in there to oversee the crime scene. Then get over to the incident room. We're set up in Chalk Farm Station.'

Anna removed a pair of rubber gloves from the box outside the front door, and put them on. She didn't see any white paper suits, so just picked her way down the hallway and over cables into the big main room.

The large bare space had the desolate appearance of a waiting room in hell. Despite police attempts to render it uninhabitable, the place had once more been taken over by dealers. A separate room leading off this main one was the secure headquarters where the dealers hung out and kept their merchandise, protected by a strongly reinforced interior door with a crude grille hacked into it, giving a view of anyone in the outer room. This door was splintered by bullet-holes. An officer was dusting and checking for cartridges while others were bagging and tagging various items. She still had not seen anyone whom she recognised.

The body of a man of about forty years of age lay on the bare boards a little way from her. His face and chest area, from what Anna could see, had taken the impact of the bullets. He was lying face down, his arms spread out in front of him. He was not some junkie; he was, in fact, exceptionally well-dressed in a smart suit. His white shirt, now covered in bloodstains, looked as if it had been pristine, and he wore gold cufflinks. Even his shoes were classy loafers.

Anna stepped over the dead man and past forensic, who were checking out the blood spattering. Filthy blankets and sleeping bags were arranged against the walls. A fire had been built in the centre of the room; there was a disposable barbecue with burned-out coals. Used takeaway cartons, bottles and cans were also strewn around.

She gingerly sidestepped the junk to reach an officer who was testing for prints around a grimy window. Anna peered out and saw a balcony below – so someone could escape that way, if they had a head for heights and were stoned enough to play at Spiderman.

'What went down here?' she asked.

He stopped dusting and looked at her over his mask. 'Maybe a drug deal that went wrong. Victim appeared to have been behind the door, waiting to get served. He took hits to the face and upper chest. We think our shooter maybe got out via the window.'

'He doesn't look like the usual druggie.'

'No, I know. I think we got an ID. I know the boss took stuff away. They'll be taking him any minute.'

'Thank you.'

'You're Anna Travis, right?'

'Yes?'

'Thought so. You were late. Mind if I give you a tip? DCI Cunningham is a real mean bitch. She can make life very unpleasant.'

'Thank you, I'll take that on board. And you are?'

'Pete Jenkins, with forensics.'

Anna gave him a brittle smile. She had never worked alongside a female boss before and already it did not bode well. She spent as much time as she felt she should at the site, before heading to the incident room at Chalk Farm Police Station. She made copious notes as always and tried, while doing so, not to get in anyone's way.

The station was old-fashioned and rundown. The murder team had taken over the second floor which had plenty of empty space: it was due to be shut down and a new building had already been earmarked. Until the move, they would entrench themselves in the allocated area. There were several small offices for the detectives; the largest corner office had already been taken by DCI Cunningham. Computers were being set up alongside an incident board, and the clerical staff were organising desks and phone lines. When Anna asked where she should unpack, she was given the closet next to DCI Cunningham's office.

The room was only spacious enough for a small desk and a swivel chair that had seen better days. No sooner had Anna taken off her coat, and wiped over the dusty desk with a tissue, than her phone was brought in and connected by a young uniformed officer.

As she took out her laptop, notebooks and pens, a red-haired detective tapped on the open door. 'Hi! I'm Gordon Loach. The boss wants us ready for a briefing in five minutes. There's coffee and doughnuts in the incident room.'

Anna smiled and stretched out her hand. 'DI Anna Travis. Nice to meet you.'

Gordon seemed very young, whether because of his almost orange hair and full complement of freckles, or his rather nervous clammy handshake. 'See you in there,' he replied, and he was gone.

Anna peered through the blinds of her small window which looked out onto the incident room. She watched the room filling up, as numerous officers drew out chairs and sat around, chatting. She still hadn't seen anyone she knew – not that she minded. It was just nice to see a friendly or familiar face when starting a new case.

She picked up her notebook and went next door, and sat down with two empty chairs either side of her. No one else sat close. She held her pencil at the ready, coffee and a doughnut beside her. She had just taken a bite when Cunningham's door banged open and the DCI strode across to stand at the incident board. With her back to the room, she made notes. Then she turned to face everyone.

'Okay, let's get cracking. First up is the call from a neighbour who lives on the estate. All we know is she heard gunfire, but I want her interviewed again, just to see if she can tell us anything about who might have been dossing down in the dump where the body was discovered.' Cunningham twisted the marker pen in her hand. 'We have an ID on the victim, but we need it to be verified and I want this kept quiet until we know the facts. I do not – repeat *do not* – want any press releases until we have that verification. According to ID in his wallet, the dead man is DI Frank Brandon.'

Anna sat bolt upright. She knew Frank Brandon: he had been on the last case she had worked on with Langton.

'Anyone know the victim?' Cunningham asked.

Anna raised her hand. She kept on swallowing to control how shocked she was. Frank of the heavy cologne and weightlifter's shoulders; Frank who reckoned he was every woman's dream; Frank who had at one time made a pass at her . . . *Frank?* What in God's name was *he* doing in a drug dive?

Cunningham continued. 'We will obviously, as soon as a formal identification has taken place, look into what case he was working on.' She looked at Anna coldly. 'Did you recognise him?'

'No, Ma'am, but he was face down. It looked like he'd taken the bullets to his head and shoulders.'

'Correct. The top of his head was blown off. We have, I believe, five bullet wounds – two shot through the door, the others we think may have been at point-blank range – but we will wait for ballistic, forensic and pathology reports for all that.'

Cunningham turned to the board, then back to the waiting officers. 'It looks, and I am only saying what I think – we won't know until we have made more enquiries – as if our victim went to the block of flats to score, was let in the front door and taken into the main room to wait, then for some reason was killed. The killer shot *through* the reinforced door, then opened it, came out and shot the victim at point-blank range, to make sure he was dead. Then he must have run back in and escaped out of the window. Right now, though, we have no idea how many people were in that squat. We wait to see if they get anything from the prints.'

Anna listened, as did everyone else. Cunningham's soft, upper-class tone was at odds with her cold attitude; she did not meet anyone's eyes, and talked *at*, rather than to them. She continued to twist the pen in her hands before writing on the board the ID of their victim and a list of the contents of his rather expensive wallet: two photographs, one of a pretty blonde woman and another of two small children; along with numerous receipts for dry cleaning, repairs to a BMW and grocery bills – nothing else.

Anna bit her lip, trying to calculate how long it had been since she had last seen Frank. He had most definitely not, to her knowledge, been married or had children. Could he, in the time she had worked on two other cases, have met someone, married them and produced two kids? She doubted it. She put up her hand and mentioned her thought to Cunningham, who nodded.

'Well, we'll know sooner or later. Anything else?'

Again Anna put up her hand. Cunningham stared at her, her dark brown eyes expressionless.

'The blood spattering, Ma'am.'

'What about it?'

'From what I could see, if the victim was shot in the head *through* the door—'

'Yes?'

'The forensic team were still checking when I left—'

'I am aware of that, Travis.'

'Well, from what I could determine . . .'

'Get to the point!' Cunningham snapped.

'The wall directly behind the victim showed only a small spray of blood.'

'So? What do you conclude?'

'Someone could have been standing behind him.'

'Thank you, well-observed. We'll obviously wait, as with everything else, for the scientists to give their report. Anyone else?'

No one else brought up any developments. By now, it was almost midday and Cunningham, with the duty manager, gave out assignments. Travis was to be accompanied by Gordon Loach to question Mrs Webster, the woman who had put the call in to the station. As the team broke up, Anna had still not been formally introduced to the main officers leading the enquiry. Cunningham had returned to her office.

Anna and Gordon travelled back to the murder site in a patrol car, with Anna driving. 'How long have you been attached to the Murder Squad?' Anna asked from behind the wheel.

Gordon flushed, which wasn't too difficult; his cheeks seemed to be pinkish all the time. 'Two weeks. This is my first time out.'

'Ah . . .'

'To be honest, I'm really sort of unsure what all the procedures are. I mean, I know from training, but being in the thick of it is different.'

'Yes.'

'My father was an officer.'

'So was mine.'

'He's now Deputy Commissioner.'

Anna turned to look at the young man. 'Really?'

'What about yours?'

'He was a Detective Inspector, Murder Squad, but he retired. He died five years ago.'

'Oh!' Gordon changed the subject. 'What do you think happened?'

'You mean the shooting?'

'Yes.'

'I can't really say. We always know more when all the tests have been completed.'

'But you think you recognised the victim?'

'No. I said I knew Frank Brandon, who owned the ID card found in the victim's wallet. I never got a look at the victim's face.'

'But if it was him, this is serious. I mean, he was a police officer.'

'Correct.'

'So what do you think happened?' the young man repeated.

'As I just said, I don't really know. Our job, Gordon, is to find out. So, we question the neighbour, see if she has anything we can work on.'

'Right. It's a terrible shithole, the Warren Estate.'

'Some people don't have a choice,' Anna said.

'Where do you live?'

She hesitated. 'I've just moved into a new place over near Tower Bridge.'

'I still live with my mother,' the young man told her. 'My parents are separated, long time ago. I want to get a place of my own eventually, but it's really hard to find anywhere I can afford. I've seen a few places, but all out of my league. Was your flat expensive?'

'Very,' she said, sounding more curt than she meant to. 'Okay, here we are.'

31

The forensic teams remained at work. Arc lamps still lit up the dingy flat and tapes cordoned off the area. The body must have been removed as there was no longer an ambulance on standby. Anna and Gordon headed up the stone staircase and branched off to where there were still residents.

'It's number 18A,' Gordon said.

'Yes, I know.' Anna walked a little ahead of him until they reached the front door. The paint was fresh, but the letterbox was boarded up; a smashed side window had a piece of board nailed across it. Anna knocked. They waited a while; she had to knock again, before they heard footsteps.

'Who is it?' came a voice.

'I'm from the police, Mrs Webster. Detective Inspector Anna Travis.'

Chains were scraped back and the door was inched open. 'Have you got identification?'

Anna showed her badge and then gestured to Gordon. 'I'm accompanied by Detective Constable Loach.' She stepped away slightly so Mrs Webster could see Gordon.

The door closed, but then the chain was released and it opened. 'Come in,' said Mrs Webster nervously.

The hallway was neat and clean, with floral carpet and wallpaper, but very narrow. The tiny woman gestured for them to move ahead. 'Go into the sitting room, please. It's on the right.'

'Thank you,' Anna said, as she and Gordon entered the first room off the hallway. The flat had the same layout as the drug squat, but that was the only point of comparison. Mrs Webster's sitting room was cluttered, with an overstuffed sofa and two chairs in front of a fake coal electric fire. There were numerous cabinets

with china and ornaments in them and a large television.

Mrs Webster had white hair, cut in a neat style rather
like the Queen's. She was wearing a twinset and pearls,
a pleated woollen skirt and stretch stockings over her
puffy ankles; fluffy suede slippers encased her feet. 'Do
you want tea or coffee?'

'Nothing, thank you.'

'Sit down, please.'

Both Anna and Gordon sat on the easy chairs. 'Mrs
Webster, you made the 999 call . . .' Anna began, then
was interrupted.

'Yes, yes, I called the police.'

'Can you tell me exactly what was happening before
you put in the call?'

'Well, I've said all this before.'

'I know, but I just need to go over a few things.'

'I was in bed and I woke up. Well, the sounds woke
me up.'

'The sounds?'

'Yes – raised voices and then a sort of loud bang, bang,
bang sound. It was so loud, I was worried Jeremy would
be woken up.'

'Jeremy?'

'My son. He sleeps in the bedroom at the back of the
flat. I'm in the front, but it was so loud.'

'Did it wake him?'

'No. Well, not at first it didn't, because there was a
sort of lull – you know, nothing happening – but by this
time, I was up.'

'What time was that?'

'It was three-fifteen.'

'So then what happened?'

'I checked on Jeremy and, just as I was closing his door, there was another pop, this time not so loud – then it went pop, pop, again. I see enough TV to know what the sound was: gunfire. So I called the police.'

'Did you leave the flat at all?'

'No, no, I was too scared.'

'Did your son?'

'No, he came in here and sat with me until the police arrived.'

'How old is your son?'

'Why do you want to know?'

'Just for the record.'

'He's thirty-four.'

'And he lives here with you?'

'Yes.'

'Is he at home now?'

Mrs Webster looked towards the closed door and back to Anna. 'He's in his room,' she said carefully. 'Is it necessary you talk to him?'

'It is, but let's just continue with you for now. You called the police?'

'I never set foot out of the front door at night; it's too risky. I've complained that the squatters have moved in and it's been going on, over and over again. In fact, when I rang 999, I didn't think they would take me seriously, because of how many times I've called them. There's needles and filth left on the walkways, and there are still children living here. It's every night, and most of the day now; they come and they go, these junkies. It's worse at night, because of the cars and motorbikes, the lights, shining into my windows, and the noise, shouting and screaming. I know two residents called the police because they found a girl doped up and being sick;

another time, a boy was found overdosed. It's like living in a nightmare that never stops.'

Anna let the woman talk on until she seemed to deflate, sighing.

'The people using the flat ... did you know any names? Can you describe anyone? Maybe someone you have seen on a regular basis?'

'No, they all look alike – hoods up, grey anoraks. They don't look at me; they just ignore the existence of anyone else living here. The council have done nothing to help us get rehoused.'

'How many would you say were living in the squat?'

'I couldn't tell you; they came and they went. Sometimes there were girls but, most times, they were just lads. Late at night the cars would pull up. I think these were bringing the drugs because then it would start, the noise, the banging, the bikes and cars, coming to get whatever they needed.'

'Last night – the night of the shooting – did you notice anything different?'

'No. Like I said, at seven, I shut my front door and I bolt it and I don't go out. I turn the TV up loud and that's it.'

'What about your son?'

'He never goes out much.'

'I'm sorry – your son doesn't go out?'

'Not a lot, unless they come for him.'

'Who comes, Mrs Webster?'

'The social services. They come and take him for his swimming and then, on Wednesdays, he goes to a special unit at Camden.'

'Is your son ill? I mean, is he disabled?'

'No.'

'I would like to talk to him.'

'He doesn't know anything.'

'He might.'

'I just don't want him upset. This has all been very stressful for him, you know. I try and keep him as calm as I can, but when these things happen, it gets very upsetting. He's afraid they might come after me because I called the police.'

'Mrs Webster, I assure you, since the shooting, I doubt very much there will be any activity there again.'

'Well, I have to say, since it happened it's been quiet, apart from all the police, and the neighbours trying to find out what is going on.'

'It must be a very difficult time for you.' Anna closed her notebook and stood up. 'May I meet your son now?'

Mrs Webster glanced at the clock on the mantel and licked her lips. 'Jeremy has autism. Sometimes he can be a bit difficult. Other times he's fine. Can you give me a few minutes?'

Anna nodded and smiled, as Mrs Webster left the room.

'It's not right, is it?' Gordon said quietly.

Anna looked at him, as if to say, 'What isn't?'

'Forced to live in this place, son dependent on you, having junkies day and night just up the corridor. It's disgusting.'

'It looks as if the council is making moves to rehouse everyone.'

'In the meantime, they have to put up with junkies and dealers.'

Anna listened: she heard raised voices. Mrs Webster was trying to persuade her son to dress; he was refusing, as he was watching something on television. They could hear a low, almost growling voice muttering, and Mrs Webster trying to cajole him.

Anna stood up and looked over to Gordon. 'Maybe we should come back.'

Jeremy was refusing to come out of his room. Mrs Webster was apologetic. 'You see, he does the trolleys in our big Waitrose – you know, collecting them from the car park. It's just a couple of mornings, but he wants to finish watching his DVD.'

Anna and Gordon made visits to the neighbours, but without much success. Everyone said virtually the same thing: they locked their front doors at night and stayed inside. A number had complained about the drug dealing and a few had called the police out many times.

They returned to the station and added to the incident board the times that Mrs Webster believed the gunshots had been fired. Anna was keen to know more about their victim, but they were still waiting on the forensic and pathology reports. For lunch she had a sandwich in her office as she typed up her report. She was surprised when her door was tapped and opened before she could say anything.

Cunningham closed the door behind her. 'Tell me what you know about Frank Brandon.'

Anna licked her lips. This would obviously mean discussing the case the two of them had been on together, which meant the possibility of mentioning DCI Langton's name. She hated the fact that, after all this time – almost eighteen months – the sound of his name still made her heart and head ache.

'We were on a really horrific case. The bodies were found in the pig pens.'

'Ah yes, I remember that. So Frank was with you on it, was he?'

'Yes. I didn't really know him on a personal level.'

'He took early retirement . . . something about a knee injury.'

'I didn't know that.'

'Before that, he had been with the Drug Squad.'

'I didn't know that either.'

Cunningham had an unnerving way of standing with her arms folded, looking around the room rather than making eye-contact. 'So you wouldn't know if he was using?'

'Drugs? No. I only worked with him once, but I truthfully didn't see any sign of him using drugs. But then I had no idea he was married, or that the children in the photograph were his.'

'We're checking that out. We still don't have a formal ID.' Cunningham pursed her lips. 'Doesn't make sense, does it? What would he be doing in that shithole? If he needed to score, then he would have had a lot of easier contacts.'

'I would think so,' Anna said.

'You got nothing from the neighbour who did the call-out for the police?'

'No, Ma'am, we didn't. We weren't able to question her son. He was also in the flat at the time, but he suffers from autism and didn't want to speak to us.'

'Anything from any of the other neighbours?'

'No. All said the same thing – that the dealers had been working there for several months. I can't believe the local cops didn't do more to bust the place. Apparently they dealt in the day as well as at night, with a lot of vehicles coming and going.'

'Wasn't Jimmy Langton on that piggery case?'

Anna felt her cheeks flush. 'Yes. He led the enquiry.'

'Right. I know him – great guy. You've heard he's been made Chief Superintendent? Virtually running the Murder Squad?'

Anna nodded.

'You liked working with him?'

'Very much.'

Cunningham now looked directly at Anna. 'We must be very different.'

'I'm sorry?'

'Is it different working on my team than Langton's?'

'Well, I can't really say. This is my first day.'

'I worked with him.'

'Did you?' Anna gave a look of surprise. They didn't, to her, seem a good match.

'Long time ago, around about the time his first wife died. He fell apart, but picked himself up again. Married again, I think.'

'Yes, I believe so.' Anna wanted the floor to open up and swallow her. Talking about him physically hurt; she felt as if she was about to have a panic attack.

Cunningham was now really unnerving her as she sat perched on the end of the small desk, her arms still folded. 'Always good to have someone like him at the top. Most of the top line are wankers, but Langton – he's the business. I admire him; got great energy, and he's fearless – doesn't take any prisoners.'

Anna felt right now that *she* was his prisoner – knowing what she did, knowing how dangerous a man he was, how he had covered up his part in a murder, albeit of the most despicable killer. It had happened on the hideous murder investigation when the bodies of a mother and

child had been fed to pigs, and Langton had, at the same
time and against all odds, recovered from a near-fatal
attack to head up the enquiry. The killer had died after
being interrogated by Langton, and Anna was certain
that Langton had engineered his death. He had made her
a part of it, because she knew what he had done and yet
kept her silence.

'He could be a mean bastard, though.' Cunningham
picked up one of Anna's sharpened pencils. 'So how did
Frank get along with him?'

'I think they were on good terms.'

'Very cagey, aren't we?'

'No, Ma'am, it's just you are asking me about things I
haven't the information to give you answers on.'

'He screw you?'

'I'm sorry?' Anna had to catch her breath.

'I said, did he screw you? All right, don't answer. I can
see by your hot flush he didn't. My, my, you are a
straight-laced little madam, aren't you?' With that,
Cunningham slid off Anna's desk and took the mere two
paces needed to get to the door. 'Okay. See you out
there; briefing in half an hour.' She closed the door
behind her.

Anna shut her eyes. She should have been angry at the
personal cross-questioning, but it had taken her so off-
guard, she hadn't been able to think straight. Cunningham obviously didn't know how close Anna had been
with Langton, but that didn't calm her. She felt sure that,
at some point, Cunningham would find out and know
that she had lied.

Chapter Three

A nna went to the washroom and splashed cold water over her face. By the time she returned to the incident room, the team had gathered and were waiting for Cunningham to join them. After a few minutes, she strode into the room and took up position in front of the board. She seemed on edge.

'Okay, let's have quiet, please,' she said loudly. Everyone became attentive. Cunningham folded her arms: a noticeable gesture, though one she did almost unconsciously. 'Right, we have a really explosive situation on our hands, as well as a tragic one.'

Cunningham, in her low, cultured voice, seemed angry at the wait for the forensic and pathology reports. They had no details on any of the suspected dealers, so the hope was they would get results from the fingerprints taken from the flat. They still had no formal identification of their victim but, as the wallet had contained his ID card, they were presuming it to be ex-Detective Inspector Frank Brandon. His fingerprints, which would have been held on file, were being checked against the body. Whether he was on drugs would only be known when the labs were through testing.

Cunningham took out a packet of Polo mints,

unwrapped the roll and took her time, carefully selecting one and sucking it, before she spoke again. 'Why was our victim there? To score – or was he working for someone else? He was ex-Drug Squad, so would have many contacts though, so far, we have not got any details of them, nor do we know if he contacted any of his old buddies. He was there for a reason and we need to find out exactly what that was.'

Anna said nothing, doodling on her notepad. It seemed to her to be obvious that the reason had to be drugs.

Cunningham continued. 'I want you all back to the estate. I want everyone reinterviewed, as we need something, anything, to give us a clue to the identity of these thugs. All we know is that at around three o'clock in the morning, an argument broke out, shots were fired, Mrs Webster called the police and, after the call, she heard a further three or four shots. This brings us to the ballistic report; they hasten to add it is a very rushed job, but I put them under pressure. Two guns were used.'

Cunningham opened her notebook and detailed how many gunshot wounds the victim had sustained. The first shots were fired through the door; this was then opened, to fire more shots into his head and neck.

Anna leaned forwards; she was confused. *Two* weapons? If gunshots had been fired into Frank's chest, they would have brought him to his knees; yet she was certain she had seen fine blood spattering on the wall behind the victim, high up, as if he had been shot in the face and head area first, before the chest. She made a note to question the forensic officer she had seen at the scene of crime.

Ballistics were confirming the make of weapon, but

had already suggested they were automatics; in other words, hand-held weapons. If two guns were fired, that possibly meant two shooters, but they still had no confirmation how many drug dealers were in the squat; there could have been three or four.

'Right now,' Cunningham went on, 'we don't have the faintest idea who we are looking for. The men seen by the tenants all fit the same description: grey anoraks with hoods drawn up over their heads, so we can't even ascertain their age, never mind their ethnic origin. These shooters, or drug dealers, also had various vehicles – BMWs, motorbikes – but, as yet, we have no details. The tenants stated they saw numerous cars parked outside, as well as cars turning up all night to score. The dealers had been living in this squat for almost three months. That's three months of complaints by residents and yet nothing seems to have been done to clear the animals away. We have various statements from the local plods saying they made plenty of visits to the squat but carried out no arrests! I want every report checked over and all the officers on these call-outs questioned.'

Cunningham folded her arms again. 'Right, I said at the opening of this briefing that we have an explosive situation. We do. We have an ex-officer down and we have a drug dealers' squat that appears to have been left to get on with its business without harassment. Do you understand what I am saying? Let's take away the scenario of tough street kids dealing and, instead, make it a much bigger operation that might have been paying backhanders to officers to keep afloat.'

She glared around the room. 'The weapons used were not the type handled by street kids. Our call-out lady, Mrs Webster, describes the sounds as loud pops; that means they were using silencers. Ballistic have said that a Glock with a silencer could have been used. Street kids? No way.'

Anna sighed, her notepad full of doodles and drawings of guns. To her mind, street kids could easily get access to this type of weapon; if they were dealing, they would have bags of cash. It was at this point that her mobile rang.

She patted her pockets hastily as everyone turned to face her. 'Sorry, excuse me.'

'I hope that isn't personal.'

'Do you mind if I go to my office?' She hurriedly made her way outside and into her own small room.

It was DS Harry Blunt. 'Travis?'

'Yes, Harry. Listen, thanks for calling me back.'

'That's okay. What can I do for you?'

'I just needed to ask you—'

'Where are you?'

'I'm on a case in Chalk Farm.'

'That's not bad. That schlep we had to go out to, that murder in Epping Forest, was a bastard. I'm in Dulwich – woman's knifed her old man with an electric meat-cutter. You tell me how she can claim it's a fucking accident – she had to plug it in! I've got one for the Sunday joint, and there is no way—'

'Harry,' she interrupted him. She had almost forgotten the way he had rambled on when they had worked together. Blunt by name and blunt by nature, he was hardly ever known to draw breath. 'I don't have much time.'

'Have you heard about Jimmy? Superintendent now – very high up. Is he on your case?'

'No, it's a DCI Cunningham.'

'Oh, her. The bull dyke. You watch she doesn't come on to you.'

'Thank you for that advice, Harry, but I didn't call about her; it's about the victim in our case.'

'Right, but word of warning: you watch out for her. In my opinion, she's full of hot air. Working with her after Langton should be a breeze,' he laughed.

'Harry, listen to me. What do you know about Frank Brandon?'

'Frank? I know he retired early. Was on some case, running after some bastard, and fell. Got a rusty screw through his kneecap – fucked him over and so he got out.' There was a pause. She could almost feel the wheels turning in Harry's square head. 'Why you asking about Frank?'

'Well, it's not been formally . . . I mean, we have no formal ID, but we think our victim is Frank Brandon.'

'What?'

'They are running tests on his prints. I couldn't be sure as he had taken some shots to his face and . . . Harry?'

'You think it was Frank?'

'We can't be sure, but he had a wallet with Frank's ID in it.'

'Shit! The poor fucker! Gets out for an easy life and . . . You really think it's him?'

'I hope it isn't, but was he married?'

'I dunno; he used to play around with a lot of women.'

'When did you last see him?'

'More than a year ago; we had drinks before he left.'

'Was he on any kind of drugs?'

'I dunno. Maybe painkillers – his knee was smashed.'

'He used to be Drug Squad, didn't he?'

'Yeah, I think so – long time back, though. What happened?'

'He was found shot in a drug squat in Chalk Farm.'

'Fuck me. That's terrible.'

'Do you know what work he was doing after he left the Force?'

'No, never saw him again. Wait a minute – I did see him once, for a few minutes on Tottenham Court Road. I dunno what work he was actually doing, but he was driving a very flash Merc. Maybe he got work as a driver or bodyguard?'

'Thank you, Harry. I've got to go now.'

'Okay. I hope it's not him; he was a good bloke.'

'Yes, I hope so too. Bye now.' Anna closed her mobile. By the time she got back to the incident room, the briefing had broken up.

Gordon approached her. 'I'm off home now. We are to go back to the estate first thing in the morning.'

She nodded, irritated that she seemed to be paired up with him. 'See you then.'

'You coming to the pub for a drink? Sort of to get to know everyone?'

'No, I have things to do at home. See you in the morning.'

Anna went to Cunningham's office and knocked. She waited for her to answer before entering. 'Sorry about the interruption in the briefing.' Anna explained that, in the hope of finding out more about Frank Brandon, she had contacted Harry Blunt.

Cunningham, on hearing his name, gave a derisive snort. 'That bigoted buffoon! Can't stand him.'

Nevertheless, Anna explained how Harry thought Frank might be working as a driver or bodyguard; he also doubted that Frank was using drugs, and recalled that Frank had once worked with the Drug Squad.

Cunningham snapped that they knew that; then she tipped back in her chair. 'He's been formally identified by his prints, Anna; it's just come in. Right now, we don't have an address, but that should be through soon enough.' Her desk phone rang.

Anna gestured that she would leave.

'No. Stay put. DCI Cunningham? Terrific – yes, yes, thank you.' She pointed to a jar of pencils.

Anna picked one up and passed it to her, then watched as the DCI listened, jotting down notes.

She finished the call and replaced the receiver. 'Frank Brandon married a Miss Julia Kendal five months ago. She has two children from a previous relationship. We'd better go and see her.'

Anna nodded, though she was eager to get home. It was already after six, and the thought of all the unpacking she would have to do made her head ache. She would have liked to have gone in her own car, but Cunningham had insisted they ride together in a patrol car with a driver.

'This isn't a social visit, Travis!'

Anna said nothing, doubting that Cunningham, she of the folded arms and classy voice, would be able to give much compassion to the poor woman they were going to visit.

Anna was surprised by the house in Wimbledon. It was set back from the Common, with pillared front steps up to a large oak studded door: modern, but expensive and quite tasteful. The carport had a Range Rover parked, leaving space enough for a second car. Anna could not imagine Frank Brandon here, but then she had never seen where he had lived as a bachelor.

Cunningham took a deep breath. 'Christ, I hate these meetings.' She rang the doorbell and stepped back, almost onto Anna's feet. 'Frank seems to have been doing all right though; this must be worth about three mill at least.'

A Chinese girl opened the door.

'Mrs Brandon, please,' Cunningham said.

The girl hesitated. 'One moment, please.' Her English was good.

'Who is it, Mai Ling?' another woman asked from inside.

'Will you please tell Mrs Brandon that I am from the police,' Cunningham said. 'I need to speak with her on a very urgent matter.'

The door was swung wider and a very attractive blonde in a chic dress and high heels appeared. 'Is it about Frank? I've been worried sick.'

'Are you Mrs Brandon?' Cunningham asked quietly.

'Yes, do you want to come in?'

'Please.'

They went into a spacious hall with a wide staircase. It was thickly and newly carpeted in a pale oyster; there was also the faint smell of fresh paint.

'I've been calling him all day,' Mrs Brandon said, as she led them into a big family room. Again, there was a new carpet, and some of the furniture still had bubble wrapping around it. 'You'll have to excuse the mess. We only moved in fairly recently.'

Cunningham nodded and introduced Anna.

Mrs Brandon knew then, by how quiet they were, that something was wrong. She touched a gold chain at her neck as she perched on one of the new easy chairs. 'Something has happened, hasn't it?'

'I am sorry, but I have some distressing news. There is no easy way to tell you this, but I am afraid your husband has been fatally wounded.'

Julia just seemed to sag, her head leaning forwards. 'Ah, no.'

'We will need you to give us a formal identification.'

'What happened?'

'He was shot.'

'Shot?'

'Yes. I am very sorry. It happened some time early this morning.'

'He's dead?'

'Yes. Do you know what he was doing last night?'

At this point, Julia lost control; she slid forwards as she vomited over her new carpet.

It took them some time to help her up, and get Mai Ling back to clean up the mess. Julia didn't cry, but seemed to be in a daze, as she was helped to lie down and a cold cloth was put on her forehead. Cunningham sat close to her, and asked the girl to call Julia's doctor.

By the time the doctor arrived, an ashen-faced Julia was holding on to Cunningham's hand. She had not said a word since she had collapsed. Her eyes were wide and frightened, and even her mouth seemed to have lost its colour. As soon as the doctor went to her side, she closed her eyes. Cunningham had to ease Julia's fingers away; her grip had been so tight, it left white marks on her skin. Julia was in a state of shock and the doctor said he would give her something to help her sleep.

Whilst Cunningham remained with Julia and the doctor, Anna busied herself, helping to clear up. The bright, happy family kitchen was full of children's toys and games, all so new and pristine. There were many photographs of the two little sisters as babies, then toddlers; there were also numerous wedding pictures of Frank with Julia, and the girls as bridesmaids, as there were in the lounge. It was hard for Anna to reconcile the Frank she had known with this proud and happy man in a pale suit and a pink silk tie.

Mai Ling, who had come down from putting the girls to bed, was placing the children's dishes into the dishwasher.

'How long have you worked for Mrs Brandon?' Anna asked her.

'One year, six months. I have a work permit.'

'I'm sure you do. Do you understand the reason we are here this evening?'

'No.'

'Mrs Brandon's husband has been found dead.'

The face remained impassive.

'How did you get along with Mr Brandon?'

'He is a very nice man.'

'Did you work for Mrs Brandon before their marriage?'

'Yes.'

'Was she married before?'

'She had partner.'

'But they weren't married?'

'I don't know; he was much older.'

'Is this house Mrs Brandon's?'

'Yes, she buy this house; we move in not long ago.'

'After her marriage?'

'Yes.'

'Do you know what work Mr Brandon did?'

'No. He go out early; sometimes come home very late.'

'But you don't know who he worked for?'

'No.'

'So – the children are in bed?'

'Yes, we have tea and then I take them up for bath and bedtime.'

Anna picked up the photograph of Mrs Brandon and the two pretty girls. 'They are lovely. They were from Mrs Brandon's previous relationship?'

'I think so.'

'What are their names?'

'Emily and Kathy.'

'Does Mrs Brandon work?'

'No, she at home.' Mai Ling turned the dishwasher on. 'He have a heart-attack?'

Anna cocked her head to one side.

'Mr Brandon? He have a gym upstairs and he work out every morning.' The girl opened a cupboard to put away the jams from the table. It was filled with vitamins and health drinks. 'He very fit man; he take all these with fresh orange juice.'

Anna looked over the mass of jars and health-food supplements and shook her head. 'No. It wasn't a heart-attack. Thank you for talking to me.'

Anna turned to walk out of the kitchen. From the array of vitamins, it was doubtful Frank would also have been pumping himself with drugs. She remembered how he was always working out; she recalled his massive shoulders and the overwhelming cologne he had always used. She was jolted out of it by the sound of the girl sobbing, sitting at the kitchen table, her head in her hands.

'Let's go.' Anna jumped as Cunningham tapped her

shoulder. 'We'll need to come back and talk to the wife. She can't string two words together right now.'

They returned to the patrol car.

Cunningham yawned. 'What do you make of all that?' she said, not looking at Anna.

'Well, it's a very nice house; they only moved in after they were married. I think she has the money. She doesn't work, and that place must have cost a fortune to furnish. From what I could gather from the au pair, Mrs Brandon's last partner was older – maybe he had the money originally. She didn't know what work Frank Brandon did; she just said he left early and often came home late. He also has a cupboard full of vitamins. It didn't look as if he was spoiling all that with drugs.'

'I know someone who works out and takes speed every morning, so you can never tell.' Cunningham tapped the driver to tell him to take her home, not back to the station. She then settled back and took out her BlackBerry, checking emails all the way to her home in Belsize Park, ignoring Anna.

By the time Anna had collected her Mini from the station car park and driven home, it was half-past nine. She had not eaten since the sandwich before the briefing, so dropped into a late-night shop on the way. Anna parked in her allocated space, then took the lift up to the top floor. Stepping out, she could hardly believe her eyes.

Stacked up outside her front door were boxes and boxes of deliveries. Attached to the top one was a note, saying they had been unable to gain access, but that the security manager had agreed the items could be left. She wanted to weep.

It was another half-hour before she had dragged

everything in from the hallway into the flat. She was too tired to begin unpacking and just wanted a hot shower and something to eat. She heated some soup and filled the fresh rolls she had bought with ham and cheese, then carried them into the bedroom. It would have been lovely to flop down on her bed and switch on the TV before crashing out, but the large plasma screen sat ominously in the drawing room, waiting to be connected. Wherever she looked were boxes; she knew there was no way she could start the marathon task that evening. She half-wished she was back at her old flat.

It got worse: there was no hot water. No matter how much she fiddled and twisted the dial, it remained icy cold. By this time, it was almost eleven-fifteen, too late to call the duty security manager.

Anna had just closed her eyes when a foghorn bellowed. She shot up. It felt as if her bed was being shaken by an earthquake. She opened the balcony window doors. It was terrifying; the whole apartment seemed to be moving. Anna's mouth gaped open: the massive bridge was closing, which was why the apartment was shuddering. As soon as both sides joined, and it reverted back to its usual position, the apartment became still.

'Jesus Christ,' she muttered, wondering if anyone else had felt it. Surely they must have, but she saw no one else on their balconies. As she returned to her bedroom, she knocked against one of the boxes, stubbing her toe. Back in bed, she bashed her pillow, but sleep didn't come easily; she was waiting for another foghorn blast.

It was her alarm that eventually woke her. She felt like hell. She was going to give it to the security manager.

Anna was still in a foul mood when she tried to get out of the garage. It didn't respond to her remote. She was swearing and cursing, when it opened of its own accord; she drove out and pressed for it to close, but it remained open. Even after she had had her breakfast in her cubicle of an office, she was still uptight. She typed up her report of the meeting with Julia Brandon and then put in a call to the security manager. His answerphone was on.

Gordon was not a morning person; he yawned so many times, it felt contagious. Cunningham had underlined that they were to question every single tenant on the estate, as one or another could have details or descriptions of the drug dealers. He didn't understand why they had such an early start. Anna pointed out that many of the residents went to work; the few they had not yet spoken to would still be at home, she hoped. It was to be another tedious round of knocking on doors and questioning the neighbours. Also, as instructed, they were to interview Mrs Webster's son.

Gordon remained silent whilst Anna did all the enquiries. She was so irritated by his constant yawning that she snapped, 'Did you have a late night or something? You seem half-asleep.'

'No, I crashed out early, but I shouldn't have eaten so much breakfast. It always makes me sleepy – well, that's what my mother says.'

'Well, in future, do you think you could just listen to what your mother says and maybe have a bowl of cereal?'

'I hate cereal, all that chewing. I like scrambled eggs and grilled tomatoes.'

'Gordon, I don't want to know.'

'Sorry.'

They went from floor to floor on the estate. This was usually a uniform job but, considering the seriousness of the crime, Cunningham had felt a show of rank worthwhile. It wasn't. Some tenants were still not at home, and most of their enquiries were carried out on the doorstep. Anna was feeling that it was all a waste of time. She had been inundated with the same complaints about the state of the building, and how many tenants had been waiting years to be rehoused.

Anna had left Mrs Webster until last. Knowing the situation with her son, she had called to ask for a convenient time. Mrs Webster had said that Jeremy would talk to them, but they had to interview him in his room. Anna felt this would be another real time-waster, but far be it from her to put a foot wrong with Cunningham.

Mrs Webster was as neat and smart as she had been on the previous visit. Anna and Gordon waited in the hall as she tapped on her son's bedroom door and then went in. They waited three or four minutes before she came out and said they could now see Jeremy.

Anna walked in ahead of Gordon – and could hardly contain her surprise.

The room was quite spacious; shelves of DVDs were built around a large desk with a computer and small TV set on it. The speakers and DVD deck were stacked on top of each other next to some expensive-looking sound equipment. The walls were lined with tapes and records, all in alphabetical order. There were many magazines, neatly placed beside the desk. The small bed was made in a military style: folded top blanket, white sheet wrapped around, with two inches showing, and a pristine white pillow on top. There was a desk chair, and two spare canvas chairs propped against a wall. The carpet was dark blue and what space on the walls was not taken up with his collections was pristine white paint. Just as Anna was taken aback by the clinical room, in complete contrast to the rest of the flat, Jeremy himself was also something of a surprise.

He was extraordinarily good-looking. He had blond hair, well-cut with a long top layer, and bright blue eyes with dark lashes; his cheeks were pinkish, almost like a child's. He was wearing slacks, a white shirt, leather slippers and a blue knitted sweater. He had the appearance of someone scrubbed clean, almost too much so.

'Jeremy, I am Detective Inspector Anna Travis and this is Detective Constable Gordon Loach. Thank you for agreeing to see us.'

Jeremy stared at Anna but made no move towards them.

'May we sit down?' Anna moved to the bed.

Jeremy stepped forwards. 'Not on my bed.' He took the two canvas chairs and carefully opened one, setting it down straight, and then the next, making sure they were exactly side by side.

'Thank you.' Anna and Gordon sat down, and she took out her notebook from her briefcase. Jeremy stood directly in front of them. 'Now, Jeremy, I am here to ask you about an incident that happened the night before last. Do you mind answering some questions?'

He nodded his head but remained standing, staring at them.

'Your mother contacted the local police station after hearing what she thought were gunshots and loud voices arguing. Do you remember that night?'

No reaction.

'We have subsequently discovered that a man had been shot.'

No reaction.

'I am here just to confirm that and check out the time the shots were fired.'

No reaction.

'Do you recall anything that might be of interest to the police?'

No reaction.

'Have you ever seen the people who were using the flat along the corridor? It's number nineteen.'

No reaction. If he was taking in anything she was saying, there was not a flicker of interest in his bright button eyes. His presence was very unnerving as he was standing so still, looking at a point just above their heads. Anna closed her notebook.

'Would you like a cup of tea?' His voice was low and guttural.

'Thank you but no, we won't keep you any longer, Jeremy.'

'I don't like to be called that.'

'I'm sorry, Mr Webster.'

'Jay.'

'Oh, Jay. Well, I am sorry to have taken up your time. I know you work two mornings a week at Waitrose. You clear the trolleys, don't you?'

No reply.

'Shall we put the chairs back against the wall for you?'

'Have you finished?' he asked.

Anna looked to Gordon and then back to Jeremy's impassive face. 'I think so.'

He almost whipped the chairs from under them both, folding and replacing them against the wall. Gordon raised his eyebrows at Anna as Jeremy took a long time making sure they were exactly on top of each other.

'Thank you, Jay.' Anna put out her hand, but he didn't touch it. He stepped back a fraction and turned to face his desk.

'Well, we will leave you to it.' Anna crossed to the door and Gordon followed.

On a large sheet of paper, pinned behind the door and therefore not seen when they had entered, was a handwritten list of dates and times, printed in different inks and highlighted with a marker pen.

'What are these, Jay?'

'Visitors,' he said.

'I don't understand. Visitors to you, or . . .'

'They do not have residents' parking tickets. It is against the law to park in the forecourt without a residents' parking permit.'

Anna glanced at Gordon and back to Jeremy, who had now turned to face them. His cheeks seemed even pinker, as if he was using rouge.

'You have been monitoring illegal cars parked, is that correct?'

'Yes.'

'And how do you know about these cars?'

'Window, of course.'

'Your window?'

'Yes.'

'May I see out from your window, Jay?'

'Yes.'

Anna passed him and went to the window. She lifted the slats of the pristine white blind. The window looked out onto the lock-up garages at the rear of the estate. She let the slats slip back into place.

'I also monitor the vehicles illegally parked at the front on the days I work at Waitrose. I collect the trolleys and stack them and replace them in a long line outside the main entrance. People leave their trolleys by the side of their cars when they unload groceries, and they are not supposed to do that. They are supposed to replace them outside the entrance, but they don't. I have to collect each one and I make a line of them to wheel them back. Sometimes, I have found our trolleys outside on the road; that's when people have not parked in the Waitrose car park but on the street. I collect them and take them back to the entrance.'

He spoke in short, sharp sentences with a low, controlled anger.

'Jay, just let me understand: are these dates of people parking illegally at Waitrose or here on your estate?'

'This is a residents' parking area. You have to have a permit.'

'Yes, I understand that, but these times and dates are from your estate and not Waitrose, is that correct?'

'Yes.'

Anna could hardly believe it. 'I don't suppose you listed any licence-plate numbers, did you, Jay?'

'I have them.'

'You have the licence-plate numbers of these cars?'

'Yes. You don't listen to what I am saying. I am a resident and these people have no right to park illegally and so I am monitoring them.'

'For how long?'

'A long time.'

Anna took a deep breath and smiled. 'Do you think, Jay, that you could pass these licence-plate numbers to me? As a police officer, I can do something about them being illegally parked in the residents' bays.'

He chewed his lip.

'I could make sure they don't block any residents' bays for you.'

'That would be good, because sometimes when my care worker comes here to see me, she can't find a space; one time she got a ticket because she had to park across the street on a yellow line.'

'Well, let's get this all written down then, shall we? Do you have the numbers?'

'Yes. *Please do not sit on my bed.*'

Anna straightened and waited as Jeremy replaced the two chairs. Again, she and Gordon sat side by side, but this time Jeremy drew out his desk chair and sat down too. He swivelled to face them. Anna took out her notebook again and gave an encouraging look, expecting him to open one of the drawers, but he remained facing them.

'Are you ready?' he asked.

'Yes, Jay, we are ready. Do you need your lists from there?'

'No, they are not the licence plates; they are the dates and times they blocked the residents' parking area. I started doing this when they boarded up the flats along the corridor.'

'Right, could you pass me the relevant licence plates and, if they match the dates . . .'

'Are you ready?' he repeated.

'Yes. Yes, Jay, we are very eager to—'

It was as if a key had been turned at the side of his head. Without hesitation, he began to list the car-registration numbers from memory. Over and over again, Anna had to ask him to pause, as she couldn't keep up. He was able to describe the make and colour of the cars as well.

Gordon was writing in his notepad too, but Jeremy spoke so quickly, as if on automatic pilot; sometimes, when they asked him to pause, it took a while for him to pick up where he had left off, but he continued reeling out registration after registration.

Anna said nothing to Gordon until they were on their way back to the station. Then: 'Do you believe that?'

Gordon shrugged. 'Did you ever see the film *Rain Man*, with Dustin Hoffman?'

Anna nodded.

'What makes a mind able to recall all those numbers, and yet he can only work pushing grocery trolleys around?' Gordon shook his head. 'Look at the way he keeps his room.'

'Obsessive compulsive syndrome. Heartbreaking really; he's such a handsome young man.'

'Yeah, his mother keeps him well turned out, doesn't she? I mean, he was immaculate: hair cut, trousers creased, even his shoes were polished. You don't think all those car numbers were just his nuttiness, do you?'

'I hope not,' Anna sighed. 'We've got pages of figures and dates. Let's hope something comes of them.'

Jeremy was still cleaning his room. He used Febreze on the canvas chairs, wiping the wooden arms down. He then wiped the window blind, especially where Anna had lifted it. He took out his own small Hoover to check over the carpet. Then he stripped naked and folded his clothes into his personal laundry basket. He showered and scrubbed his body, washed his hair and made sure his nails were clean. He then carefully got dressed. No one but his care worker was ever allowed into his room; his mother only stepped inside to pass him his meals, and to clear away his tray.

Mrs Webster tapped on his door. 'You ready for lunch, Jeremy?'

'Yes.'

'Everything go all right? They were with you for a long time.'

'Yes.'

'Were you able to help them at all?'

'I'm hungry.'

'Won't be two ticks.'

He ate grilled chicken, broccoli, mashed potatoes and gravy every day followed by fresh fruit. By the time she brought his tray, he was waiting just inside the door. He took it without a word and ate at his desk, keeping all the food as separate as possible, chewing each mouthful carefully. When she came to collect the tray, he was still sitting there, his plate empty, his cutlery placed neatly together.

'That was very nice,' he said.

'Good.' As she bent forwards for the tray, she could smell Pears soap, the only soap he would ever use. His shampoo was a brand for children, so it would not burn his eyes when he washed his hair. His freshness never ceased to move her. When she leaned forwards to pick up his tray, she was close enough to touch the soft peach cheeks that she had longed for years to kiss, but was never allowed to.

Mrs Webster returned to her kitchen and washed his dishes. It wasn't exactly a prison; he loved his room. In many ways, she was the prisoner, and had been from the time Jeremy had been diagnosed. She wondered what he had been talking about for so long with the police-woman, totally unaware that her son might have given the murder enquiry a mind-blowing breakthrough.

Chapter Four

Cunningham looked at the lists with an open mouth. 'You're not serious?'

'Yes, we are. These are all the pages of licence-plate numbers we have to check out.'

'Work backwards. Don't for Christ's sake go from the top of the list. Use whoever we need to get onto the D and V Licensing Agency. Give this over to Gordon; you can come with me to the path lab. Then we have to pay another visit to Frank Brandon's widow.'

Anna was relieved not to spend any more time with the scrambled egg and tomato gourmet Gordon, who had said not one single word during her entire interview with Jeremy. She was not sure, though, which was worse – having to partner up with him or travel with Cunningham, who unnerved her. Anna was constantly expecting her to ask about Langton.

She didn't. 'This kid is what?'

'Autistic,' Anna replied.

'Well, it could be a big break or we could be the butt of a lot of flak, taking this nutcase's word.'

'He is not a nutcase, Ma'am.'

'He isn't? Holed up in his bedroom or pushing trolleys around doesn't bode well for a witness, Travis.'

'He might not be able to stand up in court, but I believe him. You have to meet him to understand the way his mind works.'

'Yeah, well, I believe you. Thousands wouldn't.'

Dr Ewan Fielding was a thin man with bony hands and a rather high-pitched voice. As he drew back the green sheet from Frank Brandon's body, Anna had to turn away. Brandon's face was hard to recognise, the bullets having torn most of the right side of his skull apart. His mouth gaped; part of his jaw was broken and the teeth splintered. Anna couldn't help but think of James Langton. The two of them were linked in her mind as they had all worked together on the same case. She even recalled Brandon asking her out. She'd refused. Now, she wondered if Langton knew what had happened to Brandon. She shook her head, trying to concentrate.

'Three gunshot wounds to the head and face,' said Fielding, 'and lower down, we have two more: one in his upper chest and, moving upwards into his larynx, another just above his heart. He died instantly from the bullet that went into the right lobe of his brain. The bullets have been sent to ballistics. The deceased was healthy: very fit with strong organs and heart.' Fielding had found no trace of any drugs or trackmarks.

Returning to the patrol car, Cunningham seemed irritated. 'That didn't give us much. At least we know he wasn't using, so what the hell was he doing in that shithole?'

'Maybe he was working on something that took him there.'

'Yeah, maybe, but we still don't know what he was

actually doing. Let's see if we can get more from the widow.'

As they headed out of London towards Wimbledon, Cunningham rested back in her seat and closed her eyes, her arms folded. Anna kept as far away from her as possible. Even sleeping, she looked tense and angry.

Julia Brandon was wan and red-eyed. She was wearing a quilted robe and slippers, sitting on one of the plush sofas with a tissue in her hand.

'The children don't know,' she said in a heavy voice.

'They're not his though, are they?' Cunningham asked. This was somewhat unnecessary, Anna thought; they already knew that.

'No, but he was wonderful with them. It's strange, really. I was always a bit worried how he would cope. He even said at one time that he didn't want any, but then he just took to them, and they had started to call him Daddy.' Julia broke down in tears. She wiped her eyes, apologising repeatedly.

'Mrs Brandon, we need to ask you some questions and then, if you are willing, perhaps later today we will have you taken to identify your husband.'

Anna again wondered if this was necessary. They had verification that it was Brandon from his fingerprints; to subject the poor woman to seeing the terrible damage to her husband's face would be a hideous experience.

'Yesterday you said you were unsure exactly what work your husband was doing, but we really need to know anything you can tell us. Have you had any further thoughts?'

Julia Brandon looked stunned at Cunningham's question.

'We need to know what vehicle he was driving.'

'It was a Volkswagen, but he also drove my car.' Julia rose shakily to her feet and crossed to a large glass-topped cabinet. Opening a drawer, she took out a folder and flicked through it. 'These are his car insurance details.' She passed the folder to Cunningham.

'Did your husband have a life insurance policy?'

'I think so, but I don't know the details. My account-ant arranged it – he does everything.'

'Your accountant?'

'Yes, he looks after me, us – things like the house insurance. He's also my business adviser.'

'Business adviser?' Cunningham echoed again. She kept her eyes down as she looked through the file.

'Yes.'

'But you don't work?'

'No. I have money from my ex-partner for the children.'

Anna remained silent. She didn't like the harsh way Cunningham was questioning Julia.

'Can you give me his name and address?' Cunningham persisted.

'Isn't it on the file you have?' Julia replied. Anna detected a little bit of anger rising.

'Ah, yes, good. I'll just copy this down.'

At that moment, a tray of coffee was brought in by Mai Ling and placed on the table. She passed the coffee around, then left the room. Cunningham opened a note-book and made some notes.

'Were you able to get any sleep last night?' Anna asked Julia, gently.

'No.'

'This must be very distressing for you. I'm sorry we

have to be here under these circumstances, but we are trying to ascertain exactly what happened to your husband. Any help you can give us will be really appreciated, and obviously the sooner we have more details, the better.'

Julia gave Anna a wan smile, as if thanking her for her quiet comforting voice. 'How did it happen?' she asked nervously.

Anna glanced towards Cunningham, who didn't look up from the file, so she continued, 'He was found dead.'

'I know he's dead, but how did it happen? I don't know what is going on! If you told me last night, I was too shocked to remember anything that you said!' Julia's voice rose; she was losing control.

Anna was unsure whether or not Cunningham wanted to take over, but she was paying no attention, still busy reading letters in the folder. 'Your husband died in a flat in Chalk Farm.'

'A flat? Whose flat?'

Cunningham looked up. 'It was a drug dealers' squat, Mrs Brandon. There is no easy way to give you details without it being very distressing.'

'Tell me what happened to my husband!'

'He died from gunshot wounds to his head, face and heart.'

'Oh my God.' Julia leaned forward, almost resting her head on her knees.

'So you see why we need to know who he was working for. Your husband was not using drugs?'

Julia looked up, her eyes like saucers. 'I've no idea.'

'Didn't he ever mention what work he was doing, or for whom?'

'No! All I know is, about two or three months ago, he

69

got a job that he was very pleased about, as the pay was so good. He said it was driving and security, and that his past career had made a good impression at the interviews.'

'Do you have any idea where he went?'

'No, it was all happening with the house and moving in. I didn't even ask him. All he said was that it might involve long hours and late nights.'

Cunningham sighed. 'Thank you, Mrs Brandon. Now, I really would appreciate it if you got dressed and accompanied us.'

'No. I am not leaving the house.'

'Mrs Brandon, we do need you to make a formal identification, unless there is someone else that you could ask to do this?'

Julia bent her head low again.

'What about his parents? Other relatives?'

'There's no one.' She suddenly tossed her head back and took a deep breath. 'I'll do it.'

Cunningham finished her coffee while they waited for Julia to dress. She picked up the file and, when she went to the drawer to replace it, Anna saw her checking through the drawer's contents.

'She's worth a lot of money,' the woman commented. 'Frank landed on his feet with her.'

Anna tensed. Considering what had happened to him, this remark sounded crass in the extreme.

'I'm surprised you are getting so uptight, Travis. I would have thought after working with Jimmy Langton, you'd be used—'

Anna interrupted her. 'I'm sorry. It's just, considering she has only just been told her husband is dead, it feels as if we are being very unsympathetic.'

'Really ... Well, how about Mrs Brandon coming into a half-million-pound life insurance policy?'

Anna was taken aback.

'You think that she wouldn't know what he was doing? Come on, what do you think? She's a poor little rich girl about to be quite a bit richer. She knows a lot more than she's admitting.'

Anna shrugged. 'Well, maybe you'll get more out of her when she sees his body.'

'Maybe we will, Travis, maybe we will, because right now all we have is a list of vehicles from a kid with autism that might or might not give us a lead. We need one, because we have fuck all, in case you're not aware of it!'

Anna reckoned it was best to keep her mouth shut. Cunningham was not someone she wanted to tangle with at this stage of the investigation.

It was half an hour before Julia Brandon rejoined them. She was dressed in a Chanel suit and high heels, her hair swept back into a pleat with a comb. Anna noticed she also wore a very large square-cut diamond on her ring finger and diamond stud earrings. She had a pink and gold designer handbag that must have cost around four or five hundred pounds. Her make-up was immaculate and she seemed very much in control of her emotions. She insisted on calling her financial adviser, which took another ten minutes as she quietly gave him the details of why she needed him to meet her at the mortuary. She also spoke to Mai Ling about the children.

It was almost an hour before they departed. Anna helped Julia into the back of the patrol car. Cunningham sat in the front seat with their driver. Throughout the wait, she had been on her BlackBerry. Anna could barely get a handle on her. She seemed to behave as if there was no one else around and paid little attention to the well-dressed widow.

When they reached the mortuary, a smartly attired, rather polished man was waiting. He had a deeply tanned face and his balding head was almost as shiny as his flamboyant tie. As soon as Julia saw him, she gave a light cry and ran towards him. He held her in his arms, comforting her. Then Julia broke away from him, but still held tightly to his arm. She introduced him.

'This is David Rushton.'

Rushton held out his hand to shake Cunningham's. She then wafted her hand to Anna, and he looked at her with a woeful expression.

'This is a terrible thing. I'm hardly able to believe it,' he said. He asked if he could accompany Julia to see her husband's body. Cunningham agreed and, taking Anna to one side, told her to deal with the viewing as she had calls to make.

Anna hoped that the terrible injuries to Frank's face had somehow been fixed. The three of them entered the cold, bare room where a mortuary assistant was waiting. Rushton guided Julia towards the body. Anna stood to one side and quietly asked Julia to look at the body, and say if it was Frank Brandon.

Julia clung onto Rushton as the cloth was eased away from her husband's face. She stared down; her face was drained of colour, her breath coming in short sharp hisses.

'It is Frank, isn't it?' she whispered.

Rushton held her gently and nodded.

Anna guided them out of the room, still feeling that it

was unnecessary to have put the widow through the process. Rushton drove Julia away in his new Mercedes, having agreed that he would return to the station later that afternoon to talk with Cunningham.

Cunningham was standing, arms folded, in front of the incident board as everyone gathered. By now Anna had met three of the team: DS Phil Markham, who was a big, square-chested man with iron-grey hair, an old pro; DC Pamela Meadows, who was pleasant enough, with bad acne; and DC Mario Paluzzo, a part-Italian, swarthy-faced officer who had hardly given Anna the time of day.

'Right, everyone, listen up. We're doing quite well tracking down the owners of these vehicles. So far we don't have any with a police record, but we'll be running them by the Drug Squad in case they have any information that's not on the database. As you can see, we still have around twenty more to track down, so maybe one of those will give us a lead that'll tell us what he was driving – or who.

'We don't know what work our victim was doing, or who for. We think it was some kind of security chauffeur-type job, but we're hoping to get more on this when the family accountant comes in later. We are waiting, as usual, on the forensic department to bring in their results, though I know they took a lot of prints. As yet, we haven't got the full ballistic report, but we do know he wasn't using drugs, so he wasn't at the squat to score for himself.'

Cunningham went on to detail the fact that Frank's widow was wealthy and would gain a half-million on life-insurance payouts. She described the Wimbledon home, mentioned the two little girls and the ex-partner.

Anna listened intently, surprised that Cunningham seemed to have some suspicion regarding Julia Brandon. Before the DCI wound down, they were interrupted by a visitor from the forensic lab.

Cunningham smiled broadly as he approached. 'Well, we *are* getting special treatment. Everyone, this is Pete Jenkins who heads up the forensic team.'

There were murmurs all round. Anna got a smile of recognition from Jenkins, who seemed very relaxed as he joined Cunningham at the incident board.

He began by taking out files from a bulging briefcase. 'I sensed you'd be hungry for what we have to date. Obviously, you'll learn a lot more when you come to the lab, but—'

He was interrupted by Cunningham. 'How we doing on the fingerprints?'

'We have a fair amount and we're running them through the database, but that's not my department. I really wanted to discuss the blood spattering, as I think it's crucial to the case.'

Jenkins pinned up a large drawing in four parts: one showing a door with bullet marks, then three of the blood-spatter patterns at the murder scene.

He took out a pen. 'The first bullets went through this door. As you can see, I've made notes of the size of the victim. He was five feet eleven. The shooter, I would say, was much smaller, maybe five seven. He fired three shots at the victim through the door. Then I think he opened the door. Now, with the door open, the shooter fires again, this time at the head and face of the victim.'

Jenkins pointed to the red markings. 'As you can see,

the blood spattering is exactly the height of the victim, but what is important is the way the blood has hit the wall behind him. There is a clear outline: there was someone else standing directly behind your victim. This person I would say is at least six feet three. He must have been covered with the victim's blood.'

He opened a notebook. 'We've traced footprints from the area this person would have been standing in. They face at first towards your victim, then we have six, quite clear footprints in blood as he walked away from the dead man. We also traced further prints outside the premises; then they faded. The prints are from a size eleven shoe which would be about right for a man of the height I believe him to be.'

He flipped through his notes. 'We have further foot-prints made by a sneaker and, as you know, substantial quantities of fingerprints – significantly, a set that have powder burns taken from the ledge and the wooded slat of the rear window. As I said, these will all be run by the database.'

Could that someone, who had accompanied Frank Brandon to the drug squat, have been involved in the murder? Or was he the reason Frank was at the drug dealers'? Back in her office after the briefing, Anna was making notes when there was a knock at her door. It was Jenkins.

'I know you were onto that blood spatter,' he said as he shut the door, 'but I thought I should get over here to confirm it before the ritual visitation to the lab.'

'I'm sure we all appreciate it. I've never known anyone to come into the incident room before. I think it's very important, next to the fingerprints – almost equally so.'

'I was wondering if you'd like a drink one evening.'

Anna was taken aback. 'Well, I'm sure we'll be seeing more of each other.'

'Are you free tonight?'

'Erm, I'm not sure. I think we'll be under pressure here after what you've brought in.'

'Do you want to give me your number and I'll call you later?'

Anna hesitated. Then it sunk in – he was asking her out. She laughed and shook her head, jotting down her number on a Post-it note.

He stuck it against his wallet. 'Until later, then?' He gave her a grin as he walked out.

She was left with a smile on her face. His invitation made her feel good; he was a nice-looking guy. She had no more time to think about it, though, as her phone rang. It was Cunningham asking her to join her in her office: David Rushton had arrived.

The two were already in deep discussion when Anna joined them.

'I am obviously bound by client confidentiality,' Rushton was saying. 'I'm not prepared to divulge Mrs Brandon's financial situation, other than to say that she is well provided for and has substantial savings for both herself and her children.'

'Now she's in line for a heavy pay-out on her husband's life insurance policy,' Cunningham pointed out.

'I am aware of that, as I myself arranged the life insurance for her husband.'

'Why?'

'Why? I don't really think it is any of your business.'

'It obviously is. Mr Brandon has just been murdered.'

Rushton paused a moment, then shrugged. 'He was working in security as a chauffeur and bodyguard. The insurance was simply a precaution in case he was injured. As it turns out, I made the right decision.'

'Who was he working for?'

'I really don't know. All I knew is what Mr Brandon told me. In fact, I don't think he had been given the job when we discussed the policy.'

Cunningham glanced at Anna. Something wasn't right. 'So he mentioned to you that he was going for a job?'

'Yes, I've just said that he was hoping for some work.'

'But you have no idea who it was for?'

'No.'

Cunningham sighed and doodled on her notepad.

Anna leaned forward. 'What can you tell us about Mrs Brandon's previous partner?'

Rushton tensed.

'You've said she was well provided for, so could you tell us who he was? I suppose we can start checking ourselves. It would be simpler, though, if you helped us a little.'

'They were not married.'

'Yes, we know that,' Anna persisted, 'but the children are his, is that correct?'

Rushton chewed his lips.

'Mr Rushton, what on earth is the problem? You obviously know who he is, and you've stated that you take care of Mrs Brandon's finances . . .'

'The children were born two years apart, by IVF treatment. Mrs Brandon's ex-partner is now living in Bermuda.'

Cunningham looked to the ceiling. 'Terrific. Could we just have a name?'

'He's unlikely to ever return to this country.'

Cunningham leaned back, sighing. 'His *name*, Mr Rushton?'

'Anthony Collingwood . . . Well, that is the name I was told.'

'Do you also handle his finances?'

'No, I do not. I have no business connection to him whatsoever. In fact, I've never met him.'

Cunningham stood up. Rushton looked a little confused.

'Thank you for your co-operation. I'll no doubt ask you to come in again. DI Travis will show you out.' Cunningham left Anna with Rushton, who was now pinkish in the face and flustered.

'I didn't have any business dealings with Mr Collingwood. I want that made very clear,' he stated repeatedly as he left the station.

Anna returned to the incident room. Seeing Cunningham's door ajar, she went to get more details on Collingwood. She was about to knock, then stood listening.

'This case is really blowing sideways on me now. We've gone from a godforsaken drug squat in Chalk Farm to a connection with Christ knows who. I need someone from the Drug Squad over here to give me as much as they have on a guy called Collingwood. I've got a bit of a dozy team and could do with some back-up.'

Anna hung back, unsure whether or not she should make herself visible. Then she froze.

'Well, she's with me, but to be honest, she seems in

a daze. I don't know about her being sharp – I haven't seen any sign of it. She seems loath to open her mouth. In fact, I've got a young red-headed DC who seems more on the ball. Whatever happened to her when she was working for you . . .'

Anna had to take a deep breath. Was she talking to Langton?

'All right, Jimmy, but I'd appreciate a few kicks up the arse, because right now we are going nowhere, apart from some autistic kid who has given us about every vehicle licence-plate in London.'

Anna did a fast U-turn and headed back to her poky office. She was shaking with anger. Cunningham obviously thought little of her, but to compare her with bloody Gordon was outrageous. She opened her laptop and went online. She Googled the name Anthony Collingwood: it came up empty. She tried known drug dealers and soon forgot her anger as she scrolled down.

An Alexander Fitzpatrick was wanted for importation of a vast haul of uncut cocaine from the United States. His last known whereabouts were in Bermuda, but he had been sighted in Columbia. He had homes in Florida, Barbados and Santa Monica. He also had so many different aliases that it was almost laughable – but one of them was Anthony Collingwood.

Anna closed the file down, and went back online again to make sure she hadn't misspelled the name Anthony Collingwood. She then Googled Alexander Fitzpatrick himself.

He was described as a handsome, charismatic man, with high intelligence; he spoke six languages. There were many pages on Fitzpatrick covering newspaper articles dating back to his original arrest for drug trafficking. Alexander Fitzpatrick was wanted on both sides of the Atlantic for drug dealing. Next Anna requested known aliases used by Fitzpatrick, and again, amongst twenty other names, was ANTHONY COLLINGWOOD. Photographs of Fitzpatrick showed him as a slim, attractive, long-haired hippy of twenty through to his mid-thirties, and then there was nothing. It was as if he had disappeared, but he still remained on the FBI's Most Wanted lists.

Anna read and reread the attributes and stories on the website. Over and over again the words *charismatic* appeared, *Oxford-educated*, *stylish*, *literate*. Suspected of working with Mafia and Columbian drug cartels, the elusive and dangerous Mr Fitzpatrick had accumulated massive wealth, but escaped arrest for now more than thirty years.

Frank Brandon had none of these attributes but, as a tough ex-detective with broad shoulders, he must have felt capable of taking care of Julia and her children. Anna was certain, if she was correct, that Frank Brandon must have known the identity of Julia's ex-partner. Suddenly the life insurance policy made more sense. Fitzpatrick had been able to escape detection for so many years because, according to one of the articles on the website, he had tipped off the USA Drug Squad with names of other dealers. If that was the truth, then plenty of people would want Fitzpatrick dead.

Anna wondered if poor old Frank had paid the ultimate price for being with Julia. If so, she would need a lot more evidence and above all, she would have to get from Frank's widow the identity of her so-called partner. She printed off the details to take home. She didn't contemplate passing on the information just yet. As it was, she was just acting on one man's name being a connection to Fitzpatrick. *Anthony Collingwood.*

Chapter Five

Anna had no time to continue checking on Fitzpatrick as there was suddenly a buzz from the incident room. The checks into the car registrations were paying off, and the duty manager was dividing up the pick-ups of the vehicle owners. Cunningham wanted all of them questioned. A number had records: petty criminals, mostly drug offenders. It would be a hectic afternoon and a long night for everyone. Anna would have to put off her drinks date with Jenkins.

The mass exodus had been beefed up with uniforms, as they had fifty-eight licence plates to check out. Many of the cars had already been eliminated, as they were connected to residents on the estate. Other vehicles were already on the wanted list, as they had been stolen, but uppermost were the last group: those which, according to Jeremy Webster, had been parked near the site on the night of the shooting.

The hoodies brought in for questioning filled up the cells and interview rooms, but the 'smell' was wrong. Why would these smalltime punks shoot through a door? They were there, uppermost, to score – so why kill Frank Brandon? It became clear during the arrests and question-ing that the key dealers were not amongst those traced.

Anna, still seething at Cunningham's derogatory remarks, chose to take the more upmarket vehicles: one of
them might belong to the man who had accompanied
Frank Brandon. To her irritation, she was yet again
paired with Gordon. They had addresses to visit right
across London, from Hampstead to Chelsea and Brixton.

Anna arrived at the Hampstead address of her first
owner-driver at five-thirty that afternoon. Paul Wrexler
was not at home, but his pregnant girlfriend was. Helen
was nervous and agitated when faced with Anna and
Gordon, and became even more so when asked about
her boyfriend's whereabouts on the night of the murder.
He had been at home, she said, until she went to bed and
then had gone out for about an hour at nine-thirty to
pick up some cranberry juice for her, as she had a craving
for it. She had never heard of Frank Brandon, but what
interested Anna was why she was so anxious. When
asked if her partner ever took drugs, Helen broke out in
a sweat, dabbing at her upper lip with a folded tissue.

Anna eventually grew tired of being pleasant. A
man had been found murdered, she explained, at the
same location where a police witness had seen Wrexler's
BMW parked.

'Let me ask you again,' she said. 'Does Mr Wrexler use
drugs?'

Helen, in tears, stuttered out that he used cocaine, but
only occasionally. He had promised not to use it any
more, with the baby coming. She had been worried
about the people he was mixing with when he scored. It
took another few minutes for Anna to calm her down
and ask if she had ever met any of these dealers. She
shook her head and repeated that Wrexler only resorted

to taking cocaine when he was under pressure to work long hours. Just as Anna was about to get details of Wrexler's workplace, to question him there, he arrived home.

Wrexler was in his early thirties, wearing a pinstriped suit, white shirt and tie. He was a commodities broker in the City and, judging by his flat and his new car, he was earning good money.

When he learned the reason Anna and Gordon were there, he became abusive towards Helen. 'What have you been telling them, for God's sake?'

Anna asked him to sit down, and calm down. He perched on the edge of a chair, giving Helen angry glances.

'I have not used for months,' he said tightly.

'Have you ever been to the Warren Estate in Chalk Farm?'

'No, I haven't.'

'This would have been two nights ago.'

'I wasn't there.'

'That may be so, Mr Wrexler, but your car was seen parked on the estate.'

'There has to be a mistake.'

'I don't think so. We know your car was on the forecourt on the night a man was murdered.'

'Jesus Christ! I wasn't there, I swear; you must be mistaken.'

'Did you lend your car to someone?'

'No.'

'Then can you explain why we have your car registration as one of the vehicles seen parked there that night?'

'I wasn't there.'

Anna began to tap her foot; she knew he was lying.

'Perhaps we should continue this interview at the station?'

'For God's sake, why?'

'Mr Wrexler. As I said before, a man was found murdered at a squat used by dealers and one that had been in operation for some months. If you were not there on this specific night, have you ever been there before?'

Helen looked at him with an almost pleading look. 'You told me you weren't using it any more,' she said. 'You promised me!'

'I've told you the truth, for God's sake.'

Anna stood up and smiled at Helen. She suggested she make herself a cup of tea while they finished talking to Mr Wrexler.

As soon as she was out of the room, Anna went for it.

'Right. I've impressed on you the importance of knowing what time you were at the estate and when you left—'

'I wasn't there.'

Anna shook her head. 'Yes, you were, and now is the opportunity to tell me the truth. I am not concerned with what you bought, I just need to know what time you—'

'I wasn't there.'

Anna stood up. 'All we are trying to do is eliminate the people we know were parked at the estate on the night of this murder. Now, if you refuse to co-operate, then . . .'

'All right.'

Anna cocked her head to one side, waiting.

'I did go there, but I didn't score. I swear on my life, I didn't. I mean, I was thinking about it, but Helen has

Deadly Intent

been so anxious about me being out late, and she wanted some cranberry juice, and I'd had this nightmare day, and I was worn out ...' He bowed his head. 'I got there about ten-fifteen. I went up to the first landing and saw all these hoodies hovering around on the corridor, guarding the place, and I just freaked. You know the risk I was taking. So I went to the car and drove off. I was only there for ten minutes, no more.'

'I see. Can you describe these "hoodies" at all?'

'No, I never really saw their faces. They were black kids – well, most of them. There were about seven of them and I just didn't want to get into any aggravation, so I swear I just drove away.'

'What about other cars?'

'There were quite a few, but I wasn't paying any attention to them. I was more concerned with getting home.'

Anna smiled and looked up from her notebook. 'Thank you. Just one more thing. How did you know where to go to score?'

'What do you mean?'

'Well, it's simple, isn't it? Chalk Farm is a little way from here, and the dealer's flat is a boarded-up squat on a very rough estate. So how did you know you could score drugs from there?'

Wrexler twisted his body in his seat.

'Had you been there before?'

'No.'

'Then how did you know you would be able to score?'

'Oh Christ, I don't want to get him into trouble.'

'Who?'

'One of the guys at work. He used to score for me sometimes. I think he got it off one of the company

87

drivers. My mate is not a dealer, he just gets it for personal use. Anyway, it was becoming expensive – well, this is what he told me – so I said to him, wouldn't it be cost-effective for us to buy direct and split whatever we got between us?'

'I need to know his name.'

'The driver?'

'No, your friend.'

Wrexler sighed. 'Okay, but I hate to do this. Like I said, we're just small-time, and we're not addicts or anything like that.'

'His name, Mr Wrexler – then we can leave.'

'Ben Carter.'

'What car does he drive?'

'An MG Sport.'

'And the company driver's name?'

'Oh shit.' Wrexler pulled at his tie. 'Donny something. I'm unsure of his surname.'

Anna stood up and put her notebook away. Wrexler sprang up and asked if they could keep his name out of it. Anna made no reply, simply thanking him for his time.

She and Gordon returned to their car to get to their next scheduled meeting in Chelsea. It was almost seven o'clock. They drove in silence for a while. Then Gordon asked what they were going to do about Wrexler.

'Nothing, right now. I would say if he has any more coke stashed, he'll be snorting it! One day, if he keeps it up, it will take over him and his work.'

'Do you believe him?'

'Yes, do you?'

'I don't know, I've never used it. I've never even had a joint.'

'Good for you and . . . Gordon? When I'm working

these people over, it's a good idea if you made some notes as well, so we back each other up. Can you recall the name of the guy at his work who also uses?'

'Erm, no. I can't.'

'Exactly, so start concentrating. You are not along for your entertainment.'

'Right, sorry. I got so interested in how you questioned him. To be honest, I would have believed him straight off – you know, that he wasn't there. Smart flat, nice girlfriend, smart car, smart bloke.'

'No, he isn't. You think it's smart to do what he was doing? Scoring from cheap drug dealers? That's how these creeps survive, dealing with the "nice" guys who think they can handle it, cutting out the middle man – in Wrexler's case, a driver. I need to know more about him.'

The address in Chelsea was equally upmarket, a small chic house off the King's Road. Mark Taylor's car was a convertible Mercedes. They drew up outside his home as he was walking up the road, about to let himself in. He was of similar age to Wrexler and had his own business, selling bridal and wedding accessories. He was pleasant and relaxed, and invited them in.

Without waiting for Anna to explain the reason for their visit, he launched into the problems the residents had parking their cars at night. 'I've had to leave my car in Cheyne Walk, which means I've got to get up at some ungodly hour to move it before I get a ticket.'

'We are not here about parking permits.'

He blinked.

'We are here because your car was seen parked on an estate in Chalk Farm two nights ago.'

'What?'

'We are investigating a murder.'

'Christ, I can't help you.'

'I think you can, because we know your car was parked in the forecourt of the estate.'

'I don't remember.'

'Were you scoring drugs, Mr Taylor?'

It was a similar scenario to Wrexler. Taylor denied scoring drugs or ever using them, then eventually admitted that he had been to Chalk Farm at around 11.15 p.m. He had gone to the squat and scored some amphetamines. He had not been into the flat but had spoken to a boy standing on the landing outside number 19. He told him what he wanted, the boy returned with it and Mark paid him. He also admitted that he had been to the same address on two other occasions. He tried it on, saying he had a sleeping disorder, but Anna ignored the excuse; she knew Taylor was just trying to get out of the fact that he was scoring illegal drugs. The most important information to get out of him was who had given him the squat contact. He said he couldn't recall specifically but, at a party, he had met someone who had passed on the address and told him that they were dealing in anything he wanted, and at a straight price.

At last, they got their first link. Taylor said he did not know anyone called Wrexler, or Carter; all he did know was the Christian name of the driver – Donny. The latter had driven one of the guests to the party. As Anna already knew this Donny worked for the firm employing Wrexler, she was confident that they would be able to track him down. At the same time, she insisted they get the name and address of the girl giving the party. She was called Samantha Smith-Felton, was well-connected from a wealthy aristocratic family.

By the time they reached the last address, it was eight-thirty. Anna was hungry but decided to continue; the sooner it was finished, the faster she could get home. They found themselves on a council estate, almost as rundown as the squat in Chalk Farm. Eddie Court's souped-up Mini was parked in the drive of the estate. It was at least fifteen years old, not one of the new flash models. According to Jeremy Webster's list, this vehicle had been parked on the estate on four different occasions. The trace on the eighteen-year-old Edward Court had thrown up one previous arrest for burglary. He was currently working as a painter and decorator. Considering his record, Anna wouldn't have let him near a can of paint outside her property, let alone inside.

Eddie's mother was named as renting the property; he had given her address on his licence documents. When Anna knocked on the paint-peeling door on the fifth floor of the high-rise, Eddie opened it. As Anna showed her ID, he tried to shut it, but she left her foot firmly between the door and the frame. After a few terse words, Eddie opened the door wider and, begrudgingly, showed them into the front room.

It was untidy and stuffy, with a television tuned to a sports channel. Anna sat next to Gordon on a stained, broken sofa. Eddie hovered; he was wearing tight jeans, trainers and a T-shirt with zigzags across it. His hair was braided, with small beads attached to the ends. Anna went straight to the point, explaining that they were there to investigate a murder.

'Listen, I dunno what you think I done, but I never done nothink!' the boy burst out. 'I thought you was here about a ladder gone missing from the van.'

'We're not here about any missing ladder. We need to know why you were parked outside the Warren Estate in Chalk Farm two nights ago.'

It was a repeat of their previous two interviews. According to Eddie, he had never gone to the squat, he did not use drugs and they had to be mistaken about his car being parked there, 'cos he was working at a disco two nights ago. Judging by his red-rimmed eyes, he was on something; he started sweating. Anna calmly reiterated that she would need confirmation about his whereabouts and witnesses who could substantiate his claim.

'Do you know a driver called Donny?'

'No, I got me own car.'

'It's because of your car that we are here. Eddie, if you can't give me the truth about why you were at Chalk Farm, then I'll have to continue this interview at the station. We know you parked up there two nights ago. We also know you were seen there on two different occasions.'

'Shit.'

'You could be knee-deep in it, if you don't answer truthfully. All I need to know is, if you were there, what time you arrived, what time you left, and whether you can give me a description of the person you scored from. That is why you were there, isn't it?'

'My mum's gonna kill me; she's just gone out to bingo.'

'Sit down, Eddie. Let's get this over and done with and then we can leave, maybe before she returns. I am not booking you on scoring or even using, but that's not to say I won't if you don't co-operate.' Anna felt worn out; having to repeat herself was tedious. She didn't believe that Eddie could be of any more help than the previous two men – but then he started to talk.

'Okay, I admit I had gone there.'

'What time?'

'Late, 'cos I'd done my second stint at the disco.'

'So what time would you say it was?'

'Maybe two-thirty to three.'

Anna said nothing as she jotted down notes. This was close to the time of the shots heard by Mrs Webster. 'Take me through exactly what happened, Eddie.'

'Don't I need a lawyer or somethink?'

'Not unless you were involved in the murder!'

'Listen, I drive up and there are quite a few kids around and I give one a quid to stay by me car, but he tells me to get stuffed when I give him the quid, right? So I'm a bit lairy about leaving me motor and going up to the squat, so what I done was give him some lip. I sort of decided I'd not risk it – it was real dark, you know. Most of the streetlights have been bombed out, and another thing . . .'

Anna stopped writing, pencil poised.

'Well, I dunno, it just didn't feel right. I mean, I admit I'd been there before, few months back and then an even longer time before that. I didn't recognise any of the kids. Nah, it just didn't feel right.' Eddie lit a roll-up and took a deep drag. 'Before, I sort of knew some of the runners, right? And it was real easy: go up to the second floor, and they'd be with me, and then you'd get to the door. There was always a dude waiting. He'd ask what you wanted, some spliff or coke, he'd go back inside and come out with the gear, then you paid your money. Business over and done with, right? You with me?'

'Yes,' Anna said.

'But this time it was different, like there could be new blokes running it. So, I'm walking round to open the driving door. With me?'

'Yes.'

'And then this big blacked-out Mitsubishi almost knocks me sideways. If I'd been a few inches further out, it would have clipped me, and I was pissed, right, not only 'cos I'd driven all the way over there for nothing, and now this guy almost runs me down . . .'

'So you saw the driver?'

'Yeah, he parked up right in front of me and I got to give him some verbals and he turns on me, real nasty. He says go fuck yourself. I mean, he'd almost run into me, not the other way round, and he says go fuck yourself!'

Anna felt her stomach flip. 'What happened then?'

'Well, I would have taken him on but he was bigger'n me, and I just didn't want any aggro, so I turns back to me car an' I drove off.'

Anna opened her briefcase and took out the photograph of Frank Brandon. 'Is this the man?'

Eddie leaned forward and took the photograph. He stared at it for a few moments, then nodded. 'Yeah, that's him. Like I said, he was a big bloke.'

'What about the passenger? Was there someone else in the Mitsubishi?'

'Yeah, but I didn't get a good look at him. He was gettin' out and then I was drivin' past.'

'Can you just close your eyes and think back to that moment you saw him?'

'Who?'

'The passenger: the man in the Mitsubishi. You said he was getting out as you drove past.'

'Oh right, yeah. Well, what I said was, I didn't get a look at him. I was passing him, right, an' he was just sort of bending down to get out of the jeep and, like I said, it was real dark out there.'

'But didn't you put your headlights on?'

'Around there, no way. Put 'em on when I got into the road.'

Disappointed, Anna closed her notebook and stood up.

'Is that it?' Eddie asked.

'For now it is, Eddie. Thank you for your co-operation.'

Eddie seemed disappointed as well. 'Was he the geezer that got murdered?'

Anna looked at him.

'The tall guy, the passenger, was he the one done in?'

'How do you know he was tall? You said he was bending down to get out of the jeep.'

'Right, yeah, but I saw his legs – long legs; he hadda be a big geezer as well.'

Anna was considering going over it again with Eddie – the fact that the passenger could have been very tall fitted the blood-spattering marks – but then Gordon spoke for the first time since they had been there. 'You see the tall man's shoes?'

Eddie looked at Gordon, almost as surprised as Anna that he had opened his mouth. 'Yeah, I think they was polished shoes, not sneakers. They wasn't white.'

It was after eleven by the time Anna got home. Her personal parking space was taken by another car, and a flash one at that: a Lotus. By the time she had tried to contact the never-present security manager to get the offending car moved, the driver walked out of the connecting door to the apartments.

'This is a private parking space,' she said.

'Sorry, just moving it; been visiting.'

'In future, would you please not use the residents' parking bays? There are two vacant spaces for guests,' she retorted angrily.

'They were taken when I got here.' He bleeped open his car. He had a manner that really grated: upper-class, over-confident and arrogant.

Anna slammed her car door and waited for him to reverse. He fired up his engine; it sounded like thunder in the confined garage space. She adjusted the mirror to watch the Lotus, wondering how he would work the electronic garage door. He leaned out of his window, and used the manual digit box. The garage door swung open and he drove away. Tense with anger, Anna locked her car and went up to her flat. So much for the tight security, one of the reasons she had bought the flat.

There were more boxes stacked in her small hallway, along with the others she had not had time to unload. She sighed, wondering when she would ever get the chance to organise everything. Judging by the way the case was going, there would be no weekends off for the foreseeable future.

By the time she had eaten, it was one o'clock in the morning. The water in the shower was still freezing cold and there was a note pinned to the door: *Faulty heater.* Terrific, she thought, and sat down to make her list of complaints to go over with the phantom security manager, Mr Burk. She set the alarm for six-thirty, intending to have a confrontation with him before she left for work.

Morning came so fast, it was as if she had only just put her head on the pillow. She called Burk three times, each time leaving an urgent message on his answer service. On the fourth attempt, Burk himself had barked into the phone, 'Yes!'

'Mr Burk, this is Anna Travis. Would you please come to my apartment? I need to talk to you.'

'It's only seven o'clock!'

'I'm aware of that, but as I'm at work all day and not back till late, I would really appreciate it if you came up to see me now.'

'I'm not on until eight.'

Anna took a deep breath. 'Mr Burk, I would suggest that if you want to keep your job, and the accommodation that I believe is part of your deal with the company, you get yourself up to my flat as I have requested.'

There was a pause. She could hear a snort down the phone as if he was trying to control his temper. 'Give me ten minutes.'

'Thank you.' She replaced the receiver.

Anna had never had to deal with the Burks of this world in her domestic life. Her previous flat had been well-run and, when her father had been alive, he had taken care of everything. Even when Langton had lived with her, he had repaired the odd thing when necessary. Now she had no one whom she could call up and ask for help. How had she reached such a solitary point in her life, with no close friends?

Anna thought back to her time living with Langton. Their break-up had taken its toll on her. She remembered what she had overheard from Cunningham's office. Had she lost the plot because of Langton's hold over her? Lost it because of what she knew about him from their last case together? That no matter what a disgusting creature Langton's attacker had been, Langton had made sure he would never live to stand trial?

Anna began to take a good look at herself: the stupid, hurried move to sell her old flat, because of wanting to cut loose from her past; the purchase of the present apartment, with all its faults; the massive mortgage payments. The very thing that she had prided herself on was her achievement in the Met, and now she was floundering. She knew that she was going to have to get herself back on track and, with no one to help her, she would have to do it alone.

As if on cue, the doorbell rang. Anna drained her coffee mug, placed it on the kitchen counter and took a deep breath. 'Right, you little turd, I am going to start with you!'

She opened the door to the moody little man. 'Please do come in, Mr Burk. Thank you so much for coming to see me.' She smiled sweetly.

He glared at her, stepping over the packing boxes and following her into the kitchen.

She picked up her list and turned to face him. 'I have made a list of all the appliances that are not working correctly. You can start on that today—'

'Miss Travis, I am the security manager here. I am not paid to do maintenance work in any of the apartments – that's not my job.'

'Then I suggest you get whoever it is to do the work.' She listed her complaints about the garage door, the parking in her space and the fact that a visitor knew the security code.

He sat on one of the kitchen stools, frowning bad-temperedly. As she finished, he was breathing heavily, as if trying to maintain calm. 'Miss Travis, I can get someone else in to do the odd jobs, but it will cost you.'

Anna leaned over. 'No, it will not. Let me explain. It is not actually Miss; my correct title is Detective Inspector. I have been very patient, but the list of items that I require repaired should be in perfect working order. I want hot water by the time I return this evening and, if this means a new boiler has to be installed, then I suggest you get onto the owners of the block and talk to them. I would also like confirmation that no resident gives out the private entry code to their guests. I want those garage doors tested until I am confident they are secure.'

Mr Burk didn't say a word. His jaw had dropped open slightly, as he watched Anna walking around the kitchen pointing to stickers on the dishwasher, the oven and two wall plugs.

She opened her wallet and took out a fifty-pound note. 'You will get this when the packages are opened and the cardboard boxes removed. I have left details of where I want everything to be placed. You can arrange for someone to put up the blinds.'

Burk blinked.

'I need you to take very good care of me,' Anna said quietly. 'Do you understand, Mr Burk, what I am saying? What I am asking you to do?'

He nodded.

'Good, it's settled then. You go off now and have your breakfast. I will see you at this time tomorrow morning.'

★

Anna drove out of the garage. There was Burk, waving her through, almost saluting her. She smiled and waved as she passed. Having sorted her domestic problems, she was now determined that she would turn over a new leaf at work. Cunningham reckoned she had a dozy team, specifically describing Anna as being in a daze. Well, she would make her boss eat her words.

She hadn't felt this energised for a long, long time – not since Langton had left her. In some way she was back to being Anna Travis, the daughter her father had been so proud of, the officer with whom Langton had been more than impressed. DI Anna Travis was not going to be anyone's doormat *ever again*.

Chapter Six

A nna was at her desk before eight-thirty that morning. She checked over her report from the day before, and called Gordon to her office. 'You got your report of last night ready?'

'Not quite.'

'I'd like it before the morning briefing.'

Gordon hesitated. 'It's just I've not had breakfast yet.'

'That's your problem. Go on, hop it. Oh, and by the way – it was a good question regarding the man's shoes at Eddie Court's flat.'

Gordon flushed and smiled. 'Thank you. I'll get that report done straight away.'

Next, Anna called in the duty manager for an update. She was buzzing with adrenalin and he was taken aback. She asked him to arrange for the team to gather just before the briefing so she could really get to know them.

Anna had forty-five minutes before the briefing started, so she Googled Alexander Fitzpatrick again. She had a feeling about him, but she was not quite ready to share it.

Born 1948 in Surrey, into an affluent middle-class family, Fitzpatrick was educated at Eton, then Oxford, where he gained a First in PPE – Philosophy, Politics and Economics. Skimming through the mass of data, Anna tried to picture what he would look like, all these years later. The photos were at least thirty years old. Now he would be in his early sixties, and she doubted he would still look like a hippy.

Fitzpatrick had joined the local newspaper as a fledgling reporter and subsequently worked for *The Times* and *Guardian* as a travel reporter. He used this as a cover to smuggle tons of hashish into the UK from Pakistan and Thailand, broadening his sales into America and Canada. Later, he had switched his drug importation from hashish to heroin and cocaine, and built a worldwide operation, laundering money through offshore banks and fake business dealings. Making millions, he lived a luxurious life, with an extraordinary ability to maintain his profile as a journalist at the same time. At the peak of his drug dealing, he had his twenty aliases, with passports for most, and an astonishing array of phone lines: sixty that had been traced.

In the late eighties, Fitzpatrick formed a company making documentary films, which turned out to be yet another means of shipping his drugs worldwide under the cover of respectability. He had homes in Spain, Florida and the Bahamas, a fleet of cars, a jet and a powerful ocean-equipped yacht called *White Trash*. It was not until 1991 that he became the focus of the Drug Enforcement Agency; the fact that they had been monitoring Fitzpatrick for many years without success gave him the confidence of being outside the law.

It was one of his close friends who had betrayed him and eventually caused his downfall. A heroin addict, Michael Drencock had been arrested for abusive behaviour outside a night club. In possession of heroin and with even more discovered at his flat, Drencock had given police details of offshore banks and money-laundering businesses. But, before Fitzpatrick was to stand trial, Drencock withdrew all his statements and, on bail pending his own charges, he committed suicide. Fitzpatrick made another outrageous move by hiring some of his men to arrange a helicopter to lift him as he was entering the courthouse. He had been on the run ever since, remaining on America's Most Wanted list. Like a modern-day Scarlet Pimpernel, the hundreds of sightings of him in various countries gave him a mystic persona; underlined was the fact that Fitzpatrick, or whatever alias he now used, remained a very dangerous man.

Anna closed her laptop and sat deep in thought. Unlike the infamous Howard Marks, who spent time in a federal United States penitentiary for his drug dealing, Fitzpatrick had never been to prison. Marks, now a bestselling author, depicted in his books his life of drug trafficking and his career as a respected journalist, his work featuring in national newspapers. He also campaigned vigorously for the legalisation of recreational drugs.

Fitzpatrick appeared to Anna to be a very different creature. When he couldn't make enough money from soft drugs, he turned to heroin and cocaine. This meant he had to mix with more lethal partners, including the Mafia. Could Anna be right? Could Julia Brandon's partner have been Fitzpatrick? Could he have been audacious enough to return to England using the name Anthony Collingwood? She opened her notebook: it was imperative they discover just what monies Julia Brandon had access to. She made a note that they would need to bring in David Rushton again, Julia's so-called business adviser, as well as questioning Julia herself again.

Anna checked the time and went into the incident room. The team was already gathered, ready for the morning briefing. She was relaxed and confident, as DS Phil Markham shook her hand, then DCs Pamela Meadows and Mario Paluzzo. The mug of coffee that Gordon brought her was tepid, but it was a show of respect nonetheless. At last, Anna felt part of the team rather than an outsider.

One of the kids Phil Markham had brought in for questioning, whose vehicle had been listed by Jeremy Webster, had no licence and no insurance, and the steering wheel went off at a right angle. It was a death-trap on wheels, but the boy maintained that it had been in perfect working order, as he was taking his driving test in it the following day. Anna was laughing as Markham mimicked the boy's accent, and did not see Cunningham walk out of her office.

'Right, if we can just cut out the comedy and get serious.'

Anna sat back and looked attentive. Markham gave her a sidelong glance and a wink. He was attractive, with an iron-grey crew cut and bright china-blue eyes. She liked him.

'Okay, let's see what we've got from each of you and then decide how we progress today.'

One by one, the officers stood up and gave Cunningham details of their interviews. It appeared that, despite the many boys brought in for questioning, they were dealing with punk kids scoring a few grams of coke for themselves or trying to earn money as runners. They had only sketchy details on the dealers. They rarely, if ever, came out of the squat and most of the deals were done on the doorstep, as Eddie Court had described. It was clear that the squat had been active for many months; it was also suspected it might be protected. This was an uneasy suggestion, as it would involve the local police. In all like-lihood the dealers had changed over, there had been some heavy punch-ups and many of the boys said they had been warned not to get involved as the new dealers were tougher and had their own lookouts and runners.

It also transpired that, unlike a few months back when the squat had been small-time, it was now trading with more upmarket clients. Crack cocaine was being sold, plus the addictive ice and heroin wraps as the more affluent punters had replaced the street kids.

The owners of the vehicles traced all said virtually the same thing: they'd heard about the squat via someone at a party. They might be scoring cocaine and crack, but it didn't seem that many of them were out-and-out addicts. This is what marked the squat as not typical. Any bust of a similar base would bring in addicts, desperate for a fix. They would often be found crashed out in the street or in a pitiful state of begging from anyone scoring. Cunningham continued to mark up the board as they gave their reports.

Eventually, it was Anna's turn. She flicked through her notebook.

'We have to bring in a driver working for a City bank that employs a user we interviewed called Paul Wrexler. We have only a Christian name for the driver: Donny. The same name came up when we interviewed a Mark Taylor. It seems they used to score from him, then tried to cut out the middleman and go direct. The same scenario applies: no one ever went into the squat, but scored on the doorstep, paid the money and got what they came for. I don't think either of the men questioned were addicts – more weekend users – and cocaine was the drug of choice. This links back to the kids saying the dealers have changed over, that they're now dealing in the more expensive narcotics.'

Cunningham folded her arms. 'Is that it?'

'No. We got a good lead from Eddie Court. He went to the squat to score, but got frightened off. He described a jeep, a Mitsubishi with blacked-out windows; he was able to identify Frank Brandon as the driver.

'He wasn't able to give us a licence plate, and we don't have one from Jeremy Webster, but he thinks he saw the Mitsubishi at 2.45 a.m. This meant he saw Frank Brandon just before he was shot.'

There was a murmur among the assembled officers.

'We asked about the passenger in the car. Eddie did not see his face, but reckoned he had to be tall, by the way he bent low to get out of the jeep. He was wearing smart polished shoes. These fit the description we got in from forensics about the bloody footprints around Frank Brandon's body. Whoever this man was, we know he was tall – over six feet – and that he stood behind Frank Brandon when he got the fatal shots to his head and face.'

Cunningham folded her arms and perched on one of the tables, frowning.

Anna continued. 'We need to trace that Mitsubishi jeep. We need to have it verified that this was the vehicle Frank Brandon was driving.' She wondered if she should bring up what she had been working on, or was it too early? 'I would like to reinterview Julia Brandon, and I think we also need to have another session with her financial adviser.'

Cunningham stared at her.

'The reason is, she must know about the Mitsubishi. She must have documents for the insurance and if not, her business adviser will. As he arranged the life insurance for Frank Brandon, he more than likely knows a lot more than he was willing to divulge. I think we need to know what Julia Brandon's financial situation is.'

Cunningham nodded her head. She gestured to Anna and asked her to join her in her office. Once there, she rounded on Anna and demanded, 'What are you holding back?'

'Why do you say that?'

'Because I'm older than you, and a lot more experienced, and I know you've not come clean. So: what is it?'

'It's just supposition. Until I am more certain, I would like some time.'

'You don't want to tell me?'

'If you insist, but I may be putting two and two together and coming up with six!' Anna smiled.

Cunningham was not amused. 'Share it.'

Anna took a deep breath. 'Okay. Mrs Brandon – Julia – has an ex-partner. We know, because her accountant told us, that his name is Collingwood. He provided for her and the two children, who, we have been told, are not his biological kids.'

Cunningham leaned back in her chair.

'Anthony Collingwood is one of the aliases used by a bigtime drug dealer called Alexander Fitzpatrick.' Anna filled in all the details she had acquired off the Internet. Cunningham didn't say a word. As Anna concluded, there was an ominous silence.

'Shit,' Cunningham said softly when Anna had finished.

'It could be coincidence.'

'No fucking way.'

'What I can't piece together is why he would risk going to that dive in Chalk Farm.'

'Well, we are going to have to find out. First, let's you and me get over to forensic; ballistics have some details for us. Then we visit the widow again.'

'If I am correct, then she should be monitored. We don't want her doing a runner.'

'I agree.'

'With two young kids, it's not that easy to just pack up and run, but if she has access to a lot of money, then . . .'

Cunningham stood up. 'I hear you. I'll get that organised. Give me fifteen minutes and we're out of here.' Cunningham gave Anna a hooded look and then leaned forward. 'Word of warning. You were not about to spread this information until you, DI Travis, were ready. Well, don't you ever do anything like this with me again, you understand? You have any information, you pool it. I don't want you running around like a headless chicken, because I've heard that you have done so in the past.'

Anna stepped back. 'I was just not certain, that was all. I wanted to be sure.'

'That may be so, but you come to me and let me decide; do not take it upon yourself to make decisions. Is that understood, Travis?'

'Yes, Ma'am.'

'Okay. Now get back to your office and write up whatever you've got on Fitzpatrick.'

'It's all on the Internet, apart from a recent photograph.'

'Go on, get to it. I'm impressed – up to a point!'

Anna closed the door quietly; she was so uptight she could hardly speak.

Pete Jenkins looked up from a microscope as they entered the forensic lab. He smiled a welcome and indicated for them to come to his bench and see what he was working on.

'Did you know a person's left thumbprint does not match his right thumbprint? So it's possible we can get a right thumbprint at a crime scene, and it won't match any we have on the database, but we could have a left thumbprint that may produce a result. What I have here is a partial left thumb'.

'Good. What else have you got for me?'

'Well, it's off a set of prints from the window-ledge. Again, we have no match, but the prints were made from a person who has, on the right hand, an index finger minus the top section.'

Jenkins displayed the enlarged prints on a computer. 'Looks like he had some injury to his hand, apart from the missing fingertip, because there's also a big indentation on the fleshy side of his palm. Another interesting point about these prints is the width between the thumb and first finger; they used to say it meant a person was very artistic!'

Cunningham sighed and looked at her watch. 'So from all the prints taken at the murder site we have no match?'

'Correct, but if you find a suspect minus his finger-tip . . .'

'Yes, yes, I'm with you,' she snapped.

'We have eighteen different prints from the various paper cups and takeaway food cartons, but as yet no luck with a match.' Jenkins moved across the lab, to where they were examining the footprints in the victim's blood. They had marked out how the footprints faced the door of the inner room in the squat and then turned and moved out. 'Large feet – wearing, I'd say, a size eleven or twelve, a loafer with hand-stitched soles.'

Anna remarked that this would fit with the description taken from Eddie Court of the passenger in the Mitsubishi. Ignoring her, Cunningham moved over to where they had been looking at the blood spattering. As they already knew from Jenkins's visit, when Frank Brandon was shot, someone was standing directly behind him. That someone had to be at least six feet three and would have been covered in bloodstains.

Lastly, they went to stand by the vast trestle table covered in items removed from the squat. Sleeping bags and blankets were pinned out as the scientists removed hairs and possible fibres that would assist their enquiry. The items smelled of mildew and sweat and could have been left there by any of the previous dealers, Anna thought.

Jenkins stood close to Anna as they looked over the items. She didn't meet his eyes, not wanting to get over-familiar with him in front of Cunningham.

'As you can see,' he gestured to the table, 'we have our work cut out for us; judging from the stink, these could have been left *in situ* for some time.'

'Right,' said Cunningham, 'we're going up to ballistics. Thank you for your time.'

'We are doing our best,' Jenkins said, and glanced at Anna. She looked away and followed Cunningham out of the lab.

★

'Bullets fired from a Glock Meister, very nice weapon: 22LR barrel recoil, spring assembly, speed loader. We have no cartridges and we think at least six of the ten-round magazines were emptied. Mostly, I hear, into the poor chap that died.' Vernon Lee, a small solid man with crinkly grey hair, turned to a cardboard box on his desk. 'This was found at the site, which surprised me; they must have left in one hell of a hurry to leave this kind of equipment behind. This, ladies, is a very expensive item. It's a Glock Meister optic and mount, with lights and lasers. I've got onto Saber Ballistic over at Caterham Barracks to see what they can give me but, as I said, it's a very upmarket weapon and not usual here in the UK. Stateside, yes, but it's costly. Yardies might be flash enough to own one, but this was a squat, wasn't it?'

Cunningham sighed. 'Let me tell you, Vernon, you'd be surprised what weapons these kids get their hands on. From Kalashnikovs to bazookas . . .'

'I know, I know,' he said, looking down at his notes. 'Did the pathologist discuss the trajectory of the shots, because they make it interesting? I'd say your shooter was short, or knelt down, like so.' He cupped both hands as if holding a gun and bent his knees. 'The bullets to the chest area, fired from behind the door, went in at an upward angle; the head shots were literally fired at a downward angle, no more than a foot and half away from the body. There were not, as first surmised, two different weapons. All the bullets are from the same gun.'

Anna chewed her lip. 'I think whoever was the shooter knew exactly what he was doing. He looked through the spyhole, saw who it was, and fired from behind the door. Then, satisfied he'd hit his target, he opened the door to finish him off.'

Vernon shrugged. 'Possible. We've set up a laser line to help. It all looks very clever but, reality is, poor bastard took three bullets to the head and two to his upper torso.'

'Five?'

'Yes, five bullets.'

Anna frowned and recalled Mrs Webster telling her how many shots she had heard. She asked if the Glock could have a silencer. Vernon nodded.

Back in the patrol car, Cunningham yawned as Anna flicked over her notes until she found the conversation with Mrs Webster.

'I've asked for some Drug Squad officers to give us a direction on what they think we're dealing with,' Cunningham said. 'I've not brought them in before, because they could cause a lot of aggro. We pulled in a bunch of hoodies; God knows how many people scored that night. Right now, this is a murder enquiry. What I don't want is those guys stepping on our toes.' She leaned back and closed her eyes.

Anna nodded, and checked her notes. Mrs Webster had said she heard six bullets fired. She was adamant about how many, even describing the sound the last three shots made – pop, pop, pop – and a gap between them and the first lot – which she said were louder than the last. If there were only five bullets found in the victim, they were one short. Anna closed her notebook to discuss it with Cunningham, when she realised that her boss was fast asleep.

Julia Brandon opened the front door herself. She gave a half-sigh, as if to express her irritation that the police were back, then turned towards the lounge, expecting them to follow.

Today she was wearing a chic black dress, high-heeled slingback shoes, and her hair was freshly blow-dried. Her body was toned and her long slender legs were worked out, as was the rest of her. Perfect make-up, elegant jewellery; she looked today like pure class. In no way did she look as if she was in mourning. Frank Brandon just didn't, to Anna, mix and match with her on any level.

'What do you want?' she asked.

'We just need some answers,' Cunningham said softly.

'I would like some too. I have to arrange my husband's funeral; when will his body be released?'

'I am sure it will be in the very near future.'

'Will somebody let me know?'

'Yes, of course.'

There was a palpable pause. Anna was unsure how Cunningham was going to open up the interview. Julia was examining the toe of her shoe as it dug into the thick pile carpet.

'Tell me about your previous partner.'

Julia didn't show any sign that this question fazed her. She simply replied coolly: 'I have no reason to discuss my private life with you or anyone else. If that is the reason you are here, then you have had a wasted journey.'

'We are investigating the murder of your husband, Mrs Brandon.'

'I have told you all that I know. I last saw him early in the morning on the day you said he died. I didn't speak to him the entire day and went to bed early. He was often out until late, sometimes not returning until three or four in the morning. On those occasions, he used a spare bedroom so as not to disturb me. I wasn't worried when he wasn't at home the following morning. I made breakfast for the children and took them to nursery.'

Anna leaned forwards. 'Did Frank drive a black Mitsubishi jeep?'

Julia sighed. 'I'm not sure . . . He used to drive my Range Rover but, for work, it's possible.'

'But wasn't it parked outside your house?'

'No, he used a lock-up garage a few streets away. I have only room for two cars: the Range Rover and my Mercedes SL Convertible, so he rented the garage.'

Cunningham gritted her teeth as she asked for the address. Julia walked to her desk and opened a drawer. She rifled through some papers, then picked up a Post-it and jotted down the address, which was close to their home in Wimbledon.

'Thank you. Do you have a set of keys for the garage?'

'No, I don't.'

'Could I please see your spare room? The one you say your husband used when he returned home late?'

Julia shrugged. 'It's the bedroom at the end of the landing. Help yourself.'

Cunningham glanced at Anna as she left the room.

Julia went back to digging the toe of her shoe into the carpet pile. 'I don't like that woman,' she said quietly to Anna.

'Why don't you want to discuss your previous partner?'

'I don't think it has anything to do with you or anyone else.'

'What if it did?'

'It doesn't. It was over a long time ago.'

'Do you keep in touch?'

'No.'

'Not even for the children?'

'They are not his, and he was never that interested, so

no. He doesn't keep in touch with either me or them.'

'But he has made substantial provision for them?'

'Yes,' she hissed.

'And for you?'

'Yes – but again, I really can't see that this is any of your business. As I said, my relationship was over when I met Frank.'

'You know, Julia, we can, without your permission, gain information regarding your ex-partner. Wouldn't it be simpler if you just—'

Julia looked up and glared at Anna. 'Are you married?'

'No.'

'Have you ever loved someone?'

'Yes. Yes, I have.'

'If that someone lied and betrayed you and hurt you, would you want to rake it all up? I don't want to discuss this at all, I really don't.'

'I'm sorry. It must be very distressing. I do understand, but you must also understand we are investigating the murder of your husband.' Anna did not add that Julia appeared to be more emotionally connected to her ex-partner than to poor Frank Brandon. 'Your financial adviser, Mr David Rushton, gave us his name: Anthony Collingwood.'

Julia gave a deep sigh.

'Do you have a recent photograph of him?'

'No, I do not. David should not have even mentioned his name. I don't think he ever met him. So much for client confidentiality.'

'Is that the name you knew him by?'

Julia looked away.

'When was the last time you saw him?'

'Years ago; as I said, we separated a long time ago.'

'How long ago?'

'For Christ's sake, about three years ago. I have not seen him since.'

'Do you have a contact address for him?'

'No! What on earth has this got to do with anything?'

'Perhaps a lot. Do you know if he uses any other names?'

'No, I don't.'

'What business was he in?'

'He was an investment banker.'

'Which bank?'

'I have no idea. We did not discuss his business. You have to understand that when I first met him, I was only sixteen years old.'

'Where did you meet him?'

Again, Julia sighed with irritation. 'I was in Florida, staying with friends in Palm Beach. They knew him well; he came aboard their yacht and—'

Cunningham walked back into the room and gestured to Anna. 'Would you excuse us, Mrs Brandon? I'd like Detective Travis to join me.'

'Do whatever you like,' Julia snapped.

The box bedroom was very neat and tidy. There was a television and DVD unit, a single bed and fitted wardrobe. Cunningham opened the wardrobe to display a row of shirts and suits, plus shoes. 'This looks to me as if he was living or at least mostly staying in this room. I've searched all the pockets and come up with nothing; I'd say someone had a good clear-out before me. There are banks of videos and DVDs, a dressing-gown and pyjamas in the bathroom ensuite. Now, you tell me, does this look like someone who just spends the odd night in here when he's home late?' Cunningham held up a leather-bound desk diary and opened it to reveal the torn pages. 'Like I said, someone's cleaned this room out.'

Anna looked around; from the open wardrobe came a waft of the cologne that Frank used. 'Maybe we should get over to his lock-up, see if the car's there.'

'I doubt it, but we might as well. Did you get anything?'

'She agreed that her ex-partner's name was Anthony Collingwood but I didn't push it – you know, bring up the Fitzpatrick connection.'

'Yeah, we'll hold off on that, but I want to come back with a warrant. Something isn't kosher.'

'I agree.' Anna bent down and looked under the bed. A pair of slippers were side by side, but there were no dustballs, nothing. She felt alongside the mattress.

'Don't waste time – I already did that. Let's go.'

Anna hesitated. 'In the kitchen, there are wedding photographs. Maybe we could take a look at them before we leave.'

Mai Ling was polishing the floor, using an electric buffer. There were no photographs on the dresser or the side table where Anna had last seen them. Anna asked where they were while Cunningham said goodbye to Mrs Brandon.

'Put away. Emily and Kathy very sad and asking for him, so madam took them away. She upset too.'

'Do you know where they are?'

'No, I not know.'

'Thank you.' Anna walked out.

Back in the car, Cunningham's foot twitched with irritation.

'She really pisses me off. She's not going to like me when we go back for the third time, because I want that place stripped. She's lying through her teeth.' Her mobile rang.

Cunningham finished up the call. 'They traced the Donny guy, the driver. We've got an address for him, so I want him brought in for questioning. His full name is Donny Petrozzo; sheet for handling stolen goods and six months for acting as a fence. He's been clean for five years. Be interesting to hear what he's got to say for himself.'

Frank Brandon's lock-up garage was part of a substantial property divided into six flats. There was a horseshoe drive that branched off to the rear where the garage was located.

The door was unlocked. Cunningham took out a handkerchief to turn the handle and looked inside. 'Well, well, well – look what we've got here.'

The black Mitsubishi looked like a dark brooding monster with all its tinted windows. It was filthy: mud covered the wheels and sides of the doors.

Anna found the light switch; then Cunningham tried the driver's door. It was unlocked and the keys were in the ignition. 'Get this baby towed in as quickly as possible and don't touch it.'

Anna suggested they look into the glove compartment, just in case.

Again, Cunningham used her handkerchief to open it, but it was locked. 'We might have prints on the keys. I'm loath to tamper with opening it up. We leave as is.'

'Up to you.'

'If it was you?'

'I have some surgical gloves in my briefcase.'

Cunningham glanced at her. 'My, my. Old Langton taught you well, didn't he?'

Anna didn't wish to get into whether or not Cunningham knew her father Jack Travis, but he had been the one to remind her always to keep a spare set with her. She shrugged and gestured to their patrol car.

'Should I get them?'

Cunningham nodded as she called into the station to arrange for the jeep to be towed. Anna snapped on the gloves, secretly pleased with herself. She removed the keys from the ignition, selected the smallest and opened the glove compartment. It contained a torn envelope with the insurance documents for the jeep in Frank Brandon's name, a parking ticket and a creased, folded map. Inside the map was a page torn from a small notebook. Written on it were five scrawled numbers and letters but no obvious words. Then Anna looked in the back seat.

It was empty, but there was a smell, one she had grown used to since joining the murder team. She got out of the car, handing the map to Cunningham and walked to the rear of the jeep. Due to the blacked-out windows, she could see nothing in the storage section at the back. 'I think we should take a look inside.'

Cunningham was eager to leave.

'Can't you smell it?' Anna persisted.

'Okay, let's open it up.' Cunningham grimaced as she stood beside Anna.

Covered in black bin liners wrapped around with thick masking tape was, they both knew, a body. 'Don't touch it. If we open it up, we might lose evidence.' Cunningham moved well away; she obviously found the stench difficult to deal with. It surprised Anna; as much as she was revolted by it, she had been on enough murders not to be that repelled.

It wasn't long before police cars were drawing up with the tow truck. The jeep was to be driven to the station yard, the body removed and taken to the lab for forensics to start work.

When the Mitsubishi had been taken away and the garage secured, the two women began checking out the residents of the house. Out of the six flats, they were able to gain access to only two.

First they interviewed a smart, elderly, rather deaf gentleman called Alfred Hall who lived in the basement and ground floor. The flat smelled of mothballs, urine and stale food. He complained bitterly that the original owners had not included the garage facility but, to his knowledge, rented it out for an exorbitant price. Numerous vehicles had used it over the years he had been living there, but he had not met any of their owners. He did know about the Mitsubishi, because it was often driven in late at night, and he was woken up by the lights and noise. He couldn't really recall the last time he had been woken, but he thought it was within the last couple of days.

The second tenant was a woman who was reluctant to let them in. Arlene Thorpe was in her mid-forties, thin, and with a yapping Jack Russell dog, which she had to shut into a bedroom. She was able to describe Frank Brandon and the Mitsubishi, as she had met him once when she was heading out to Wimbledon Common with her dog for his morning walk. He had been washing the jeep down and seemed quite pleasant. As far as she could recall, he had only been using the garage for the past six months; before that it had been used by the local estate agents who handled the rental.

Cunningham and Anna interviewed the estate agents, a local firm who were able to confirm that Mr Brandon had seen the rental advert in the local paper and contacted them. He had paid six months in advance, at five hundred pounds per month. He had given his address as the house owned by Julia and said that he would probably require the garage for year-round rental but, until he had more details, it would be for six months only.

By the time they returned to the station, the body had been removed. After grabbing something to eat, Anna yet again accompanied Cunningham to the mortuary.

There were no identification papers or wallet: the dead man's pockets had been emptied. He was wearing a cheap grey suit and a white Marks & Spencer shirt with a black tie. He had black lace-up shoes with navy-blue socks. His age was put at around late forties, early fifties. Cunningham asked for his prints to be rushed through to see if he had any form. Anna, however, was certain she knew who he was. The grey suit and black tie was almost like the uniform of a chauffeur.

By four o'clock, she was proved correct. The prints from the dead man matched those of a Donald Petrozzo, his record for burglary and fencing on file. The forensic team reported back that someone had done a very thorough cleaning job of the interior of the jeep. They were coming up empty-handed so far, but had only just begun stripping down the seats.

Cunningham held a briefing to discuss the new developments. The case was opening up, its loose ends dangling like stalks. Whoever accompanied Frank Brandon on the night of his death drove his jeep away from the drug squat. The connection to Donny Petrozzo had to be drugs. Anna would have to re-question Wrexler and Taylor. She returned to her office and sat brooding, making a jigsaw of her notes. She constantly came back to the possibility that Anthony Collingwood, the man Julia Brandon admitted was her ex-partner, could be the kingpin dealer, Alexander Fitzpatrick. Langton had always said there were no coincidences; Anna was beginning to think he was right. The key, to be certain, had to be Julia Brandon.

She checked that the surveillance was still in operation. If Julia was the vital link to Fitzpatrick, her life could be in danger. It was still not clear why he would not only be with Frank Brandon, but accompanying him to the drug squat. It didn't add up. She was certain they were overlooking something: the question was – what?

DS Phil Markham had been monitoring the surveillance on Julia Brandon. She had not left the house other than to collect her children from their little private school and then, with Mai Ling, to do some grocery shopping. There had been no visitors.

'What about phone calls?' Anna asked.

'We haven't had the go-ahead to tap into her landline.'

'We should. What about her mobile phone?'

'I've no idea. Right now, they are just keeping watch over the house. Her accountant has called us a couple of times asking for the release of Brandon's body, so they can arrange the funeral. So far they are keeping him on ice, so to speak.'

It felt as if everything was on hold as they waited for the autopsy result on Donny Petrozzo, and for forensics to report on any findings from the jeep. Anna went in to see Cunningham, asking if she could take off home.

'Sure, we'll have more developments to crack on with tomorrow.'

'Good night then,' Anna said, relieved that she could get back to do some unpacking.

She had intended going straight home, but instead decided to call in at the murder site. The crime-scene tapes were mostly still intact, but a couple of them were loose and flapping. The teams taking evidence from the squat had long gone, but there were still two uniformed officers on duty. It was dark; the corridors of the boarded-up areas of the estate had no lights left intact. Forensics had removed their arc lamps. Anna walked over broken glass and debris to show her ID to the bored uniformed officer. She asked if they had booked any of the kids trying to score and he shook his head, pointing to the crime-scene tapes across the front door of the squat. 'They see those and they get their skates on fast!'

'You mind if I just take a look around? Do you have a torch I could borrow?'

He handed over a high-powered torch and she ducked under the tape. With only the beam of the torch, she made her way into the dank, dirty corridor, now cleared of food cartons and beer cans.

The heavy bolted door to the dealers' room had been removed and taken into ballistics to examine the bulletholes. On the floor, she could see the forensic chalk marks, the white tape showing where Frank had fallen. The blood spattering on the walls was marked with chalk numbers, from one to fifty.

She could see more numbers, where the officers had taken prints from the window and window-ledge. Standing in the wretched, stinking room, she still couldn't put the pieces of the jigsaw together. Why, if she were correct, would a man like Alexander Fitzpatrick come to such a small-time den? She shone the torch around, and stood in the position where the door would have been. She knew there was a spy-hole in the door, so whoever used the gun had looked through it, seen Frank and opened fire. No cartridges had been found – the gunman must have picked them up. Would a street dealer have picked up the shells? Would he care?

Anna aimed the torch slowly around the room. Way above the outline of Frank Brandon's body was an old square air vent. Anna shone her torch up, holding the beam on the vent. She wondered if it had been checked out, but could see no chalk marks to indicate that it had been examined.

The only piece of so-called furniture left in the squat was a wooden crate. She carried it to the air vent, climbed up and examined it more closely, standing on tiptoe. Each square of the vent was large enough for her to insert her index finger; she poked and prodded, then felt in her pockets for a pen. She wiggled it around, and was about to give up when she felt something blocking the vent.

When she shone the torch directly at the hole she could see something glinting. The pen was no use; she got down to open her briefcase and took out a manicure set. She didn't like doing it, because they were very good tweezers, but she stretched them wide and then climbed back up again. It took some time, standing on tiptoe, and she had to balance the torch in her left hand – but, at last, she was able to tease out the sixth bullet.

Cupping it in her hand, she was afraid to clutch it too tightly, as she could see the dried blood on it. She almost lost her balance as she stepped down, and gently wrapped it in a tissue. She had a strange feeling in the pit of her stomach. If the blood was not Frank Brandon's, it had to be from the man standing behind him. Was that man Alexander Fitzpatrick?

Chapter Seven

Pete Jenkins at forensics was, as usual, friendly and offered coffee, but Anna declined, saying she would have to move fast to get over to the station in Chalk Farm. When she showed him the bullet, their heads were close as she eased back the piece of tissue. 'I think it's blood,' she said.

'Soon be able to tell you. Where did you find it?'

'The air vent.'

'Whoops. Someone's gonna get rapped over the knuckles; probably me.' He took a small swab stick and prepared for a blood test.

'How long will it take to confirm whose blood it is?'

'Not long. Do you want to wait?'

'I should get moving.'

'You free for dinner tonight?'

She hesitated, then smiled. 'Can I talk to you later – see what I've got lined up?'

'Sure. I can cook – do you like Italian?'

'Yes, I do.'

'Well, why don't we say my place at eight, unless something crops up?'

Again she hesitated, but he was so easygoing, she

couldn't understand why she was being so unsure. She agreed that they would talk later.

'This is my address.' He jotted it down. When he had finished working on the bullet, he promised he would get it over to ballistics.

Cunningham was holding forth when Anna joined the team. She broke off to look at her watch. 'Nice of you to join us, DI Travis.'

'I'm sorry, Ma'am.'

'So am I. I am not going to say everything again, so catch up, will you? We go over to the mortuary in an hour.'

Anna raised her hand. Cunningham gave her a dismissive glance.

'I went back to the murder site last night,' Anna announced, then explained how she had been constantly thinking about the statement from Mrs Webster. She told the team about the discovery of the bullet, and that forensic were working on it and would be in touch that morning.

Cunningham remained, arms folded, staring at the floor, until Anna had finished. She then looked up and gave her a strange, direct stare. 'Good work.'

'It is possible the bullet clipped the man we are trying to identify, the one standing behind Frank Brandon,' Anna went on. 'If it *is* someone else's blood, then—'

'Yes, that's obvious, Travis, but let's not get too excited until we hear back from the lab. Right now, it's just speculation.' Cunningham walked off.

Just speculation! Anna's mobile phone rang; the caller was Harry Blunt. She hurried into her office.

'Listen, Anna, this may be nothing, but I've been

thinking – you know, about Frank. Sort of feel bad about him; he was a pain in the arse, but he was an okay bloke. You liked him, didn't you?'

'Yes, I did.'

'I'm not too far from you – want to have a coffee?'

Anna checked her watch. She wasn't due to go to the mortuary with Cunningham for another hour. 'Sure.' They arranged to meet in the nearest Starbucks.

Harry was already tucking into a doughnut and giant latte. He grinned when he saw her, his mouth full, and held up a small black coffee. 'You can get your own cream if you need it,' he said, chewing, as she perched beside him.

'Black is fine; I've not got much time.'

'Nor have I. I'm gonna interview a bloke we think chopped up his wife, so I wanted to get something to eat before we drag him in.'

Anna smiled – typical of Harry.

'Fucker used a meat cleaver; we got bits and pieces of her all over London. You want one of these? I got three.' He proffered a doughnut and she took one, as she hadn't had time for breakfast.

'Okay, I was in Oxford Street getting the wife her birthday present, and I bumped into Frank's ex; she works in Selfridges on the perfume counter. To be honest, I didn't remember her. I'd met her a couple of times but, if you recall, old Frank used to put it about. Anyways, her name is Connie – lovely-looking, great figure, big tits. You know old Frank liked them top heavy.'

'I didn't,' Anna said.

'Well, we had a bite to eat one night – me, Frank and Connie – and so she recognised me – calls me over, right?' Harry demolished his doughnut and started on the next. 'First, she is showing me all these offers on perfume. I said I was looking for the wife's birthday, so she only sprays me so I smell like a whore's bedroom, then suddenly, she says she's really desperate to contact Frank.'

Anna listened as Harry, between mouthfuls, explained that, at first, he was wondering how he was going to tell Connie that Frank was dead. Then she showed him an engagement ring – nothing too flash, a nice little three-diamond job. Frank had apparently told her that he would have to be away for a few months; he had got this blinding job, driving some big shot around. Part of the deal was, he was to be on duty twenty-four seven, so it meant that he wouldn't be able to see her until the job was over. He might also have to travel abroad. Frank had then asked her if she would stand by him; they would get married when it was over. Connie had agreed.

'She tells me that Frank buys the ring: they were living together, right? Then, a week later, he goes off to work. He said he would have his mobile on and she could call him if something urgent cropped up, but to wait for him to contact her. He was worried that, if he didn't come up to scratch, they'd fire him. She never heard nothing, so she called a couple of times, but it was dead.' Harry finished the second doughnut. 'Anyways, I am just about to tell her that so was he, when she says that he'd been working for a chauffeur firm. She'd called them; said he had been wheeling around in a flash Merc. Now, that would have been when I saw him. Remember, I said I saw him in a flash Merc in the West End?'

Harry rummaged in his jacket pocket and took out a crumpled card. 'She said he was working for this bloke but, when she called him, there was no answer.' He passed over the card, *Chauffeur Hire, Donny Petrozzo*, and a mobile number. 'She said he worked for big money blokes in the City; I tried the number and got nothing.'

Anna pocketed the card as Harry continued. 'I told her, Anna. I said that as far as I knew, Frank had met with an accident, but I didn't have no facts – just that he was dead. She broke down. I felt terrible. Left without getting the wife's perfume, I was so uptight.'

'Listen, thank you for this, Harry – I appreciate it.'

'Okay. I'd like to know when they're burying him; show him respect, know what I mean?'

'Yes, I do. I'll be in touch.'

Cunningham was about to have another tetchy go at her, but Anna didn't waste time. Giving Cunningham the details from Harry Blunt, she said she felt it was important enough for her to meet up with Connie.

Cunningham tapped Anna's desk with the Petrozzo card. 'Okay. Follow this up, Travis, and take Gordon with you.' She lightly touched Anna's shoulder. 'It was good work on the discovery of the bullet, but you were out on your own. I don't want to have to tell you again: I do not want you acting like a loose cannon, running around London alone. Maybe the bullet will give us a lead, but it could also come back and slap us in the face. You should have had a witness and you should have discussed your concerns about Mrs Webster's statement.'

'Ma'am, I did write it in my report.'

'Don't interrupt! I do not want you going out on your own fucking enquiry. This is a murder investigation, not Anna Travis proving herself to be better than anyone else. As from now, any misgivings you have, any single thing that crops up in that little red head of yours, you discuss with me and the team – do you understand me?'

'Yes, Ma'am.'

'Good. I don't want to stunt your obvious ability, but I will get you off this case if I feel you have disobeyed my direct order one more time. I am fully aware of the problems you had with Detective Chief Superintendent Langton – or, should I say, his problems with you. You consistently flaunted his authority. In case you are not aware, it's on your record sheet. If you ever want to get promotion, Travis, I should warn you that I'd add my ten cents in, as well as Jimmy Langton's.' She left the room.

Anna had to grip the sides of her desk to keep control. Langton had to be protecting his own backside, conferring with the arm-folding Cunningham. Anna was so angry that she wanted to pick up the phone and get him on the line there and then. Suddenly her phone rang.

She snatched it up. 'Travis,' she snapped.

'Hi there, it's Pete. You were right: the blood on the bullet is not Frank Brandon's. We are running tests and seeing what the database throws up, so I'll be in touch later.'

'Good. Thank you,' she said, still hot with rage.

'You know if you will make dinner tonight?'

Anna had to take a deep breath to be civil. 'Not yet. Can I call you later?'

'Sure. Don't make it too late, though, because if I am cooking, I need to get the food in—'

'I'll talk to you later!' She felt bad about being so uptight, but she just couldn't contain herself.

She picked up the phone again and dialled an internal number. 'Gordon, can you check out if they have a record of the marriage between Frank Brandon and Julia?

And Gordon, write this up on the bloody incident board, and give the duty manager details.'

She slammed the phone back down, and started her report on the meeting with Harry Blunt. If Cunningham wanted her to go by the book on every single detail, she would do so. The phone rang again. It was Gordon asking if she had Mrs Brandon's maiden name. She snapped that it was in the file; he should find it himself.

Cunningham arrived at the mortuary with DS Phil Markham. They had not completed the post mortem on Donny Petrozzo, but she was putting the pressure on for any new evidence. Ewan Fielding was irritated by their arrival, he loathed to hurry and complained that he had stated, innumerable times, that he was not able to give any details until his work was completed. Donny Petrozzo's body had already been 'sliced', and his organs removed and weighed, so Cunningham was somewhat surprised by Fielding's annoyance. Looking over his notes, he said that the victim was a rather unhealthy individual. His last meal had been a hamburger and chips. He also had quite a high blood–alcohol level. The victim had been quite a heavy cocaine user. His septum was weak; there were still traces of cocaine inside both nostrils. Death had occurred some three days previously, but they had so far been unable to ascertain the actual cause. 'I will obviously require time to do more examinations. That is about all I can give you at this moment.'

'Was it a drug overdose?' Cunningham demanded.

'I'm unable to confirm that,' Fielding said wearily.

'But you have found cocaine?'

'Yes, traces. It appears that he was a regular user, but I don't have, as yet, evidence to prove he overdosed on that particular drug. I don't want you to take this as verbatim – but my gut feeling is that he *has* overdosed; on what exactly, I am unable to tell you, but I think it was some kind of opiate.'

'Why do you say that?' Again, this was from Cunningham.

'From his heart. I am just about to run some tests. Until I have done so, that is about all I can give you.'

DS Markham looked over the body and then asked if whatever drug Petrozzo had died from could have been self-administered.

Fielding glanced at him and shrugged. 'Quite possibly, but even if his death was self-inflicted, I doubt he would have been able to place himself in the black bin liners – four of them, to be exact – and wrap them around his entire body with masking tape!'

Cunningham had heard enough.

Markham hurried after her. She banged through the doors, removing her protective green overall and tossing it into the bin provided. 'Those pricks make me so pissed off. Pompous arsehole,' she muttered.

Markham removed his overall, then had to hurry to catch up with her once more as she headed towards the forensic department.

Pete Jenkins looked up as the double doors to his lab slammed open and Cunningham strode in. 'Hi!' he greeted her. 'I was just about to call. We're pretty swamped with work on your case, but we have the clothing from Donny Petrozzo on the benches. Downstairs, they're stripping down the Mitsubishi.'

'You get something from the blood on the bullet from the murder site?'

'Yes. I was just about to contact DI Travis.'

'Well, I'm here, so what have you got?' Cunningham demanded.

Jenkins picked up his report. 'The blood is not a match for the victim. We have run it through the database but we have come up empty-handed; in other words, there is no match on file.'

'So what is your take on it?'

Jenkins shrugged. 'Pretty much the same as DI Travis: your gunman fired six shots, five into your victim. One shot clipped the man we believe was standing behind him. We've made a few more tests on the angle of the bullets and the spattering.'

'No, no! Let me look over Petrozzo's clothes. Found any bloodstains on them?'

'Not as yet, I believe, but we're still checking them over. His pockets were empty. We had no papers or identifying documents, but we got his ID from his prints.'

'Yes, I know. What about the bin liners and the tape?'

Jenkins led them over to a trestle table. 'We have four bin bags. Pathology department sliced through them as neatly as possible to help, but the bags and the tape are a common variety and hard to trace. Also, I would say whoever wrapped him up – and, by the by, did it very well, the body was quite well-preserved – I think must have worn gloves, as we have as yet no fingerprints. Often we get a good result from duct tape but, in this case, nothing.'

Cunningham sighed and looked to Markham. 'You want to ask something?'

Markham nodded and pointed to the shoes. 'Any bloodstains on these?'

'Nope. We have mud particles, but no blood.'

'So he wasn't at the murder site?'

'The footprints we have from there are not his size. He is, or was, size nine shoe and, I think I was told, around five feet nine, so he wasn't the man standing behind your victim Frank Brandon. Travis and I have ascertained he had to be over six feet two or three—'

'Really? DI Travis seems to have spent a lot of time here,' Cunningham said sarcastically. She gestured to Markham that it was time to leave, and walked off without so much as a thank you to Jenkins.

Their next stop was Vernon Lee, the ballistics expert. Lee had little to add, apart from the fact that the bullet was from the same Glock pistol and, as with the other bullets, they did not have the casing. Frustrated, Cunningham and Markham returned to their car.

As they left the car park, Cunningham switched on her BlackBerry and began checking her messages. Then she looked at Markham. 'You ever worked with Chief Superintendent James Langton?'

'No, Ma'am.'

'Travis worked three cases with him. He rated her, but said she was a bit of a solo artist; got into some trouble with a journalist on one case. I need you to watch over her. I don't want her creating any more problems for me than I've already got.'

'Yes, Ma'am.'

'And we do have problems, Phil, big ones. We're now four days into the investigation with fuck all, and Frank Brandon being an ex-cop is starting to create pressure from the Chief. We need to get some kind of a result, and fast, so all weekend leave will be cancelled.'

'Yes, Ma'am.'

'You see Travis acting like she's running this investigation, you report straight back to me – understood?'

'Yes, Ma'am.' Markham didn't like this at all, and decided he would have a quiet word with Anna when he returned to the station.

Anna and Gordon went back to question Paul Wrexler and Mark Taylor, who had both scored drugs from Donny Petrozzo. Again, they were spun virtually the same story. Donny always insisted that he was not a dealer; he could just get a few grams for when they needed it. Both the companies they worked for had used Donny's firm of chauffeurs when they required clients to be collected from the airport, or for special functions. Donny was not on a permanent payroll, but worked freelance; due to his good record, they had used him for over eight years. He owned a Mercedes Benz and a Ford Escort which he and his wife used for personal driving. Donny's Mercedes had not been recovered.

When Anna and Gordon called into the station, Cunningham had still not returned. Anna made sure that the duty manager reported to Cunningham, when she did get back, that she and Gordon were going to see Mrs Petrozzo.

Donny Petrozzo's address was in Fulham. As they were arriving, Gordon got a call from the station. When they saw Mrs Petrozzo, they should tell her that a car had been arranged to take her to the mortuary. She was required to identify her husband.

Anna was stunned that no one had yet been to see Mrs Petrozzo to give her the news. 'You know, DCI Cunningham should have sorted this out.'

'Well, I suppose as we only found him yesterday . . .' Gordon said uneasily.

'We had him identified fast enough by his prints. His wife should have been told straight away. It's really disgusting.'

'I suppose so.' Gordon checked his *A–Z.* 'Next right. The flat faces the Palmers Green Park. Nice area.'

They drove round to the bays at the rear of the block. Parked underneath a cloth cover was Donny Petrozzo's Mercedes and, next to it, his Ford Escort. Anna had lifted the cover to check the number-plate and then, being on best behaviour, called into the station to suggest they remove the Mercedes to be checked over by forensics.

Mrs Petrozzo lived on the top floor. The stairs and corridors were well kept, with buckets of flowers on each landing. Flat 10 had a freshly painted front door, with a polished brass letterbox.

'You ever done one of these before?' Anna asked Gordon.

'One of what?'

'Telling someone that their loved one's dead, then trying to get information out of them?'

'No.'

'Okay. This is the way I am going to work it: we keep the death until last – "we are not sure", et cetera – I need some answers first.'

'Right,' Gordon said, as Anna rang the doorbell.

Mrs Petrozzo was a pale, nervous woman with straight, unflattering hair pinned to one side with a clip. She was quite well-dressed, if rather drab, and she had an Irish accent.

'Mrs Petrozzo?' Anna said pleasantly, at the same time showing her identification. 'This is Detective Gordon

Loach, and I am Detective Inspector Anna Travis. I wonder if it is convenient for me to ask you some questions?'

'What is it about? Only I was just going out.'

'It is important. Could we please come in and talk to you?'

'Is it about Donny?'

'Yes.'

'I've been waiting for him to call me,' she said, gesturing for them to go down the immaculate little hallway, to a large sitting room overlooking the park.

'Oh, this is a lovely room,' Anna said.

'Yes. I've lived here nearly all my life. My parents had the flat, then when they died, me and Donny moved in.'

'You own it?'

'Yes, my father did, so we took over the mortgage. Can I get you tea or coffee?'

'No, thank you. Mrs Petrozzo, this is a very serious matter we are here to discuss. When did you last see your husband?'

'About four days ago. He was working. He often goes away – well, not often, but he sort of said this was a possibility. He usually calls me, but I've not heard from him and I'm worried.'

'Do you know who he was working for?'

'No.'

'Did he mention any names at all?'

'No, he keeps his business very private. I knew some of it, but he never really bothers to talk to me too much. He's often out early and back very late. I know he was collecting someone from Heathrow.'

'But you don't know who?'

'No.'

'Does Mr Petrozzo have an office?'

'He has a phone and a desk next door.'

'Mrs Petrozzo, I really need to see your husband's office.'

'I'm afraid I can't let you; he will go mad. I hardly ever go in there accept to hoover and dust. It's his business, you see.'

Anna braced herself, and then leaned forwards. 'Mrs Petrozzo, your husband might have met with a fatal accident. We are here to ask you to accompany a police officer—'

'Accident?'

'Yes. We have someone at the mortuary—'

'I don't understand.'

'It's possible your husband is dead. I am so sorry.'

Anna was not prepared for the reaction, because there was hardly one at all. The woman just sat there, with her hands in her lap.

'I really do need to see your husband's work room,' Anna repeated gently. 'Would that be possible?'

The lack of response was unnerving. Still Mrs Petrozzo sat, with her rather big raw-boned hands folded in her lap. She then made a soft coughing sound, as if clearing her throat. 'I am afraid that is not possible. If you insist, then you will have to get a search warrant. I would like you to leave, please.'

'I'm sorry, Mrs Petrozzo—'

Anna was interrupted as the reticent woman suddenly stood up, her face now twisted with rage. 'I allowed you to come in here, because I thought you were coming to talk about that bloody CCTV camera right outside our block of flats. It swivels and looks straight into the flats – it's outrageous they can just set one of those intrusive

140

things up without ever getting permission from a single tenant, and I know they are looking into the bedrooms. I know that for certain, because we have two young girls in the flat next to us and they are complaining about it.'

'If you would like me to make you a cup of tea . . .'

Mrs Petrozzo turned on Anna, her big hands clenched into fists at her side. 'You will not set foot in my kitchen! I want you to get out. My husband is going to make you pay for this. I don't believe you are from the police. I think you've come here to steal from me, that's what this is all about. I know about you people, I know . . .' She was like the mouse that roared. She began thrashing at her sides with her fists, and spittle formed in the corners of her mouth as she hurled abuse at them.

It took an hour. They had to call a doctor. Gordon found the address in a book by the telephone. Anna rang into the station to request a search warrant be issued. All the time, Mrs Petrozzo shouted and argued with them, and screeched and threw cushions. Even with Gordon trying to calm her, she was unstoppable. By the time the doctor arrived, she had quietened down but was still unstable.

The poor woman had a history of mental illness and had been sectioned numerous times. She was sedated and taken to her bedroom. The doctor knew of a niece who had often stayed to care for her; he was dismissive of Donny, saying that he kept his distance from his wife at all times. By the time they had arranged for the niece Ella Douglas to leave her work and come to the flat, another hour passed. When Anna told Ella the reason for their visit, her response was equally shocking. She just said that she hoped Donny was dead, the way he had treated his poor wife.

Anna glanced at Gordon, who was even redder in the face than usual. 'Look, Gordon, this entire scene is not the usual,' she told him. 'I've never had a reaction like it, but we just have to sit it out.'

Ella tended to Mrs Petrozzo and handed Anna a set of keys to the office. 'These are what you want. I will go and identify Donny. She can't be put through that.'

The small room was neat and orderly, with a desktop computer and a filing cabinet. Donny was meticulous: a large desk diary listed his clients and his commitments. He wrote in different coloured pens his airport drops and pick-ups, city functions and dinners. The last entry was a collection from Stansted Airport. This was four days ago; he had added to the entry a note of a payment in cash, then underlined *no tip*. He had picked up the passenger at 8.15 a.m., dropped them at Claridges, and returned home. There were a few future dates, but nothing of interest. His bank statement, however, was very interesting.

Donny Petrozzo had savings of seventy thousand pounds. In another account, they found even more money: over a hundred thousand pounds. There had been large cash deposits; the last one for twenty thousand pounds.

Anna listed the items she wished to take away, then contacted the station for the computer to be removed and checked. There were two mobile phones and these were taken too, plus his address books and files. It was late afternoon by the time a patrol car arrived with a female officer to accompany Ella Douglas to the mortuary for the formal identification of Donny Petrozzo. Anna wanted to go over the diary entries in more detail, so once a neighbour had agreed to sit with Mrs Petrozzo who was sleeping, she and Gordon returned to the station.

Although it wasn't on the way back, Anna wanted to stop at Selfridges. She needed to pick up something and asked Gordon to wait in the car park there.

Anna went straight to the sea of perfume counters and asked if she could talk to someone called Connie. Anna was directed to the Dior counter. Walking around, she couldn't see any well-stacked blondes as Harry Blunt had described. She eventually asked a girl with the nametag *Sharon* where she would find Connie. Sharon said she'd got some bad news and was at home.

'Was it about her bloke?' Anna enquired.

'Yeah, but I dunno much else. She got into a state a few days ago and she's not been back.'

'Do you have her phone number? I would like to call her – I know him well and I might be able to help.'

Connie agreed to see Anna that evening at seven. She lived in Notting Hill Gate, close to Portobello Road. As Anna wrote down the address on the back of her hand in the car, Gordon glanced at her. 'Got a date?'

'Yes,' she smiled.

She would have to cancel poor old Pete Jenkins once again. As the car continued across London to the station, Anna called the forensic lab. An assistant told her that Pete had gone out for a while, but would be back later. Anna didn't leave any message, deciding she would call him later from her office.

By the time Anna had made copious notes and typed up her report, it was after six. She went into the incident room to mark up the data and was surprised that they still did not have the completed autopsy report on Donny

Petrozzo. They had no match on the blood found on the bullet and, as yet, no forensic details on the Mitsubishi. Anna still had Donny Petrozzo's diary in her briefcase, keeping hold of it until she had finished checking it over. The rest of the items removed from his house were now with forensics. She knew from Pete they were already inundated; now they had even more to contend with.

Anna called Pete's mobile as she was leaving the station. Before she could say that she would not make dinner, he told her that he had started cooking and was looking forward to seeing her. When she heard that, she said simply that she might be a bit late as she was still working. She didn't want to let him down again.

Anna was fifteen minutes late for her meeting with Connie. The woman lived in a first-floor flat, with a dingy threadbare carpet on a rickety staircase. Connie was, as Harry had described, very well-endowed but with a small waist, accentuated by a wide elastic belt. Her blouse was flimsy and frilly, and she wore black pedal pushers with pink ballet shoes. Her hair was dyed blonde and held up in a loose bun with a comb. Her attractive face was blotchy and her eyes were puffy from crying. She was nowhere near as sophisticated as Julia Brandon.

'You want a drink or anything?' she asked in a cockney accent, leading Anna into the flat.

'No, thanks. I don't want to take up too much of your time.'

'Well, I got enough of it. I've not been into work – just can't function. I dunno nothing except for what that bloke Harry told me. I keep on trying Frank's mobile number. I just dunno what to think. I mean, why don't someone call me and tell me what's going on?' She slumped onto a large leatherette sofa. 'Is he dead? I mean, is that true?'

Anna sat opposite on a matching chair. 'Yes, I am afraid he is.'

'Oh Christ.'

'I'm so sorry.'

Connie hung her head and broke down sobbing. It was some time before Anna could really ask any pertinent questions. Connie became even more distressed when Anna gently broke the news that Frank had been murdered and that he had been identified by his fingerprints. She could not bring herself to go into the details of his relationship with Julia.

She and Frank were engaged to be married, Connie said; they had been living together for over a year. Between tears, she explained how they were saving to buy a place, as the flat was only rented. Gradually, Anna turned the conversation round to what work Frank was involved in. Connie knew that he had been taking employment as a chauffeur with Donny Petrozzo. It was not full-time, but he was on call for when he was needed. He would often work late and sometimes would be gone for a few days at a time.

'Did you ever hear any names of the people he was driving?'

'No. He said that sometimes they'd come into Heathrow and he had to drive them up North. You know, long journeys that Donny said he didn't want to do.'

'Did you ever meet Donny?'

'No.'

'What about the last job Frank was on?'

Connie sighed and leaned back on the sofa. 'He come

in an' he was real up, said that he'd just landed a big gig, but he was gonna be away for weeks on end. I didn't like it, but he said the money would be enough for us to get married and put down on a place of our own so, I mean, I couldn't not want him to do it, could I?'

'I understand.'

'Well, it was more'n a few weeks; it was starting to be months. I only ever heard from him a few times at weekends, like, and he didn't like me callin' him. He used to say he had "POB" – that meant "person on board", like, so he'd ring off.'

'When was the last time you saw him?'

Connie closed her eyes. 'Long time. Months – gotta be months.'

'Did he ever say anything about who he was working for?'

'Not really, just that they was mega-wealthy and he was coinin' it in.'

'Could I see his things?'

'Yeah, if you want.'

Connie got up. She seemed sluggish and so despairing that Anna felt truly sorry for her. They went into the bedroom next door. The double bed was new, and there was a white fitted wardrobe with long mirrors on the doors. 'Frank done this room up; we picked the bed and things between us, and me mum ran up the curtains and bedcover.'

Anna smiled and said it was very tasteful. It wasn't – it was rather tacky, with mounds of frilly cushions. Connie's décor and Julia's were poles apart. Connie opened a wardrobe to reveal Frank's suits, shirts and shoes, with rows of sweaters next to them on the hangers. Her side was crushed with clothes and she gently touched one of Frank's jackets. 'I come in and hold them sometimes. You know – make it like he's still here.'

Anna nodded. Again, she could smell Frank's familiar cologne. She looked around the room. 'What about papers, documents . . . did he keep his diary and things here?'

Connie crossed to her dressing-table, and stared at herself in the mirror.

'I need to have anything you've got that might help our enquiry, Connie.'

In the small kitchen, there was a Formica table stacked with two boxes of Frank's documents, from car insurance to old pay slips from the Met, his pension details and bank statements, envelopes stuffed with petrol receipts, and a large foolscap notebook with addresses and pick-up times.

'Donny would just call, like, and Frank would go round to his place, pick up his car – it was a Merc – and leave his own car there as he said it wasn't good enough for the clients.'

'What car was Frank driving?'

'It was a VW – a pale green one.'

Anna noticed the file on the car and its insurance; she also saw that it was after eight-fifteen. 'Connie, do you mind if I take these boxes? They'll be returned to you as soon as I have looked over them.'

Connie shrugged. 'Whatever.'

Anna asked if she could check through Frank's clothes to see if there was anything to indicate who he was working for. Connie said she'd been through them and there was nothing.

'Did he take clothes away with him?'

'Yeah, took 'em in a suitcase.'

'I am so sorry, Connie, really I am. You seem to be a lovely girl and Frank must have felt very fortunate in knowing you.'

'Yeah, he was ever so good to me. He was always buying me little presents. Last thing I ever heard from him was he sent me flowers on my birthday.'

'When was that?'

'Two months ago. I kept the card; they come from Interflora.'

Anna asked to see the card, jotting the florist's name down in her notebook. The message was affectionate: it said he would be home soon and he loved her. Anna passed the card back. She didn't like doing it, but nevertheless she asked if Connie had ever heard Frank mention a woman called Julia.

Connie immediately became wary. 'Why you askin' that?'

'Just that we think he may have been working with a woman called Julia.'

'Who is she?'

'She lives in Wimbledon.'

'Wimbledon?'

'Yes. Did Frank ever mention her to you?'

'No! Is she connected to him? I mean, is she something to do with his death?'

'Possibly. I can't really say any more.'

'I mean, are you saying he was with this woman?'

'Working for her, yes.'

'Well, you gotta know what he was doin' then!'

'Not quite. He was driving for her – that's all we really know.'

'How did he die then?'

Anna really didn't want to get into this, but she could

feel Connie becoming more and more tense in her desperation to know.

'I gotta right to know. I mean, if he was involved with another woman, I have to know.'

'He just worked for her and her children.'

'Oh, she got kids then?'

Anna could not bring herself to tell Connie that Frank had married Julia.

'When is his funeral?'

'I don't know. His body has not yet been released.'

Connie chewed her nails, and looked angrily at Anna. 'I don't have no rights or nothing, do I? But he loved me, and I loved him, and something isn't right 'bout this. I mean, who is this woman? Why was he not tellin' me about it, if she only lived in fucking Wimbledon? He said to me he was gonna have to go abroad. Why couldn't he stay here with me?'

'I really don't know, Connie, but when I do know more, I will contact you, I promise.' Anna looked at her watch and said that she would have to leave. Connie helped her take the boxes down to her car and put them in the boot. As Anna drove away, Connie was standing on the pavement, still chewing at her nails.

Anna now had to drive across London to Pete's for dinner. It was the last thing she needed; she had so much paperwork to sift through from Connie, as well as Donny Petrozzo's diary. By the time she had run a comb through her hair and put on some lipgloss in the car, it was nine-fifteen.

Pete lived in a tree-lined street in Hampstead, behind the cinema. Anna was surprised that it was such a pretty house; she had somehow thought he would live in a flat closer to his work over in Lambeth. She rang the doorbell, feeling guilty that she had come empty-handed.

Pete opened the door and put his hands on his hips. 'Well, I had just about given up on you!'

The front door opened straight into a large room with a kitchen-diner at the back. It was well-furnished, with big white easy sofas and a massive plasma TV beside banks of DVDs, surrounded by pine bookshelves. The floor was stripped pine; even the kitchen had pine tops and a rustic pine table, with a bowl of fresh flowers.

'This is very nice,' she said, as he helped her off with her coat.

'I might have "pined-out" a bit,' he said, laughing.

'How long have you lived here?'

'Two years. This was three rooms and a little closet hall, so I knocked them all into one room. There's just a bedroom and bathroom upstairs, and a small box room I use as an office.'

Anna joined him in the kitchen area, where he passed her a large, long-stemmed wine glass of chilled Pinot Grigio.

'Cheers,' he said, tapping her glass. 'I've managed to drink half the bottle waiting for you.'

'I'm sorry. Something came up.'

'Always does. Anyway, sit down. I'm going to serve up straight away – I am starving.'

'Me too. I don't think I had any lunch.'

First, Peter dished up a salad with nuts, chopped apple and sliced orange, with warmed fresh bread. Then he looked into the oven. 'It's lasagne, done a bit to a crisp.'

Anna tucked into her salad. 'I love it when the cheese is crispy on top.'

'It is, very much so.' He sat down opposite her.

Anna beamed. 'This is delicious; you are obviously a good cook.'

He cocked his head to one side and laughed. 'It's just a salad.'

'That may be, but the dressing . . . and the fresh bread!'

Again he laughed as he watched her lathering butter onto the bread. 'We have a good bakery down the street – it's a very cosmopolitan little enclave round here.'

Anna chewed and licked her lips. He had said 'we'. 'Do you live with someone?'

'That was a slip of the tongue. I used to live with someone – my wife, actually.'

'You're married?'

'Was. We are in the process of divorcing.'

'I'm sorry.'

'Don't be. It's very amicable. Fortunately, we don't have children, so there's no hurt on either side – just working out who gets what. You can sort of tell, by the sparse furnishings. Ellen has moved to Surrey, close to her work; she is a mathematician and teaches at Kingston College. What about you? Where do you live?'

Anna had him laughing a lot with her description of her new flat, the noise from the bridge, the fog-horns, the unpacked boxes and her interaction with Mr Burk, the so-called security manager. As she talked, he refilled her glass, and cleared the salad plates away to bring out the lasagne. He had a lovely warm giggle that was infectious; she was becoming more and more relaxed, and pleased she had turned up.

As he served the main course, he asked if she was living with anyone. She went into details about selling her old flat and making a new move to get rid of memories. She was grateful that she didn't have to explain about the 'memories'; instead, their conversation wound round to discussing the case.

'We had an interesting turn-up. Well, *we* didn't – old Ewan Fielding did over in the path lab. I stopped by there earlier and he had just come across it.'

'Come across what?'

Pete explained how perplexed Fielding had been about the cause of death with Donny Petrozzo, so had really put in the hours. Eventually, he had asked his assistants to do an inch-by-inch check of the body. 'They were coming up with nothing – basically, Fielding said he had just stopped breathing – but then, he checked inside Petrozzo's mouth and found a pinprick under his tongue. Someone had injected him. He's been running tests trying to find out with what.'

'Any luck yet?'

'Not when I was there, but he called me later. You know how straight-laced he is. He actually sounded excited, but he stressed that he wasn't a hundred per cent sure.'

'What was it?'

'A minute trace of a drug called Fentanyl. It had been quite brutally injected and left a slight residue on the two front lower teeth.'

'What is Fentanyl?' Anna asked, clearing her plate.

Pete got up to proffer a second helping, which she accepted; he took another bottle of wine from the fridge.

'It's a very powerful opiate, incredibly potent. If you consider that morphine is given in dosages of milligrams, Fentanyl is prescribed in micrograms – that's how strong it is. Very fast-acting, it's used a lot in the USA for emergency surgery. It's a strong painkiller, but it's out of the system very quickly. For example, a hit from heroin would last maybe an hour or so; with this drug, the high hits fast and you get total relief for about a minute or so.'

Anna put down her fork. 'So Donny Petrozzo was injected with it?'

'Yes – well, possibly – and probably with enough to kill him. I'd say he was held down and injected, then wrapped up in the bin liners.'

'And shoved into the back of the Mitsubishi.'

Peter collected the plates and started to make some coffee.

'What else do you know about this drug?' Anna asked.

'Only what I've told you. Do you take sugar?'

'Nope, and I'll have it black as I have to drive home.'

Pete wasn't looking at her as he finished stacking the dishwasher. 'You could stay here.'

Anna flushed. She said it too quickly. 'No, no – I'll go home.'

'Okay, up to you.' He still had his back to her.

'Fentanyl,' she repeated.

'Yep, but don't quote me. You know Fielding – he's now doing a full toxicology report, so it won't be passed on until he's totally sure, and that'll take eight to ten weeks.'

'But why did he say it to you if he wasn't positive?'

'He wasn't; it was just a possibility. Maybe I shouldn't have mentioned it.' The coffee-grinder went into action, so they couldn't really continue the conversation until it was finished.

'Do you know if they got anything from the Mitsubishi?'

'I think there was a residue of blood, a very small swipe on the side of the front driving seat, but it's not been tested yet.'

153

'Was it wiped clean apart from that?'

'Yeah, but they may have something from the glove compartment; apparently there was a map inside which they want to test.'

Anna had opened the glove compartment and looked over the map. She hoped she hadn't smudged any possible prints. 'I was wearing gloves,' she said, and he turned to her. 'I opened it up and looked at the map. There was also a torn piece of notepaper.'

'Naughty! You know how fragile prints are to get off paper.'

'Sorry. At that time, we didn't know there was a body in the back.'

'Coffee, and some nice chocolates,' he said, placing a cup down.

They sat opposite each other again. This time, there was an awkward pause.

'You *can* stay here, you know,' he said again. 'That's a very comfortable sofa.'

'No, I should get back – it's been a long day.'

'For both of us.'

'Yes, but I've really enjoyed this evening.'

'Good.'

'Maybe I could cook dinner for you at my place?'

'I'd like that.'

Anna sipped her coffee. 'I'm not sure when. I don't think we have any weekend leave – maybe next week sometime?'

Pete looked at her, his head to one side. 'Whenever.' He picked up his coffee cup and gestured for them to go into the lounge area, saying it was more comfortable. Anna hesitated, wondering if he was going to slide onto the sofa next to her and make a pass.

He didn't. He sat in one of the easy chairs. 'What's your take on this?' he said.

'My take? You mean, as a whole on the case?'

'Yeah.'

'I'm unsure. It's very much a jigsaw puzzle at the moment, with a lot of missing pieces.'

'Like what?'

She suddenly felt very tired, and didn't really want to get into explaining herself or discussing the case. 'Just things that don't add up,' she said.

'Like what?'

She sighed. 'Well, for one, my biggest issue is: what was Frank Brandon doing in that squat?'

'Scoring for someone?'

'Maybe.'

'When you're hooked, you'll go to any dump to score, be it in Chalk Farm or wherever, so it doesn't surprise me that he was visiting the squat. People take big risks.'

'Yes, I know.'

'You don't want to talk about it, do you?'

'To be honest, Pete, I'm whacked out.'

'Sorry.'

'It's okay, it's just having to deal with Donny Petrozzo's mentally disturbed widow, interviewing the guys who were scoring from the drug squat, talking to the girl who hoped to marry Frank Brandon . . . it takes its toll.' Anna finished her coffee. It was almost eleven o'clock.

'I'm sure it does.' He stood up, and smiled. 'You should go.'

She nodded and reached for her briefcase. 'Thank you for tonight.'

'My pleasure, and Anna – I'll wait for you to call me, okay?' He kissed her cheek and walked her to her car. 'Good night.'

She smiled and put the key into the ignition, starting up the engine. He stood, watching her drive away, before he went inside to roll a big fat joint.

By the time Anna was ready for bed, it was after midnight. Sleep didn't come easily; she kept on listing in her mind the many loopholes and loose ends of the case, then thought about the evening, and about Pete Jenkins.

She really liked him, she decided, and couldn't quite understand why she was so reticent about showing it. He was such a different creature to James Langton – and, she was certain, far nicer – but even the comparisons meant her last thoughts before she fell asleep were of Langton. He was a hard act to follow. After all these months, he still had a stranglehold over her emotions. She knew that she was still in love with him, no matter what he had done.

Chapter Eight

Anna had only enough time to check over a few of Frank Brandon's papers before leaving for work. His bank statements were interesting: judging by the amount of money in there, Frank and Connie would have had more than enough to get married and make a down payment on a property. But where did that leave his marriage to Julia? Anna made notes as she read, underlining the fact that Frank began working for Donny Petrozzo, but did not own a suitable car. She wanted to cross-reference with Donny's diary, as Frank drove Donny's Mercedes for the clients. She would check through the registration numbers taken from Jeremy Webster's list, though she doubted it would be amongst them. She had barely started cross-referencing Frank's papers with Donny's diary before it was time for her to leave.

Anna's flat was strewn with packing cases and boxes, but at least her shower was hot, and the garage doors opened and closed without any problems. She was at the station by eight-thirty, ready for the briefing session with Cunningham. Before it began, she went to check out with the officers a few of her queries. She got one hit straight away.

157

One of the cars listed by Jeremy Webster as being parked in the forecourt of the estate was registered to a Miss Ella Douglas. As the car, according to Webster, had not been parked there on the night of the murder, they had not pressed to get the details. One quick phone call to Ella told Anna that Donny had insured the car for her to drive his wife to her various doctors; he had registered it at Ella's address. This was a step forward. It meant that Donny Petrozzo could have been to the drug squat in that car.

Anna returned to her office and put in a call to Pete to see if there were any new details on the fingerprints taken from the squat, and whether Donny Petrozzo's were amongst them. She spoke to one of his assistants. As with the car licence-plates, it was a slow process of elimination and match. Anna reminded the assistant that they had identified Donny Petrozzo by his fingerprints and that, as they were on record, they could easily check with the databank. She was told that they had thirty prints being tested. Anna was frustrated by the delays, but knew that forensics had their work cut out for them.

Another step forward was that the swipe from the Mitsubishi had now been verified as the same blood-type as the blood found on the bullet. Anna marked this detail up on the incident board. There was now a mass of data, with red arrows, linking the evidence gathered to date.

Anna was joined by Gordon, who had not found evidence of a marriage certificate issued to Julia Kendal in the UK. He had found out birth dates of her two children from the registration. No father was listed on the birth certificates. Was the marriage to Frank Brandon a sham, as seemed likely now? Why the wedding photographs, then?

There was still no post-mortem report back from the lab for Donny Petrozzo, as they were waiting for the toxicology report. Nor was there any reference to the drug, Fentanyl, that Pete had mentioned as a possible cause of death. The surveillance report on Julia Brandon offered up no suspicious outings or visitors; however, they had by now gained access to her finances – despite the interference from her accountant, who had tried to block them at every level. Julia Brandon was a lot wealthier than they had first believed.

The lists of different accounts and deposit facilities presented them with a maze of names and offshore companies. She had access to big money; however, she was unable to withdraw it without notifications. Some accounts were in her daughters' names, but most were off-the-shelf companies. The ballpark amount, and this was still being assessed, was in the region of fifteen million pounds. Added to these investments was her ownership of properties, including one in the Isle of Wight.

Anna sat with the officers who had been assigned the job of digging. They were flabbergasted by the complicated paper trail. Where had this money come from originally? At the moment, they had no idea. What they did have details of, however, was how the money moved around. With the value of the dollar so low, a lot of monies were being moved into accounts in the USA. Then no sooner had the exchange taken place, than the money was moved to another bank in another city.

'It's got to be drug money,' Anna said, and the others agreed.

They had little on Julia Brandon's previous financial situation, but they had traced a small account in the name of Julia Kendal in Oxford, where she had been born and brought up. Both her parents were deceased, but there was a sister living in a village just outside Stratford-upon-Avon. Honour Kendal was married to Damien Nolan, a Professor of Chemistry at Oxford. As far as they could ascertain, the Nolans were a respectable married couple. They had no children, nor did they have a property in their name, and money was tight. Academics were badly paid, and Honour did not have a full-time job.

At the briefing, Cunningham seemed her usual lack-lustre self. Arms folded, propped on the end of a desk, she asked the team to give an update. Anna sat through all their findings silent, waiting for her turn.

'DI Travis, you got anything new for us?'

Anna stood up and went to the incident board. 'As you can see, I've added some of the information that I have been working on. There's nothing that really stands out, other than the possible links – but again, it could all be coincidental.'

'Like what?'

Anna took a deep breath. 'Okay, this is just surmising, as I have to do some cross-checking with Donny Petrozzo's diary and with some items I got from Frank Brandon's fiancée . . .'

This created a murmur, because no one had heard about any fiancée.

Anna pointed to the board, where she had written up Connie's details. 'She was very distressed, obviously. What is interesting, is that Frank told her that he had some big job on. However, he didn't want her to know what it was; he said only that the job was one that would pay a substantial amount – enough for them to marry and buy a place.'

'Did you find out anything about this job?' Cunningham interjected.

'No. All I know is that it was connected to Donny Petrozzo, whom Frank worked for. Frank owned a VW Golf, which we need to trace; it was not a car to chauffeur clients in. We have him working for Donny up until about six months ago. This takes us back to Julia Brandon. When did they first meet? When, or how, did he start to work for her? We have no UK marriage licence. We know he lived at her home in Wimbledon, but it's possible he just slept in the spare bedroom. However, she claims to be his wife; her accountant even arranged a big life insurance policy.' Anna referred to her notes. 'We need to verify if the money does go to Julia, or whether Frank arranged for his girlfriend to be taken care of, if anything happened to him. If he did, then he was obviously aware of the job being risky.' As they had nothing yet from surveillance, Anna suggested that Julia be brought in for further questioning.

Anna held the floor as she talked about Julia Brandon's mega-bucks, and why it didn't quite add up. Cunningham was staring at her. Anna licked her lips, turning over a page in her notebook. 'Okay, this is what I'm spinning. If Julia's ex-partner, as we have discussed – or I have, with the Chief – could possibly be Alexander Fitzpatrick, then her money is from drug dealing going back twenty or thirty years.'

There was another murmur around the team: they were not privy to who Fitzpatrick was. Anna gave a brief rundown of his drug-trafficking career, and then continued. 'Fitzpatrick has remained on the Most Wanted lists since then, but what if he has returned? Could *he* be the man seen in the Mitsubishi? Whoever it was got clipped by a bullet. We now have a match from the bullet and from the jeep. He might even be quite badly wounded – we don't know – but the main query is, if this was the kingpin drug dealer, *why return*? If he is the money behind Julia, then he could easily live a life of luxury and remain undetected. We also, to date, have no verification as to who exactly owned the Mitsubishi.'

Cunningham stood up, then sat back down, folding her arms. 'Why, if you think he's here, would he want to score from a shithole drug dive?'

'Maybe he didn't want to score. Maybe there was something inside that drug squat that he wanted.'

'Like what?'

'I don't know. Our big loose end is we still do not know who was inside that squat. We've been tracing all the owners of the vehicles, and the prints, but they're small fry. We don't have any that would give us a possible reason.' Anna could feel the room tense, the officers listening and making notes for themselves.

She crossed back to the incident board. 'The link is, I believe, Donny Petrozzo. We know he was a small-time drug dealer, so he would maybe know the guys dealing in the squat.' She hesitated; this was all supposition. 'What if Donny knew Alexander Fitzpatrick? For us to get confirmation of this, we'll have to go way back into his background and records. In one of Donny's pick-ups at the various airports, did he collect Fitzpatrick? He would only be in this country for something big, or emotional – which brings me back to Julia Brandon.'

'Wait a minute.' Cunningham shook her head. 'Would someone like Fitzpatrick use a lowlife like Donny Petrozzo? I don't think so. I'm really not going along with the suggestion that a man wanted on every country's lists is going to drop into the UK and then hire a small-time guy like Petrozzo.'

'Maybe he had no option,' said Phil Markham.

Anna felt the team was backing her theory, but Cunningham wasn't. She certainly made as much clear when she called the briefing to a halt, requesting Julia Brandon be brought in that afternoon. She gave out assignments to various officers to run a final check on all the licence plates; she would put the pressure on the labs to come up with something they could work on. She wanted Frank Brandon's VW traced and she wanted to know who owned the Mitsubishi that Donny Petrozzo's body was found in – the same jeep as seen at the drug squat. They seemed to be treading water; she gave them a short sharp lecture to all pull their socks up and to return to base for another briefing that evening.

Anna went back to her poky office, and decided to use the rest of the morning to check out Donny's diary.

Phil Markham knocked and entered, closing the door. 'She's weird, you know. Why sit on everything you just said?'

'Maybe because it's just supposition?'

'But what if it isn't? We know Donny dealt in cocaine and grass to anyone that wanted it. He had to score, so it would make sense that he used that drug squat.'

'We've not put him in there yet, though,' Anna replied. 'We do have his car licence numberplate, listed by Jeremy Webster, but *not* on the night of the murder.'

'That fucking lab is really dragging its heels. I've been on to them and so has the rest of the team.'

'Yeah, well, they are a bit snowed under.'

'You can say that for the autopsy report as well. Donny Petrozzo was found how many days ago – and they still can't give us anything. The only big move we got was you finding that bullet, and Petrozzo's body. Surely we should know by now who owns the Mitsubishi?'

'They say it's got stolen licence plates.'

'Right. We're running around like headless chickens.'

Anna leaned back in her chair. 'I think Julia Brandon has the answers to a lot. I mean, look how much money she's got. No way does she match up with Frank.'

'Cunningham's got me checking out A and Es at the local hospitals for anyone coming in with a bullet wound.'

'You may get lucky.'

'I doubt it. If you've got a load of cash, you go to a private doc in Harley Street.' He put on a posh, upper-crust voice. 'Out shooting; just got clipped instead of the ruddy pheasant.'

Anna laughed.

'You want a drink at lunchtime?'

She shook her head. 'No, thanks. I'm on the visit later to Julia Brandon's sister. I've got to schlep all the way out to Oxfordshire but I'm quite looking forward to it.'

'Another time, then.'

'Okay.'

Phil grinned and winked. 'Good work, Travis. You're keeping us all on our toes.'

Phil left and Anna went back to Donny Petrozzo's diary. Donny listed pick-ups, drops, deliveries and functions; she started to see some kind of code by certain names. There were black dots – nothing else, just dots – which coincided with times he drove Paul Wrexler and Mark Taylor. Both, she knew, scored from Donny. The dots were also alongside entries for various other names; then sometimes a square with a dot inside. She ploughed on, page after page, until she reached eight months ago and saw the name and initials of Frank Brandon.

FB was used about four times a week for long-distance drives and airports, hauls that Donny obviously didn't want to be bothered with. Then, eight months ago, Donny had four Heathrow airport trips in one day. FB took two and he took the other two. Beside the last one, Donny had done something that he hadn't on any other page: put a red ring around Flight 002 BA Miami. The red ring was deep, as if he had pressed the pen into the paper hard.

Before Anna could continue reading, someone tapped on her door and DC Pamela Meadows popped her head around it. 'We have a possible connection for you regarding Donny Petrozzo and Alexander Fitzpatrick.'

'You do?'

'Yes. It's not like they were buddies or anything like that, and maybe they never even met, but previous to his other charges, Petrozzo was sentenced for burglary at the Old Bailey in 1979.'

'Go on?'

'Well, Alexander Fitzpatrick was being tried in court one, for drug trafficking after a massive raid: twenty million quid's worth.'

'You're kidding me!'

'No. Fitzpatrick jumped bail and has been on the run ever since. Petrozzo served a few years and then went straight for seven years, before he was picked up again for fencing stolen property and got an eighteen-month sentence . . .'

Anna interrupted. 'Wouldn't Fitzpatrick have had to give a blood test?'

'I don't think so. I can check, but there is nothing on

record about that. Back in 1979, they were not even aware of DNA; it was before the Holmes database. But, like I said, it is a possibility that Donny would have crossed paths with Fitzpatrick. Added to that, there was a lot of press and photographs. He was called the "Hippy Drug Baron".'

Anna nodded her thanks and Pamela left her office. She opened up the website again to look at the pictures of Alexander Fitzpatrick. Would someone be able to recognise him after such a length of time? She stared at the photographs and then closed her eyes, trying to imagine what he would look like now: hair white or grey, thinner, older. The size of him would be a giveaway – six feet four.

Cunningham tapped on her window and peered between the blinds. 'Interview room two. Julia Brandon's here with a solicitor.'

Anna opened her office door.

'She's got Simon Fagan with her. You know who he is?'

'No.'

'Top-notch, hard-nosed solicitor from the most expensive firm in London. He's a real bastard, so we won't get much joy, but that doesn't mean we won't try. Okay, let's go.'

The interview room was bare and the green walls gave a chill to the atmosphere, as did the single light bulb hanging over the table. The only furniture was a Formica-topped table and four chairs. The tape recorder and video camera were on a shelf, ready for use.

Simon Fagan was a tall, elegant man, with dark receding hair and a small toothbrush moustache. He had dark, liquid brown eyes, expressionless; his face was tanned, but his hands were not. Anna suspected he was probably a morning gym-and-sunbed client!

Cunningham introduced Anna and gave a brittle smile to Julia who looked stunning in a light fawn leather suit with a cashmere sweater. Her hair was loose, swinging in a silky sheet that she constantly brushed aside with her manicured hands. She was wearing her large square-cut diamond ring, with a diamond eternity ring, and her Cartier watch was the new diamond-cluster style with a thin black strap. She wore little make-up but her full lips were a pale coral shade of gloss. She was a very beautiful woman, more so today than before.

'Shall we get down to why you have, to my mind, been harassing my client who, as you must be more than aware, is still deeply distressed by the death of her husband,' Fagan began.

Cunningham pressed her back against the hard chair, but did not fold her arms. 'By all means, Mr Fagan. As you are obviously aware, we are simply asking Mrs Brandon to assist us in our enquiries into the murder of her husband.'

Fagan nodded but remained silent.

'Firstly, we have been unable to discover a marriage licence issued between your client and the victim.'

Fagan clicked open his briefcase and took out a brown manila envelope. He withdrew a licence issued in the Isle of Man and passed it across to Cunningham. The latter showed not by a flicker that this had taken the wind out of her sails. She calmly checked over the document and then passed it to Anna, who glanced down at the date and recorded it in her notebook. It was dated eight months ago.

Fagan again held a pause that was as cold as the room.

'Do you own a black Mitsubishi Jeep, registration—'

Before Cunningham could finish, Fagan interrupted her and said that Mrs Brandon owned a Mercedes Convertible and a Range Rover. He produced more documents from his shiny briefcase; it was as if he enjoyed snapping it open and closed.

'Mrs Brandon, have you ever seen this vehicle parked in or near to your property?' Cunningham passed her a photograph of the Mitsubishi.

'No.'

'Your late husband owned a pale green VW Golf. Have you seen that vehicle recently?'

'No. I wasn't aware that he owned one.'

'But you must have seen this Mercedes Benz?'

Again a photograph was passed to Julia; she glanced at it and then shrugged. 'I may have seen one of these, but not parked at my house.'

'Your husband used this car.'

'Perhaps that was before I knew him,' she said softly.

'Have you ever seen this man?' It was a photograph of Donny Petrozzo.

'No. No, I haven't.'

'Do you rent a garage in Wimbledon?'

'I told you about that garage!' Julia said irritably. 'Yes, I rented it, not for myself, but for Frank. I never even went there. I park my own cars at the house. They are inside the garage at the moment, as Mr Fagan drove me here.'

Cunningham leaned forwards. 'Could you tell me how you met Frank Brandon?'

'I advertised for a chauffeur and he answered the advert.'

'Could you give me details of this advertisement, and when and where you placed it?'

Julia sighed and said that it had been in the local paper and in *The Times*. She could not recall the exact date, but felt sure that if they enquired with the papers, they would be able to give more details. She did not have a receipt for payment of the advert. She then went on to say that she had subsequently employed Frank to act as her driver and bodyguard.

When asked why she required a bodyguard, Fagan held up his hand. 'It is quite obvious. My client is a very wealthy woman with two small children.'

'Had there been any threats against you?' Cunningham pointedly looked at Julia, who shrugged.

'No, but as Mr Fagan said, I am a very wealthy woman and I have a great deal of jewellery and antiques, so I required more than just a driver, in case anything untoward happened.'

'Why was there such a substantial life insurance policy taken out for Mr Brandon?'

Fagan held up his hand. 'Mrs Brandon has already answered this question; in reality, she did not instigate it. Her accountant and business adviser suggested that it be taken care of. I believe it was Mr Rushton who suggested the amount. My client just pays the premiums.' He snapped open his briefcase again and showed them the documents for the life insurance policy.

Cunningham passed them straight to Anna, who skim-read them to see if Connie was named anywhere, should anything 'untoward' happen to her boyfriend. Julia was the sole beneficiary.

'So at what point did your relationship with Mr Brandon turn from a professional one to—'

169

Fagan was jumping in again. 'It is obvious, as you can see by the date on the policy; it was arranged after the marriage, as by then Mr Brandon was living with my client and the possibility of something untoward occurring would affect him.'

'But you had had no threats. There is no police report that you had been burgled, or your children threatened. Isn't that correct, Mrs Brandon?'

'Frank was worried when he knew how much jewellery I kept in the house. It was, as I have said, simply looking out for anything that could possibly happen.'

'I see.' Cunningham was edgy, her foot tap-tapping against the side of the table. 'Well, something untoward did happen: your husband was murdered.'

There was another cold pause.

'Could you just take me through what happened on the day of the murder, Mrs Brandon?'

'I already have. Frank got up very early, as he said he had some business to attend to. As I have also told you, he continued to work as a chauffeur whilst married to me. I didn't like it, and he obviously didn't need to do it, as I have substantial monies of my own, but he wanted to retain his independence. He left before I got up and before the girls went to school. I didn't hear from him during the day. I wasn't too concerned, as on occasion he had worked, driving long distances, and often didn't come home until very late. On those occasions, he would sleep in the spare room rather than wake me. I never saw him again.'

Anna watched her. There was no sign of emotion. Julia was composed and calm – in fact, almost bored.

Fagan was drumming his fingers on the table, as if he was impatient to leave.

'I don't think you are being very truthful with us, Mrs Brandon. I think you had a marriage of convenience; that Mr Brandon did not share your marital bed, but lived in the spare room of your property. You have declined to say why you required a bodyguard, but if there is a reason, you should be honest with us.'

'My client has told you the truth,' Fagan interjected.

'So we are to believe that, when Mr Brandon was interviewed for the job, you took him on and then within three weeks married him? Is that really what happened?'

'Yes. We fell in love and Emily and Kathy adored him. To you it may seem fast – perhaps it was – but there is nothing illegal about falling in love.'

Anna spoke for the first time. 'It is rather confusing, though, considering Mr Brandon was engaged to someone else.'

Julia avoided her gaze. 'He never mentioned it to me,' she muttered.

'His fiancée loved him, and she was certain that her love was reciprocated.'

'It obviously wasn't,' snapped Fagan. He made an expansive gesture. 'Mrs Brandon obviously has nothing to do with the tragic death of her husband. She was at home all that night and morning, with witnesses to prove it. She has stated that she had no threats or fears of any kind. If Mr Brandon did, as you say, have another woman, my client knew nothing about it, as he did not inform her of this relationship. I would now ask you to finish this meeting: it is becoming very tedious. I am at a loss as to why Mrs Brandon is even being subjected to this, considering she has just been through a very harrowing ordeal.'

'I really appreciate you being here,' Cunningham responded. 'As I have said, we just need to clear up a few things.'

'I would say they have been, wouldn't you?'

'Not exactly. We would now like to know about Mrs Brandon's ex-partner. I believe you said his name was Anthony Collingwood, is that correct?'

Fagan began to dominate the interview. 'Whoever my client's previous relationship was with, is of no concern to this present situation. She has no need to answer that question.'

'I am simply trying to ascertain her ex-partner's name,' snapped Cunningham.

'Whoever it was, he is no longer connected to Mrs Brandon.'

'Was it Anthony Collingwood?'

'No comment.'

'I cannot understand why this seems to be a problem. Either it was Mr Collingwood, or it wasn't.'

'No comment.'

Cunningham sighed. 'I need to know how Mrs Brandon's wealth was accrued.'

'No comment.'

Cunningham shook her head.

This time, Fagan leaned across the table. 'If you have any evidence that involves my client with the murder of her husband, I suggest you disclose it immediately. If you do not, then this meeting is over. Mrs Brandon's previous relationship and her financial situation are private matters. I know you have approached her financial adviser, which is an infringement of her rights; so are surveillance vehicles that have been parked twenty-four hours a day near her property. I want them removed forthwith, or I will take out charges for invasion of privacy and harassment. I fully intend to report to your superiors this entire very distressing situation.'

He got up and held out his hand to Julia; she clasped it tightly and then stood up. She was, in high-heeled boots, at least five ten.

'Mrs Brandon would also like to be informed as to when her husband's body will be released, as she wishes to arrange his funeral.'

'We will be in touch,' Cunningham said, walking to open the interrogation-room door. She held it wide as they passed, then waited for them to head down the corridor, before she let it swing closed with a bang. 'What do you make of the marriage certificate?'

Anna closed her notebook. 'Quickie job, Isle of Man. We should look into it, because aren't you supposed to read the marriage banns for a certain number of weeks?'

'That's for a church wedding, I think. I also want to know her previous address – she's only just moved into the Wimbledon property. As it is, we're not getting very much, are we?'

'No comment.'

'What?'

'Well, it's obvious she's hiding something. I mean, she admitted that was his name, so we now check out if there are any records of him anywhere. Collingwood was one of Fitzpatrick's aliases, along with about twenty others. One of the things she did say to me was that she had been betrayed.'

'By the ex-partner?'

'I presumed that's who she meant. She got quite emotional about it and implied that she had been very much in love with him.'

'Mmm.' Cunningham paced around the room. 'She was shocked when we told her Frank was dead, but she's no grieving widow. If she was doing something with the ex's money then that could create a threat, and could be the reason why Frank worked for her.'

'I agree, but it doesn't link to the drug squat or to Donny Petrozzo, as far as I can see.'

'Well, let's see what her sister turns up for you this afternoon.' Cunningham opened the door again. 'You getting anything for us on the Petrozzo diary?'

'I think he had some code for his dealing: little black dots and a square with a dot in it. What it means, I haven't the slightest idea, but the dots coincide with the people I interviewed who scored from Donny. Also, he had substantial savings in a deposit account – as did Frank – so somebody was paying them; maybe Donny for drugs and Frank for—'

'Protection?'

'Could be.'

Cunningham sighed. No way was she prepared to pull the surveillance off the house in Wimbledon. 'This is a fucking nightmare case; it's like an octopus with all these tentacles flailing around one central dead man.'

Anna wondered if she should mention what she had been told by Pete Jenkins, but thought it better to keep her mouth shut as he had said it was not confirmed. Maybe the centre of the octopus was not Frank Brandon, but Donny Petrozzo.

Chapter Nine

Anna, once more accompanied by Gordon, drove her own car to Oxfordshire. They had a good clear run on the motorway with little traffic, and even less conversation. Gordon had tried to discuss the case, but Anna didn't want to get into it, partly because the drive reminded her of all the times she had driven to Oxford to the Met's rehabilitation home. This was to visit DCI Langton, after he had been in such an horrific knife attack he had almost died. His recovery had been long and he had been a nightmare patient. Like everyone else, she had doubted that he would ever return to work. She wondered if he was still suffering and how he was coping; then got cross with herself for caring. At that point, Gordon tapped on her arm to say she was hitting over ninety miles an hour.

She slowed down. 'Sorry.'

'I love Oxford,' Gordon enthused. 'There are some beautiful villages, especially the ones outside. You drive through the main town, past all the colleges, and then about twenty miles on is a fantastic restaurant.'

'Really,' she said flatly.

'I also love going to Stratford. When I was a kid, my father took me regularly every season. The best production I ever saw was *Richard the Third*, with Anthony Sher; he was brilliant! He had these walking sticks and this hump on his back, and he moved like a spider.'

'Really.'

'Do you know that the swans around the Avon are constantly found wounded and tortured?'

'No.'

'I always think it's strange. You have all that classic theatre, all that beauty – and obviously the Shakespearean history – yet someone attacks these innocent creatures.'

'Yes.'

'Mind you, they can be quite vicious. I never go near them. The way they can run at you, with their wings flapping and their feet paddling – they can take a slice out of you.'

'Is this the turn-off for Honington?'

'Sorry? No, it's the next one on our right, I think.'

She continued driving. Whilst she had been a student at Oxford she had never had the luxury of a car, and had rarely if ever left the city centre. She had been a very diligent and dedicated student, and her weekends were spent with her parents in London. Her father had been so proud of her and had never ceased to praise and congratulate her on gaining a place at the prestigious university. In reality she had often been quite lonely. Many of her fellow students were far more affluent and she was not the type of girl who enjoyed drinking in one of the many wine bars and pubs the undergraduates frequented. In fact, she had disliked the drunken antics they got up to and couldn't even recall ever mentioning that her father was a police officer.

'Nice village, isn't it?' Gordon said, and Anna was jolted back into concentrating on the route.

The village was straight from a picture postcard. There were white picket fences and velvet lawns, with tubs of flowers dotted around. Anna felt it was a trifle manicured, but nevertheless very lovely.

'I doubt they ever allow any dog-walkers around here; there's not a turd in sight,' Gordon commented. 'Even the pub looks as if Emily Brontë is about to emerge and wait for her carriage.'

'This isn't right,' Anna said. She did a tour of the village and then saw a small sign leading to Lower Honington. They followed the road until they came to another sign that directed them towards a narrow lane, which soon turned into a dirt track. They passed a cottage draped in ivy, with a garden in flower, lattice windows and trailing roses over the door. Beside the cottage, set back, was a large garage, with its own small drive and gate.

'Go and see if we're heading in the right direction,' Anna said to Gordon. As she waited for him to return, she checked the map and the address: Honey Farm, Honington, was all they had written down. The map didn't even show the dirt track. Anna looked impatiently up the garden path to see Gordon having a conversation with an elderly woman who was gesturing with her arms, pointing to further along the track.

Gordon returned and slammed the car door so hard she winced.

'Okay, we're not far. We continue down this road for about a mile, then take the right fork and it should be on our left, past a wood: it's an old farmhouse.'

They drove slowly up the track, reached the fork and

continued as instructed, passing a wooded area and a copse of high brambles. Eventually, the road became flatter and less bumpy.

Honey Farm had a double-barred gate, which had been left open. Part of it was rotted away. They came through it into a very narrow drive with ditches on either side.

'Wouldn't like to do this with a few beers inside me,' Gordon said, winding down his window. They passed a dilapidated barn and two greenhouses that hardly had a pane of glass left intact, and parked outside the farmhouse, a long, low building with small lattice Bishop's Mitre windows. It was covered in thick ivy that crept up over the tiled roof and seemed to be taking over the entire building. There was a huge tub of flowers by the front door, which was round at the side: an old stable door split in two.

'Doesn't look like anyone's at home,' Gordon said.

'Should be; I called ahead to the University.'

There was an old iron bell ring. Anna pulled it but the bell was missing. She called out, 'Hello!' and waited. She then rapped on the top half of the door.

'Can I help you?'

The voice came from behind, and made them both turn in surprise. A young man in jeans and a filthy T-shirt was standing by the barn.

'I'm looking for Honour Nolan,' Anna said.

'She's round the back, in the henhouse.'

Anna smiled and was about to ask who he was, when he turned and walked away down a small path at the side of the house. It led to a big kitchen garden, overgrown but evidently still productive. There was a rickety henhouse, on stilts, with a ladder up to the small gate at the top.

Emerging from the back of the henhouse, carrying a large straw basket, was a striking-looking woman. Her dark hair was worn in two big braids down to her waist and she was wearing a long print cotton dress and open-toed sandals. 'Hi there, won't be a minute,' she called.

They watched her climb the steps and lock the henhouse gate, then come down. 'We have to keep our eyes open; the foxes still manage to get in, even up the ladder.' She walked towards them with a wide smile. 'I'm Honour Nolan.'

Anna introduced herself and Gordon. Up close, she could see the likeness to Julia Brandon: the two sisters had the same tall, willowy figures, but Honour was totally natural, with obviously very different colouring. 'Come into the kitchen and I'll make some tea.' She walked ahead of them and pushed through the half-open door, gesturing for them to follow her inside.

The big, old-fashioned kitchen had two massive threadbare sofas, with throws over them. There were a number of moth-eaten kilims scattered over the York stone floor. Painted cupboards of sky blue and green, with glass fronts and a mish mash of crockery, surrounded the pine kitchen table, piled high with books and newspapers. There was a large open-brick fireplace with last night's logs left charred in the grate. It was a big warm family room, with heat coming from the bright red Aga. Herbs were drying on strings above it, and there were bowls of wild flowers and fruit everywhere. Honour brewed up a pot of tea and placed home-made scones onto a rack to put into the oven to warm. Anna had to sit forward on the sofa; it was so deep her feet lifted off the ground, if she sat back. Gordon was sitting in an old pine chair at the table.

'Damien said it was about Julia, the reason you wanted to talk to me?'

'Yes. If you don't mind, I'd just like to ask you a few questions. I suppose you know why?'

'Something to do with her husband?'

'Yes. He was murdered.'

'Jesus, she didn't tell me that! When?'

'Six days ago.'

'Oh God, that's awful. I mean, I didn't know him – in fact, I never met him – but nevertheless . . . She must be feeling dreadful.'

'She hasn't called you?'

'No. There's no point in hiding the fact that we don't get along. It's not that we don't love each other – of course we do – it's just that we have very different opinions about the quality of life.' Her laugh was soft and gentle. 'That sounded so crass. I'm sorry, but you must have met my sister, so you can obviously see for yourself that we live very different lives.'

As she talked, Honour removed the warmed scones, saying that they only needed a few moments; the Aga was hot because she was baking bread. She buttered them and set them out on a big oval plate. She moved like a dancer around her kitchen, fetching jam, milk and sugar, and setting out cups and saucers on the table, as she cleared the newspapers away.

Her arms full, she gestured to Anna. 'My husband! These are last Sunday's; it takes him an entire week to wade through them all. Still, they make jolly good fire-lighters.'

'This is really very kind of you,' Anna said.

'Well, you've had a long drive; I just hope it's not a wasted journey. That said, I can't for the life of me think how I can help you, as I haven't seen Julia for months.'

'Did you go to her wedding?'

'No. She didn't invite me.'

'And you never met her husband?'

'No. As I said, we don't get along – or, more to the point, we don't mix in the same social circles.'

'He was also her driver and bodyguard.'

Honour shrugged and took a scone for herself, passing the plate to Gordon so he could take another.

'What about Julia's ex-husband – or partner, rather? She said they never married.'

Honour bit into the scone, leaving a small trace of jam on her upper lip. She licked her finger to remove it. Anna noticed that her hands, unlike her sister's, had not been near a manicurist. They were rather raw-boned, with square-cut nails, and looked as if she needed some hand lotion on them. 'I don't think she did ever get him to put a ring on her finger; he was not the type.'

'So you met him?'

'I didn't say that. It's just that I know she cared about him a lot – or, let's say she liked the lifestyle he introduced her to. He was apparently very wealthy.'

'Did he leave her?'

'I think so. I know she said he was a lot older, but I didn't meet him either, so I couldn't really tell how much older. She was always jet-setting around – Barbados one minute, South of France the next. I think he had homes in Florida and Los Angeles. To be honest, I couldn't really keep up with her postcards, not that she ever sent very many.'

'How long was she with him?'

'I don't know exactly . . . maybe ten years? She was very young when she met him.'

'Where did she meet him?'

'Couldn't tell you. As I said, we were, and are, very different creatures. I couldn't stand to live in London, she couldn't be a country girl – well, not for more than ten minutes. She hated it.'

'So she came here?'

'Yes, once or twice, but she was no sooner here than she wanted to leave.'

'Do you own this property?'

'No, we rent it. I'd like to own it but we don't have the money. It may look rundown, but there's a lot of land and it would cost a few million.'

'Your sister certainly has the finances to help you.'

Honour reached for the teapot. 'Well, maybe she does, but I would never ask her for any. I am married; my husband provides for me.'

'You have any children?'

She stirred her tea and then shook her head. 'No. Sadly we don't.'

'What was his name?'

'I'm sorry, whose name?'

'Your sister's ex-partner.'

'Oh, I'm not sure. Maybe my husband can remember.'

'Did your husband meet him?'

'No, but he has a better memory than I have. More tea?'

'No, thank you.'

Gordon was about to pass his cup across for seconds, but dropped his hand back onto the table as Anna stood up and took her teacup over to the sink.

'Oh please, leave them. I do have a dishwasher!'

'It's a wonderful spot, hard to find.'

'Yes, we don't get many ramblers, thank God.'

'In fact, if you didn't know the farm was here, you'd never find it.'

'Exactly.'

'Do you work?'

'No, it takes all my time looking after the animals. I like to paint. I used to run a small antique shop in Oxford, but it was mostly junk. Unlike my sister, I have never felt the need to be materialistic.'

Anna opened her briefcase and took out the photograph of the Mitsubishi. 'Have you ever seen this jeep before?'

Honour glanced at the photograph and shrugged. 'No. We don't have many visitors, especially ones driving that kind of vehicle – it's hideous.'

'Have you ever heard of a man called Donny Petrozzo?'

'No.'

'Alexander Fitzpatrick?' Anna stared at the beautiful, wide eyes.

There was not a flicker of recognition. 'No.'

'Anthony Collingwood?'

'No.'

Lastly, Anna showed Frank Brandon's photograph. 'This was your sister's husband.'

'Really? Well, as I said, I never met him.'

Anna replaced the photographs, as Honour looked to Gordon. 'Don't you have anything to say?'

'Not really.'

Honour gave a friendly laugh, then fetched a tray and began to clear away the tea things. It felt as if the interview was over, but Anna wasn't through yet. She slipped a note to Gordon as she passed him.

'Could you show me around?' she asked politely. 'I'd love to see the rest of the house.'

Honour gave a rather tight smile. 'Why not? There's not a lot to see, but please . . .'

Anna followed her out into the hallway, full of Wellington boots and umbrellas, old folding chairs and some browned prints on the shabby flocked wallpaper.

'We keep meaning to do something out here, but we never get around to it.' Honour opened a door to a large, rather musty-smelling lounge. 'We don't even use this room much; it faces north and doesn't get much sun.'

Honour led Anna up the small staircase. There was a large master bedroom, with books lining the walls, but the furnishings were modern, especially the king-size bed. The other room was a small single bedroom, taken over with canvases and an easel and Honour's painting equipment. Anna thought it was not difficult to see why her sister didn't come to stay.

'This is where I work. I have a small kiln in one of the outhouses, as I'm trying my hand at pottery.'

'It's so peaceful,' Anna said, looking out from the lattice windows. She was taken by surprise as Honour moved close to her.

'What is it you want? I mean, I really don't understand why you are here.'

'Just part of the enquiry into your sister's husband's murder; we often have to make what appear to be unconnected interviews.'

'Well, I'm sorry you had to come such a long way.'

'It was quite a relief to get out of the station,' Anna

said, as she followed Honour back towards the stairs.

As they entered the kitchen, Gordon was sitting on the sofa.

'What time do you expect your husband home?' asked Anna.

'That depends. If he has lectures, he's often quite late, as he stays in Oxford for dinner with his cronies.'

'Is he lecturing today?'

'I'm not sure.'

'Could you call him and ask?'

Honour hesitated and then shrugged. She walked back out into the hallway.

Anna looked at Gordon and then sat beside him.

'There's a room off the side of the kitchen: an office, or what looks like it – they've got computers and mobile phones in there, and . . .'

Anna wondered why Honour had gone into the hall and not used the room Gordon was referring to. 'Any photographs?'

'No.'

This was strange – there were no photographs anywhere in the house. They remained silent as they heard Honour saying, 'Thank you,' to someone, then she walked back into the kitchen.

'He's not in his office; he left about an hour ago.'

'So is he on his way home?'

'Don't know.'

'Does he have a mobile you can call?'

'No, he hates them.'

Anna stood up and looked at her watch: it was after five. She smiled and thanked Honour, and walked towards the back door. 'You have a lot of barns and outhouses.'

'Yes. Some we use, others are rented out to farmers who leave their tractors here occasionally. Do you want to walk around? Only it's a bit muddy underfoot.'

They heard a car pulling up. Honour said it sounded as if her husband was home.

Professor Damien Nolan was a tall man, at least six foot, dressed in a tweed suit, with a checked shirt and a thick knitted tie. As he walked in, he dumped a bulging briefcase on the floor. He was a handsome man, with dark hair flecked grey at the temples and sideburns. He was tanned and looked fit, almost athletic.

'Hello, there. I'm sorry, I did try and get home earlier, but I had a tormented student to deal with.' He smiled with white, even teeth; like his wife, he had a relaxed air about him. 'Is it too early to have a glass of wine?'

Anna refused, but he opened a bottle and poured himself one. Honour sat at the table watching him with open adoration. He stood beside her, resting one hand on the nape of her neck.

'So, this is all very intriguing,' he said, smiling.

Whilst Anna explained the reason for the visit, Honour excused herself – she wanted to check the henhouse and close up for the night.

Damien took his wife's seat as Anna joined him at the table; she went through the same scenario as she had done with Honour. Like his wife, Damien was shocked to hear about the death of Julia's husband, but had never met him, nor had he any knowledge of Donny Petrozzo, or Julia's ex-partner.

'You know, Julia is a gorgeous woman but, to be truthful, she's a pain in the arse. On the few occasions she has stayed here, it was very tedious. One can't really have an intellectual conversation with her. The only thing she seems to be interested in, apart from herself, is her wardrobe.'

'What about her children?'

He seemed nonplussed by the question and then shrugged. 'I've not met them. To be totally honest with you, it's quite an area of . . .' He hesitated. 'My wife can't have children, so . . .'

Anna noticed the way he moved his long legs for comfort beneath the table. She wondered if he could possibly be the man in the Mitsubishi but then dismissed it: he was obviously in the peak of health, with no outward show of any injury.

When Honour walked back in and went to the sink to wash her hands, Anna stood up.

'Thank you both so much for your time,' she said, shaking the Professor's hand. It was a strong firm grip. He was head and shoulders above her.

'If there's anything else, do call,' Damien replied.

Driving back down the now dark lane, night drawing in, Anna took a deep breath.

'Nice couple,' Gordon said.

'Yes, very nice.'

'Good-looking pair.'

'Yes.' Anna began to chew her lip. 'But there's something I don't feel easy about.'

'Really?'

'Yes. That place is a perfect hidey-hole; almost too perfect.'

'He drives a pretty rundown old Range Rover.'

'Yes.'

'They don't seem to have a lot of money.'

'No.' Anna didn't want to discuss them any further.

She had a gut feeling there was a lot more beneath their relaxed and charming exterior. First thing in the morning, she would see how much she could dig up on the duo.

It was nine when Anna got back to her office. She typed up her report, and then went to look over the incident board. A skeleton night duty was working and she saw that yet another of Cunningham's briefings was to be held at nine the following morning. As she was walking out, she noticed that Cunningham's office light was on. She decided she would go in to see her, just to make a show that, at nine-thirty, she was still busy. She passed the half-drawn blinds, looked in – and froze.

Detective Chief Superintendent James Langton was sitting with Cunningham. She was leaning forward, listening, as Langton talked. The shock to Anna's system, seeing him, was like a panic attack. She didn't want to be caught listening, so she backed away. She had to gasp for breath and then skedaddle out fast, as Langton stood up as if he was about to leave. The last thing Anna wanted was a confrontation with him: she was simply not ready for it. She felt so inadequate as she hurried back to her office to collect her briefcase and coat. She had shut down her laptop, and was about to turn off the light, when she heard his laugh. Her heart was pounding as she heard Cunningham saying he could look over the incident board. She knew that if he decided not to, he would have to go past her window to leave and, if he looked into her office on the way, he would see her. She sighed with relief as she heard him saying that he would like to get up to speed.

'Dear God,' she murmured, 'please don't let him

come onto this case.' She physically jumped when her door was opened.

Phil Markham looked in. 'You want a drink?'

'Yes,' she said, hastily grabbing her coat. 'I'd love one.'

'See you in the pub then.'

'I'll walk out with you.'

He grinned and waited as she turned off her lights and shut her door. 'You see who's busy on this?' he said, as they headed down the corridor.

'No.'

'That guy Langton, the new Chief Superintendent. He's been holed up with the boss for hours.'

'Don't tell me he's taking over the investigation.'

'No way, he's got his hands full – there's a serial-killer case over in Hemel Hempstead – but he was certainly putting old Cunningham through the wringer. He was just going into the incident room when I left.'

Anna relaxed as they entered the car park. She saw Langton's old, beat-up, brown Volvo parked erratically as usual across two spaces. 'You know, maybe I'll take a raincheck on that drink,' she told Phil. 'It's been another very long day.'

Phil looked at her, then shrugged. 'Okay. See you in the morning.'

'Yeah, see you then.'

In the confines of her Mini, she started to breathe more freely, knowing she would not have to see Langton. She drove out of the station, longing to get home. Then she reprimanded herself. This had to stop.

She *had* to come to terms with the fact that she would have to confront Langton at some time; it was just that she wanted to be in total control, and not taken by surprise. Yet as she drove home she began to think, not about him, but about Damien Nolan.

By the time she got home, she understood why she had been so unsettled by Nolan. It was because he reminded her of Langton. He had the same charm, the same handsomeness; they were even similar in looks. She knew not to trust James Langton and she was certain that the Professor was one of the same breed. They were both dangerous men.

Chapter Ten

Anna did some sporadic unpacking before having an early night. Just as she was turning her bedside light off, she remembered something: the scrawled writing found inside the map from the glove compartment in the Mitsubishi. The torn piece of notepaper had only numbers and odd letters written on it. She had copied the information down, but done nothing about it. She doubted if anyone else had, because it had not been brought up; the forensic team still had it to check for fingerprints along with the map. She closed her eyes, trying to recall what area the folded map was for, but couldn't remember. It was already after eleven-thirty; there was nothing she could do but wait until morning.

Anna was the first of the team in the station. She went back over the incident board. There were the lists of items removed from the Mitsubishi, but no further details. Frustrated, she went into her office and called the forensic lab. She waited for what seemed an age before Pete Jenkins came onto the phone.

'Morning, Pete. I'm sorry to be such an early bird, but can you give me any details on the map removed—'

'What?'

'It was sent over to you for fingerprints.'

'Christ, I don't think we've got round to it yet.'

'Is it at hand? Can you just check something for me?'

'Sure, like what?'

'Where is it for?'

'The map?'

'Yes, it's very important.'

She waited another few minutes before he came back on the phone. 'It's still bagged up.'

'Can you just tell me if it's for Oxfordshire, that area?'

'Hang on.'

Again Anna had to wait; then Pete was back on the line. 'That's right.'

'What about the note that was sent in?'

'Do you know it's only eight-thirty? I've not had my coffee yet.'

Anna hadn't had any breakfast herself. She was getting impatient; even though she was certain she was correct, she wanted verification. Five minutes later, she got what she wanted. She gave Pete instructions to work on both items as soon as possible. He sounded tetchy, but she didn't care.

'Do you want to have dinner with me again?' he asked.

'Yes – yes, I do.' She was eager to get rid of him.

'Talk to you later then.'

Anna replaced the phone and almost hugged herself. Before she could go up to the canteen, Gordon knocked on her office door. 'You got a minute?' he asked.

'Just one, what is it?'

'I've had the photographs printed up.'

'What photographs?'

Gordon held up his mobile phone. 'From when you

went upstairs with Honour Nolan and I did a snoop job.'

Anna looked impressed and then laughed. 'Good for you, Gordon!'

He laid out six photographs. She didn't say anything because they were of the kitchen, the outhouses, the henhouse . . . 'These are of the rooms off the study.' He placed down three more.

Anna picked one up and scrutinised it. 'What's this?'

'His books and papers on the desk, computer and—'

Anna held the photograph closer. 'No, no, not on the desk — the picture on the wall behind it.'

'Oh. I dunno.'

'It's a painting of a boat.'

'Oh, is it?'

'Listen, get this blown up, will you? I want to see the picture more clearly.'

'Okay, will do. When do you want it for?'

'Like now!'

As the team grouped for the briefing, Anna ate a bacon sandwich. When Cunningham asked for any developments, it was painfully obvious that they were getting nowhere, until it was Anna's turn. She took great pains to cover the interactions with Honour and Damien Nolan. At the end, she left a theatrical pause; she had learned a lot about delivery from Langton, and she had everyone's attention.

'I think they were lying. I believe they *are* involved. Their farm is a perfect hideaway; you could stay there for weeks and not be discovered. If Alexander Fitzpatrick has returned, he could be living there. Found in the Mitsubishi jeep was a map: it detailed the area in which the farm is located, and the numbers on the scrap of torn paper that we recovered, I think, are actually directions to Honey Farm. It's not easy to find.'

With perfect timing, Gordon joined the team. It would have been even better if he had had the blown-up picture to show, but he had been unable to get it done in time. Anna described the painting of a large yacht in the farm office. It could mean that the Nolans had been in touch with Fitzpatrick. Cunningham was impressed.

Coming up after Anna was Phil Markham. He had also been busy. He gave a mock bow as he listed his new developments. First up, was the verification that a set of prints from the squat, found on a crumpled plastic take-away carton, belonged to Donny Petrozzo. There was no evidence as to the time or date the prints were left. They could have been there from before the night of the murder. From the residue inside the carton, however, they could perform further tests. Secondly, there was at long last a set of prints from the squat that came up on the database, identifying Shane Browne, a known addict with a long record for drug abuse, a Bernard Murphy and Julius D'Anton. The last two had record sheets for theft and housebreaking, D'Anton for domestic violence as well.

As Phil continued to detail the trace on the three men, which was already underway, Anna jotted down their names. None were big-time, and none had a record for using weapons. The forensic teams still had many more items to check for prints before they started on the Mitsubishi, which had now been taken apart. The number-plates were false and the vehicle identification number had been destroyed by acid. It had also been customised, the black windows tinted darker than was legal. It was no more than a year old, so it was probable they would get a trace on it through dealers quite quickly.

Phil reported that the blood swipe did match the blood spattering from the squat, so it must belong to the man who was standing behind Frank Brandon, but, as yet, forensics had no further evidence for them. Tests were still being done on the road map and the scrap of paper, as Anna had mentioned. He then turned over a page in his notebook and grinned.

'Saving the best for last . . . We suspected that, after the shooting, either the shooter or his cohorts left via the back window of the squat. This had been nailed down, so they'd used a wrench to get it open. We have a right-hand print, half the palm and four fingers; the tip of the right index finger is missing. They did not have a match, but we started sifting through any known drug dealers with similar injuries, specifically before the database was compiled. We were coming up with a big fat zero, until we got a break from chatting to a few blokes from the Drug Squad – and we got a name.'

Phil looked around the incident room, really milking it. 'Stanley Leymore, secondhand car dealer. No previous, but known to the squad because at one time he was a useful informer – this was until eighteen months ago. His connection is to Donny Petrozzo, as he sold him the Mercedes; we know this from Donny's documents. I wouldn't be surprised if we found out that the Mitsubishi also came from his garage.'

There was a buzz around the incident room; at long last, they appeared to be making some headway. Cunningham gave out the details for tracking down and bringing in the men named by Phil, and the search for Shane Browne, Bernard Murphy and Julius D'Anton went into overdrive.

Phil, accompanied by DC Pamela Meadows, left to pick up Stanley Leymore at his garage. This was situated behind Kings Cross Station and occupied three of the old railway arches. They had sent someone to his home address, but with no luck. As they parked up, it also looked as if the garages were not in operation either: the three massive double doors on each of the arches were locked and bolted. They made enquiries on either side of the garages and talked to the mechanics, who said they hadn't seen Leymore for days. Armed with warrants, Phil used a crowbar to force open the centre of the three arches.

The dark, damp caverns went back under the arches for at least sixty yards. There were numerous cars parked nose to tail in various degrees of repair. They looked like wrecks that Leymore had probably bought for the parts. Finding nothing but vehicles in the first garage, they went to the next.

This was cleaner, with a few vehicles that looked polished and in working order; two even had canvas covers to protect them, as the ceiling was dripping water. Paint-spraying equipment, vacuums and hosepipes were coiled along the brick walls. It looked as if this was where Leymore prepared the vehicles for sale.

The last garage was filled with old cabinets and spare tyres. They could see a small kitchen with two gas burners and a filthy sink, and a makeshift office sectioned off with metal sheeting.

Inside was a desk propped up with telephone directories; one leg was broken. There was a telephone and an outdated computer, and old diaries and ledgers. Phil and Pamela looked over the dusty, oil-streaked office, then Phil paused, lifting his head to sniff.

'You smell it?' he asked Pamela.

'Yeah. I thought it was the damp, but it's stronger in here.'

Phil looked around, then walked out of the office. At the back of the garage, there was a portable toilet, the type used at building sites. He and Pamela walked cautiously towards it. The door was shut but, as they got closer, the stench was stronger. Phil took out a handkerchief and covered his mouth and nose as he tried the door, then inched it open. The smell hit them like a vile blanket – so pungent, Pamela had to turn away.

Stanley Leymore was sitting on the toilet, his pants round his ankles, his head resting back. The bullet wound was in the centre of his forehead. His eyes were wide open. They knew it was him: his right-hand index finger was minus the tip.

'Shit,' Phil muttered.

Anna was in her office, checking over Petrozzo's diaries, when the news came in. The team had, so far, located two of the suspects: Shane Browne and Bernard Murphy. They were being questioned by Cunningham and Gordon in the interview rooms. Anna had seen the two boys being brought in and somehow knew they would not be of importance. Both wore grey anoraks with hoods, dirty trainers and baggy pants. The third suspect, Julius D'Anton, was still being hunted. She was not finding anything of interest in the diaries; it was tedious, trying to fathom out Donny's scrawled writing, and the series of dots and dashes that represented the users for whom he had scored. There was no reference to Fitzpatrick, nor any clue to Julia Brandon's connection.

She put in a call to Pete to ask what he had found on

the map and scrap of paper. The news was also dis-
appointing. Whoever had handled the map recently had
worn gloves, and these had smudged any prints that had
been on the paper. However, Pete was sure, like Anna,
that the scrawled letters on the note were directions to
the farmhouse. It was likely the Mitsubishi driver had
either been intending to go there, or had been there
already. Anna asked for the tyres to be checked for mud,
or any other evidence that could be matched to Julia's
sister's rented farmhouse.

'Do you know if the toxicology report is anywhere
near ready?' Anna added.

'Ask Fielding, but these things always take at least six
weeks.'

'Yes, I know. Thanks anyway.' Anna replaced the
receiver as Cunningham walked in.

'The kids admit to using the squat, and scoring dope
from there, but have alibis for the night of the murder.'

It was as Anna thought. She asked about the third guy,
Julius D'Anton, but as yet they still had no trace of him.

'You heard about the bloody garage owner?' Cunningham grunted. 'Been dead a few days, judging by the
stench.'

'Yes, I heard.'

'Phil's bringing in all the ledgers to sift through. It's
possible this guy had the Mitsubishi.' Cunningham
hesitated, then, as an afterthought, said they had also
found Frank Brandon's VW parked in one of the garages.
'I dunno. We get these links, and then it flatlines,' she said
angrily.

'Have we still got surveillance on Julia Brandon?'

'Nope, had to pull it off, invasion of friggin' privacy;
that bastard Simon Fagan's been onto the boss. To be

honest, I don't think we'd get anything out of her.' She looked at Anna. 'What?'

'I disagree. I think she knows a hell of a lot more than she is coughing up – ditto her sister and her husband.'

Cunningham folded her arms. 'Well, we need something to indicate what that is, Travis.'

Anna told her about the map and the directions.

Cunningham ran a hand over her short hair. 'Yeah, well – if Donny Petrozzo drove out there, or Frank, we don't have any evidence.'

Anna felt otherwise, but declined to say so.

Cunningham was edgy, stepping from one foot to the other.

'Leymore was shot between the eyes, close up; blew the top of his head almost through the portable toilet. Fielding's going to work on him as soon as he's delivered, but it looks like a very professional job. Judging from the fact he was taking a crap, he either knew the shooter, or they came in and caught him unaware.'

'What about the Mitsubishi? *Was* it from his garage?'

'Don't know yet, but I'd say so. I think Frank Brandon drove there in his VW, parked up and took the Mitsubishi – but thinking isn't good enough. We need to . . .'

Phil opened the office door. 'From what we've been able to check, Leymore was dealing in stolen cars: respraying, doctoring plates and engine licence numbers. We've got a sales receipt for Donny Petrozzo's Mercedes eighteen months ago – Leymore took another one in part-exchange – and, last but not least, we have the Mitsubishi. We've got some intelligence that it may have been stolen eight months ago from Brighton, but we're still checking it out.'

Anna repeated that she had asked for forensics to check out any soil particles on the tyres to see if they could match it with soil at Honey Farm.

'That'll take effing weeks,' Phil said tetchily. 'You know they gotta send it out to a different lab. We're still waiting for the toxicology report on how bloody Donny Petrozzo died.'

Cunningham shrugged. 'Yeah, well, that's the way it is. We wait.'

Anna watched them both leave her office. She noted that Phil, the golden boy at the briefing, was seeing his hard work result in bugger all. They had a few more pieces of the jigsaw, but none of the corners, just a small section. Those pieces in a jigsaw that were always the most difficult, like the sky or the sea, were still missing.

Thinking about the sea, she went into the incident room to ask if Gordon had the blown-up picture of the yacht from the farm. He passed it over. Back in her office she took out an old eyeglass that had belonged to her father and checked over the painting. It was quite good quality – the painting, not the enlargement. The boat had both sail and engine, and was enormous, with a speedboat winched onto the stern and two jet skis. She squinted at the small section of black writing on the bow, then took the painting over to the small dirty window, trying to get more light. There was a D and then an A, a clear R and something she couldn't make out . . . but then another D, E, V . . . She put the eyeglass down. Could it be *Dare Devil*? Even if it was, she wasn't sure what it meant.

She logged onto the computer, looking up Alexander Fitzpatrick again. She scrolled through the various newspaper articles written at the time of his arrest, and found a short paragraph about his prowess as a yachtsman when he had escaped via his boat back in the eighties. She kept scrolling through, to see if there was ever a mention of what the yacht was named, but found nothing. She sat back. Could the painting be of his boat? It would, she doubted, be in his possession now, as it was many years ago and ocean vessels had become much more sophisticated since then. However, if this was Fitzpatrick's boat in the painting, it gave an obvious link to Honour Nolan. She surely knew Fitzpatrick a lot better than her noncommittal 'never met him'.

Ballistics were able to ascertain very quickly that the bullet taken from Stanley Leymore was a match for the bullets that had killed Frank Brandon: it came from a Glock weapon. Pathology estimated that he had been dead for at least four days. He left a widow and three teenage children. Mrs Leymore had not reported her husband missing, because she said he had told her he was going to be away on business.

Anna physically jumped as someone rapped on her door. Gordon poked his head round. 'You heard the latest?'

'You mean about Stanley Leymore?'

'No, Julius D'Anton.'

'What about him?'

'Fished him out of the Thames four days ago.'

'What?!'

'Boss wants you and me to go over to the Richmond mortuary.'

A fisherman had seen the bloated body of Julius D'Anton floating over the weir in Teddington, caught in weeds beneath Richmond Bridge. Wrapped around one ankle was a rope; it appeared to have been attached to something at some point, but it must have broken loose and the body floated to the surface, aided by the gases trapped in the swollen belly. Anna stared at the hideous face.

D'Anton was not like the other kids they had interviewed. A mature man, he had been wearing a tweed sports jacket, polo-neck shirt and cord trousers; even his shoes looked good quality. He had no wallet or identifying papers in his pockets, and cause of death was listed as unknown! No water had been found in his lungs, so he had not drowned, and was therefore presumed dead before being tipped or falling into the Thames. D'Anton had been initially ID'd by his fingerprints, due to previous arrest sheets. His wife, Sandra, had also identified him. Anna and Gordon went to interview her.

The house was in Chiswick, a substantial property on three floors. Sandra D'Anton was an attractive blonde in her early forties. She had decorators in, and apologised for the mess in her hallway. She had large, sad brown eyes, and a weight of depression clung to her. She was wearing slacks and a loose sweater with old leather slippers. She led them into a pleasant kitchen and offered them tea, but both declined.

'I am very sorry about your husband. I really appreciate you agreeing to talk to us,' Anna said quietly.

'I've wondered if someone else would come – you know, after they came to tell me they had found him.'

'I need to ask you some questions.'

Sandra shrugged and sat down at the kitchen table.

'When was the last time you saw your husband?'

'Over a week ago.'

'So were you worried when you didn't see him?'

'Not particularly; he often went off for days on end.

He was in the antique business, so frequently travelled up North or wherever.'

'Do you have a shop?'

'No, he had regular customers he bought and sold for. We sort of worked doing up properties, like this place; soon as it's all finished, we sell and start all over again. Well, we did . . .'

'So you own this house?'

'Yes, but it's mortgaged up to the hilt.'

'So you believed he was buying antiques?'

'I presumed he was.'

'He used to just take off?'

'Well, yes. This time he said that he was . . .' She threaded her fingers together. 'It's the way he was, you know, always going to find something that would get us off the treadmill. Out of debt, to be more exact.'

'So you are in debt?'

'You could say that. I don't think we have ever not been, not for the past ten years.'

'Before that?'

'He was successful; we had a shop on the King's Road, but that went.' She sighed. 'My husband was arrested for dealing drugs. He served time, but always said when he came out, it was over. He tried to straighten out, but it was hard and he was always chasing the dream. When he did deal drugs, he had money he could throw around.'

'Do you know Donny Petrozzo?'

'No.'

'How about Stanley Leymore?'

'Never heard of him.'

'Julia Kendal?'

'No.'

Anna hesitated. 'Frank Brandon?'

'No. I don't know any of these people.'

'Anthony Collingwood?'

'No.'

'Alexander Fitzpatrick?'

Sandra closed her eyes. 'Well, I know who he is. I never actually knew the man but Julius knew him years ago – I mean years, like thirty, maybe even more.'

'How well did he know him?'

'They were at Oxford together – Balliol. I think he was pretty infamous. Julius used to dine out on stories about when they were undergraduates.'

'Did he keep in touch with him?'

'Good God, I doubt it.'

'Did he mention recently that he might have seen him?'

'No. Look, if you must know, and I see no reason why I shouldn't say it, my husband was quite a sad character. He came from a very good family but blew his inheritance before I even met him. Then he got caught up in drugs.'

'Was he still using?'

Sandra nodded. 'He tried to quit, but then he'd make some money and go on a bender. It drove me to distraction, but he wouldn't listen to me. He was a very sweet guy, so generous. For all his faults – and there were many – he was always kind to me.' She sighed. 'Even though he was older than me, he just never grew up.'

'I'm sorry.'

'Yeah, but you know, all the time we've been together, I always felt something bad would happen to him. In the end it did, didn't it?'

It was strange. Sandra didn't seem that distressed; there was just a sad resignation. Perhaps, just as she said, she had always been expecting this. Anna knew that one of the charges against him had been for domestic violence, but she didn't feel that this was the time to bring that up. She didn't have to.

'He hit me, you know,' Sandra said. 'It was a long time ago. He was high on crack and he lost it, started wrecking the house – not this one, another place we had. Anyway, when he attacked me, I called the cops and they arrested him. I never meant it to be such a big thing. I mean, he had punched me around, but they found his stash of drugs, so he got a six-month sentence. He was in Ford Open Prison; in a way, it was the best thing, because he got clean whilst he was there. When he came out, we started over. For a while, he was on his best behaviour but then, as always, he started using again. You know, recently, he'd been trying to stay straight. Then, when he said he'd got this big thing going down . . .'

'Did he ever hint at what this was?' Anna asked.

Sandra got up and went to the fireplace. It was being rebuilt; there were tiles and bricks stacked beside it. She looked along the dusty mantelshelf and sifted through some letters. 'You get so fed up that you don't really ever believe someone like Julius. You know the promises – he was always going to sort himself out, go into rehab, when he came out of prison things would be different . . . but you get used to empty promises. They sort of deaden any real feelings.'

'But you loved him,' Anna said softly.

'I guess so, but the terrible thing is, I feel a kind of relief. That may sound awful, but it's the truth. I mean, we lived together but he was impotent – had been for years – and I was getting tired out from propping him up.'

'Are you looking for something specific?' Anna asked, watching Sandra hunting through the papers.

'Yes. It was a few months back – he said he was onto something. He'd been away for a couple of days antiquing, going to odd fairs up and down the country . . .'

'Something he wanted to buy?'

'I'm not sure. All he said was, things were going to turn around and he would be able to buy the lease on a shop he had seen – you know, really start afresh. But if you knew how many times he'd said that . . .' Sandra held onto one opened envelope and placed the others back onto the mantelshelf. 'Those are mostly bills, unpaid, and will have to stay that way until I know what I'm doing.' She opened the envelope; tucked inside was a pink flyer with lists of antique fairs. 'This is the flyer they leave at the London fairs, giving details of the ones out of town. He bought a few things, but it was after that trip he said he was onto something. Whether or not he went back there, I really don't know.'

'May I see it?'

'Yes, take it.'

Anna glanced at the advertisement. A couple of fairs had rings around them and were underlined. One, Anna paid particular attention to: a trade fair in Shipston on Stour. 'Isn't this near Oxford?'

Sandra looked over her shoulder. 'Yes, but it's not a big one: just a village hall. Sometimes you can pick up good stuff if you're lucky. I doubt if Julius would have found anything of great value there, but I think he was going back to one of the shops.'

'Not the antique fair?'

'I think the guy may have had a stall there; often

shop-owners take stalls at these fairs. You get to see a regular bunch of people.'

'Did he stay in hotels?'

'No, he used to sleep in the back of the van. He never had enough money to stay in hotels. Drink in them, maybe . . .'

'The van, do you know where it is?'

Sandra shook her head. 'It was a wreck. Julius drove it into the ground. I think the back end or something went, so he might have dumped it somewhere.'

'What was he driving the last time you saw him?'

Sandra puffed out her cheeks, trying to remember. 'I don't know. He said he'd borrowed someone's jeep, I think. Whose, I have no idea.'

'Did you ever see this jeep?'

'No.'

'Could it have been a Mitsubishi?'

'I don't know, and he could have been lying. All I remember is, he said he was going to pick it up.'

They drove in silence back to the station, Anna's mind churning over everything they had discussed with Sandra. Gordon, as usual, had not said more than a few words, but he was at least onto the fact that the antique fair was not that far from Honour Nolan's village.

Anna gave him a sidelong glance. 'Yes, my thoughts exactly. It's another link, because Julius D'Anton also knew Alexander Fitzpatrick.'

'What if he was hiding out at the farmhouse and somehow D'Anton saw him?'

'But if he was hiding out, he's not likely to have been wandering around an antique fair, is he? It's another schlep to check it all out; it'll mean contacting all those dealers that had a stall, especially the guy that Sandra said owned a shop. It might be local, it might not, but that's what you have to start on as soon as we're back at the station.'

'Okay.'

Anna decided that she would go over to the forensic lab and see if they had any results from the tests being done on the Mitsubishi. This time, she wanted to find out if there was any crossover from the clothes worn by Julius D'Anton – anything that would place him in the jeep.

Pete listened as Anna outlined what she wanted tested. He shook his head. 'You must be joking. We've had it stripped down, and it was given a very thorough clean, apart from the small blood swipe.'

'What about the map?'

'There were prints, but nothing clean enough for us to run by the database.'

'The note?'

'Ditto. It does look as if the numbers were, as you thought, directions to the farmhouse. We're testing soil samples, but they will take a while. Then we've got to match them with samples taken from the farmhouse.'

Anna sighed with impatience.

'You can well sigh, Detective Travis, but have you any idea of the amount of forensic work going on? The body count keeps on growing every time I turn around. This guy brought in from the Thames: his clothes are all pegged out, so are Donny Petrozzo's clothes, then there's the guy shot on his toilet . . .'

'Stanley Leymore.'

'Yes, him – we've got all his gear being tested. The cost is mounting. We've brought in three extra assistants and the path lab is screaming blue murder. They are as inundated as we are.'

'What about the toxicology report?'

'Jesus! Ask Fielding, I don't know. I'm aware he's getting in extra people too, but the costs – do you know how much it is just to get the soil samples tested?'

Anna wondered if Cunningham was under pressure; her budget must be through the roof. Maybe that was why she was so bad-tempered all the time.

'So, we still on for dinner sometime?'

Anna suddenly relented and smiled. 'I'm sorry. Yes, of course we are.'

'When?'

'Why not tomorrow evening?'

'Great. You want me to bring anything?'

'No. Say about eight?'

'I'll be there.'

Anna jotted down her address and asked if there was anything he couldn't eat.

'Nope. See you tomorrow night.'

By the time Anna got back to the station, it was almost four. She hadn't had lunch, but didn't have time to go up to the canteen, as Cunningham had asked for yet another briefing. These were starting to get on everyone's nerves: usually an enquiry spaced them out, to give the team time to do their jobs. There were a lot of disgruntled people banging down chairs. Anna could see that the incident board had more information, but much of it was eliminating the vehicle owners, whose number-plates had been listed by Jeremy Webster. It was the wait for evidence from the forensic and pathology reports that was holding them up. The body count was, as Pete Jenkins had said, mounting: Frank Brandon, Donny Petrozzo, Stanley Leymore and now Julius D'Anton.

Anna was quickly marking up the information on D'Anton that she'd got from his wife, the possible link to the farmhouse, and his association with Alexander Fitzpatrick, when Gordon hurried over to say that he had tracked down five stallholders' names and addresses. He was waiting for the organisers to give him more details, but he had the name of two who also had antique shops in the area, one in Oxford and another in the village of Shipston on Stour. Anna told him to form a new section on the board and write up everything.

He was busy doing so when Cunningham made her usual scowling entrance. 'Okay, everyone, listen up. I am getting a lot of pressure regarding the mounting costs. We have to really concentrate on . . .' She turned to the board as Gordon finished writing. 'What the hell is this?'

Anna stood up and explained that Julius D'Anton might have been in the area of Honour Nolan's farm, and that he might also have been driving the Mitsubishi.

'Might?'

'Yes, it's possible, but my interest is that D'Anton knew Alexander Fitzpatrick—'

'Right now, we do not have any evidence that this man is involved, Travis. We have not a shred of evidence that he is even in this country. What we do have are four dead men and very little else. The killer, or killers, are dropping these bodies like flies without anything that helps us with the murder of Frank Brandon.'

'I'm sorry, but I disagree with you. We know Frank worked for Donny Petrozzo, we know Donny bought hot cars from Stanley Leymore, and we know that at one time Julius D'Anton knew Fitzpatrick.'

'What exactly does that give us?'

'A link!'

'Bloody fantastic, a link. We still don't know who was the main dealer in that stinking squat, nor why Frank Brandon was there, and we don't have any clue as to who the man was possibly standing behind him. I don't buy that it might have been Fitzpatrick. You tell me why an internationally infamous drug operator would risk entering the UK to schlep over to Chalk Farm, and for what – to score some cocaine? It doesn't fit. He is on our Most Wanted lists. All this supposition about this couple and their farmhouse has not brought in any connections.'

'Bar the fact that Honour Nolan is Julia Brandon's sister.'

'So what does that give us? We don't have any connection between Julia Brandon and the dead men, apart from a dodgy marriage to Frank Brandon. We're going round in circles.'

'But the circles keep on joining up,' Anna said defensively.

'Do they hell! Show me – I am all ears. We need a break, and I can't see us finding it by constantly bringing in supposition instead of hard evidence.'

'I think both Honour Nolan and her husband Damien lied about how well they knew Alexander Fitzpatrick.'

'But, Travis, what does that give us?'

'Well, there is the painting of a boat.'

'Painting?'

'Yes, it's of a very large, ocean-going yacht called *Dare Devil*, painted, I think, by Honour Nolan. If she didn't know Fitzpatrick, as she claims . . .'

'Is it his boat?' snapped Cunningham.

'I don't know. I am still checking it out.'

'Did she actually paint it?'

'I don't know that either,' Anna said lamely.

'So all this is still just your supposition. It's no good going off to interview these suspects if you just come back with "possibles", for Chrissakes. Get your head down and check it all out.'

'We have asked for the soil from the wheels of the Mitsubishi to be tested, prove it was on the Nolan farm.'

Cunningham folded her arms. 'Okay, and that, we know, is going to take weeks. We are waiting on fucking forensics to bring us something – and running around like blue-arsed flies is not, to my mind, bringing us anything we can get to grips with.'

Anna sat back in her chair, furious at the way she had been spoken to.

Phil Markham raised his hand. 'What do you suggest we do, Ma'am?' His sarcasm was obvious.

'I want the Frank Brandon and Julia Brandon relationship delved into. I want to know where she got her millions. I want her under the hammer – put as much pressure on her as possible.'

'Hard with that bastard Simon Fagan watching over her,' Phil muttered.

'Then put the pressure on her weasel-faced accountant. Get whatever warrants we need to make him squirm,' Cunningham continued. 'Above all, I want to know who was running that fucking drug squat. Any vehicle still not traced, get out there and find who owns it and who was inside that squat.'

'Well, we know Leymore was there at some point,

because of his missing fingertip and the prints.' Again this was Phil.

Cunningham folded and refolded her arms. 'Small fry, dealt in stolen cars. So, we are now going to focus on why Frank Brandon was shot? Why were they at this drug squat?'

Anna coughed. 'Maybe the scoring of drugs is not the reason. Maybe there was something else inside that squat.'

'Like what?'

'I don't know.'

'Terrific, thank you, Travis. Now, all of you get back to basics. This is a murder enquiry and the main development has to come from why Frank Brandon was shot.'

'Because maybe he was protecting someone?' Phil said.

'Find out who.'

'But what if Travis is right? What if Fitzpatrick *is* back in the UK?'

Cunningham sighed and threw open her arms. 'Then give me proof!'

She then gave the main team the following day off, saying she wanted them all to take a breather and come back refreshed, with details and not supposition. Hopefully, by that time, they would at long last have some details from the labs.

Anna packed up her briefcase. At least she would be able to sort her flat out and buy some groceries for dinner with Pete. Just as she was about to leave, Gordon called. There was someone she should talk to on line two – a Michael Sudmore, antique dealer and owner of the shop in Shipston on Stour.

Mr Sudmore had a very fruity voice. Anna held the

phone away from her ear, as he spoke so loudly. Sudmore had known Julius D'Anton quite well and was not that fond of him, as he often took a long time to pay for goods. D'Anton had such a poor record that Sudmore refused to sell him anything unless it was for cash. Sudmore had been at the village fair and met D'Anton, who was interested in a table but, as usual, tried his bouncing cheque routine. When Sudmore had refused, D'Anton had agreed to come to his shop with the money within the next week. He had left twenty pounds for Sudmore to hold it for him. Sudmore was really not expecting D'Anton to show, as he had done this many times before.

He also reckoned he had undersold the table, and was hoping D'Anton would not actually turn up to buy it. It was almost three days later when D'Anton returned with a large wedge of fifty-pound notes. He paid over the cash but said his van was in the garage, so he would not collect the table until the following week.

Sudmore recalled that D'Anton was driving a black Mitsubishi jeep; it was not large enough for the table to fit in the back. He described D'Anton as being very full of himself, a bullshitter, saying that he would soon be opening up a shop in Chiswick as he now had financial backing. Sudmore recalled as best he could the clothes D'Anton was wearing – a polo-neck sweater and tweed jacket. He suggested that they call his assistant, who had met him, and ask her if she could remember anything else that might help them. When she asked for the woman's name, Anna almost dropped the receiver.

'She lives quite locally; she's an artist and only works part-time when I need her. Honour Kendal, lovely lady.'

Anna asked him to repeat the name, to be 100 per cent sure.

'Honour Kendal. Her married name is Nolan.'

Anna replaced the receiver. She was buzzing. Could it have been coincidental that Honour Nolan was working in the same antique shop that Julius D'Anton walked into? Was it coincidental that perhaps Alexander Fitzpatrick was there? Did D'Anton recognise him? Was he paid money to keep his mouth shut until they could get rid of him? Anna sat back in her chair. Coincidence? Langton always said there were no coincidences, just facts.

This time she would make Cunningham wait until she was positive. She was certain that Alexander Fitzpatrick was in the UK, and he had to be here for a reason. If she was correct, he was taking out anyone connected to him. Uppermost in her mind, though, was still the question of how it all linked to Frank Brandon's murder in the drug squat on the Chalk Farm Warren Estate.

Chapter Eleven

Friday morning, and Anna really intended to do a grocery shop before cooking dinner for Pete Jenkins. She had even attempted to clear some of the packing boxes, but she kept on thinking about Honour Nolan and the possibility that she and her husband were involved with Fitzpatrick. Eventually, she decided that, contrary to what she had been instructed to do by Cunningham, she could legitimately pay another visit to Oxford, to check on the antique shop and to follow up on Honour Nolan's meeting with Julius D'Anton. She rang Pete.

He sounded as if he was half-asleep. 'Hello?'

'Pete, it's Anna.'

'Oh, don't tell me you want to cancel dinner.'

'Well, not exactly. It's just I sort of need to take a trip to Oxford and I won't be sure what time I'll get back.'

'This got something to do with the case?'

She said that it did, in a roundabout way.

'You want company?'

She hesitated.

'There are some really great restaurants,' he said persuasively. 'One called The Bear, something like that – it's got Michelin stars up the yin-yang. I've always wanted to try it out. I could drive?'

'Well, if you can take the rest of the day off, then great,' she said.

They arranged to meet at his house in Hampstead, as he said he would need to take a shower and have a shave. They would then drive from there in his car, as he said it needed a 'blow out'. She was unsure exactly what he meant but agreed. An hour later, Anna parked outside Pete's house and was concerned that there was no response when she rang his doorbell. The sound of his Morgan sports car roaring into the street made her turn; he also blasted the horn.

The hood was down; it was already a pleasant morning, which she hoped would bode well for a sunny day. She parked in his garage around the rear of the house and then, armed with a bag of fresh fruit, water and chocolate bars, they set off towards the M40.

'This is a great car,' she said, above the noise of the engine.

'Yeah, I've had it for years, but don't drive it into work as it's too much aggravation. It'll be good to get a long drive, blow the cobwebs off the engine; these old cars need to be driven.'

The interior smelled of old leather and mildew; the dashboard was a lovely polished wood, with a few bubbles and cracks. Pete drove fast, but was competent and didn't take any risks. It was refreshing to drive into the country after picking their way through the city and onto the motorway.

This time, Anna didn't think of the many trips she had made to see Langton in the rehabilitation home. With the wind making her hair stand up on end, she rested back with her eyes closed, the sun on her face, glad Pete had come along. They didn't make much conversation, as they couldn't really hear each other, until they branched off and headed towards the village of Shipston on Stour.

Michael Sudmore's antique shop was on the High Street. There were a number of items on a table outside the shop and an antique rocking chair with embroidered cushions. The shop was well-stocked, with a lot of spindle-backed chairs, small Edwardian tables, and many prints and cabinets covering the walls; on one table, a large china dinner service was set out with a bowl of fresh flowers. The florid, fruity-voiced Sudmore was sitting behind a small counter, reading *The Times*. He was wearing half-moon glasses and peered over them as Anna and Pete entered the shop.

Anna introduced herself, and left Pete to wander around the shop, as she went over everything they had discussed on the telephone. Sudmore could add little, apart from a few anecdotes about Julius D'Anton and his notoriously bad cheques. He did say that D'Anton had a great charm to him and was always very affable; yet, over the years had become rather seedy, and was mistrusted by the other antique dealers. For all his faults, Julius did have a very good eye and considerable knowledge.

Sudmore then showed Anna the table Julius had put twenty pounds deposit down on. It was an oval shape with cabriole legs and a folding arm, and it resembled a small version of the old hunting tables used by the gentry when they were served drinks after a fox hunt. He had, as he had said on the phone, undersold it.

'He was a wily old sod, asked me where I had bought it. You know, dealers have this nose – maybe where I had got it from, there could be more bargains – but I told him he wouldn't get anything else. The old lady has an eye for Ikea! She lives in a cottage not far from here. This table was about the only thing left of value and it was in a terrible state, standing outside her kitchen door!'

Anna took down the exact dates of Julius's visit and worked her way round to asking about Honour Nolan.

'Adorable! She used to have her own little shop, but closed it up years ago. Now she just does odd days for me when I am off buying. As she lives close by it's convenient for me; sometimes I sell some of her paintings.' He raised an eyebrow. 'Not what I would call works of art, but very colourful, and she buys some of my old frames. I have a couple of pots she's made. She had a kiln in one of her barns. But they don't sell. Well, anyone coming in here is not after anything modern.'

Anna glanced over to Pete. He had walked out of the shop and was sifting through the items for sale outside. She could see that anyone standing in the shop had a very good view of the front and road, even over to the local pub and car park where they had left their car.

'Do you ever socialise with Mrs Nolan?'

'No. I have been over to Honey Farm once. I was in the area and I needed to see if she could come in and watch the shop for me. She rarely answers her phone and they don't have an answer machine.'

'You have met her husband?'

'Oh yes, he often collects her. Lovely man, very pleasant, but they are a very private couple. In fact, I hardly ever see them, even at the local pub. They keep very much to themselves.'

'Did you ever meet her sister?'

'No, I didn't. I know she came to stay once. I only

remember because I needed Honour, and she said she had people staying.'

'People?'

'Well, her sister. I saw her in the village with Honour but, as I said, I didn't really get to meet her.'

'Did you ever see the black Mitsubishi jeep, before D'Anton turned up in it?'

'No, and we do get some flash cars. We even had one of those huge Hummer things here the other day – bright orange. Ghastly.'

There seemed nothing else to gain from Sudmore, so Anna thanked him and went out to join Pete. He had wandered further along the road and was looking into a Cancer Research charity shop; he turned and grinned as Anna approached.

'There's a great hat in the window. I was thinking of buying it for you.'

It was green velour, with a long pheasant feather sticking out of the side, and a silver brooch.

'You think that's my style, do you?'

'It'll keep your head warm on the drive back.'

She laughed. They crossed the road to find the car, then drove out of Shipston on Stour, heading for Honington and the farm. Even with the map, and even having already been there, they missed the turning. Anna was still unsure they were on the right track until she saw the first cottage covered in ivy.

'Okay, keep on going and take the right fork,' she instructed Pete.

'That adds up.'

'What?'

'The note: there's *RF* written – must mean right fork!'

Anna nodded, knowing they were correct that the

note found in the glove compartment of the Mitsubishi contained scrawled directions to the farm. The old Morgan creaked and groaned as it bounced over the dry cartwheel indentations in the dirt track. They passed the wooded area and came onto the narrow lane with a ditch either side.

'This is right, we're almost there.'

'Thank Christ. Any more of this rough track and my back end will collapse. I wouldn't like to do this drive at night – there's no street light. It must get pitch black.'

Anna smiled and chewed her lip. Julius D'Anton's van – hadn't Sandra said something about him saying the back end had gone, which was why he couldn't take the table? She wondered if the van could have been left in a local garage. She would have a wander around after they left the farm. She didn't mention it to Pete, as he was carefully trying to manoeuvre the Morgan round the deep potholes.

'Christ, this is a terrible road,' he swore again as they splashed through a deep puddle.

'We should be there any minute,' Anna said as the lane evened out.

They drove through the broken gates and parked outside the front door of the farmhouse.

Anna got out and looked around. 'They don't use the front entrance; we'll walk around to the back. It's down the lane beside the farmhouse.'

Pete looked over the sides of the Morgan. They were covered in mud. 'I'll have to take a chisel to get this mud off, look at it!'

Anna did and then smiled. 'Take samples – I want them sent over to the lab for testing against the soil from the Mitsubishi tyres!'

Pete laughed and then took her elbow, helpfully guiding her beside him, as they walked to the back of the farmhouse.

The stable door at the kitchen was half-open and Anna whispered to Pete that she had seen Honour Nolan's face at the window, so she knew they were there. Could he think of some excuse to get Honour out of the kitchen, as she wanted to look at something.

Anna called out, and Honour came to the door, with a look of surprise. 'Hi there! You gave me quite a fright.'

Anna apologised. 'I'm sorry to bother you again, but I need to ask some more questions.'

'More? Well, you'd better come in. Damien is out riding but he'll be back shortly.'

'It was you I really need to talk to,' Anna said, following Honour into the kitchen. She introduced Pete, saying he was a friend who had agreed to drive her. She asked about restaurants, making it seem very casual; Honour said she would jot down a list of some of the best to try. Friday and Saturday nights they might need to book.

'Oh, we'll just take pot luck,' Pete said affably, as he sat at the table. Honour offered tea, and more of her home-made scones, but Anna declined, saying they wouldn't be taking up too much of her time.

Honour drew up a chair to sit beside Anna, moving away stacks of what looked like exam papers. 'So, what do you need to know?'

Anna went into the Julius D'Anton scenario, asking if Honour could give her details of when she had served him in the antique shop.

'Oh, well, when you said his name I wasn't sure who he was, but now . . . yes, I remember him.'

'He was buying a table?'

223

'Yes. I work part-time, or whenever Michael needs me, and I happened to be in the shop when he came in. I had been warned about him, that he might try to pass off a cheque, and I was not on any account to accept it as payment.'

'Just take me through what happened.'

'Can I ask why?'

'Yes. He was found dead two days ago, in the Thames near Richmond.'

'Oh, that's terrible! I'm sorry.'

'Yes, that's the reason I'm here. He'd been in the water for a while, probably since around the time you had seen him.'

'Really? Well, I can't see how I can help you. He came into the shop and asked to collect the table, as he had put down a deposit. As Michael had warned me about him, I asked that he paid the purchase price in cash, as I was not allowed to accept a cheque.'

'How did he react?'

'Well, he sort of shrugged, you know, as if he expected that; he didn't seem put out. He was quite chatty and friendly, and said he would come back to talk to Michael.'

'Did you see what he was driving?'

'No, but I suppose he must have had a van or something to fit the table in as it was quite large.'

'Did he come here to the farmhouse?'

'Good heavens, no! Why would he?'

'Had you ever seen him before?'

'No.'

'So you didn't recognise him?'

'No, it was the first time I'd ever seen him at the shop.'

Anna smiled. 'Well, that's it then. I'm sorry to have bothered you.' She glanced at Pete.

He stood up. 'Could you show me to the bathroom, please?'

Honour gestured to the hallway. 'Straight through, off the hall; it's a cloakroom.'

Pete hesitated and then walked out. Anna wanted to go into the office room that Gordon had seen, but Honour remained seated, so she kept asking questions.

'Did your husband meet Julius D'Anton?'

'No, he was at work.'

'You have a kiln in one of the barns.'

'Yes, but I'm a real amateur; it's just something I like to do.'

'I saw some of your paintings at the antique shop.'

Honour laughed. She hadn't sold more than one small canvas.

Pete returned. 'Sorry – I think the cistern is playing up. I couldn't flush your loo.'

Honour shook her head and walked towards him. 'It's tricky – you have to yank it down hard.'

She walked out and Pete followed, as Anna made a quick move to the room off the kitchen. She opened the door and looked in: there was the desk and computer, as Gordon had photographed, but there was no painting on the wall. That in itself was suspicious; they would need a search warrant to explore further.

'Thanks again,' Anna said, when they left a few minutes later. She paused and turned back to Honour. 'When I was last here there was a young man, blond hair, in your yard?'

Honour looked puzzled and then smiled. 'Oh, that'll

be one of the local farm boys. They muck out the stable and exercise Damien's horse.'

'Thank you.'

Pete started up the engine; they reversed and drove out, Honour watching them leave.

'What did you think?' she asked.

'About what?'

'The set-up here?'

'Rather pleasant, if you like this kind of thing, but it's really out of the way. I wouldn't like it.'

'What did you think of her?'

'Seemed nice; must have been a real beauty, very friendly.'

Anna nodded and then asked Pete to stop at the ivy-covered cottage. He stayed in the car as she walked up the tiny pathway to the front door. It was a long shot, but nevertheless, she wanted to make sure of something. The same elderly lady opened the front door who had given Gordon the directions to the farm. Anna introduced herself and Mrs Doris Eatwell patted her arm rather than shake hands, as she was very arthritic. Anna told her that she was making enquiries about an antique dealer called Julius D'Anton. Mrs Eatwell said she had never heard of him, but knew Michael Sudmore, as he had bought a number of items from her.

Anna was invited inside, and knew she had the right place.

'Oh, this is nice,' she said, as she was shown into a small sitting room with a very modern sideboard and table.

'Thank you. I've got a new bathroom, too – I sold off all the old things I had.'

'Did you recently sell a table to Mr Sudmore?'

'Yes, I did. He's a lovely man – he came by to see some china I was selling, and he saw it outside the back door.'

Anna was gone for over half an hour.

'Guess what?' she said when she returned to the car. 'Michael Sudmore buys the table, does it up and puts it into his shop, I would say asking a hell of a lot more than he paid for it. Julius D'Anton goes to the fair – as Sudmore said, he had a real eye for antiques – puts a down payment on the table and sniffs out where it came from.'

Pete started up the Morgan and they drove on down the lane.

'So, this is what I think might have happened: Julius D'Anton drives here to see if Mrs Eatwell has any other antiques that he can buy for peanuts. It's not far from here to the farmhouse, right?'

'Right,' Pete said, concentrating on manoeuvring the car round the potholes once more.

'What if he pays a visit and was, according to Mrs Eatwell, driving a van? She had no idea what make or colour, but she said it was a van – you with me?'

'Yeah.'

Anna leaned back; it was all supposition yet again.

'Go on,' Pete said, all ears now.

'Okay, what if he ran into trouble – maybe hit one of the ditches? I don't know, but what if he continued on from Mrs Eatwell's to the farmhouse? Nobody answers at the front door – the bell doesn't work, so again this is just possible – what if he walks around to the back of the farmhouse to the kitchen?'

'Yes, still with you.'

227

'It's a big coincidence, but Julius D'Anton would know Alexander Fitzpatrick from his days at Oxford. What if he saw him here? What if he was hiding out here and Julius recognised him?'

'Then what?'

'Well, I don't bloody know,' Anna snapped.

'So this guy Fitzpatrick is hiding out, and up comes someone from his past: "I say, I say, I say, I recognise you, matey" – and then what? "My van has broken down and do you have a vehicle I can borrow, like the Mitsubishi"?'

'Oh shut up. It's possible.'

'Sure, anything is – but you'll need to match the dates this Julius was seen in the Mitsubishi to when he went belly upwards in the Thames.'

'Yes, I know. Let's just ask around any garages and repair shops in this area and see if we can find the missing van.'

Anna was doubting herself; she was certain that Pete thought she was adding two and two and coming up with Christ knows what. However, an hour and a half later, in McNaulty & Sons crash repair shop and restoration yard, they found the van.

It was an old Post Office van, re-sprayed a dark navy blue, with more dents and bangs than a stock car racing vehicle. The entire bodywork was a mismatch of filler; it didn't look remotely roadworthy. The back end had indeed gone. The van had been towed into their yard, but remained in the same condition, as the owner had given them a dud cheque to repair it. The cheque was signed by Julius D'Anton. Anna gave instructions to the garage that they should leave the van as it was; she would have someone tow it to London.

Pete had shaken his head; yet another vehicle the

forensic lab had to check over. It was filthy, mud spattered, and inside were used coffee beakers and takeaway
food cartons, mounds of newspapers and a few odd pieces
of bookcases and ornaments. These could possibly have
been bought at the antique fair, as there were also some of
the flyers on the passenger seat, along with an old T-shirt
and jeans, and a rolled-up sleeping bag. In the ashtray
were also some roaches. They left everything as it was.
Anna knew she would have to work out a timeframe of
when D'Anton was last seen alive by Michael Sudmore,
with what looked like quite a wedge of cash, to when his
body was discovered in the Thames. She would need to
go back to talk to Sandra, his widow, about the exact
dates when Julius had said he was onto something big,
and the fact that his fingerprints were found in the drug
squat in Chalk Farm. They knew when his van had been
taken into the breaker's yard at McNaulty's: it was two
weeks before the murder of Frank Brandon.

Anna and Pete found a table for dinner in a small Italian
bistro in Oxford city centre. They had not bothered to
drive any further afield to the famous, Michelin-starred
eateries outside the city. The food was delicious and,
apart from a few rowdy students, they had an enjoyable
meal without mentioning the case once. Anna relaxed,
helped by a very good bottle of Merlot and Pete's equally
good company. Anna told him about her student days
here, and how she had rarely ever had enough money to
dine out further than a McDonald's. She never brought
up the times she had driven back and forth to see Langton
in the rehabilitation home. In fact, it never crossed her
mind, and she enjoyed telling Pete about her old bicycle
that she had ridden around the city until it had been

stolen. From then on she had walked, even though she had been certain she'd seen another student whizzing past on it.

The case finally reared its head when, as they left the restaurant, Pete had asked for some tinfoil. From his glove compartment, he took out a plastic knife, then took copious scrapings of mud from around the hubcaps, wheels and sides of the Morgan.

'I'm impressed,' Anna said, watching him.

'Yeah, well, it looks like it may rain, so better to do it now.'

The rain started coming down about half an hour later. Pete had put the roof up, and despite a few areas where tape covered some cracks, they could hear each other. They ran into heavy traffic on the motorway, as a truck had overturned, and spent over an hour inching along. They found themselves discussing the case, all Anna's theories and suppositions. Pete queried many of them, but became fascinated and also slightly in awe of her productive detective mind.

'I take after my father,' she said. The conversation turned to her personal life, and she found herself telling him more than she could recall telling anyone else. How her father had been such a powerful force in her life, and her delicate mother such a loving support to them both.

'You are lucky,' Pete said. He gave a few details about his own childhood. He had been brought up mainly by his grandmother, who had doted on him, until he was twelve years old. After she passed on, he went to live with his father in Devon. He was a builder and carpenter, who would spend whatever he made in the pub. His mother had been a nurse, who had left his father for a doctor, and emigrated to Australia. The broken promise of her sending for him had hurt him deeply, but thankfully his grandmother had always made him feel very loved. When he did eventually fly out to Australia to meet his mother and stepfather, she was a stranger.

'It's odd. I went out there with every intention of forming a bond with her – you know, wanting her to be special – but she was a strange, cold woman. Maybe she regretted leaving me, but I don't ever recall her holding me in her arms.'

'That's awful,' Anna said, remembering how her mother would be at the gate waiting for her to come home from school: always there, always with her arms out for a hug.

'The way I was brought up made me wary of relationships. Women were either like my granny or the type my father used to bring home from the pub – and he had a real variety. He was never too particular: blonde, brunette, fat or thin. I don't think he liked to sleep alone, or cook or do any household things like washing up, so whenever I got back from school, there was always a strange woman hoovering and dusting.'

'Is he still alive?'

'Nope. He committed suicide eighteen years ago. Went out to his hut, where he would supposedly do his carpentry, and threw a rope over a beam.'

'Did you . . .'

'Yeah, I found him – not a pretty sight. But I called the police and they took care of everything. From then on, I was sort of on my own. I inherited what little he had – the cottage and a couple of outhouses and fields. I got about fifty grand. I went to university in Liverpool; no idea why I chose that one, because I could have had the pick of a number, but off I went, money in the bank, good digs and a sort of freedom I had never really felt before. I had a terrific time – there's nothing like the Liverpool sense of humour – and I made great friends there; we still keep in touch.'

'Did you meet your wife there?'

'No, I was back in London when we met. In fact, we only really knew each other for a few months before we moved into the house in Hampstead, and then got married a year or so later.'

Anna stared from the window as the rain lashed down.

'Have you ever been married?' Pete asked her.

'No. Not even close.'

'How come?'

'Well, I'm not that old for one thing – I'm only twenty-eight.' And yet it did sound old to her, and she was shocked.

'You ever lived with anyone?'

Anna suddenly didn't want to talk. 'Not really.'

'Oh, I see. You can pump me for my seedy background, but you don't seem to want to go into yours.'

'Your background didn't sound seedy to me. I told you, I had a great relationship with my parents.'

'But what? You gave everything to your career?'

'Yes.'

He laughed and gave her a sidelong look. 'You must have got hurt hard.'

'No, I didn't.' She really didn't want to get into the Langton relationship, and was beginning to get irritated by his persistence. At last, the traffic thinned out and they could pick up some speed.

He reached over and took her hand, giving it a squeeze. 'Sorry. I just want to get to know you – I suppose that's obvious.'

She smiled and released her hand. 'Well, I've never been very good at expositions, so let's just say maybe I will give you the gritty details some other time.'

'Gritty?'

She sighed and then shook her head. 'I was joking. There's really nothing else to know about me.'

'You going to stay with me tonight?'

'No, I'd like to get home – but how about I cook you breakfast tomorrow at my place?'

'Okay, it's your call.'

Anna still didn't really understand why she was keeping Pete at a distance. She did find him attractive, and she was getting fond of him and enjoying his company.

She was still pondering it when she drove herself home after collecting her Mini from Pete's garage. He had kissed her briefly – it had felt good, but not passionate – not like she had felt with Langton. The 'gritty' truth was that she was unable to let Langton go. She hadn't wanted to continue the relationship, and she was certain that he didn't either, but why was she so tentative about making more of her friendship with Pete?

Undressing and getting ready for bed, she felt terribly sad. She curled up like a child in her big new bed. The few sexual relationships she had had in her past had meant nothing compared to her infatuation with Langton. In many ways, that was what it had been: never a steady or serious affair. He had never been a friend, but a demanding lover. She wondered if that was why she couldn't move forward with Pete. He was just too damned nice! He didn't excite her.

Langton had certainly done that. In bed, at work, in every way, he had dominated her – at times, really frightened her – but she had thrived on his ability to make every nerve in her body tingle. She wondered if she would ever feel the same way about anyone else, even knowing what a dangerous creature Langton was. Instead of making her reject everything about him, it made her long for him to wrap her in his arms and make love to her. She didn't think about what had gone on that day with Pete, the discovery of D'Anton's van, the possibility he had met Alexander Fitzpatrick at Honour Nolan's farm. All she thought about, as she cried herself to sleep, was how much she missed James Langton.

Chapter Twelve

Pete arrived at nine o'clock with croissants and fresh fruit. Anna made them both omelettes and brewed up some coffee. Once again, they were totally at ease with each other. Pete helped unpack her boxes and put up the plasma TV; he was helpful and considerate, and very adept at checking plugs and carrying all the cardboard boxes down to the bins in the basement.

He worked alongside her, washing china and ripping off the bubble wrap from various pieces of furniture. He loved her new flat and, when they took a coffee-break, they sat on the small balcony looking out onto the river. Anna was wearing old jeans and a stained T-shirt with sneakers. He was similarly dressed; they could have easily been mistaken for a loving couple. But he didn't make any moves on her; in fact, apart from a kiss on her cheek when he arrived, he had not touched her.

She was surprised how disappointed she felt when he checked the time and said he should be making a move. 'Do you have to go? I owe you dinner.'

'I'll take a rain check. I'll probably be pretty tied up next week.'

She smiled. 'Okay. Thanks for helping me out this morning.'

She watched him leave, feeling at odds with herself. She was unwrapping the few items still left to put into the kitchen when she came across a painted mug. It was nothing special to look at, but what made Anna sit back, thinking, was its shape. She had seen one similar – far better painted, and with a more professional glaze – in Michael Sudmore's antique shop.

Honour Nolan had said she was a beginner at pottery, and twice had mentioned that she had a small kiln in one of the barns. What if that was a lie? What if there wasn't any kiln, but perhaps a stove: something to give heat to the barn, if someone was living in it? It would be a very good cover. After looking over the farmhouse, Anna was pretty certain there was no one else living there – but what if one of their barns was being used? She again went over the possibility that Julius D'Anton might have had problems with his van and somehow inadvertently come across Alexander Fitzpatrick. He could have given D'Anton money and the Mitsubishi to drive, yet knew he would have to get rid of him, so dumped him in the Thames.

Anna showered and changed, and drove to Chiswick to talk to Sandra D'Anton. She really needed to get her timeframe in order. She knew the dates of the antique fair and how many times D'Anton had visited the shop, but had no clear date for when he returned to London. His fingerprints were matched to ones found in the Chalk Farm squat, but were they there before the murder? Had she been wrong about the passenger in the Mitsubishi with Frank Brandon: could it have been Julius D'Anton? That didn't quite add up. D'Anton was tall, but not six feet four. However, she made a mental note to test his shoes against the prints in blood at the scene of crime.

Sandra was surprised to see Anna, who was wearing casual trousers and a sweater, rather than her usual suit. She invited her into the kitchen, which was in even more disarray, with most of the windows removed. There was a burly guy working in there, and Sandra asked if he would take a break for fifteen minutes. He put down his tools and took himself over to the pub.

In response to Anna's questions, Sandra found a rather moth-eaten-looking diary that was two years old. All she could recall clearly was that Julius had said he was going to the antique fair. The next time she had spoken to him was when he had called to say he had found something special, and was going to check out some possible buyers. The next call was to tell her he had trouble with his van. 'He was onto something really promising, but he didn't say what it was. He was, in his words, "hanging out with some friends".'

Sandra shrugged. Usually, this meant he was getting stoned, but she had no idea who these friends were or where he was. When Anna asked if she had seen him after that, Sandra sighed. 'Look, I've honestly told you everything I know. He could have returned here, but I wasn't around.'

Anna looked up from her notebook.

'Julius and I were really just sort of cohabiting, if you know what I mean. I'm living on and off with Hal, the builder you saw. With all the work going on in the house, I stay over at his place. Jules could have come home, I don't really know, but I never saw him again.'

'Did your husband know about your relationship with Hal?'

'Yeah – he didn't mind.'

'So he could have come back here?'

237

'Yeah. I didn't check his clothes or anything. I mean, as far as I knew, he was still off scouting for antiques, which is why I never mentioned any of this when you first came to see me.'

'But when you did talk to him, he said he was onto something special?'

'That's right, but he was always onto some scam or other, so I didn't give it much thought. He said it was going to make us a lot of money, maybe he even said he had some money already. I don't really remember, he just sounded a bit high; you know, he gabbled a bit. I have got so fed up with these promises over the years, I just said, "Yeah, yeah, see you when I see you." I told you this.'

'He said his van had broken down?'

'Yes, he was waiting to get it fixed. It was a dreadful old thing, an old Post Office van he got for peanuts; he used to drive it into the ground. He said he'd gone into a ditch or something. I honestly didn't pay that much attention.'

If the damage to D'Anton's van had been caused by driving it on the narrow lane by Honour Nolan's farm, this would place him close to the farmhouse. From there, he might have walked further up the lane and towards the farmhouse. He could then perhaps have seen Fitzpatrick. Anna knew that, without proof, all her stitching together of this information was supposition; nevertheless, she had traced the old Post Office van and she did now know for sure that D'Anton had called into the ivy-covered cottage. So, he had to have been very close to the farmhouse. The significance of all this hinged on whether or not she was correct about Alexander Fitzpatrick being there.

★

Anna drove into the car park at the Lambeth laboratories and went into the building to see if Pete was around. She was disappointed, and a trifle confused, to be told that he hadn't been in. She could see by the extra assistants that work was being done over the weekend. The number of trestle tables with victims' clothing laid out for testing made it look like a jumble sale. She asked a young Asian scientist if she could look over the clothing from the body of Julius D'Anton.

The polo-neck sweater was cashmere, but very worn and frayed around the neck. The socks had holes in them, and the old tweed jacket had leather patches over the elbows. They had not as yet begun testing and retaining fibres. Anna asked if the shoes had been matched to the bloody footprints left at the drug squat in Chalk Farm. There and then, the scientist, whose name was Shara, picked one up and carried it over to the far side of the room. The footprints had been transferred onto sheets of white paper with markings showing the stitching on the soles. It was obvious that D'Anton's shoe did not make the imprint; it was nowhere near the same size.

Anna decided that, as she was at the laboratories, she would see if the pathology lab had any results. Passing the office, she saw that Ewan Fielding was sitting eating a sandwich at his desk; he looked up with annoyance when she tapped and entered.

Apologising for interrupting, she asked if it would be possible for her to see the corpse of Julius D'Anton. Fielding sighed, muttering that it was his weekend off; he was already tired and planning to leave, having had to work long hours to accommodate the extra workload.

'I don't know if your boss is collecting every corpse from all over London and dumping them on my lap, but the body count supposedly connected to your case is becoming ridiculous,' he grumbled. 'I've had to ship in another pathologist to give me a few hours off!'

They walked to the cold storage section, Fielding still complaining, 'No one seems to understand that until I have tests completed, there is nothing I can report.'

'Did he drown?'

'No, and I believe you've already been told this,' he snapped, as he walked to drawer four and gestured for an assistant to open it up.

'Have you any thoughts on how he died?'

'Thoughts? *Thoughts?* We don't surmise, Detective Travis, we get everything tested. We don't think, but produce the facts.'

D'Anton's body was uncovered down to his chest.

'I don't know what you'll gain from this,' Fielding said, looking down at the dead man.

'So what killed him?' Anna persisted.

Fielding shook his head. 'I am not one hundred per cent sure. I'm waiting for the toxicology department to finish their tests. I'm also waiting on them from the body of Mr Petrozzo. All I can tell you is that this chap was not a very healthy specimen, far from it. He had at one time been injecting himself, as we have a lot of broken veins – probably heroin – and he was, I would say, a heavy cocaine user, as his nostrils have almost collapsed. His heart was also enlarged, probably due to his drug intake. Basically, all I can verify is that he stopped breathing!'

'Before he was dumped in the river?'

'Yes. There is no water in his lungs, but . . .'

Anna turned to him. 'But?'

'I discovered a similar injection mark beneath his

tongue as found on the body of Petrozzo. I am not able to confirm what drug was used.'

'But you have an idea?' Anna knew that Fielding had called Pete to say he had found a trace of a drug. 'With Petrozzo, did you have any clue as to what had killed him?'

'I am not confirming anything. All I can say is, like this poor chappie, Petrozzo stopped breathing! You will have, Detective Travis, all the information from toxicology in due course. I am not in a position to give you any details.'

Anna could not bring up what Pete had told her, as she knew it could get him into trouble, so she thanked the disgruntled Ewan Fielding and returned to her car. Adding to her 'stitching' was the possibility that both Petrozzo and Julius D'Anton had been killed by an overdose of a drug she couldn't remember the name of.

It was after four when Anna drew up outside Pete's little terraced house. She rang the doorbell and waited. She was about to give up, when the door opened.

'Wow, twice in one day! I am flattered,' Pete said, beaming.

'I was just passing,' she lied.

'Really? Well, you had better come in, as to just pass is quite a drive from your place to here.'

Anna laughed and followed him into the sitting room. Newspapers and coffee mugs were spread all over the floor, and the fire was lit.

'Coffee is on,' he said, fetching a clean mug and carrying the dirty ones to the sink.

'I dropped by the lab, but they said you hadn't been in.'

'Ah, I got back here and needed a shower as I'd built

241

up a sweat moving your boxes around. Anyway, after the shower, I felt knackered, so I had a snooze and then decided to read the papers and take my day off.'

Pete handed her a mug of steaming black coffee.

'You didn't see much inside the antique shop, but there were mugs in there that Sudmore said had been made by Honour.'

Pete sat on the floor and placed another log onto the fire, trying to straighten out as fast as he could: he was stoned, hence he had taken so long to open the front door.

Anna explained about the mugs she had painted as a child with her mother. He was finding it all hard to follow. 'What if she didn't have a kiln? What if it was a cover?' Anna was saying.

'Right, yes,' he said.

'The barn would be a perfect place to hide someone, but it would need to be heated – so what better excuse than to say she had a kiln in there?'

Pete couldn't help himself; he started to giggle.

'What's so funny? It's possible.'

'I know, I know – yes, it is.' Pete tried to look serious, but was having a hard time not only keeping his face straight, but also trying to understand what she was talking about.

Anna was in full flow, but she was getting such an odd response from Pete that she eventually gave up. 'Well, I'm obviously not getting through to you,' she said, sipping her coffee, which took her breath away it was so strong.

'No, I'm sorry. It's just it's so much to take on board. I am sure you must be on to something!' Again he chuckled.

'Why is it so funny? You know what I found out from Fielding? Both Donny Petrozzo and Julius D'Anton have injection marks beneath their tongue and, in both cases, he is unable to give the post-mortem report on how they died – apart from saying sarcastically that they stopped breathing!'

'Well, that's pretty conclusive,' Pete said, trying to look serious.

'You told me about the drug Fielding thought he'd found traces of – what was it called?'

Pete licked his lips – they felt bone dry. He sipped his coffee. 'I've forgotten, but you know he said that he wasn't certain what it was, and not to repeat it to anyone. Did you bring it up?'

'No, because, as I just said, I couldn't remember what it was called.'

'Nor can I.'

Anna sighed and drained the coffee mug. 'I wouldn't have asked him anyway, and got you into trouble.'

'Would you like a glass of wine?' Pete got unsteadily to his feet.

Anna looked up at him. 'Are you all right?'

'Yes, puuuurfect. I'm going to open a bottle.'

She watched him weave his way to the fridge and select a bottle of chilled white. He then rummaged in drawers to find the bottle opener. Anna took a look around the room and saw the ashtray; it was partly shoved beneath a chair. She looked back to Pete as he took down two wine glasses from a cupboard. 'Are you stoned?'

Pete placed the glasses onto the counter.

'You are, aren't you?'

'Well, Your Honour, I do admit to having a large joint this morning. I can't deny it.'

Anna stood up. 'A joint?'

'Yes, Ma'am! Can't you smell it? It's very, very good grass.'

'Is this a regular thing?'

Pete poured the wine.

'Pete, it's illegal! You must be crazy.'

'It's just weed, for God's sake! Any day now they'll make it legal. It's not as if I am shipping it in by the ton.' He passed her the wine. 'Don't look so shocked.'

'Well, I am. I mean, do you ever smoke it when you are at work?'

'Don't be so crass. I just use it to unwind; it helps me sleep.'

Anna sat down again. She was unsure what she should do.

'Cheers,' he said, as he sipped the wine and then put another log on the fire. 'What are you going to do, Anna – arrest me?'

'Now *you're* being crass. I just think someone in your position shouldn't take such a risk. I mean, if anyone was to know, you could lose your job!'

'Have you ever had a joint?'

Anna looked flushed.

'You haven't, have you?'

'I've never felt the need to.'

'Even when you were at university?'

'No! It was not for lack of opportunity. To be honest, the crowd that got stoned every night were not my type, and if my father had ever found out, I think he would have throttled me.'

'Daddy's girl!'

'That has nothing to do with it. I respected him and wouldn't do anything that could not only upset him, but have repercussions: he was a very well-respected police officer.'

'You sound so self-righteous.'

'Maybe I am, but I also take my job very seriously. If I was foolish enough to start smoking dope, I could jeopardise my career. You only have to be caught once, you know.'

'I dare say that is true, but I'm in my own home and I use it to relax. And, may I say, it would do you a hell of a lot of good to try it. It would maybe let you relax and get off this case for a few minutes.'

'What you don't take into consideration is that you have to score it from someone, which means that he or she is also aware of your addiction.'

'I am not a fucking addict.'

'Nevertheless, the risk of it being known to another party means they could have a hold on you.'

'In what way, for Chrissakes?'

'Well, for example, say you get some evidence that is detrimental to one of these people you score your dope from – they could get in touch with you and say that they would like you to lose the evidence.'

'Blackmail me?'

'Yes, that's a risk.'

Pete leaned back against the sofa. 'Well, I'll have to warn my brother.'

'What do you mean?'

'He grows it.'

Anna finished her wine. 'You don't have a brother; you told me about your family.'

'Ah, this is my Australian stepbrother. He lives in Dorset.'

'You get it from him?'

Pete turned to look at her. 'This is getting really boring, Anna. I smoke dope, and I will continue to do so. I am at risk only because I let you in and you are a police-woman – a detective, no less! Any risk I am getting into will probably come from Miss Super Sleuth. Now, can we change the subject?'

'I'm going home.' She stood up.

Pete remained lying on the floor, his head resting back on the sofa. He watched her put her empty wine glass on the counter.

'I'll show myself out.'

'Fine.'

Tight-lipped, Anna walked to the front door. Pete made no effort to get up, so she let herself out. He stayed on the floor for a while longer, then crawled to the ash-tray and took out the half-smoked joint. He was about to light up when the doorbell rang again.

'It's me,' Anna shouted.

Pete opened the door and stood back in mock horror. 'Oh Christ! You've come to arrest me!'

'Very funny. I've got a bloody clamp on my car.' She slammed the front door closed. 'I'll have to call and get it taken off. How long will it take?'

'I have no idea. Could be hours – depends on where the clamping buggers are.'

Anna sat down and opened her briefcase, taking out her mobile. Pete poured her another glass of wine and topped his own up.

Keeping her voice controlled, she explained that she wanted the clamp taken off her car immediately. She was a police officer interviewing a suspect and required her vehicle to return to the station.

She snapped off her phone in a fury. 'They said it'll take at least an hour! I don't believe it.'

'Am I the suspect you told them you were interviewing?' Pete said, grinning.

'Oh, shut up. They won't let me off the fine because it's a private vehicle. It's bloody outrageous.'

'Double yellow lines, sweetheart – you know about the parking. You should have driven round to the garage at the back of the house.'

Anna accepted a fresh glass of wine and sat on the sofa.

Pete lay prone beside her. 'I was just about to light up.'

'For Chrissakes, don't do that! If they come, they'll smell it.'

'I'm not going to let them in! Your car is outside – they won't smell it from there. Besides, they're clampers, not police.'

Anna sighed with frustration.

Pete lit up the joint, took a big lungful and then held it up. 'You know, you should just try it at least once, so you're experienced in the field of marijuana smokers. It will give you a better insight into the farce of it being illegal. You know as well as I do the cops go easy on it; it's the hard stuff they are trying to stop.'

'Well, they say it's the stepping stone to hard drugs.'

'Bullshit.' Pete leaned on one elbow and held out the joint. 'Go on, try it. Heave in the smoke, just as if you are smoking a cigarette and let it out slowly.'

'No way. I'll go and stand by my car.' Anna drained her glass.

'You're over the limit,' Pete said, grinning.

'I am not.'

'Yes, you are. Women can only drink two very small glasses of wine and you've had a large double measure.'

'I also had that glue coffee you made.'

'Ah, it won't count, sweetheart.'

'I wish you wouldn't call me that.'

'It's just a term of endearment.'

'I hate it.'

'Well, dearest, I won't call you sweetheart again.'

Langton had always called her sweetheart. He probably called most of his women that.

Anna reached forward. 'All right, let me try it.'

She coughed a lot to begin with. Then Pete rolled a smaller and thinner joint, without tobacco. The clampers arrived and Pete dealt with them as Anna was unable to stand up straight.

He left her lying on the sofa, listening with headphones on to The Doors. She said, very loudly, when he returned, 'I really like this band!'

He grinned and opened up a bar of chocolate from the fridge. Anna was lying back, eyes closed.

She wafted her hand, singing, '*I'll never look into your eyes again, my friend.*'

He popped a slice of black, ice-cold chocolate into her mouth and then rolled another joint. The room was hot and the fire blazing, as he kept on stacking more logs onto it. They opened another bottle of wine and finished the bar of chocolate. The curtains drawn, Pete lit scented candles and then lay beside her on the sofa. She was loath to part with the headphones, but he switched discs and put on his favourite compilation of seventies and eighties rock music. They lay together, wreathed in smiles. He found her adorable, as she burst into song, singing the odd lines.

The first kiss was light. She eased her body round to face him, pressing herself against him. She cupped his face in her hands and they had a long, lingering, passionate kiss. There was no thought of James Langton, no jigsaw puzzle of facts and suppositions of the case. In the warmth of the room, wrapped in his arms, Anna felt incredibly happy. She also felt safe and, he was so gentle and considerate, she felt loved.

The following morning, Anna knew they had made love – in fact, a number of times – but wasn't too clear about how she came to be in his bed. She remembered talking about mundane things like childhood memories of holidays with her parents. She had never had this experience of sharing so much of herself, nor had she ever been stoned, and with more wine than she had ever drunk in one session before. She didn't, at first, regret a moment but, as she slowly woke up to exactly where she was and who she was with, she had terrible misgivings and, when she tried to sit up, and her head felt as if it was about to explode, she questioned how she could have allowed herself to be so foolish.

Pete lay beside her, still deeply asleep; she eased back the duvet and inched to the edge of the bed. Slowly, she swung her legs over and got to a sitting position. This made the room spin and her head throb. Wrapped in a towel, Anna moved slowly down the narrow staircase into the living room. She drank some water and then started to collect her clothes, which were strewn around the room. Each time she bent to pick up an item, she felt dizzy and, by the time she had managed to track down her knickers and bra, she had to sit down on the sofa. It took her even longer to dress and when she caught sight of herself in a mirror, she had to look away fast.

Her hair was standing up on end and she had black rings beneath her eyes from her mascara. She looked really wretched. She splashed cold water over her face and used a dishcloth to pat it dry. She combed her hair and, with her head still throbbing, brewed up some coffee. There was not a sound from above, for which she was thankful, because she wasn't sure if she could talk. By the time she'd downed two cups of black coffee and found a bottle of aspirin to ease her headache, she at least felt as if she could function. She cleared the room, washed up the wine glasses, emptied the ashtray of its roach stubs and was about to pour her third cup of coffee when she heard movement from the bedroom.

'Anna?' Pete called out. He came thudding down the stairs; his hair, like Anna's, was standing up on end, and he had pulled on a pair of jeans but was bare-chested and bare-footed.

'I've made some coffee,' she said, not looking at him.

'Great. Don't you want a shower?' he said, as he looked around the room.

'No, I'd better get back home to change.'

He peered at the clock on the mantel. 'Is this the right time?'

Anna looked at her wristwatch; at least she hadn't taken that off. 'Oh my God – it's half past eight. I'm going to have to go straight to work.'

'Me too. Do you want some toast?'

'No, I'll get something from the canteen.'

He came to stand behind her, reaching around her for his mug of coffee. 'You okay?'

'Yes, my headache is fading fast. Want an aspirin? I found some in your cupboard.'

'Nope.' He slurped his coffee, then wrapped his arms around her, nuzzling her neck. 'Any regrets?'

'No, of course not,' she said, but still turned away from him.

'Look at me,' he said gently, and turned her to face him. 'What's the matter?'

'I haven't cleaned my teeth,' she said.

'I've got a spare toothbrush in the bathroom.'

'I'd better just get going.'

'Not until you've looked at me. Stop turning away.'

She sighed, and slowly turned to him, looking up into his face. He bent down and kissed her softly. 'Last night was special,' he said, and cupped her face in his hands. 'No regrets?'

'You already asked me that.'

'Well, have you?'

'No.'

'Good, I'll call you this evening.'

'Okay.'

He turned away and picked up his coffee; she moved quickly to collect her briefcase and handbag.

'You sure you don't want to have a shower with me?'

Anna lifted up her coat. 'I really have to get going, or I'll be late. As we had the weekend off, I don't think Cunningham would appreciate it. She's sort of got it in for me anyway.'

'You going to give her the update from what we picked up at the farm?'

'Not straight away.'

'Well, if you want that van towed in to be checked over, you'll have to give details.'

251

'Yes, I know, but just let me get sorted and I'll call you later this morning.'

Anna made her way to the front door, where the Sunday papers protruded out of the letterbox.

'It's Sunday,' she said.

'What?'

'I said, it's Sunday!' She felt such relief, she laughed.

'Christ, it's bloody Sunday!' he repeated.

'I don't have to go into work until Monday!'

'Nor do I,' he laughed. He then came to her and picked up the papers. 'Tell you what. Put your stuff down, I'll go out and get some fresh bread and we'll have bacon and eggs or bagels and smoked salmon.'

'No, I think I should get home.'

'I can't tempt you? How about we meet for lunch?'

She hesitated. She still had a load of clearing up to finish.

He shrugged. 'Up to you. I could come over and help you out?'

'Let me think about it.' She opened the front door.

'Well, you know where I am,' he said.

Anna took a long shower, trying to get her head around exactly what had happened the night before. She changed into a tracksuit, made herself some tea and toast, and sat on her small balcony. It was after eleven when she began to unpack some more cases and it took her by surprise: she was humming. Suddenly, she realised that she felt really happy. Was it because of Pete? Because they had made love all night? Or was it because it felt as if she was, at long last, freeing herself from Langton's domination?

At just after one, Anna called Pete. It had to be telepathy, he said, as he had his hand on the phone to call her.

They agreed to meet for a late lunch at San Frediano's, just off the King's Road. Anna dressed in jeans and a pale blue cashmere sweater that she knew always made her eyes seem bluer. Again, she felt a sort of warm glow: she was eager to see Pete again. She had a new relationship blossoming. For someone like Anna, who had had so few, it gave her confidence in herself – a confidence that had been lacking for so long.

By the time she had driven to Chelsea, it was exactly two-fifteen. Pete was already there waiting; she noticed he had shaved and washed his hair. He had on a denim jacket and check shirt, tight jeans and cowboy boots. When he saw her, he opened his arms to give her a big hug. 'You look fabulous,' he said. Arm in arm, they went into the restaurant and were directed to a small corner table for two.

As they were perusing the menu, a lovely tall blonde girl came over. 'Pete, how are you?'

He lowered the menu and half-rose from his seat. 'Daniella, good heavens! It's been ages.'

'I'm living in Spain,' she said. Judging by her golden tan, she was taking in a lot of sun.

'This is my girlfriend, Anna.'

'Nice to meet you,' Daniella said, then gestured towards her table, where there were several young men with sweaters slung around their necks. 'We're all going to a funfair on Wimbledon Common after lunch.'

'Sounds fun,' Pete said, smiling.

'Well, look me up. I'm here for a month before I go back.'

'I will – you look terrific!'

Daniella gave Anna a smile before she sashayed back to her table.

'You chosen what you want to eat?' he said, picking up his menu.

'She was very glamorous.'

'Yes, and her sisters are even better-looking. I've known them for years, but I'm not really in their league. They are stinking rich and just want to party. They have a big yacht . . .'

'Pete, if someone has a boat, do they have to record ownership? You know, like a race horse?' she asked when they had ordered their food.

'How do you mean?'

'Well, no two race horses can be called the same name – they have to be recorded at Wetherby's. I wondered if it was the same with a boat. Do owners have to register the name for permits and things, or when they come in and out of this country?'

'I don't know. I can ask Daniella, but I doubt she'd know.'

'Never mind – I just wondered.'

Pete sat back as the waiter brought their wine. He picked up his glass and tapped Anna's. 'Cheers. To us?'

She smiled and sipped her wine. She had felt so touched when he had introduced her as his girlfriend; in fact, she could not recall anyone ever doing so before. Certainly not Langton – he was even loath to admit he was having an affair with her.

'What are you thinking about?' he asked softly.

She flushed and shrugged her shoulders. 'You introduced me as your girlfriend.'

'I'm sorry.'

'I liked it.'

He cocked his head to one side, then he gave that

lovely warm chuckle, reaching over to take her hand. 'That's good. You know something? I have never been so grateful for a Sunday before. I think if it hadn't have been for you, I would have gone off to work like a grouch, and I would have had a hard time persuading you to agree to ever see me again.'

'I called you, remember,' she said.

'So you did. Maybe I underestimated myself. I have in the past. So why do you want to know this stuff about a boat registration?'

As their lunch was served, Anna described the oil painting of the yacht at Honour Nolan's farmhouse and how Gordon had taken a photograph of it. It was not clear if it did have the same name or was in fact the boat that they knew Alexander Fitzpatrick had previously owned, but there was, she felt, a possibility that it could link him to Honour and Damien Nolan. They had no way of checking as the painting had been taken down when Anna had returned with Pete to the farmhouse. Which in itself was suspicious, as both had denied knowing Anthony Collingwood, the man Anna believed to be Alexander Fitzpatrick.

Throughout, Pete listened and threw in the odd suggestion. Anna loved being able to talk about her work with someone who understood it. Though his own connection to the police was scientific, they nevertheless had so much in common.

Anna and Pete were one of the last couples to leave the restaurant. Hand in hand, they walked to her car and he agreed, without any pressure from her, to let her go home and have an early night, so as to be refreshed for the morning.

She hesitated, unsure how to approach the subject but,

yet again, he seemed to intuitively know she wanted to say something. 'Go on, what is it?'

'Well, this situation between us. I want to see you and I think you feel the same way, but Pete, I can't if you continue to smoke. It would be unethical for one, never mind illegal, and I am not prepared to take the risk or try it again. So really, it's up to you.'

'I hear you, and I promise no more. I think I want you more than any gear – agreed?'

'Thank you.'

He stood on the pavement and waved her off, then returned to his Morgan. He lit up a joint, smoking it in his car, before deciding that a night at the funfair in Wimbledon might be entertaining.

Chapter Thirteen

Anna didn't just feel relaxed and rested, she felt like a new woman. She had taken care when dressing, and blow-dried her hair; she was even wearing a little more make-up than usual. Her suit was one of her best, grey Armani, and she wore a crisp white linen shirt, the collar and cuffs pressed and starched. She had arrived at eight-fifteen and made a report about the weekend's activities. She did wonder how she would get around to presenting the findings without a snide put-down from Cunningham about her solo investigations; however, she knew she had made a lot of progress. When she got a call from Cunningham to be in her office immediately, however, she wondered exactly how she would pass on the details.

Cunningham was sitting at her desk, leaning her head on her hands, elbows resting on the desk. She looked up when Anna knocked and opened her door. 'Come in, sit down.'

Anna sat opposite. Before she could say anything, Cunningham gave a deep sigh. 'Travis, I have a personal problem. I need to take the day off. Can you take my notes and handle the briefing for me?'

'Yes, of course.'

'Good. I will try, if possible, to get back by this afternoon, but it'll more than likely be the morning.'

'Is there anything else I can do?' Anna asked, wondering what the 'personal problem' could be.

'No, I'm going to take off now but if you need me, I'll
be at the Harley Street clinic. You can contact me on my
mobile.'

'Okay. I hope there's nothing wrong.'

Cunningham stood up and fetched her jacket from
the back of her chair. 'Not with me – it's my partner.
She found a lump in her breast last week. I want to be
with her when she sees her doctor. If it's malignant, she'll
have to go in straight away for treatment.'

'I'm sorry.'

'I would appreciate it if you kept this to yourself,
which is the reason I've asked for you to stand in for me
and not Phil. But keep me informed. As I said, I'll have
my mobile turned on.'

Anna stood up.

'You have a good weekend?' Cunningham said, as she
picked up her briefcase.

'Yes, thank you.' This was not the time to bring up
the developments.

'Well, I'm glad you had a restful time; it's been hideous
for me. I had bloody Langton giving me a grilling all of
Saturday and then, when I got back, Sheila had the news
about the tests. Still, the good thing is she has medical
insurance . . .'

It was the first time Anna's heart hadn't jumped at
hearing his name mentioned.

'Still, I think we are making progress, albeit at a snail's
pace. I'll keep in touch.' She passed Anna a file as she
headed for the door.

As Anna followed Cunningham out of her office, she couldn't help wondering just how much of a grilling Langton had given her. She also wondered if her name had cropped up, but she didn't ask. 'I'll just look over your notes, then crack on.'

'Good.'

She watched Cunningham walk down the corridor and out of the building, before branching off to enter her own office. She remembered how she had felt when her father had been diagnosed with lung cancer. It had been a terrible moment. He had joked, warning her never to start smoking as he lit up one of his ever-present Silk Cut cigarettes. She couldn't reprimand him. It was a sad show of defiance and all she could do was wrap her arms around him and tell him that she would be there for him. The disease had taken its toll fast, and watching him waste away in hospital had broken her heart. As much as she didn't really like Cunningham, she hoped that she would not have to go through such an ordeal with her partner.

Anna forced herself to get back to her work.

The typed notes were a run-through of the case to date, nothing new. Anna had time to find herself a coffee before she stood by the board and began to write up her notes from the weekend's trip to Oxford. The discovery of D'Anton's van was a plus; it had by now been towed to the forensic yard. She arrowed the connections to the antique shop, then to Honour Nolan's farmhouse. She also arrowed the connection of the Mitsubishi with D'Anton, that he might have returned home whilst his wife was away. She then underlined the possibility that D'Anton could have been at the farm, and that tests would be made on the mud from his Post Office van and the Mitsubishi.

Phil joined her. 'Somebody didn't have time out this weekend!'

Anna smiled, and finished writing on the board. By this time, the team had gathered and were talking quietly to each other; only Phil was paying close attention to the added details. Anna then asked for everyone's attention. As Cunningham was not available, she said, she was giving the briefing to update them all on the weekend. They listened attentively as she outlined the links, then opened the floor for a discussion. She did not refer to Cunningham's notes as they related the possibility that D'Anton had been killed because of who, or what, he might have seen at the farmhouse.

'I think we need more pressure on Frank Brandon's widow. I also think we need to find out more about her finances. If, as we know, she does have ten million or more, then this must be checked out. If it was drug money paid into her various accounts over the years, we need the accountant to be requestioned. The fact that she has admitted that her ex-partner was Anthony Collingwood, one of the names used by Alexander Fitzpatrick, makes it possible that he is in the UK.'

Phil gestured that he wanted to say something. 'But if, as we are led to believe, Fitzpatrick has mega-millions stashed in the USA, why is he back here? Also, what is the connection to the drug squat in Chalk Farm?'

Anna looked at the board. 'I keep on coming back to the possibility that it was something or someone inside the squat he was after – that is, if we can prove that the man who accompanied Frank Brandon was Fitzpatrick.'

To date, Phil interjected, the people identified and murdered were all lowlifes. Why would a man like Fitzpatrick want to be involved with the likes of Donny

Petrozzo, let alone Stanley Leymore, and even Julius D'Anton? D'Anton may have been a cut above the others, but not much: he was a junkie, living hand to mouth, buying and selling antiques.

Anna turned back to the board. 'Okay, I hear what you are saying, Phil, but D'Anton was at Balliol at the same time as Alexander Fitzpatrick; he dined out on the fact that he used to know him. By coincidence, he went after an antique table at a local fair in Shipston on Stour, then tried to find out where the table came from – a cottage not far from the farm where Honour Nolan lives. D'Anton's van breaks down; it's a really narrow lane with ditches either side, maybe he walks to the farm . . .'

'And maybe sees Fitzpatrick?'

'Yes.'

'That is, if he is there, or even in the country.'

'Let's say that he is,' Anna said tetchily.

Phil continued. 'D'Anton next gets to borrow a Mitsubishi – from the farm?'

'We don't know, but he is seen driving it. The table wouldn't fit into the back, remember.'

'So D'Anton, without his table, returns to London; his wife is off with her builder; he gets dumped in the Thames; then we find Petrozzo's body inside the Mitsubishi!'

Anna chewed her lips. 'We'll have more details as soon as the tests have been done on the samples of soil taken at the farm.'

'Yeah, but in the meantime, we're still waiting on toxicology reports – how long is that all going to take? Right now, we have no confirmation on what killed Donny Petrozzo or our junkie friend from the Thames.'

'What about the boat, *Dare Devil*, seen at the Nolans' farmhouse?' This was Gordon asking.

Anna said they would need verification of ownership, as it did not have the same name as the boat they knew to have been previously owned by Fitzpatrick. She again brought up the fact that the painting of the boat had been taken down from the study in the farmhouse.

'So what is that going to give us?' Phil again.

'That both Honour and Damien lied about how well they knew Fitzpatrick.'

'Even so, *what does that give us*? I mean, maybe they knew him a long time ago; he was with Honour's sister for years – if he is the man she calls Anthony Collingwood.' Phil was getting rattled.

'How many Anthony Collingwoods are in the phone book?' Anna was starting to get angry herself. 'Has anyone tried to trace him?'

Pamela Meadows said that she had been running through the Anthony Collingwoods listed in the telephone directory, but to date they had all checked out as legitimate.

'Keep going. If Julia Brandon admits to living with him or someone using that name, there has to be some kind of record that he existed,' Anna said briskly.

Phil gave an open-armed gesture. 'Why? Right now, Julia Brandon is not a suspect for the murder of her husband. The fact she lived with someone doesn't give us anything, even though you believe that man could possibly be Alexander Fitzpatrick. Let's say he was: we have not a shred of evidence in our case that involves him. What we *do* have are three dead men.'

'And we've made a connection between all of them,' Anna snapped, her patience at breaking-point. 'What we do not have is the identity of the man we know entered that drug squat with Frank Brandon, and the reason I am constantly bringing up Alexander Fitzpatrick, is because there is a strong possibility it was him.'

'In your opinion.'

'Yes, in my opinion!'

'Why? Why does an international drug dealer, a man wanted around the world, a man known to have stashed away millions from his drug trafficking, want to be back in the UK? In addition, for me, the big question is still what the fuck is he doing with Frank Brandon in that shithole in Chalk Farm? All we've got are small-time drug dealers. Yes, they do all link together, but none link back to your kingpin. You think he'd bother with this lowlife? That is, if he is even in the country? Far be it from me, but all you are bringing up is supposition without any firm evidence. I mean, I may eat my words when we eventually get the bloody forensic reports in, but I can't jump the hoop of coincidences with you.'

Anna took a deep breath to calm herself. 'Okay, if that is the consensus, let's concentrate on how we proceed until we do have the toxicology reports and the geographic tests. We are still hanging loose with a number of registration numbers of cars known to have been parked around the drug squat, so push for tracing those outstanding.'

Anna continued to outline the work for the team, tight-lipped. In the meantime, she would attempt to firm up her suppositions, and would start by requestioning Julia Brandon and her accountant. She caught the look Phil gave to two members of the team and her irritation boiled over: she said crossly that, to date, they should all pay notice to exactly what she had personally produced for the case. They broke up and a trolley of coffee was wheeled in. Phil kept well away from her.

Anna returned to her office, furious. She sensed that part of the reason Phil had been deriding virtually everything she said was because he felt that he should have been handling the case in Cunningham's absence.

Her office door opened and the man himself put his head around the doorframe. 'I'm having meetings with the Drug Squad – checking out what they can give us on the occupants of the squat, see if they have any leads for us. You want to come along?'

'No, I'm going into the West End to meet with Mr Rushton, Julia Brandon's financial adviser.'

Phil gave a non-committal shrug and walked out, as Gordon entered.

'I should have brought this up at the briefing; you're taking your time checking out that boat from the painting, Gordon.'

'I'm sorry. I've already done some digging. I've got a call into the Registry of Shipping and Seamen, they're in Cardiff. Apparently, all ships are registered and given a number which never changes. A registered ship must also have a name different from any other ship and these numbers are carved into the main beam of the ship.'

'For Christ's sake, Gordon, get on with it – see if you can trace *Dare Devil*. I'll be on my mobile.'

'It'll cost twelve pounds for a current search of ownership and, if we want photocopies of the ledgers, that'll cost twenty-three pounds. These searches will show mortgages of the boats and—'

Anna sighed. 'Just do it, Gordon, and get back to me.'

'Okay, I just wanted your permission to pay them.'

'You've got it. Now go on, get moving.' A minute later Anna snatched up her briefcase and was leaving the office, when her desk phone rang. She hesitated and then answered.

It was Gordon again. 'Look, this is going to take some time. Any ship used outside UK waters, or over twenty-four metres, has to be registered, but it's quite a haul, as any ship can be owned by up to five people or companies. Those five can be divided up into as many as sixty-four shareholders.'

Anna closed her eyes. 'Gordon? Are you saying that you've traced the boat?'

'No, not yet, but I am just saying it might take a lot longer if there are, say, sixty-four shareholders and maybe four or five owners.'

'Just do it, Gordon, and also check out Fitzpatrick's previous boats listed on his website. One was a big power cruiser – see who bought it from him.'

'Okay, I'll get cracking.'

'Thank you!' Anna slammed down the receiver and walked out.

David Rushton's offices were located in Jermyn Street, on the fifth floor of a small, but smart, office block. Anna noticed how much security there was, from the CCTV cameras to the double locking device on his reception door. She had to wait to be buzzed in by a receptionist who was very guarded, as Anna did not have an appointment. Anna said she would wait until Mr Rushton was available.

She sat in the reception area on a gilt and leather chair, having a good look around. Mr Rushton was obviously very successful; numerous smart young men passed to and fro, and two attractive girls, carrying mounds of files, and wearing tight black skirts and high heels clicked past, flicking back their blonde hair. Anna was pleased she had taken time dressing. Then she saw Rushton guiding out a young man in a bomber jacket and jeans. Rushton glanced at Anna and ushered the man out before he acknowledged her.

'Sorry not to have made an appointment,' Anna said, standing.

Rushton glanced at his large gold-faced wristwatch and told the receptionist to ask his next client to wait. 'I am very busy,' he said coldly.

'So am I,' Anna said, picking up her briefcase. She was led into a large, comfortable office with a leather sofa and matching armchair. The desk was oak with carved legs; the top was covered in thick glass and rows of telephones. On the walls were many certificates in gold frames, listing Rushton's credentials and awards.

'Do sit down.'

'Thank you.' Anna perched on a leather chair in front of his desk; Rushton moved around to sit in a large swivel office chair. 'We can do this informally here, or at the station. I need verification of exactly how your client Julia Brandon came to be such a wealthy woman.'

'That is a preposterous invasion of privacy. Mrs Brandon pays her taxes; her wealth is no one's business. If you require details of her various companies, then you could do that without my help. Just go to Companies House and check – it is all legitimate.'

'We have her bank statements from the time she lived in Oxford.'

He shrugged.

'You have given us the name Anthony Collingwood

as Mrs Brandon's previous partner, and told us that he had engineered her finances – is that still correct?'

'Yes.'

'Did you ever meet Mr Collingwood?'

'No.'

'But if you never met Mr Collingwood, how did he do that?'

Rushton sighed. 'Telephone, email, fax ... I never knew where he was contacting me from.'

'Did this Mr Collingwood arrange for Mrs Brandon's finances?'

'Yes. She was left a considerable fortune by him.'

'Is he deceased?'

'Not that I am aware of, but my association with Mrs Brandon is as her financial adviser. We do not have any social connections.'

'How did you become her financial adviser?'

'She contacted me. I think she may have met one or two of my clients.'

'When was this?'

He rocked in his chair. 'About ten years ago.'

'You have handled her fortune since then?'

'That is correct.'

'Did she ever disclose where this money had come from?'

'She was given it, but that is really governed by client confidentiality.'

'So this very wealthy lady just contacts you?'

'Most of my clients have considerable wealth, some far more than Mrs Brandon. She required my assistance in protecting her finances.'

'From what?'

'Taxes.'

'So when Mrs Brandon contacted you she had what, this money in a bank account?'

'Yes, various accounts.'

'We would like access to these accounts.'

'They are dormant. I have, as I have already said, as Mrs Brandon's financial adviser, ensured that her monies are in the most productive and beneficial accounts. Added to that, her investments are substantial.'

Anna crossed her legs. 'But didn't you ever enquire where these monies came from?'

'That is not my job. There did not appear to be anything illegal; I am obviously aware that is exactly what you are trying to imply. All I know is Mrs Brandon was left this fortune, I believe, by a Mr Collingwood. As I have said, I did not meet him, but he did very early on make contact with me. He basically left everything to Julia and me to deal with.'

'You say you are not on social terms with Mrs Brandon?'

'Yes, that is correct.'

'Then why did she contact you, before anyone else, to be with her at the mortuary to identify her husband, the late Mr Frank Brandon?'

He shrugged.

'She appeared to be very dependent on you, and you were very protective of her.'

'Under the circumstances, that is understandable; her husband had just been murdered.'

'You also arranged a substantial life insurance policy for Mr Brandon.'

'Yes,' he hissed angrily.

'Why did you do that?'

'I also arrange her house insurance and pay her household bills, so therefore it would only be natural that she would approach me with regard to her husband. Again, this was all done in the proper manner, with medical tests, et cetera.'

'But why would she want her husband to have such a large life insurance policy?'

'It may appear to be a large amount to you, but it isn't. Her children also have life insurance policies, as does she.'

'Her children?'

'Mrs Brandon travels a lot; they all have medical insurance. This really is a waste of my time. I truthfully cannot understand why you want to know about my client's insurance policies.'

'Because her husband was murdered.'

'And Mrs Brandon had nothing whatsoever to do with that tragic event.'

'What is she afraid of?'

'I'm sorry?'

'I said, what is Mrs Brandon afraid of?'

'I really couldn't say, but if her husband was murdered, perhaps she is fearful for herself and her daughters.'

'Mr Brandon was working as a chauffeur when they met.'

'I believe so.'

'He was also acting as a bodyguard?'

'I believe so.'

'Why do you think she required a bodyguard?'

Rushton sighed. 'She has a lot of money, she has valuable jewellery, she is a careful lady and very protective of her family. In this day and age, I can't really see that it is unusual – far from it. The fact that Julia then married Mr Brandon is her private business.'

'Not approved by you?'

'I never said that. I had only one meeting with him and he seemed a very pleasant man, very caring.'

'Did you meet her sister?'

'No.'

'Her sister's husband, Professor Damien Nolan?'

'No – my relationship with Mrs Brandon was, as I have stated, purely a business one.'

'Had she recently asked for any of her monies to be released?'

For the first time, she saw a flicker of hesitation. 'Mrs Brandon's finances are carefully constructed. To take out any lump sum – any large amount – would take time.'

'Did she ask for any large sums?'

Again, there was hesitation. Eventually, he conceded that Julia had asked him to release some money. He explained that he had warned her that she would lose a considerable amount by withdrawing money from the companies.

'How much?'

He was uneasy, loosening his tie. 'I advised her not to do so.'

Anna had taken enough of the pompous man's attitude and she leaned forwards. 'Mr Rushton, you know I can get this information and I could also get a warrant . . .'

'That won't be necessary,' he said immediately. Picking up the phone, he asked for Mrs Brandon's file to be brought in. He then went to a water fountain and poured himself a small cup of water.

Anna could see he was sweating. One of the blondes she had seen pass in the reception area tapped and entered, carrying a file; she put it down on his desk.

He waited until she had left before he opened it. 'As

I said, I advised Mrs Brandon against withdrawing any monies, particularly as I have spent many years building up her profile so she would live comfortably off her substantial investments.'

Anna waited as he sifted through the file and eventually withdrew two sheets of paper. He put on his glasses and read through the information. 'Mrs Brandon requested two substantial withdrawals. The first was nine months ago.'

'How much?'

'Four million.'

Anna sat back, stunned. 'The next?' she asked quietly.

'Six months ago, she requested a further two million. I was unable to complete the transaction.'

'Why?'

'It was actually a mutual decision.'

'Did she say why she needed this amount of money?'

'No, she did not.'

'Didn't you ask her? It's a lot of money.'

'I obviously said that it was not advisable, as I have explained, and she then agreed with me.'

Anna leaned back in her chair, trying to calculate the timeframe of when Julia married Frank Brandon. It added up: she was married to Frank around the time of the second request for money.

'So when she agreed not to go ahead with the next withdrawal, did she seem worried? I mean, are you saying she never explained to you why she would want so much money released? I presume it was cash?'

'Yes, cash, but she did not disclose to me why she needed the money. I don't recall her being worried, though.'

'Did she at any time say to you that the fortune she

had when she came to you as a client was not actually hers?'

'No, of course not.'

'But would it be possible that the sums she had accrued did not actually belong to her, but were someone else's? That she may have just been looking after them?'

'She did not at any time give me reason to believe that her money was not left to her by her ex-partner. She simply said that it was to take care of her and her children.'

'But when she first came to see you, she did not have children!'

She'd got him again; he loosened his tie as if it was throttling him. 'It was obviously after her relationship with her partner had broken down and she was very distressed about it.'

'How much of Mrs Brandon's money was in cash when she first approached you, Mr Rushton?'

He swallowed. After a beat, he said he recalled that there was a considerable amount in cash, but he could not recall the exact sum.

By now, Anna had heard enough to gain a warrant for access to Julia Brandon's accounts and business dealings. Mr Rushton knew he could be in a shedload of trouble; he was a very different man ushering her out. He was sweating and exceedingly nervous, repeating that he had never done anything illegal and if necessary he could prove it.

'I am sure you can, Mr Rushton. Thank you so much for your time.'

Anna was buzzing as she collected her car from a meter a short distance away from Rushton's office. It was after eleven, but she decided she would drive straight to Julia Brandon's home in Wimbledon.

Phil had spent two hours with the Drug Squad, sifting through all the known dealers arrested from the Chalk Farm area. They were mostly young kids. They had on record a previous bust of the squats over a year ago. Phil had to tread on eggshells as he questioned the Squad about how the squat, even after a bust, was still active when the murder had occurred. He was told that they no sooner cleaned up a squat on the estate and boarded up the flat, than within weeks another group had set up dealing.

The empty high-rise blocks earmarked for demolition were anathema to the Squad. They thought that the area had been used by heavy dealers of heroin and cocaine, but they could not be certain. The flood of class A drugs coming onto the streets was a constant nightmare. Phil asked if any of them had ever come into contact with, or knew, the infamous Alexander Fitzpatrick. He virtually got a repetition of his own feelings.

The Drug Squad knew of Fitzpatrick, but queried why such a kingpin would bother with a small-time drug squat. They doubted he would have been there, and doubted that he was even in the country. Rumour had it that Fitzpatrick had upped his drug trafficking in the US and was stashing millions, working with cartels in Columbia – that was, if he was still active. They doubted it: he was still on the USA's Most Wanted list. More than likely, Fitzpatrick was sunbathing on some glamorous yacht in Barbados. As he would be around sixty odd, he might have retired from the high life. They wondered if he was living in Spain, or even the Philippines. There had been no sighting of him for over twenty years. They also knew the man had numerous aliases, and more properties than even he could probably count.

Phil left as they started swapping stories about the audacious Fitzpatrick. Although it was of some concern to the Drug Squad, it was generally agreed, with some resignation, that Fitzpatrick had got away with it.

Julia Brandon was none too pleased to see Anna. She was just entering her house as Anna drew up. This was good, as it meant that Rushton might not have been able to contact her. She waited at her front door as Anna parked behind her Mercedes in her drive. Anna followed her inside and helped her carry some of the groceries.

'Mai Ling is picking Emily and Kathy up for me, so I had to do the shopping.' Julia dumped the bags down on the kitchen counter. 'Do you want anything to drink?'

'No, just a few minutes of your time.'

Julia walked past Anna back down the hall. Anna saw her lock the front door and switch on the alarm, before she returned to the kitchen. Anna also saw her checking the back door, and then she made herself a cup of mint tea. Julia carried her tea into the drawing room and gestured for Anna to sit down.

'What is it now?'

'I want to clear up a few things.'

'They still haven't released Frank's body for his funeral.'

'I'm sorry.'

'Yeah, well, so am I.' Her foot was twitching as she sat perched on a hard-backed chair.

Anna opened her briefcase and took out her notebook. Julia was sipping her tea, but her foot kept on twitching.

'I met your sister.'

Julia suddenly got up and put her tea down.

'I went to her farmhouse.'

Julia looked away. 'We don't get along. I hardly ever see her. I think she is envious about the kids. She can't have any, so maybe that's why she's always so difficult.'

'I liked her.'

'Yes, everyone does.'

There was a pause as Anna searched for a pencil.

'Why did you go to see Honour?'

'Just making enquiries.'

'About Frank? She never met him.'

'I know, but I was there just to check over a few things.'

'Like what?'

'Did your partner own a boat?'

Julia blinked and then nodded her head.

'Did you know the name of it?'

'No. I always get seasick on boats, so I only ever went on it once.'

'Where?'

'It was anchored in Cannes. His crew used to take it wherever he wanted it but, like I said, I get seasick, and with two small children, I don't like the risks.'

'Did your sister ever go on it?'

'No.'

'How about your brother-in-law?'

'Well, if Honour never went on it, I doubt Damien would; they're joined at the hip. It was he, you know, who made her change the way she spelled her name. It used to be just Honor, with no U in it, but then she started spelling it with one, as in "Honour thy husband" shit.'

'I saw a painting of a boat at her farmhouse.'

Julia shrugged.

'So I just wondered if perhaps they *had* been on the boat – maybe when you weren't around?'

'I doubt it.'

'But why paint a boat?'

'I have no idea. She paints all sorts of things – cows, hens, sheep, fields . . . Why are you asking me about my sister?'

'Just checking out a few things.'

'Like what?'

'Really, it's connected to you. You see, we are trying to trace your ex-partner.'

Julia stood up. 'Why?'

'Because it's part of our enquiry.'

'But he has nothing to do with Frank or me! I just don't understand.'

'Well, we don't understand quite a few things either, Julia.'

'This is ridiculous. My relationship was over years ago – not that I can see why it has anything to do with Frank.'

'Would he have been jealous?'

'Of what?'

'Your relationship with Frank.'

'I have told you, it was over many years ago. The last time you were here you were asking me about him. I explained then he left me, it broke my heart.'

'He left you very well provided for though, didn't he?'

Julia pressed her hands down her sides, as if smoothing her tight black skirt. 'So what? That is my business.'

'But it could also have been Frank's; it could be a motive for his murder.'

'No way. They never met.' Anna watched Julia as she picked up her cup. Her hands were shaking.

'Why did you need to liquidate so much money?'

The tea spilled as Julia spun round to face Anna. '*What?*'

'Why don't you sit down, Julia. I think you heard what I said, and I need some answers from you.'

Julia moved to sit on the arm of a large easy chair. 'I have had a lot of extra expenses because of moving house. I'm shocked that David Rushton has spoken to you about it. It is of no concern to anyone else but myself. What I do with my money is my own business.'

'It was a lot of money and you wanted it in cash.'

'Yes, because it's still the best way to make deals. You'd be surprised what builders and decorators will accept, and then of course, there are all the furnishings.'

Anna looked around the room. It was certainly beautifully furnished and the house was very elegant. For a brief moment, she even wondered if it could possibly be the truth. But four million and in cash? The property wasn't that sumptuous. 'So that was what you needed the first withdrawal for. But what about the second?'

'Well, as it turned out, I didn't need it, so I didn't bother.'

'I don't believe you.'

'Really? Well, that's your problem.'

'Do you have one?'

'Do I have one what?'

'A problem. That is a great deal of money. Is someone putting pressure on you? Is that why you needed Frank Brandon to look after you?'

Julia gave a nervous laugh. 'I just can't believe what you are asking. No one is putting any pressure on me to do anything. I loved Frank; that is why we got married.'

'I think you are lying. I am trying to fathom out just why.'

'Well, do tell me what you fathom out, because I am bored and I really don't have the time to waste.'

The doorbell rang and Julia froze. It rang again twice. She hurried out of the room. The bell sounded again two times in rapid succession, as if it were some kind of a code. Anna heard her letting the children in with their au pair. The girls were rowdy and screeching as they were led to the kitchen for their lunch.

Julia returned. 'I feed them at home, as I like to monitor what they eat. Nursery food consists of chicken nuggets and French fries, or fish fingers and French fries, so if you don't mind, I'd like you to leave.'

Anna paid no attention but flicked over a page in her notebook. 'Fifteen years ago, you had a small bank balance in an account in Oxford.'

'Jesus Christ, you people make me sick. Just what business is that of yours? My husband has been murdered and you appear to be incapable of finding out who did it to him. I have given you all the information possible. I have been at all times totally co-operative and willing to speak with you, but this is nothing more than harassment and I won't stand for it. I would like you to leave.'

'Do you have a forwarding address for your ex-partner Anthony Collingwood?'

'No, I don't. I told you I have not seen him since he left me.'

'Did the money belong to him?'

'He gave it to me.'

'In cash?'

'Some of it, yes, but mostly in properties and companies.'

'And you don't have any contact with him?'

'No, I have told you.'

'He must have been a very rich man.'

'He was, and very generous.'

'Do you have a photograph of him?'

'No, I do not. When he left, I tore everything up. He walked out on me.'

'Leaving you a fortune?'

'Yes,' she hissed.

Anna folded her notebook. 'Could I see the pictures of your wedding to Frank Brandon?'

'No. I don't have them any more.'

'Why not?'

'Because I destroyed them; they were too painful.'

Anna gave a soft laugh. 'You really are an exceptional liar, Mrs Brandon. I think you needed Frank to act as a bodyguard. Why you actually married him is confusing; maybe as some kind of extra protection? Because I think your ex-partner wants his money back! Is that true?'

Julia's mouth was a thin tight line. 'Please go away, just leave me alone.'

'If I am correct . . .'

'You are not!'

'I will go, Mrs Brandon, but I will keep on returning until I get to the truth.'

'You just try it. I am going to call my solicitor and make a formal complaint. You have no right to come to my home and make these accusations. The money I have is mine. No one is threatening me or trying to take it from me. I can look after myself.'

'Frank Brandon was murdered, working for you. Doesn't that frighten you?'

'It had nothing to do with me. I don't even know who he was working for.'

'For you, wasn't he? You benefited from his life insurance policy: that's half a million.'

'I also paid the premiums. I've already told you this, so we are now repeating ourselves.'

Anna took out her card and passed it to Julia. 'If you want to talk to me, here's my direct line.'

Julia tapped the card against her teeth. 'I don't think you will be hearing from me, Detective Travis.'

She stood in the hallway, hands on hips, waiting for Anna to join her. As they reached the front door, she pressed the security codes and unlocked the door.

Anna looked at the lock. 'You are certainly taking precautions.'

'I have to. I have spent so much of my money on the house, it's a precaution against burglary.'

Anna smiled and walked out. The door shut so fast behind her it almost clipped her briefcase. She heard the locks being put into place as she went to her car. Bleeping it open, she turned back to look at the house. She was certain Julia was lying. From Rushton she knew that Julia had needed a lot of money: four million. She got into her Mini, tossing her briefcase onto the passenger seat.

She wondered if she was right – whether Julia's ex-partner needed money, or wanted some of his cash back. But if he was the kingpin drug dealer, Alexander Fitzpatrick, surely he already had mega-millions? If Anthony Collingwood was Fitzpatrick, which she was presuming, then he must have been in and out of England, forming a relationship with Julia. Could he really have been that audacious? Or was she becoming, as Phil had implied, so preoccupied with her own theories that she was losing the plot?

Her mobile rang: it was Gordon. 'Can you talk?' he asked.

'Yes.'

'Okay, this has taken me all morning.'

'Fire away. I presume it's about the boat?'

'Talk about the ownership being submerged in so many different companies and shareholders. To sell a ship, you have to have a bill of sale. The bill of sale is in a special format and copies are available from the registry. Alexander Fitzpatrick's first big yacht was sold over twelve years ago to an Italian; the bill of sale was handed over to this guy, Carlo Simonetti. He was the sole owner, and the boat was anchored in Florida. There is a second boat, also from Florida and called *Dare Devil*, which was owned by five different people.'

Anna closed her eyes, wishing Gordon would get to the point.

'All five are names that had at one time been used by Alexander Fitzpatrick; his name is not on the registry. The boat cost a staggering fourteen million dollars. Joint owners are considered as one party – are you with me?'

'Yes, Gordon, I'm just about keeping up.'

'Okay – and this is the same boat – it has been divided up into twenty-two shareholders. A single shareholder could be at least five people. It's a plethora of names, which makes it very hard to trace.'

'Where's the boat now?'

'Well, this was a hard one; it was last docked in the UK at Southampton in 1997, and that took me over an hour to find out. It was also docked in Puerto Banus,

Spain in 1997. I'm still trying to find out more about any ports in the UK.'

'Who was on the boat – do you know?'

Gordon huffed and puffed at the end of the phone. 'Well, it was chartered – that is, rented out – and I'm still trying to find out the people who handled it.'

'Go for the crew and see if you can get anything from the Spanish authorities. They would have to have had passports.'

'I'm trying! It's taken me all morning to get this far and I have a feeling the boat might have been sold.'

Anna shut off the call. Gordon's tracking of the boat was yet another possible wild-goose chase but, at the same time, it could also mean that, in 1997, Alexander Fitzpatrick, using any one of his numerous identities, could have been in the UK. Anna started to back out from Julia's drive. She was forced to brake as a Mercedes Benz drove up behind her.

Simon Fagan got out and rapped on the window. 'Detective Travis, I have already made a complaint regarding the surveillance vehicle positioned outside my client's premises—'

Anna said that, as far as she knew, it was no longer present.

'But you are harassing my client. I want to know exactly why you are persistently questioning Mrs Brandon and causing her great distress.'

Anna got out of the Mini to face him. 'I have every right, Mr Fagan. We are still investigating the murder of her husband and certain information has arisen that required me to reinterview Mrs Brandon.'

'I'd very much like to know what this is.'

'Your client has withdrawn very large sums of money.

My concern is that she may possibly have been black-mailed or if not, this has some connection with the death of her husband.'

Fagan stepped back from the Mini and said aggressively, 'If you wish to speak to Mrs Brandon again, then you will do so in my presence, is that understood?'

Anna shook her head, smiling. 'It will then be a formal interview at the station. Mrs Brandon may of course request you to accompany her.'

Fagan glared and returned to his Mercedes. He backed out into the road to allow Anna to drive past. His presence made Anna even more suspicious; she reckoned that Julia had put a call into him as soon as she believed Anna had left. Fagan had certainly got to the property fast; she would have liked to have been a fly on the wall to overhear their conversation.

Anna drove into Wimbledon village, parked in a pub car park and went to get a coffee and a sandwich. Sitting outside, in front of the pub, she had only just taken a bite when she saw Simon Fagan's Mercedes pass, only a few feet from her. Julia Brandon was in the passenger seat, obviously crying: she had a handkerchief to her face, wiping her eyes. She had shown no emotion whilst being questioned by Anna, which made her wonder just what the woman had learned from Fagan that had upset her so much. Anna could see the silver Mercedes at the traffic-lights. They were waiting as four horses and riders passed, heading towards Wimbledon Common.

Anna grabbed her sandwich and, ramming the lid on her coffee, ran to her Mini. She drove out of the car park, turning right into the High Street; she could still see, four cars ahead, the Mercedes. She tailed them about a mile up the road before she saw they had turned left into Old Windmill Lane. Still keeping her distance, afraid that Fagan would recognise her car, she drove slowly up the lane. The lane branched out into a large car park. Worried she would easily be seen, she quickly parked between two stationary cars, and used her wing mirror to look for Fagan's car.

He was parked at the far side of the car park; both he and Julia remained inside the car. Heading into the car park, and passing Anna, was a navy-blue Range Rover. She could clearly see the two burly occupants looking around; then Fagan got out of his Mercedes and waved towards them.

The Range Rover parked alongside Fagan's car. He bent inside to talk to Julia, as the two men got out of the Range Rover and joined him. Fagan was clearly introducing the two men, Julia leaning across the driver seat to acknowledge them. They wore cheap grey suits and ties; both were muscle-bound and looked like ex-Army. Anna jotted down their licence-plate number and then had to duck down as Fagan appeared to look directly towards her, but she was mistaken; instead he walked around to the passenger side and helped Julia get out. The two men shook her hand, and one guided her to the passenger seat of the Range Rover. She got in; the two men talked for a few more moments to Fagan, before they got back into the Range Rover. Fagan drove out, passing Anna as did, shortly afterwards, Julia and the two men in the Range Rover.

Anna waited a while before she left the car park and drove past Julia Brandon's house. The Range Rover was already parked outside. The men beside Julia took a covert look around before they stepped inside her house. Their presence confirmed to Anna that Julia might well have hired Frank, and now these two goons, for protection. The question was, *from whom?*

Anna knew she was stepping on Phil Markham's toes but, before returning to the station, she decided to see if she could talk to someone from the Drug Squad. She needed to know more about Alexander Fitzpatrick, and she hoped they could help her. She was, yet again, certain that he was behind Julia Brandon's fear.

Chapter Fourteen

Anna waited in a small outer office for over twenty minutes. A rather scruffy officer, wearing denim jeans and bomber jacket, eventually joined her. Sam Power was an undercover officer, and one with quite a reputation; he had busted a very big cocaine ring in 2002 so, for his own protection, he was 'paperworking' until the heat of the trial died down. They were up to their ears, he explained, and having spent some time with Phil Markham that morning, the officers didn't want to cover the same ground again.

'So you got me,' he grinned. He was rather good-looking, with sandy hair and bright blue eyes, and a very confident manner.

Anna thanked him for seeing her. She then came straight out with it. 'I have this gut feeling that Alexander Fitzpatrick is back in the UK. I'm sure you know who I'm talking about.'

'Of course I do – he's the one that got away. But we don't act on gut feelings. To be honest, he's been dormant for so many years, we've kind of dismissed him as having any hand in trafficking big-time any more. He made a lot of money; he's probably lying low and enjoying the proceeds of his ill-gotten gains.'

'How dangerous was he?'

Sam shifted his weight in the hard-backed chair. 'Well, you can't compare him with Howard Marks, not the same animal. Marks was never violent; never, to our knowledge, killed anyone. He's kind of a hero to the pot-smoking oldies who still maintain a hippy attitude to soft drugs. I don't agree with any kind of leniency regarding hash or marijuana – I've seen too many kids fall into the trap of moving up the scale to use heroin – and nowadays, Christ only knows what they mix up with so-called class C drugs.'

Anna nodded, letting him expound his personal theories with regard to drug taking, and flushing as she recalled her time with Pete the other evening. She waited for the opportunity to bring the conversation back to Fitzpatrick. It took a while; Sam seemed to like the sound of his own voice.

'Did you ever meet him?'

'No, he was before my time. He's at pension age now; no one's heard a dickie bird from him for at least fifteen, twenty years. The guy made millions. He is either living a life of luxury, or he could even have been topped – he was known to mix with the Columbian cartels and the Mafia, and you don't mess with those types. In the mid-eighties, they reckoned he mobilised the law-enforcement agencies in fourteen or fifteen different countries. That's the US, UK, Spain, the Philippines, Hong Kong, Taiwan, Thailand, Pakistan, Germany . . .'

'Good heavens,' Anna interjected.

'Yeah, good heavens. He also shipped to the Netherlands, Canada, Switzerland, Australia and Austria – a lot of dope, and a lot of money. He was rumoured to have something like twenty homes around the world.'

'And boats?'

'Yeah, Christ knows how many yachts – maybe as many as his different identities. After he'd flooded the market here and skipped bail, he went onto bigger deals, trafficking cocaine and heroin into the US. They couldn't capture him either; he's still on their Most Wanted list.'

Anna tried not to sound as if her supposition regarding Fitzpatrick was implausible. 'His ex-partner, a very beautiful woman, lives here. She has two children. Whether they are fathered by him or not, I don't know.'

Sam tapped her knee. 'He had beautiful women all over the world; with his money and his drugs, he could get any woman he wanted.'

Anna continued, even though she could feel Sam almost laughing at her insinuation that Fitzpatrick would want to be with this woman or her children. 'He possibly has close friends here?'

'No way would he risk it. No one was his close friend; he couldn't afford the risk that they would give him up! There are rewards out for him in the States . . .'

Nothing Anna said appeared to dent Sam's over-confident attitude that she was wrong about Fitzpatrick. In fact, he made her feel almost foolish in suggesting it.

When she brought up the yacht and the fact that it had been docked in Southampton, he shrugged. 'Listen, whether or not he had speedboats, yachts and Christ knows what else, any boat would have to be registered. If it came into UK waters, we'd have nabbed him.'

'What if you didn't know the boat? What if it was chartered to someone else?'

Sam agreed that it was possible, but he was dismissive of whatever she said. In his opinion, Fitzpatrick had no good reason to be in the UK.

289

'So he was very dangerous?' Anna prompted.

Sam did another of his shrugs. He conceded that, in his prime, Fitzpatrick took no prisoners; to maintain his drug trafficking in the US, he would have had to have an army to protect him, or kill for him. 'Nowadays, I don't think he would be any threat. We've not had so much as a rumour that he's still active – he's an old-age pensioner, for Chrissakes!' Sam stood and hitched up his jeans. 'If you want to leave me with the details you've got on this yacht, I can check it out for you, see if we have anything on it, but we're up to our ears with Yardies and gang wars; they've got weapons nowadays that'd make your hair stand on end.'

Anna wanted to discuss the drug squat in Chalk Farm but, by now, she sensed that Sam was eager for her to leave. She gave him the information she'd gained from Gordon that morning, but didn't mention the Oxford-shire farm or even Julia Brandon.

By the time Anna was back in her office, it was after four. Phil was waiting in the corridor.

'Can I have a word?' he said.

'Sure, just let me get my breath; I've only just walked in.' She could feel his animosity as she put her briefcase onto her desk.

'I've just had the fucking guy I spent half the morning with at the Drug Unit calling me. What is it with you?'

'I don't understand the question.'

'I was checking them out, then you turn up. Now they've got back to me about a fucking yacht. You know these guys don't like to be messed around.'

'Yes, well, I only just got the details this morning and we are still checking it out.' Anna looked at him. 'Can you just wait for the briefing, Phil? You'll get everything

I have. If you want to talk to Gordon, he can give you the information on the boat, which I don't have.'

'Too fucking right we need a briefing: we've got four dead bodies, and one an ex-cop. Instead of working on his case, you are running around on some crazy investigation into a guy that even the Drug Squad thinks is long dead. If he isn't, he's not likely to be getting his leg over a hard bitch in Wimbledon or hiding out in a barn in Oxfordshire!'

'That hard bitch cashed four million nine months ago! And if you haven't tracked down the man she calls her ex-partner, Anthony Collingwood, then bring it up at the briefing.'

'What's *he* got to do with the murders?'

'Because, as you well know, it is one of the aliases used by Fitzpatrick. Phil, if no one can find the bastard, then it could be for a bloody good reason!' Her desk phone rang and she reached for it. 'Can you give me fifteen minutes?'

Phil slammed out of her office as she picked up the phone.

'Hi there, it's me – it's Pete.'

She sat down. She really didn't want to talk to him.

'I've got a result for you, my darling.'

'I need one, Pete. What have you got?'

'The soil particles – and you may ask how this has come through so quickly; it is because yours truly has been pressing for details. Okay, are you ready for this?'

'I am.'

'The Mitsubishi, D'Anton's Post Office van and even my dear old Morgan all have matching soil particles. Not one hundred per cent confirmed – you know what wankers they are, far be it from them to commit to anything on paper yet – but I'm telling you, and it's not just mud, it's also horse shit! This made it even easier: shit is shit . . . Hello, are you still there?'

Anna leaned back in her chair and grinned. 'I am, and thank you.'

'Do I deserve dinner tonight?'

'Maybe you do, but can I see how the rest of the day pans out?'

'Okay, call me back.'

Anna said she would and replaced the receiver. She got her notes together and, with knots in her stomach, because she knew this was not going to be easy, made her way to the incident room.

The entire team were gathered. Anna went to have a quiet talk with Gordon. He had made no further progress in tracking down who had actually chartered the boat to Carlo Simonetti, the name they had from Spain. He had also been unable to, as yet, track down any crew members, but the shipping registry office was confident they could give more details eventually. Gordon had some information about the boat being sold in Florida, but again lacked any confirmation as to who had bought it. He had not, as yet, listed his findings on the incident board. Anna said he should mark up what he had so far before the briefing.

Phil was sitting, thumbing through his notebook, and DC Pamela Meadows was writing up on the board the name Anthony Collingwood: no known address, not on any voting register, but a passport had been issued to someone of that name in 1985. Anna joined her, and asked if she would also check with passport control all the other aliases used by Alexander Fitzpatrick. Phil glanced up, as if he had overheard Fitzpatrick's name, then took a deep breath and looked back down to his notebook.

'Okay, everyone. Can we kick off with you, Phil?'

Phil went over his dealings with the Drug Squad. He had been given short shrift over the possibility they had 'overlooked' the dealers at the squat. He listed the number of times the police had been called to the estate, and how many arrests had been dealt with; he then reiterated the problems they had encountered. No sooner was a drug squat raided and boarded up, than another reopened in another empty flat. He did not believe that either the local police, or anyone from the Drug Squad, had turned a blind eye to the dealing in the flat where Brandon was killed.

They had now succeeded in tracing virtually all the vehicles listed by Jeremy Webster, though a few more interviews were outstanding. 'The delay in tracking these vehicles, and owner/drivers,' Phil continued, 'is due to the fact that three were stolen; two more had no tax or insurance, and were used by kids for joy riding.' Two motorbike riders had also been traced, but again, neither had any connection to the murder of Frank Brandon.

Anna looked at the incident board and then back to Phil. 'We still do not have an ID on the dealers from the squat. Somebody has to have known them, so we need that covered.'

The rest of the team gave a rundown of what their allocated workload had produced. They now had confirmation that the still unidentified man, who they presumed had accompanied Frank Brandon, had not presented at any of the hospitals suffering from a gunshot wound or graze. The diary of Donny Petrozzo had been checked and all names taken from it interviewed but, as most of them were legitimate clients who had simply used Donny as a chauffeur, they had been eliminated. Pamela repeated that she had not been able to trace Anthony Collingwood and had no luck from telephone directories or voting registers. She was now proceeding to check with passport control all the aliases used by Alexander Fitzpatrick, as they knew that Collingwood was one of them. Phil almost snorted, only just managing to restrain himself.

Anna waited until everyone had finished, then did a Langton pause before she began.

'Frank Brandon's widow withdrew four million in cash some months ago. According to her financial adviser, David Rushton, she was advised not to, as it would mean a considerable loss of premiums, but still she went ahead. She then attempted to withdraw another large sum but this time, acting on Rushton's advice, decided not to. The dates for the withdrawal and attempted withdrawal coincide with her marriage to Frank Brandon – which I believe to be a marriage of some kind of convenience. Frank's life insurance policy was arranged by Rushton; Julia paid the premiums.' Anna paused for another moment, then continued, aware that the team already knew most of what she was saying, but she wanted to underline its importance. 'Frank, as we all know, was murdered at the drug squat. He was accompanied by someone we have been unable to identify – but we do know they drove there in a black Mitsubishi jeep. This jeep featured again, when the body of Donny Petrozzo was discovered in the back of it. The same vehicle, as you can see, features *again*: this time driven by Julius D'Anton in the village of Shipston on Stour.'

Anna waited as they all took in the links on the board.

'D'Anton's body was subsequently found in the Thames. It has been ascertained that he did not drown; we are still waiting on the results from toxicology to give us the precise cause of death. We are also waiting for the same department to give us details on how Donny Petrozzo died. We do know that Stanley Leymore was shot – and here we go with the links: the bullet that killed Stanley has been matched to the bullets that killed Frank Brandon.'

She gestured to Stanley Leymore's name, and the red arrow that linked it to the black Mitsubishi. They had found papers in his garage that meant he had sold it; they knew the vehicle had been originally stolen from Brighton.

Anna pointed to the Post Office van used by D'Anton. 'Okay, here is another link: we have traces of the same horse shit . . .'

Phil muttered, showing his boredom at the repetition.

She turned to stare at him. 'I mean real horse shit, Phil: the same *dung*, for want of a better word, has been matched on the Post Office van, and the Mitsubishi – and, guess what?' Anna drew an arrow from the two vehicles to the names of Honour and Damien Nolan. 'Their home – Honey Farm! So why was the Mitsubishi there? And did D'Anton – who, coincidentally, had been at Balliol with none other than Alexander Fitzpatrick – by accident approach the farm and perhaps recognise Fitzpatrick hiding out there?'

Anna placed down her marker pen as the team muttered. She continued by saying that, although the Drug Squad found her hypotheses about Fitzpatrick almost laughable, she had not backed down. Even if he was at pension age, she believed he had returned to the UK.

Anna next discussed the painting of the yacht at Honour's farmhouse: it had been taken down, but not before Gordon had photographed it and subsequently traced it. They did not yet know, however, if the yacht *was* Fitzpatrick's, nor whether he could have been in England in 1997.

Anna next turned back to the widow, Julia Brandon. 'She has two children: she has admitted both were by IVF treatment. We have no named father. She insists her ex-partner was Anthony Collingwood; as we all know, we have no trace on him.'

Anna was in full stride. She now began using another coloured pen to arrow the next set of links. 'Julia Brandon is Honour Nolan's sister. Honour denied ever knowing Fitzpatrick, and yet there was a painting of the yacht *Dare Devil* at the farm.'

Phil interrupted. 'You know, I see all these links – in fact, it's looking like a tube map right now – but I can't see how this all adds up to a string of four murders: an ex-cop, a chauffeur, a crooked car dealer and a junkie antique dealer. I mean, if this Fitzpatrick *is* here – which I do not believe for a minute – what does it give us? Why is he here? Why would this infamous drug trafficker be visiting a shithole of a squat in Chalk Farm?'

Anna could feel her exasperation building. 'Phil, I don't know why Frank Brandon or Alexander Fitzpatrick were there. I am trying to bloody find out. I have said from day one that maybe, just maybe, it's not anyone in the squat they wanted – it was something they had and that something, whatever the fuck it was, links all the dead men together and may, ultimately, link to Fitzpatrick.'

It was at this point that Langton walked in. Anna almost had heart failure.

Cunningham, who accompanied him, threaded her way between the tables and chairs to the front. 'In case any of you don't know, this is Detective Chief Superintendent James Langton.'

Langton nodded as he unbuttoned his navy pinstriped jacket. He took it off and hung it over the back of a chair, then loosened his tie before turning to Cunningham with his hand out. She passed him a file. Langton coughed, and opened it. 'We now have a toxicology report. Donny Petrozzo was killed by a massive overdose, as was Julius D'Anton. The same drug killed both victims, linking them directly: Fentanyl. For those of you who don't know, it is a very potent, fast-acting, opiate pain medicine, mostly used in hospital emergency wards and not, thank Christ, as yet on the streets. Fentanyl is used by the microgram, it's that potent; unlike morphine, which is used in milligrams. So you understand what we are dealing with!' He grinned.

'Cocaine gives you a high for maybe an hour, heroin ditto; Fentanyl gives you no more than five to ten minutes but, because it's so strong, addicts are starting to play around with it. The US have begun to get feedback on the use of this drug: addicts are mixing it with low-grade morphine and, in a number of cases, scopolamine, which is used for motion sickness. Fentanyl is also being mixed with heroin and OxyContin, a painkiller. Its nickname is Polo, the mint with a hole, but in this case, the hole is an almighty high!'

The room was silent, listening intently to his commanding manner and his low gruff voice.

'We have a number of reports from the States that

three warehouses containing packages of Fentanyl have been raided. We are in the process, with the FBI Drug Unit, of looking into the drug surfacing over here. We are also checking out if there are any known thefts of Fentanyl from hospitals.'

He gestured with his hands to indicate the size of a package. 'One this size – because it takes only a microgram to get a high that is very dangerous as it is guaranteed to lift the roof off your brains – is worth millions.'

A murmur lifted slightly as the team took on board what he was saying. He waited for them to settle.

'If this is coming into the UK, it is a frightening new development. It is short-acting and comes out of the system quickly; take too much, and it will kill you just as fast as the high.'

Langton then turned to Anna. His eyes seemed to bore into hers. 'DI Travis, you've been doing some very intuitive detective work. I'm impressed. DCI Cunningham and I would like to go over the details; I've asked Detective Sergeant Sam Power to join us.'

He asked Cunningham which would be the most suitable office to use. She gestured towards her own.

'Good. I'd like some coffee, and to get on with it as soon as possible.'

Anna had not said one word. All she could think of was being thankful she had dressed well that morning. Langton looked even more spruce than she remembered. There was no hint of a limp from his injuries; on the contrary, he bristled with energy and vitality, unlike Cunningham. He strode to the door, as he saw Sam Power hovering. Anna picked up her briefcase and put her notebook inside. She went into her own office to give her hair a quick comb and straightened her jacket. She checked her make-up, putting on some lipgloss, then wiping it off in case Langton noticed she had done so!

As she made her way to Cunningham's office, she caught Langton talking to – or talking *at* – Phil Markham. It sounded like he was lecturing him on not being so tight-arsed.

Phil was sweating. 'I'm sorry, I just didn't reckon this Fitzpatrick guy was in the frame. It was a long shot—'

'He might not be, but something stinks in that farmhouse besides the horse shit. And you shouldn't ever dismiss anything that DI Travis comes up with. She has more brains in her little finger than this entire team put together! If she's right, you've all lost valuable time. Fitzpatrick was an evil sod who'd knife his own mother to get what he wanted; maybe even his kids.'

'If they are his.'

'Yeah, *if*! We've got a fucking nightmare on our hands and we shouldn't be wasting time putting another officer down. No matter what you think or what you feel, just learn to button it!'

'Yes, sir.'

Langton pulled at his tie. 'I want this boat *Dare Devil* checked over. I also want any updated photographs of Fitzpatrick.' Then Langton walked off, leaving Phil ready to explode.

He looked at Pamela. 'He wants an updated photo of this bastard Fitzpatrick; where am I gonna get that from? He's only been on the wanted list for fifteen years. If the US don't have one, where the fuck are we going to get one from?'

Pamela pointed at the incident board of aliases used by

Fitzpatrick and suggested they try to track them down via passport and immigration. If Fitzpatrick had, as suspected, entered the UK in the past few years using these aliases, they might have a recent photograph. She also suggested that Fitzpatrick might have had plastic surgery to disguise his looks; living in Florida, it would have been easy to accomplish.

'Terrific! Now we don't have any idea what the bastard looks like!'

'Can't change his height though; six feet four,' Pamela said, smiling.

Closeted in Cunningham's office, Langton was certain that Anna had stumbled on a situation bigger by far than they realised. The murder of Frank Brandon, he believed, was part and parcel of the atrocious intention of someone, perhaps Fitzpatrick, preparing to import quantities of Fentanyl into the UK. A kilo of the drug, worth millions, would be very easy to move through customs.

He sat listening to Anna run through the reasons why she had begun to believe Fitzpatrick could be in England. She spoke quietly, head bowed, as she recalled all the events to date, occasionally referring to her notebook. She did not, at any time, gloss over the suppositions and the doubts that even she had, but listed the loose tentacles. Her doubts were the same as Phil's: although the amount of money to be made from the sale of Fentanyl would obviously be substantial, was it enough to draw Fitzpatrick back into the world of drug trafficking? There had been no sighting of him for over fifteen years. Anna did not have any evidence, but she did say – very firmly – that she really felt a key to their enquiry lay with Honour and Damien Nolan and Julia Brandon. However, to date, she had not been able to get Julia to talk – and she had not had the backing from Cunningham to press for warrants to search the farm.

Langton turned to stare at the downcast Cunningham, who sat on a chair by the wall with her arms folded.

'I didn't mean that to sound as if I was in any way querying DCI Cunningham's investigation – the new developments only really arose today and over the last weekend – but I do think we need to search both sisters' premises.'

'So this Julia situation, with regard to the four million – you only found out today?'

'Yes.'

'Take me through the Frank Brandon marriage again.'

Anna repeated all she knew about his marriage to Julia, the girlfriend he was supposed to marry, and what she had seen in the Windmill car park that morning in Wimbledon.

'You think she is scared of something or someone?'

'Why hire Frank as a bodyguard if she didn't need protection? These two goons looked like ex-Army.'

'Maybe she just wanted to fuck him,' Langton said.

'You haven't met her,' she snapped back.

Cunningham glanced at Anna, surprised at the way she had spoken to Langton, but he didn't seem in any-way fazed, far from it: he laughed. 'I'll take your word for it, then.'

Sam Power had remained silent throughout the entire interaction. Now he got up and leaned against the wall. 'I've got my team digging up anything we can get for you, but it is a lot of supposition. I'm not that confident that DI Travis is correct about Fitzpatrick. If it pans out, and we get a sighting or any concrete evidence, we will have to work together.'

Langton glanced at him and then back to Anna. 'What we need is fingerprints; don't tell me a guy is up for trial without there being a single set of his prints retained on record.'

Sam shook his head. 'It was before the database. Even if there were, they'd not be on file twenty odd years later.'

'Course they would; he skipped bail, didn't he?'

Anna coughed. 'I've already made enquiries and, to date, we have no prints on Fitzpatrick.'

Langton clapped his hands as if to draw everyone's attention back to him. 'Okay, let's not waste time. You move on that, Sam; in the meantime, we should structure surveillance on the farm and on Julia Brandon – perhaps this time not making it that obvious! We also need to get more details on Fentanyl and the thefts in the US. Right now, you have four dead men and no suspect! So we are really going to have to put pressure on, all round.'

He stood up and turned to Cunningham, thanking her for coming in as he knew she had personal issues. Cunningham assured him that, as from that evening, she would not require any further time off.

'Can I see you in your office?' he said to Anna. She gave a small nod.

'Right. Tomorrow, we'll outline how we proceed in more detail. Thank you both.' He nodded to Sam and back to Anna; it was a cue for them to leave.

Sam and Anna walked along the corridor. When they got to her office, he stopped and said, 'Look, I'm sorry if

I appeared dismissive about your investigation when you came to see me this morning.'

'That's okay.'

'It isn't. Now with Langton breathing down Cunningham's neck, he'll also be coming on to my lads. It's not going to be easy: Drug Squad and murder teams like to work their own cases.'

Anna opened her office door, eager for Sam to go. 'Sam, we have four dead men. If the lead to their murder is drugs, then it's obvious we have to work as closely as possible.'

'Yeah, I know – but we will want to control the surveillance.'

'That's not my decision. I think tomorrow we'll all have our work cut out for us by Langton. The sooner it's set up, the better; I also think you need to go over all the old cases of busts at the Chalk Farm estate. Maybe the same guys could be involved.'

'I agree. No doubt I'll see you in the morning.'

'Good night,' she said, entering her office. She was relieved when he walked on down the corridor. She closed her door and not until she was alone did she feel as if she needed something to calm her nerves. She had not shown a single sign of how much tension she had felt with Langton, but now it was obvious: her hands were shaking.

No sooner had she sat at her desk than her door banged open and Langton walked in, carrying two beakers of coffee. 'Thought you might need this,' he said, placing her beaker on her desk and sitting down. 'Cunningham's partner's having to undergo chemo. She's all over the place – I doubt she's going to be steady enough to run this enquiry.'

'Will you be taking over?' Anna asked with trepidation.

'No, but I'll be overseeing it. I've got Christ knows how many other cases. This happens to be quite an extraordinary one, I'll agree, but nevertheless, DCI Cunningham stays put. From what I've gathered, you've been slogging away regardless.'

'That's not true. I've always referred my findings—'

'Bollocks. You think I don't know? You've been at it again, Anna, going off solo. This has to stop, do you understand me? From now on, you are going to have to work with the team.'

'I have been!'

'Anna, I listened to you and Phil Markham having a go at each other. You work together or you don't work at all.'

'Fine.'

He shook his head and sipped his coffee. He put it down on her desk and leaned back in the chair. 'Okay. Give me your take on how these dead men link, not by what you've got on the incident board – I can see the obvious connections between them, there's enough arrows to make it look like a kid's colouring chart. Give me what you believe might have taken place.'

It was as if they had never been lovers. It helped her calm down. 'Okay, and this is still sort of fermenting . . .'

'I'm listening.'

Anna took out her notebook and picked up a pencil. 'Petrozzo was at one time on trial for burglary. His trial coincided with that of Alexander Fitzpatrick, back in the late seventies. It is very possible that he may not have known him, but he could have. Fitzpatrick is, from his old photographs, someone you'd remember; he cuts quite a strong figure, at six feet four . . .'

Anna continued, describing the possible scenario that Donny recognised Fitzpatrick; he might even have been the passenger Donny had to collect. 'If his arrival was to prepare for dealing in Fentanyl, he would require contacts. He would not likely use Donny, since he was a small-time dealer – but it's possible. Donny was supplying cocaine to a lot of city slickers. Donny also used Stanley Leymore to buy his cars from, one of them a Mitsubishi. Did Fitzpatrick require a car? If so, there could be another link. Fitzpatrick gets the jeep and either goes to visit Julia, or even the farm in Oxford, as he makes preparations to deal. At some stage, Donny introduces Frank to Julia. Did Frank pick up Fitzpatrick to take him back to Heathrow? It's possible. Julia, at the same time, released four million pounds from her inheritance; was this to pay Fitzpatrick? She hires Frank Brandon to protect her, or protect her money. She marries him in a quick ceremony at a register office on the Isle of Man and Frank moves in to live at her new property in Wimbledon. This would also coincide with Julia trying to release more funds, but is persuaded not to by her business adviser. Who needed that cash?'

Langton gave a long sigh then gestured for her to continue.

'I've always thought that Frank Brandon's murder was not because he was scoring drugs, but because there was something inside the squat. Was it Fentanyl? We know Donny Petrozzo scored cocaine from there. What if Fitzpatrick used Donny to collect for him? Fitzpatrick was very unlikely to risk bringing it in himself.

Meanwhile, Fitzpatrick holes up at the farmhouse with Julia's sister and her husband waiting for the delivery.'

'Which never arrives?'

'Right, because Donny misguidedly reckoned he could pull a fast one. He might not have even known what he was carrying. As you said, this is not a well-known street drug.'

'So, Donny Petrozzo collects the package and, instead of delivering it to Fitzpatrick, he takes it to the low-life drug squat that he has been using to score from?'

'It's a possibility.'

'So Fitzpatrick has to go to the squat to get it back.'

'Yes.'

'Using Frank Brandon as a driver?'

'Yes.'

'This is all supposition, Anna.'

Anna tossed down her pencil. 'Look – you wanted to hear what I thought.'

'Okay, okay – don't get tetchy. Go on, I'm all ears.'

Anna sighed, but continued. 'Frank had told his girl-friend, Connie, that he was onto a very big earner. Whether it was Donny who killed Frank, we don't know; we do have his prints from the squat, so we know he had been there at some time. We also know that the same gun used to kill Frank was also used to kill Stanley Leymore, the car dealer.'

Langton nodded.

'Both Donny and the antique dealer Julius D'Anton were killed by an overdose of Fentanyl. At this time, Frank is driving the Mitsubishi – he parked it in a garage near to Julia's house in Wimbledon. What if he used the jeep to drive Fitzpatrick to the drug squat? I don't know

– I'm just making this up now as I go along, but we have no trace of the man who was with Frank. All we know is, whoever it was, was injured and had to be covered in Frank's blood.'

Langton puffed out his cheeks, and ruffled his hair.

'We now find the dead Donny stashed in the back of the Mitsubishi. Next, we discover our car dealer shot with the same weapon that killed Frank. Then, we have the junkie antique dealer, Julius D'Anton: another big coincidence, since he was at Oxford with Fitzpatrick, who I think was hiding out at Honey Farm. Again, like Donny, could we have someone who recognised Fitzpatrick, and this gets him killed? I'd say our man has got his hands on the Fentanyl. Both men died from a lethal injection of it. I think that by now Fitzpatrick has to have it.'

There was a long pause. 'Mmm.' Langton looked at his shoes.

'I know it all sounds far-fetched.' Anna closed her notebook.

'You can say that again.'

'It all hinges on whether or not I have the right man in Alexander Fitzpatrick. We don't know if he is the father of Julia's two children. Nor do we know if he was also Anthony Collingwood, but I think he was.'

'Sorry, you've lost me,' Langton yawned.

'Julia admitted that her ex-partner was called Anthony Collingwood.'

Langton nodded his head. 'Right, right – one of the aliases used by Fitzpatrick, I'm with you.' He drained his coffee and crumpled the beaker, tossing it into the waste-bin. 'Well, we have a lot to iron out.'

Her phone rang: it was Pete asking if they were on

for dinner. She told him that she would call him back directly.

Langton was standing, straightening his tie. 'I was sorry to hear about Frank. Sad way to go out; he was a nice bloke.'

'Yes.'

'I'll be in first thing in the morning. In the meantime, I'll mull over everything you've told me.' He walked to the door and had his hand on the handle to open it, when he turned. 'How's things with you?'

'Fine.'

'Good.' He stared at her, then cocked his head to one side and smiled. 'Good night.' He closed the door quietly behind him.

She sat, listening to his footsteps receding down the corridor. This was the first interaction she'd had with Langton since she had pieced together what part he had played in the death of the suspected killer on their last case. Langton, she knew, had played his hand so carefully that she was the only person who knew just what lengths he was prepared to go to. It was revenge for what had been done to him; to have been sliced almost in two by a machete would make anyone want retribution. He had perverted the law to gain his own justice.

It was an act of madness, but one she knew he did not regret. She had walked away from their relationship, accusing him of betraying everything he stood for, and yet she had been unable to walk away from him personally. He had remained in her thoughts and heart ever since and, try as she might, she was unable to free herself from wanting him. It made her feel depressed and angry that he still had such a hold over her emotions.

Anna reached for her phone and dialled Pete's

number. She would pick up some takeaway and meet him in half an hour. He was as affable and as easygoing as ever, agreeing to see her outside her flat and bring some wine.

'You sound a bit uptight,' he remarked. 'Everything all right?'

'Yep, fine. I'll see you later.'

It wasn't fine at all, but she needed to be with someone who took her mind off Langton. From the way he had behaved with her, she doubted that he even gave her a few moments' thought, but all she could think of was him. Langton was out of her reach and he had to stay there; she could not ever allow him to come close again.

Anna forced herself to make a quick exit; Pete would be waiting.

Chapter Fifteen

The second glass of wine had eased a lot of Anna's tension, but she was still wound up. Pete had asked if she was all right a couple more times. In the end, she snapped that she was fine, then she apologised and explained.

'I just had a long tedious session explaining away all my suppositions.'

After the third glass, she finally started to really chill out. Pete was as relaxed as ever and she was glad she had suggested he come over.

Whilst she cleared away, he put up some shelves. He was good at carpentry, but not very careful about the mess he made whilst working, so she got out the Hoover and cleaned up as he took a shower. She laughed when he appeared in her towelling dressing-gown, which was very short, the sleeves reaching just below his elbows. He hurled himself onto her bed with the remote and switched on the TV, relaxing back on her pillows.

After her shower Anna joined him on the bed, wrapped in a big white towel. He lifted his arm for her to snuggle beside him. 'You want to talk about your "suppositions"?' he asked.

'Not really. My boss has personal problems and had

the day off – until the briefing, when she came back . . .'
Anna hesitated.

'Go on.'

'Well, we had the Chief Superintendent come in
and, instead of my suppositions being swept aside, he sort
of . . .' Again, she paused.

Pete looked at her. 'Sort of what?'

'Well, agreed that I might be on the right track.'

'You mean with this Fitzpatrick guy?'

'Yeah. Until we have it confirmed, it's still up in the
air; main thing is trying to understand why he would
take such risks, coming back into the UK.'

'He's got to have a reason.'

'I know, but it's still sounding far-fetched. Whether or
not it is connected to the Fentanyl, we don't know, but
two of the victims were killed by an overdose of it . . .'

Pete tilted her chin up and kissed her. Then he leaned
up on his elbow to look into her eyes. 'That's enough.'

'What?'

He kissed her again. At first she didn't respond, but
then he slowly began to remove her towel and kiss her
breasts. She closed her eyes and murmured as he kissed
her belly and then slowly moved her legs apart. She
hated herself, because it was Langton's face she held in
her mind, Langton caressing her, and she was ashamed.
They climaxed together and he lay beside her, panting,
then reached out to draw her to him.

He sat up. 'What's the matter?'

'Nothing.' She turned off the bedside light.

He reached across her and turned it back on. 'Tell me.'

'Pete, there is nothing to tell. I'm just really tired and
I need to get some sleep.'

'Okay.'

Anna turned the light off. Pete lay on his back, staring at the ceiling, as she curled up with her back to him. Eventually she heard his breathing deepen and knew he was asleep. She was glad he wouldn't hear that she was crying.

Pete was frying eggs and bacon by the time she joined him in the kitchen. 'Good morning, light of my life,' he said, grinning.

'Morning. I didn't hear you get up.'

'You were out for the count. If you want to put some toast on, we can eat – everything is ready.'

She kissed his cheek and then went over to the toaster. By the time she had fetched the butter and marmalade, he had wolfed down his eggs and bacon. She didn't really feel that hungry, but nevertheless managed to clear her plate. Pete poured coffee and fetched the toast, as he eulogised about breakfast being the best meal of the day. He explained how to cook French toast, beating up the eggs and making a frothy batter, then dipping in the slices of bread before frying them in butter.

'It's called ready steady heartburn,' she said, smiling.

'Ah, but not if you also eat mounds of fruit. I chop up loads and stick them in a plastic bag, so you don't have to bother with all the peeling and chopping. That's what you need, by the way – a chopping board.'

Anna gestured to one of the drawers. 'There's one in there, I think.'

'Ah, I'll know for next time.' He stood behind her and wrapped his arms around her. 'I'm going to get off. I want to go back home and get a change of clothes. Maybe see you after work tonight?'

She smiled and nodded. 'Let's see how it goes.'

'I'll call you later.' He kissed her again and was about to leave when he paused in the doorway. 'Is there something you want to tell me?'

'Me? No. Why do you ask?'

'Just a feeling I get. Do you not want me to call you?'

'Yes, of course I do.' She turned away, not wanting to discuss arrangements for the evening.

'Okay, I'm off.'

She heard him whistling as he let himself out and felt guilty, so much so that she was almost about to hurry after him, but then she saw the greasy frying pan and grill, and the dirty dishes stacked in the sink. He was even more untidy in the kitchen than Langton had been.

She banged the frying pan down and swore – she was thinking about Langton again. She washed up with a fury until the kitchen was spic and span, then returned to the bedroom. Yet again Langton crossed her mind: the bed was unmade and wet towels from Pete's shower were left strewn over the floor. By the time she had tidied up, she was going to have to get her skates on so as not to be late for work.

Langton had put the pressure on. Warrants were to be issued for a search of Julia Brandon's house and her sister Honour's farm. In the meantime, surveillance teams had been organised for both properties and were already in position – hopefully, this time, far more covert in Julia's case; they really didn't want another terse visit from her lawyer, Simon Fagan. Anna had no sooner sat at her desk when Cunningham called to say she would like a few words.

Anna could feel the tension as soon as she entered Cunningham's office.

'Langton's breathing down my neck,' the DCI said. 'We really need to cover some of his suggestions. First up is the need to get more details on the drug squat. As you know, we're still unable to find out who was running the place; all we have succeeded in doing to date is tracking down people trying to score. I want you to see what you can dig up, even if it means going back to all the people you interviewed. One of them has to know.'

Anna shrugged. 'I doubt if anyone I questioned will be of much use. They weren't regulars and usually scored through Donny Petrozzo—'

Cunningham interrupted her. 'That's Paul Wrexler and Mark Taylor, correct?'

'Yes; there was also Eddie Court.'

'Right, go back and see if they withheld anything.'

'Do you also want me to go back and talk to Jeremy Webster, the boy who gave us all the details on the vehicles we've been tracing?'

'If you think it will be productive, yes.'

Anna waited a moment and then stood up. She had the distinct feeling that she was being sidelined; she would have preferred to have been privy to the surveillance and house searches, but when she asked about them, Cunningham was tetchy.

'Langton doesn't want us to go in yet, just monitor what they're up to as we try and firm up the loose ends. Phil is co-ordinating that side, and the rest of us are trying to get confirmation from passport and immigration of all the false passports and aliases we know were used by Alexander Fitzpatrick. If we can get verification that he has been in the UK, then we act on that, but it is still only supposition.'

'You don't think the longer we leave putting pressure

on Julia and her sister means the more time they have to get him out of the country? Because I am sure that he is behind all this.'

'I know you are, Travis, I heard you last night, but we have to have proof, otherwise we are running around like headless chickens. Our priority is to find out who killed Frank Brandon, then I think it could all fall into place.'

'Like a pack of cards,' Anna said, unable to hide her sarcasm. She returned to her office, where Gordon was waiting.

'The team are picking up where I left off, trying to track down the last guy that rented the boat *Dare Devil*,' he told her. 'They are also checking into the possibility that it might have been sold a few years ago. I got ear damage from the hours I was on the phone.'

'So, you're with me today, are you?'

'Yes – back to the Chalk Farm estate, right?'

Anna sighed and picked up her briefcase. 'Can you get me the lists of vehicles that Jeremy Webster recounted, as we'll also need to talk to him again.'

Gordon rolled his eyes. 'Okay, but we've pretty well covered every listed vehicle, and traced the owner drivers.'

'I am aware of that, Gordon, but maybe, just maybe there's more to get out of him!'

Anna had just left the station when Phil got a call from Langton. Digging back into Fitzpatrick's past, he had discovered a previous arrest – for drunk driving – whilst he was at university. He had been charged, fined and given a suspended sentence. Langton wanted them to see whether the Oxfordshire police might have retained on file Fitzpatrick's fingerprints. If that was unsuccessful, they were to contact the US and see if the police there had anything that might assist in identifying their man. They still had unidentified fingerprints taken from the Mitsubishi: a part bloody thumbprint, and a smear of blood with a part-palmprint.

The team were taken aback at how fast Langton was moving, firing off instructions and demanding results fast. Because of the pressure, they had already arranged the surveillances and warrants; he had also requested they talk to Julia's lawyer regarding the two men seen in Wimbledon, and yet again question her financial adviser. Cunningham was handling the pressure, but appeared edgy. Phil was aware that she seemed to be sidelining Anna on yet another wild-goose chase over at the Warren Estate. He had even hinted that, with so much going on, they needed her, but got the sharp response that Travis was going to have to buckle down and work with the team. She was too close to Langton and she didn't need any one of them telling tales! The fact that Anna Travis, whether working solo or not, had brought in major results, Phil declined to mention. If the two women were in competition, then he would let them get on with it.

The estate was looking even more wretched. The rain was lashing down and, as Anna parked up, she could see that even more flats had been boarded up. Whether or not the flapping police cordons had put off any fresh drug dealers, the place still had a desolate feel. Deep puddles formed across the parking area, rubbish had been left out in black bin liners and dogs or cats, or maybe vermin, had been ripping them up, so garbage was strewn everywhere.

Anna hopped over the puddles with her umbrella towards Mrs Webster's flat. Gordon followed, holding his raincoat over his head. Mrs Webster's immaculate stone step and front door stood out amongst the other flats. She was very hesitant about letting them come inside, as they were both dripping from the rain. Jeremy was at work. Anna spent a few moments talking on the doorstep with Mrs Webster before she and Gordon returned to her car and drove to Waitrose.

They took a parking ticket for the Waitrose car park and drove over to the allocated parking bays. The rain was still pouring as they looked for Jeremy. There was a long line of gathered trolleys left by a wall, but no sign of him. No wonder, Anna said. He was probably taking shelter inside. Then, just as she was about to get out of the car, she saw him.

He was entering from the exit gate, pushing five trolleys that had been left outside the car park. He was wearing a draped green plastic cape, the hood drawn up, almost hiding his face, and shiny black rubber overshoes, as he plodded through the puddles. Anna told Gordon to approach him and ask if they could talk to him for a few moments. She watched as Gordon hurried over to Jeremy; he didn't appear to even acknowledge him, but continued pushing his row of trolleys, collecting two more.

Gordon returned to the car, and got in beside Anna. 'Well, he's a hard one to have a conversation with. He said he was working and couldn't talk to me, or anyone else.'

'Go and speak to the manager; see if they have a staff room we can use.'

Gordon sighed. 'Okay.'

She watched him trudge back across the car park and go into the store itself. He was gone for over ten minutes but then reappeared with a large blonde woman, who went to talk to Jeremy while Gordon came back to Anna. 'They've got a staff room at the rear of the store; we can use that. She'll give him an early tea break – she said he won't go in there unless it's for his tea break.'

The manageress led them through the aisles towards the staff quarters. Two assistants were having coffee when they entered; the manageress said they could finish their break in her office.

Jeremy walked in and gave the two assistants a beaming smile. 'Hello, Pauline.'

'Hello, Jay.'

'Hello, Carol.'

'Hi, Jay. Bit wet out there for you today.'

He looked genuinely pleased to see the two women; then his face became stern as he carefully removed his wet cloak. He took it to a peg, hung it up and then removed his rubber overshoes. Anna was sitting at one of the tables, Gordon standing. Jeremy crossed to the small kitchen area, and took a mug with his name on it. He checked it was clean, and then took an age to measure sugar, milk and use the tea urn. He still had not even glanced at Anna; he passed Gordon to place his mug down on another table. He took out from his pocket a packet of disinfectant wipes to clean the table, but only the area he was going to use. He then placed down his mug, walked to a rubbish bin and deposited his wipe.

'Mr Webster,' Anna said quietly. He ignored her, as he took out a small plastic container and placed it next to his mug. He sat down and carefully opened it to re-move two biscuits, which he set down side by side. 'Mr

Webster, we met when I came to see you at your home.'

Jeremy nodded and bit into one of his biscuits. 'I am on my tea break.'

'I really need to talk to you, and you were very helpful.'

He didn't look at her, chewing with a studied look on his face.

'It's about the lists of cars you provided for our investigation.'

He sipped his tea.

'We've been able to trace almost all of them. You really did a great job. If you don't mind, I would just like to check over a couple of things.'

Gordon glanced at Anna; she could have been talking to the wall. Jeremy finished his second biscuit, carefully picking up the crumbs, then he sipped his tea. Anna had to sit patiently as he washed up his mug, placed it back on the hook and washed his hands.

She tried again. 'The manageress said that we could have a few moments to talk to you.'

He still did not make eye-contact. Instead he took a deep breath, sighing and staring at the floor. 'What do you want?'

Anna tried to explain as quickly as possible the reason she was there, and how much she appreciated him talking to her and helping their enquiry. She took out the list of car number-plates he had passed on to her, and asked if there were any more, or anything he could tell her about the vehicles.

'They were illegally parked,' he said.

'Yes, I know.'

'They are not from the estate; they do not have parking permits.'

'Yes, we know that.' Anna had highlighted the

vehicles where she had interviewed the owners. 'Is there anything else you could help me with?'

He didn't want to handle the piece of paper, so she laid it flat on the table.

'I mean, maybe you saw the cars there more than one time?'

Jeremy glanced down and stared at the rows of numbers. He then lifted his left hand, pulled back the sleeve of his sweater to look at a large watch, then pulled his sleeve back and straightened it.

'You see, Mr Webster, we have not as yet been able to identify the people using the flat to sell drugs.'

He walked back to his rain cape and shook it out. He stepped into his rubbers like a dancer. Anna glanced at Gordon and rolled her eyes.

'Can I help you with that?' Gordon said, with his hands out towards the cape.

Jeremy swished it aside like a bullfighter. 'No.'

The sheet of paper fluttered to the floor. Jeremy stepped forwards to pick it up. Anna thought he was going to put it into the bin, but he replaced it onto the table and returned to fastening his rain cape.

He didn't actually point; it was more an odd jerk up and down of his right index finger. '621 APS,' he said, as he pulled up his hood.

Anna looked to Gordon, trying to check which of the rows of numbers he was referring to. Then he repeated the date, time, and month in numbers only, and repeated the time – 8.07 – then he turned and swung open the door, walking out.

'Shit! Which car – did you get the number?' Gordon said.

Anna glanced down the paper. 'Here you go – 621

APS . . . Eddie Court, our witness for the tall man in the smart shoes in the Mitsubishi.'

'He also identified Frank Brandon,' Gordon said.

'Right; he admitted to being at the squat late that night, but Jeremy just stated that earlier time of seven minutes past eight.'

'Well, if you can trust what he says,' Gordon scoffed.

'He came up with all these, didn't he?'

'Yeah, I know.'

'If Jeremy's correct, that little bastard was lying: he went to the squat twice in one night.'

Jeremy was back pushing the trolleys, all neat and perfectly lined up, staring ahead as his eyes caught sight of a stray trolley a few yards across the car park. Anna smiled and waved, but his brilliant blue eyes gave no hint of recognition as he herded them back for the shoppers to use.

'He's got to be bloody fit to handle them – they're heavy,' Gordon commented.

Anna said nothing, angry that Eddie Court had lied to her. On the night Frank Brandon died, he had scored drugs from the squat. Had he also lied about how much he had actually seen?

'You okay?' Gordon asked, as they waited by the barrier.

'I am going to look like a right idiot if this pans out. I'd like to get that bloody Eddie Court and wring his neck.' She flashed her ID card to the man inside the booth, and he lifted the barrier.

Eddie had moved out of his mother's place and was sharing a basement flat in Maida Vale. His mother said that he didn't have a mobile, which Anna didn't believe, and he no longer had his old Mini. The basement had a steep staircase going down from the pavement, with big iron railings and a cast-iron gate. The door was quite modern, in varnished pine, with a stained-glass insert held together by white Band-Aids.

They rang the bell to the flat but could hear no sound, so banged on the door. Still no response. They looked through the windows but could see little other than grey dirty nets and some kind of heavy curtain. Anna banged with the flat of her hand; Gordon tapped her arm to listen. Then locks were being moved, one at the top of the door and one near the bottom. The latch drew back, and the door inched open. There stood a girl with dyed black hair; her face was a pasty white, with thick black mascara and eyeliner making her look like a badger.

'Eddie Court – in, is he, love?'

She screwed up her eyes as if trying to focus. Anna showed her ID, and gave her name and Gordon's.

The girl didn't seem that concerned. 'What do you want?'

'To talk to Eddie; is he in?'

'Is he the DJ?'

'Yeah, that's right. Can we come in?'

The girl stepped back, wrapping her robe around herself. She was bare-footed, and obviously suffering from a hangover.

'Which room is he in?'

'Back room, I think – straight through, past the kitchen.'

'Thank you. What's your name, love?'

'Megan Phillips. I live in the front room, with my boyfriend. It's his place, but he's out.'

'Megan, can you go back to your room, please? I'll knock on the door if I need to talk to you.'

There was an overpowering smell in the place – a mixture of mildew, joss sticks and body odour. The kitchen was filthy, with dirty pots and pans and cutlery and leftover takeaway cartons. A bin spewed out stale food; even the lino seemed to have a film of grease.

'Ugh,' Gordon said, pulling a face.

The end door had a large poster of Alice Cooper pinned to it; the wall beside it was covered in names and phone numbers. A pair of old Wellington boots lay tossed in the corner, alongside a broken umbrella and a Hoover with a split bag. Anna banged on the door and waited. Gordon tried the doorknob, and it turned; a safety chain hung loose. He pushed it open wider, but it was hard to see anything. The walls were a dark blue; there was a blue, threadbare carpet, but this could hardly be seen for the mounds of dirty clothes: jeans, shirts, shoes, sneakers, cowboy boots, smelly socks and vests. The room was a pigsty and the smell disgusting.

Anna eased her way further into the room; there was a chink of light coming from the drawn curtains. The bed was a mound of old blankets and a stained orange duvet. Anna looked over the room, then gestured for Gordon to cross to the bed. She lifted the duvet and then both of them pulled it back. Curled in a ball, wearing socks, underpants and a torn T-shirt was a comatose Eddie Court. He didn't wake, even when they pulled the curtains back. The light streamed in as best it could through the dirty windows, but still he remained curled up.

'Is he dead?' Gordon whispered.

'No, I think he's sleeping one off though.' She nudged

the bed. It was astonishing: they banged the bed and shook him but he remained out of it.

Gordon was becoming freaked out that he might have overdosed. 'Come on, Eddie, wake up!' he said loudly.

Anna turned as there was a loud blast of the Muppets' theme tune. It came from a dirty pair of jeans by her feet. Somehow this got a reaction. Eddie gave a low moan and grunted. Totally unaware that Anna and Gordon were in the room, he flopped over the side of the bed and reached, with shaking hands, to his dirty jeans.

'It's probably your mother,' Anna said, snatching the jeans away.

Eddie flopped back and squinted at the light coming in from the window. 'Fucking hell, what's going on?'

'Just need to ask you a few questions.'

Anna sent Gordon out to get some coffee, while Eddie went into the bathroom. There was broken frosted glass set into the door, so Anna could see Eddie's shadow as he tried to wake himself up. There was no possibility he could make it out of the window as there were bars across it. She gave him five minutes before she rapped on the door for him to come out. He had dragged on a pair of jeans; at least he was more awake.

'Get out of it last night, did you?' Anna said, following him back into the disgusting bedroom.

'Yeah, smashed.' He flung himself back on the bed, rubbing his hair.

'Okay, we have a few minutes before Detective Constable Loach comes back.'

'He gettin' me some coffee?'

'Yes, but that's a plus for you – I wanted a few words with you alone. If you give me what I want, then we won't take you in.'

'For doing what?'

'Lying, withholding evidence – you can get into big trouble for that.'

'I never done nothing.'

She moved closer. 'Don't play any more games, Eddie. I want the truth this time.'

'About what?'

'The night you went to visit the drug dealers in Chalk Farm.'

'I told you, I never went in.'

'Not the second time you were there; that was when you were able to identify this man.' She showed him the photograph of Frank Brandon. 'But you went to the same place earlier that night, didn't you?'

'No.'

'Eddie, we know that you did. Now, I am not interested in what you scored – I just want the name of the dealer.'

Eddie closed his eyes, shaking his head.

'It's up to you, Eddie. Give up who was dealing or you'll be arrested.'

'I can't.'

'Yes, you can.'

'If it ever got out, I'd be fucking dead meat.'

'Oh, so you do know?'

'I never said that!'

'Give me the name, Eddie. It doesn't mean they'll know it came from you. Any more lies and I will lose my patience.'

'They don't deal from there no more.'

'Yes, I know that. The place was closed down.'

'You'll look out for me?'

'Yes.'

Eddie chewed his lips. A cold sore on his upper lip started to bleed. He used a corner of his filthy sheet to dab at it. 'I only ever seen one of 'em – since, that's Delroy Planter.'

Anna jotted the name down; it wasn't one she knew. She looked up as Eddie still messed with his lip. 'The second?'

'He's a mean bastard but, like I said, I've not seen him since. It was a bloke called Silas Roach.'

Anna pressed for descriptions of both men. Eddie shrugged and muttered, but eventually gave Anna some idea what the men looked like. Both, Eddie thought, were Jamaican. The front doorbell rang and it made them both jump.

Gordon had left the door on the latch and was already heading down the dingy corridor with coffees. Anna asked for the address where she could find the dealers. Eddie muttered and moaned, but gave it up, as Gordon held out his coffee.

'Okay, Eddie. If this doesn't add up, we will be back.'

Anna ran both names by Sam Power. He had no record of either of the men, and no information on the squat they were now using to deal from. The address was in Kensal Rise, not that far from Chalk Farm, nor from Maida Vale; it hung between the two. Sam knew the area well, as they had busted a row of shops there two years previously. They had swooped on two hairdressing salons and a grocery store, and made over twenty-two arrests, including runners, delivery boys and girls, customers trying to score. The stash of drugs was impressive, from heroin to crack cocaine, hash and marijuana. It was a well-publicised raid and the row of shops had since been closed and boarded up. Sam was surprised that the two dealers would be either stupid or audacious enough to operate from there again.

'Two years ago? Maybe the businesses have reopened.'

'Yeah, in more ways than one.'

Sam suggested they take it quietly. He and Anna should first stake out the area, as neither knew what their suspects looked like, apart from Eddie's descriptions. Silas Roach had dreadlocks and always wore a multi-coloured, knitted bobble hat, whereas Delroy Planter, 'the muscleman', was lighter-skinned and often wore a leather jacket and trousers.

Anna and Sam, with two other members of the Drug Squad, went to Kensal Rise. They used a dental practice overlooking the semicircle of shops to set up their surveillance. Three were still boarded up, but the central one was now a café with a board outside, advertising all-day breakfasts. Sam still had all the maps of the previous bust, so they could ascertain the ways in and out of the premises. The other building to have reopened was a hair salon operating specifically for ethnic customers, hair and nail extensions. However, the flat above still had boards across the windows.

Sam used binoculars to check over both the properties from the window in the dental surgery. He handed them to Anna. 'There's our man now, outside the café.'

Their undercover officer was a short skinny black guy, wearing dirty jeans, trainers and a cap pulled down low over his face. He appeared to be in deep conversation with a very young black boy who was wheeling his bike around him. There were a number of kids with bikes, both male and female, who entered the café, came out and went into the new hair salon.

'They should be in school,' Anna said.

'Yeah, but they'll be earning a lot of cash, running the drugs back and forth.' Sam straightened up as a BMW drew up and out got a massive guy with a muscular body and bald shaved head. 'I'd say that's your Delroy.'

Anna drew up a chair to sit beside Sam at the window.

'Second target just driven up in the Mercedes. From the description, that's got to be Silas Roach.' Anna passed the binoculars back to Sam. They watched as the two men conferred on the pavement, and then strolled into the café, shortly followed by the undercover Drug Squad officer.

They maintained surveillance for over two more hours until Sam received a call from his officer and left the building. Anna stayed at the window, watching, her nerves at breaking-point; she couldn't understand why they didn't simply arrest the pair. There was also something very uncomfortable about remaining closeted in the small dental surgery with its central leather chair and tray of dental equipment.

Sam eventually returned. 'Okay, they're dealing from a back room in the café. It's got a bolted door and access over the yard into the hair salon – I'd say for a quick getaway if needed. There's a fire escape, with another possible exit route. Both cars are registered to different names than our targets, plus addresses we're checking out.'

'When are you going to make an arrest?' Anna asked.

'Not for a while; we want them dealing. Apparently they are waiting on a drop – our man was told to come back in an hour. Right now, they are sitting down to a full breakfast!'

'But we know they were dealing from the Chalk Farm estate.'

'So your informant says, but we've got no prints that match any records. These two are clean and maybe very mean, according to our man. He reckons they have weapons, and they've got heavies inside as well. I'll need back-up and, if we get them, handling gear. It's going to make interviewing them a lot easier if we have something to deal with, if you'll excuse the pun.'

Anna nodded and looked at her watch. It was after two. Putting in a call to the station, she was told that most of the team were out, but Gordon was there. They had a development with the boat, *Dare Devil*, he told her. It had been sold more than eight years ago and was now registered to a charter company working out of Malta. The same charter company had also rented it out to Carlo Simonetti, who was a legitimate businessman. The company had bought the boat when it had been anchored in Cannes, and still did charters there for the film festivals. They had no record of Alexander Fitzpatrick using it; the sale had gone through with a man named Stephen Anderson. This was possibly another alias used by Fitzpatrick, as they had so far been unable to trace him, and as yet had no luck from passport and immigration.

Anna was frustrated. They had no details on the surveillance of either Julia Brandon or the Oxfordshire farm, but a trace had been put on the Range Rover driven by the two men that Anna had seen at the Old Windmill talking to Julia Brandon and her solicitor. They were possibly ex-Army – or Marines, as the Range Rover was registered to a mercenary agency. As yet the police had not had confirmation of either of the men's names as the company just had a box number – but they were being checked out.

Cunningham had interviewed Simon Fagan, who was still accusing the police of harassing his client. He said that he had instigated the hiring of the men to protect Mrs Brandon from unnecessary invasion of privacy. Cunningham believed he was unaware of any further surveillance now operating. That was about it; in other words, nothing had really moved forwards.

Anna wondered if Simon Fagan could have an ulterior motive for his championing of Julia Brandon, either financial or sexual. She went for the latter. She asked if there was any more information from Rushton, and was taken aback to be told that Langton was handling the next interview.

It was almost four when Sam was confident that they should move in. He had two wagons with drug and weapon sniffer dogs, and had orchestrated the entire bust along the same lines as the massive one two years previously. He was still astonished that the two targets had brazenly taken over the café and hair salon, knowing they had been the focus of a previous drug bust. It was either arrogance or stupidity, or gross misjudgement and inexperience.

Anna said nothing. If these two men also worked out of the Chalk Farm drug squat, then that was how they operated – taking over rundown properties. From their luxury cars, they were obviously making money hand over fist. Could one of them be the killer of Frank Brandon?

Sam turned to her, adjusting his earpiece. 'Okay, it's going down. It makes it a lot easier in broad daylight.'

Anna stood up, but he gestured for her to remain sitting.

'Watch from here! I don't want you in the thick of it. Let me do my job.'

Anna frowned. The hours she had been hanging out there, and now she was told she wouldn't be in on the arrest! It really infuriated her, but there was nothing she could say.

The two police people-carriers suddenly drove up and moved into position, blocking off the road exits at either end. At the same time, armed officers moved in from the front and rear of the building.

Anna stared from the high window as the suspects came out with their hands on their heads. A few women were screeching and shouting abuse, as they had been removed from beneath the dryers. The hairdressers, wearing bright pink overalls, were also shouting and yelling as they were led out. They formed two lines along the pavement as the officers with the dogs held back the yapping, barking animals. The young kids were herded out and lined up; next came two mean-looking men with muscles and black shirts and trousers, struggling as they were cuffed. It was like a bizarre Noah's Ark, with people being brought out two by two.

The last out were their two targets, Delroy Planter and Silas Roach. Both men were handcuffed to heavyweight officers and forced to stand facing the wall. The sniffer dogs were then released inside both the café and the hair salon. The weapon sniffer dog weaved in and out of the lines of men and women. It was extraordinary to watch; if the dog picked up the scent of a weapon on someone, it sat down in front of them. The dogs were switched every fifteen minutes to keep their sense of smell clear.

Whilst weapons were being recovered this way, from flick-knives to machetes to small-calibre pistols, armed officers with large boxes were removing a further array of weapons from the café. Then came the uniformed officers, ready to remove the men and woman, take down statements, and generally pave the way for clearing the area. They took the first load away as Delroy and Silas remained facing the wall.

When Sam rejoined Anna, he was grinning, and looked elated. 'Well, our guys are something else! They both claim they were at the café to just score a bit of hash. Not illegal, and for medicinal purposes only!'

Anna smiled, but became serious as Sam held up a plastic bag containing a large silver Glock pistol. 'Where did you find it?'

'In the café. In fact, Silas Roach tried to reach for it, then acted all innocent as if he didn't even know it was there!'

Anna looked out of the window just as Silas Roach was being turned from facing the wall. He had both wrists cuffed, and kicked out as the weapon dog barked and sat in front of him. She could feel her adrenalin pumping. Might she be looking at the man who had shot Frank Brandon? If she was, he'd also shot the man standing behind him. Would he be able to identify Alexander Fitzpatrick?

Chapter Sixteen

The incident room was filled to bursting as the team received the update. Anna and Gordon were now waiting for their turn to interview Silas Roach and Delroy Planter, who had both been charged with dealing and possession of class A drugs – heroin and cocaine, and a large quantity of hashish and marijuana. A bulk of hash had been discovered hidden in one of the old-fashioned hair-dryers.

Roach and Planter were in real trouble, as the kids were so terrified that they talked freely; some were as young as eleven. A few girls who were legitimate hair-dressers also spilled the beans. The non-talkers were their heavies and six Jamaican servers, who were the guys who would pass the gear and take the money to Delroy and Silas. Three were illegal immigrants; the other three had records for drug offences and burglary. Also dis-covered was a considerable amount of cash in a suitcase, with lists of numerous names and addresses.

It would take hours to process the offences against the dealers. It was imperative for the Murder Squad to question the two men with reference to their case, but the Drug Unit were not prepared to release them into their custody until they were sure they had charges against them. Cunningham was furious, and eventually had to get Langton to secure the release of the two suspects into their custody. They were to be delivered the following morning and held in the cells at the station until they had finished being interrogated. They would then be returned to the Drug Squad to complete their charges.

By this time, it was after nine o'clock. Cunningham called it quits for the night but wanted the team back early the following morning. Anna wrote up her reports and did not get home until after ten-thirty. It had been a long but productive day. Already the two suspects' fingerprints were being matched with those from the drug squat, and they would have verification of any hoped-for match by the following morning. Suddenly the case was starting to move – yet again down to Anna's diligence, in re-questioning Jeremy Webster and Eddie Court.

The next morning, however, Cunningham reprimanded her for not gaining the two dealers' names from Eddie Court in her initial interview. If she had done so, it would have taken the case forwards far more quickly. This time, Anna stood her ground and, trying hard to retain her composure, said that it was her initial interview with Jeremy Webster that had steered the case. If it had not been for him, they would not even have had the link to Eddie Court.

'Well, I want the little bastard brought in and charged for withholding evidence. I am not satisfied.'

'I did give him my word that if he gave me information, he would not be prosecuted,' Anna said angrily.

'That was not your prerogative. Bring him in.'

Anna gritted her teeth. She wanted to be privy to the

interviews with Delroy Planter and Silas Roach, however, so kept her temper. It was still only eight-thirty, and they had not as yet been brought over to the station. Both suspects were to be taken before a magistrate to answer the drugs charges; there was no hope of either being granted bail. Anna gave instructions for Gordon and two officers to bring in Eddie Court. They wanted a statement from him saying that he had scored from both the men, and that they were in the Chalk Farm squat the night of Frank Brandon's murder. This was confirmed at ten o'clock. They now had a match with their prints from those taken from the squat.

There was a buzz as the two suspects were delivered at eleven-fifteen. They were taken to separate cells while their solicitors met with Cunningham. They would be questioned separately. Both were informed that there was strong evidence that one of them had committed a murder. Fingerprints on the Glock automatic were confirmed as belonging to Delroy Planter; ballistics had already confirmed that the weapon was the one used to kill Frank Brandon. This detail brought the incident-room tension up a notch. Everyone was eager to know the outcome of the forthcoming interrogation.

Only Anna was doubtful that Delroy was the shooter. He was such a big man. Frank Brandon had been shot through the drug-squat door; the two bullets had entered his chest at an upward slant. When she mentioned this to Phil, he dismissed it sarcastically, suggesting that the bastard could have been sitting down – or that maybe they should look for a dwarf, because Brandon had also been shot whilst he lay on the floor! Like Cunningham, he also brought up the fact that she had questioned Eddie Court days ago.

His attitude infuriated Anna. 'Well, at least I proved that Mr Webster was of value!'

Phil shrugged. They had, he murmured, wasted hours of time tracking down the vehicles listed by Jeremy Webster. Anna gave up. There was no way Phil was going to give her credit for anything she had done, but she didn't have a row with him, remembering Langton's warning about getting along with the team, especially Phil.

It was not until twelve-thirty that Cunningham gave the team the line-up for the interviews. She would take Delroy Planter into interview room one, and Anna was to interview Silas Roach in room two. Cunningham had Phil with her, and Anna was with Gordon. Both suspects would have their solicitors present: Elwyn Jones was representing Planter and Margery Patterson was acting for Roach.

Silas Roach had overpowering body odour. He was still wearing his knitted hat, and had not had any change of clothing since his arrest. He was belligerent and totally unco-operative, repeatedly sucking his teeth and kicking against the table leg. Anna read him his rights, but he wasn't listening. Patterson was trying her best to make him pay attention, but he didn't seem interested; he kept on saying that he had been set up and was not going to say anything else. He had never been at the Chalk Farm estate and his arrest the previous day was a frame-up. He was at the café having a cup of coffee.

Anna let him rant on as she took out her notebook and files. 'Mr Roach, we have confirmation that your prints were found at number nineteen in the Warren Estate. We also have a witness to your presence on the night of the murder.' Anna showed the photographs of Frank Brandon.

Roach was pushing his chair back and clearing his throat as if he was going to spit on the floor in front of him. 'Fucking lies, fucking lies.'

Anna tried to maintain her calm as she ploughed on, bringing out more photographs from ballistics showing the bullets and saying that they now had verification that the weapon used was the one Roach had in his possession; since it also had his prints on it, they were certain he had been the man who pulled the trigger and killed Frank Brandon.

'I fucking didn't, I was never fucking there. It's a fucking set-up.'

Cunningham was having a similar session with Delroy Planter. He had constantly refused to answer any questions, saying nothing but, 'No comment.' He denied ever using the Warren Estate to sell drugs; even when told they had witnesses, he still denied it. He also denied that he was dealing drugs from the café and said that, like Roach, he was only there for a coffee.

'Mr Planter, we are not interviewing you about the drug raid. This is an entirely different case. You are here to answer questions regarding the murder of an ex-police officer, Frank Brandon.'

Phil took over and, like Anna, he showed the mortuary pictures and the murder site. He got the same denial. It was at this point that the interview-room door banged open, and James Langton barged in.

Whilst Cunningham explained into the tape that he had now joined the interview, Langton banged his fist down on the desk.

'Take a good look, Delroy. He was a police officer; he

was also my friend. You'll get time for this and your life won't be worth living, I'll make sure of it. Start talking – you got five minutes before we charge you with his murder. Your prints are all over the fucking weapon, and we have a witness who says you fired the shots. Don't think your pal next door isn't going to save his own skin.'

Langton dragged over a chair and sat opposite Delroy. Elwyn Jones, Delroy's solicitor, asked about the evidence. Langton glared at him. 'Take a look.' He swiped at the papers on the table.

'I am advising my client not to answer any further questions until I am satisfied.'

'I am not wasting any more time,' Langton said. 'You can play out the "No comment" game but, like I said, we have a witness. You are being charged with the murder of Frank Brandon.'

'I never fucking shot him, man! It wasn't me!'

Langton leaned over the desk. 'Then tell us who it was. You help us, Delroy, and we can give you a break, a big one.'

Delroy shook his head, sighing.

Anna was not having any luck with Silas Roach. He still maintained that he was never at Chalk Farm and that he had never met Frank Brandon. No matter what angle Anna tried with him, he was dismissive and becoming more and more abusive. Langton again banged into the interview room, wafting sheets of paper.

As Anna reported his entrance into the tape, Langton leaned close to Roach. 'Your pal has just put you right in it. You want to read his statement? You fired the Glock automatic into Frank Brandon's body, you then opened the door and stood over him, firing three more shots into his head and face.'

Patterson demanded to see the paperwork and to have a discussion with her client. Langton dragged up a chair and banged it down. Gordon got up and stood against the wall, as Anna gave Langton more room at the table. He was as she remembered him: loud and brash, leering into Silas's face as he listed the charges they were going to slap on him. 'You fucking shot a police officer, Silas. He was a friend of mine, and I can guarantee it'll be twenty years.'

Suddenly Silas stopped his bragging; he hung his head and stared at the floor.

'Start talking, sunshine, because we are not fucking around any more. Selling dope to a few street kids is nothing compared to what we are wrapping around your neck. Your pal next door doesn't want to get blamed for what you did. You opened fire, straight through the door. You never gave Frank Brandon a chance, did you? *Did you?*'

Anna glanced at the documents brought in by Langton: they were old statements, including an office memo about cleaning up coffee cups after a briefing! No matter how much Silas's solicitor tried to halt the interview, she was ignored. Langton did his leaving act, pushing back his chair and rising. It was at this point that Silas Roach started talking.

They could have heard a pin drop as Silas, still with his head bowed, staring at the floor, explained his part in the murder of Frank Brandon. He swore that he did not use the Glock; he said it was a man called Donny Petrozzo. Piece by piece, he recalled what had taken place. Donny, who was well-known to both him and Delroy, had told them about a package he had got; he said it contained drugs worth millions and he wanted them to deal the gear and cut him a big slice. The only problem was that he didn't know what the stuff was, and had to ask around.

Silas was asked if the drug package contained Fentanyl. He hesitated, unsure even now what the stuff was called. Delroy had made enquiries and been told it was a very powerful opiate. Donny had turned up at the squat to discuss where and how they would deal. He was very hyper, and Delroy was uncertain about dealing with him, as he refused to explain where he had obtained it from. Donny said he had tried it out, that it was mind-blowing; they all reckoned he was still high on the stuff, as he was acting so crazy. The three of them were arguing about it when there was a rap on the door. A henchman slid open the small caged opening and Donny had gone crazy. He had grabbed his pistol, pushed his way to the door and opened fire.

'He just shot through the fucking door! It was mayhem; we was all trying to get the gun off him, and he was screaming and shouting. Then he picks up the silencer, kicks open the door and starts shooting again. I grabbed him and I got me gun back – it's a fucking Glock, right? And he was spitting and screeching and there is this dead geezer on the floor.'

Anna leaned forwards. 'What about the man with him?'

'What?'

'There was someone else with Frank Brandon – did you see him?'

'No, but Donny did a runner, and Delroy says we had all better fuck off out of there. That's the God's honest truth; there was blood and fucking brains spattered all over the place. I got out through the window.'

Cunningham and Phil were just finishing taking Delroy's statement. His story was very close to Silas's: Donny Petrozzo, high on drugs, had been at the squat, wanting to get them to deal and cut him in. The next minute, Donny picked up the gun and opened fire; they had all been freaked. Delroy had stood over the dead man, even tried to find out if he was from the Drug Squad, then, certain the scream would go up, he had run. As far as Delroy knew, Petrozzo had escaped; he had even tried to contact him, but couldn't get any answer on his mobile. He had decided that it was best to keep well away from him.

When Phil asked about the package, Delroy said that, as far as he could remember, it was still in Donny's possession. He wasn't interested in it, as it was some drug he didn't know about. All he was certain of was that Donny had got away. He was also unable to recall the man who had accompanied Frank.

At the next briefing, Langton sifted through both men's statements. He was of a mind that they had both told the truth. The series of gunshots also confirmed what Mrs Webster had said: first the loud bangs, and then pop, pop, pop, after Donny had fixed the silencer to the weapon. The question was whether Donny had taken the package with him when he escaped, or had he not brought it to the squat in the first place? Langton believed he had had it with him, and had done a runner carrying it.

They were still no closer to identifying the tall man

accompanying Frank Brandon. They were also trying to fathom out why Frank Brandon, who worked for Donny as a chauffeur, and therefore would have known him well, was shot. Anna interjected that, although they knew that Frank did work for Donny, at some point he became employed by Julia Brandon; it could have been that Donny had not seen him for some time. The shots were fired upwards. Donny was short, maybe he wasn't aiming at Frank but the man behind him? Langton shook his head. Donny had pumped more shots into Frank, making sure he was dead.

Anna frowned. 'I know you believe their story, but Delroy said that he had tried to find out who Frank was. Maybe Donny just ran, then Delroy took a look at the dead man, maybe searched his pockets. Frank had his old ID card, which would scare the shit out of him, so possibly it was Delroy who fired the next shots with the silencer to make sure he was dead.'

Anna decided that she would check out the vehicles again. How had Donny got to the squat? On foot? She doubted it; they knew that Frank had driven up in the Mitsubishi. She was trying to fathom out when Frank had taken possession of the Mitsubishi that they knew was connected to Julius D'Anton and Stanley Leymore. She wanted to talk to Frank's girlfriend Connie again. She looked up: Langton was bringing up exactly what she had just queried in her mind. He was pointing to the incident board and the arrows linking the jeep to the dead men; then he moved along to ring Julia Brandon's name.

'So far, we have nothing of interest from the surveillance teams. She takes her daughters to school and picks them up, either with or without the au pair. She does grocery shopping, accompanied by the two heavies, and that's about it. We're still trying to get an ID on them from this company they work for, but we're getting no response from the box number their Range Rover's registered to. She remains at home every night; the only visitor is slimeball Simon Fagan – he has called on her three times, stayed for a few hours, and then left.' Next, he moved onto the Oxfordshire farm. Damien Nolan went to work every day at the University. Honour Nolan remained at Honey Farm or went grocery shopping on a bicycle; there had been no visitors.

Langton twisted his pen in his hands, then tossed it aside. 'Let's go through a possible scenario. Donny Petrozzo may have recognised Alexander Fitzpatrick at the airport; he could have even driven him, or was hired to drive someone else and saw him. Did he then follow him, approach him? I dunno. Next, we have Frank Brandon working for Donny. It's possible that he could have driven Fitzpatrick, or even collected something for him: the package of drugs. We do know that Donny had in his possession a package of Fentanyl – we know he died of an overdose of it; we also know that Julius D'Anton died in the same way. What we don't know is if this is what Fitzpatrick is handling, was handling, or even if he fucking features in all this! Travis is keen on the idea that he does, but we still have no evidence that confirms he is back in the UK and involved in all this mess. What we do have are four dead men who all link together; and then we have these two ladies, Julia Brandon and Honour Nolan.'

Next, he drew a line under the name Anthony Collingwood. No one had been able to trace Julia Brandon's ex-partner, nor had they had any joy with the other aliases used by Fitzpatrick; passport control were taking their time. Langton removed his jacket and tugged at his hair. For the first time, Anna noticed that he seemed to be tired and in pain. He rubbed his bad knee and asked for a chair. 'So, as we are going round in circles, I think we have to kick some ass; put some pressure on both our ladies. We use the search warrants now. I have a feeling we'll come up empty-handed, but it's about the only way we can proceed.'

Gordon went to answer a call, as Langton continued, saying that Eddie Court's statement had been taken and he had been released; he had withheld evidence, but it was too much paperwork to waste time on prosecuting him. He went on to say that they should give some kind of commendation to Jeremy Webster. Then came the breakthrough from the police station in Oxfordshire. Gordon had taken the call and returned to the incident room even more flushed in the face than usual.

Alexander Fitzpatrick had been arrested for drink driving whilst still at college. He had also been charged with disorderly conduct. The local Oxfordshire station, for some unknown reason, had retained the file dating back to the seventies. They now had a set of Alexander Fitzpatrick's fingerprints. These were on their way to the lab for testing, specifically against the blood swipe in the Mitsubishi and the part-thumb and palmprint.

Langton looked at Anna with renewed energy and smiled. 'Well, ladies and gentlemen, we will now see if DI Travis has been correct all along: that the kingpin is back in the UK. If we get a result, then the search of both women's homes is going to be very interesting.'

The day concluded with checking on the thefts of Fentanyl. There had been no report of any in the UK.

The FBI had no suspects for the thefts from the three factories in the US, but they had done a check on four properties known to have been owned by Fitzpatrick. It had taken some time, as they were buried in layers of aliases and companies. The Florida property had been repossessed by the Bank of America. The other three had also been repossessed, as recently as a year ago, due to the properties being heavily remortgaged, their leases held by a bank in Germany that had collapsed with massive debts.

Langton was keen to get more information, now privy to the fact that Fitzpatrick had lost millions when the BCCI bank had collapsed. He wondered if the man had switched to laundering money via the German bank, which like BCCI had gone belly upwards. This could be a reason for his possible return to the UK: their kingpin might be needing cash. This would coincide with Julia Brandon's release of the four million. It was possible. But they still needed confirmation that they were hunting for the right man.

Anna was in her office, preparing her reports, when she got the call from Pete. He wanted her to be the first to know. 'The part-palmprint – the one from the Mitsubishi – is no go, but the small section from one left-handed index finger is a match with the ones sent to us from Oxford. You've been right all along, Anna: that bloody guy is back in London.'

Anna wanted to yell, she was so thrilled. She banged her desk with the flat of her hand. 'Fabulous.'

'Come over later, will you?'

She doubted she could. With this new information, none of them would be released until late. She was just replacing the phone when Langton banged in and leaned over to grip her by the arms and kiss her.

347

'Fucking brilliant – we just had verification that a print matches Alexander Fitzpatrick!' She sat back in her chair as he made a big expansive gesture, grinning like a schoolboy. 'You've never let this go, have you? And you've been on the ball from day one!'

She was flushed, not just from the kiss; she was so chuffed about being proved correct.

Next to congratulate her was Phil. 'I guess I owe you an apology.' She smiled as he came to her desk and held out his hand. 'Sorry!'

'That's okay. It's certainly making this a really big case.'

He leaned closer. 'That's why Langton's hovering around. I think Cunningham could cheerfully wring his neck, but with this new development, he's going to want a slice of the kudos. They've been after this son of a bitch for over twenty years.'

'We have to find him first.'

'Yeah, Langton's arranging a dawn swoop.'

She frowned. 'What?'

'On both Julia's and Honour's homes. I'm off now. Back at the crack of dawn, so I want some sleep.' Phil walked out, hands stuffed into his pockets, whistling.

The news of this step forward had given everyone a buzz, but it irritated Anna that she had not even been told the dawn raid was going down. She was about to call Cunningham when she, like Phil, appeared in the doorway. 'Langton is over everything like a bloody rash. We have instructions to go into both women's homes at dawn.'

'That's good,' Anna said quietly.

'So which one do you want to head up?'

Anna smiled. She wanted the Oxfordshire farmhouse.

'That means you are going to have only a few hours' sleep.'

'I don't mind.'

Cunningham tapped the edge of the door with her foot. 'Good work, Travis. You've had this bee in your bonnet about Fitzpatrick from the start.'

Anna gave a rueful smile. Cunningham was about to walk out, when Anna asked if Langton was taking part in the raids. 'No. I know it looks like he's running this enquiry, but he's just overseeing it and on my back like the proverbial monkey. At least he's not poking his nose in tomorrow, so go get some sleep and I'll see you there.'

'Good night.' Anna was disappointed. She would have liked him there. She had liked him being around; he somehow spearheaded the team, and gave it the thrust and energy that Cunningham could not.

She had just packed up her briefcase when he walked in. 'You up for a drink?'

She hesitated, and then nodded.

'Good. The Huntsman – it's a pub in Hampstead by the Heath, far enough away from this mob. Do you know it?'

Anna nodded, not really certain of the address but she'd check it out.

'I'll see you there.'

'Okay, see you there.' She knew it was stupid – she knew she shouldn't have agreed – but she had been unable to stop herself. It would be just one drink, then she would have to leave; tomorrow was going to be quite a day.

The first person Anna saw as she entered the bar was Langton; he was leaning against the counter with a pint in his hand. He turned towards her and smiled. Standing beside him was Pete. Anna could have kicked herself; of course this would be his local pub! He only lived a few minutes away.

'Do you know Pete Jenkins from forensic?'

'Yes, of course.'

Pete leaned forwards to kiss her cheek. 'Hello, there. Many congratulations.'

'On the print?'

'What else? It's proof that you've been right all along. I hope the rest of the team make apologies, especially Phil,' Pete said. She felt herself blush as he slipped his arm around her shoulders. 'Let me buy you a glass of champagne,' he continued, and signalled to the barman.

'It's only a partial print, maybe not good enough to stand up in court but it was a match.' He held up his hand to indicate the small section the match had been made from.

Langton looked from her reddening face to Pete, who still had his arm casually around her shoulders.

'Did you go over to my place?' Pete asked.

'No, I just needed to talk over a few things here with Detective Superintendent Langton.' Her face was even hotter.

'Oh, right!' Pete released his arm and asked the barman for a glass of champagne. He leaned against the bar, looking at the pair of them.

'Anna and I have worked on a few cases together,' Langton said.

'I should leave you to it then.' Pete took out his wallet as if to pay, but Langton rested his hand over it.

'This is on me. You want another, Pete?'

'No, no, I'll be getting off.' He gave Anna a strange

look and then leaned forwards to kiss her neck. 'You can pop over later, if you like.'

'No, thanks. It's just one drink, then I need to get off home ready for the morning.'

Pete downed the rest of his pint as the barman appeared with her glass of champagne. 'Keep me updated,' he said, as he headed past them.

Langton passed Anna her champagne. 'Congratulations.'

'Thank you.'

Langton looked around for a place away from the noisy bar. Anna suggested they go outside, to the garden area with its chairs and tables.

'Not too cold for you?'

'No, and it's more private.'

They headed out and sat on one of the benches. It was cold, but it was also quiet.

'Listen, Anna, I know you want to be on the Oxford stakeout, but I think you might get more of a result from Julia Brandon. You've been the one interviewing her, and probably have a better relationship with her.'

'I wouldn't say I *have* a relationship with her.'

'Just one with Pete, huh?'

She sipped her champagne, looking away from him. 'That's my business.'

'I know; I was just curious. He seemed put out at my presence. He's a good guy, if he stays off the wacky tobacco.'

'What?'

'I've known him for a while; he's very good at his job, but I know he's a bit of a groover – nothing against it, unless it interferes with work. Sometimes the pressure gets to him.'

'Really?'

'Does to us all.'

'Can we talk about the case?'

He nodded.

'I don't think my having interviewed Julia is that beneficial. I would prefer to do the search of Honour and Damien Nolan's farmhouse.'

'I want you at the Wimbledon house.'

'Cunningham actually gave me the choice.'

'Well, I'm not.'

She hesitated. 'The henhouse at Honey Farm: when I was there, Honour was very keen to point out why it was locked – foxes getting to the hens, she said – but maybe there's something else inside.'

'I'm sure the lads will cover everything.'

She finished her glass of champagne.

'You want another?'

'No, I should get as much sleep as possible.'

Langton shrugged; he still had half of his pint left. 'Julia Brandon, from reports, seems very keen to get Frank's body released for burial.'

'Well, he was her husband,' Anna said.

'Maybe it's the death certificate she wants. Something just sort of niggles if, as you believe, it was a marriage of convenience.'

'Well, she does come into half a million life insurance.'

'I know.' Langton drank his beer, then placed the glass down carefully on the table. 'She's also got quite a tidy sum, right? Even though she took out four million quid?'

'Yes.'

'I wonder if this is all down to money.'

'I don't quite follow. What is?'

'The reason Fitzpatrick is back. What if he's running

out of cash? To stay on the run costs; he's lost houses all over the US, sold his boat a few years back. If he was the partner who left her all the dough – and it's looking as if this Anthony Collingwood could be Fitzpatrick – he could be putting pressure on Julia to release her cash back to him. Maybe she doesn't want to lose it.'

Anna smiled. As always, Langton was putting his finger onto the motive that had not even been brought up by the investigation. She pulled her coat around herself to keep out the chill. 'You know, the house in Wimbledon might not reveal any evidence that Fitzpatrick was there. She only moved into it about eight months ago.'

'Which would coincide with her hiring Frank Brandon.' Langton pulled at his hair. 'I need you to get the bloody timeframe ironed out. It's important we know the exact dates Frank started to work for her, and we need the date that Donny Petrozzo died. It has to have been after the murder of Frank, right?'

'Yes.'

'And Julius D'Anton died after Petrozzo?'

'Maybe. It's not been verified; they're not sure how long he was in the water. All we know is that both of them died from an overdose of Fentanyl.'

'Yes, I know that,' he said impatiently. He continued trying to co-ordinate the series of murders. If Donny had died first, then D'Anton, Stanley Leymore was shot when? They had found the Glock pistol used to kill Frank Brandon still in the possession of Delroy Planter! Therefore his statement, along with Silas Roach's, didn't add up.

Anna closed her eyes, sighing. Yet again, Langton was coming up with queries that even she had overlooked.

'Get me the co-ordination ironed out,' he said.

Anna agreed. Both dealers were still being held by the Drug Squad, so it wasn't as if they could do a runner.

Langton stood up, buttoning his jacket. 'I'm cold. We should either go back inside or . . .'

'I should get moving,' Anna said.

They walked in silence to the car park, Langton deep in thought, Anna equally so. She wasn't thinking about the case, but why he had wanted to see her alone. She got to her car and bleeped it open.

'You've moved,' he said quietly.

'Yes.'

'Where to?'

'Over by Tower Bridge.'

Langton held the car door open for her. 'Thanks for coming to see me. Sorry if I chose the wrong pub, but I'm sure you'll iron it out with Pete.'

'There is nothing to iron out,' she said tetchily.

He cocked his head to one side, stared at her, then looked at his watch. 'You'd better go. Good luck tomorrow.'

She was about to close the door when he leaned in. 'This guy Fitzpatrick is a real nasty piece of meat. Christ knows how many people he's used and abused. He'd kill anyone who stands in his way, so I'm warning you, Anna, behave yourself. No going off if you get the scent of him. Work as a team, and make sure you have back-up, understand me?'

'Yes, sir!'

'Good night.' Then he slammed her door and walked off towards his old brown Volvo.

She started the engine and reversed past him, but he didn't acknowledge her; he was talking on his mobile phone. She felt depressed. Had he really asked to meet her to warn her to behave herself? If that was the only reason, he could have told her in the office. She couldn't suppress her mixed emotions, yet he had not shown her any.

She went over everything they had discussed, first the case, then when he had asked if she had moved. She wondered if he had tried to contact her. If he had wanted to, he could have done so easily. Had he been jealous about her friendship with Pete? Just thinking about it made her feel as if she owed Pete some kind of apology. She had refused to see him that evening, saying she was working late; then he had been confronted by her with Langton.

Anna was close to where Pete lived in Hampstead so, instead of heading for home, she turned off towards his house. She thought she would just drop by and say she was sorry but, as she turned into his road, she saw Daniella, the attractive blonde girl he had introduced her to in the coffee-shop paying a taxi driver outside Pete's house. Anna had to pull over, or she would have driven past just as Pete opened his front door. Pete ushered Daniella inside, closing the door.

'Bloody men,' Anna muttered, angry that she had even felt bad about bumping into him. She felt angry the entire drive back across London to Tower Bridge. Angry with Pete, angry that Langton had asked to see her for a private drink but had made no reference to their previous time together. Then angry with herself. What was it she wanted? For him to make an approach, and try to rekindle their love affair? As her anger subsided, she felt a strange sadness. She was not going to even contemplate the fact that, deep down, she wanted Langton to give her some indication that he still cared. He had behaved merely as her superior officer. It finally dawned on her that he was never going to be anything other than that.

Chapter Seventeen

It was 4.30 a.m. when Anna drew up outside Julia Brandon's house. The surveillance team, parked some distance away, said that there had been no movement. The two heavies were inside the house. Anna gave instructions for two officers to move around to the back of the house, and two to stay beside her. Armed with search warrants, she waited for radio contact to confirm that the men were in position outside the back door. Security lights had come on: the gardens and garage were almost floodlit. Also waiting was a team of three forensic officers, parked directly outside the house. As soon as Anna gained entry, they would follow her inside. Anna pressed the doorbell, then lifted the knocker and let it bang hard five times.

Lights came on in the house; the door was opened by one of Julia's bodyguards. When shown the warrant, he backed into the hallway. Julia, in a satin nightgown, appeared on the landing, looking terrified. The children's au pair started screaming; from the nursery, Emily and Kathy started howling for their mother. Anna asked that everyone remain calm. She showed the warrant to Julia, and told her to bring the children downstairs with the au

357

pair. They were all to stay in the lounge together with the two bodyguards.

Julia screamed at Anna over and over: 'Why are you doing this to me? Why are you doing this to me? Why, why? What have I done?' She was like a needle stuck on an old 78 record; it was as if she could not stop repeating herself. Anna insisted that Julia remain with the children.

The officers were to search every drawer and cupboard, taking back to base anything that appeared to connect to the case, including possible bloodstains, fingerprints, unusual fibres. Anna was to supervise the search, on occasions agreeing whether or not to remove items. It was a very large house; the garage was to be searched too, as well as the garden and small garden shed. It would be a long, painstaking process. Anna was like an army officer watching the progress but, after an hour, she could see nothing that aided their enquiry.

She herself worked her way through drawer after drawer of documents in the kitchen: kitchen appliance insurances; household bills, telephone, gas and electricity; gardener's invoices; invoices for electrical work and carpet laying; a thick wad of invoices from furniture stores; delivery arrangements . . . She had to check every single one of them. She was sitting at the kitchen table when Julia barged in, demanding to speak to her.

'My lawyer is coming. I want to know what right you have to do this. Emily and Kathy woken up and taken out of their beds, it's outrageous! I still don't know why you are here.'

Anna didn't look at her, but kept on going through papers. 'Well, Mrs Brandon, we don't think you have been totally truthful with us. As a result we need to make sure that—'

'I have told you everything I know! I just don't understand. I mean, my kids are crying in there.'

'Feel free to heat up some milk or cereal, whatever you need.'

Julia banged open the fridge, took out some milk and filled a jug; she banged open another cupboard to take down cereal packets. Anna had to check them; she got one packet of cornflakes hurled at her head, the contents spilling over the kitchen floor.

In total contrast, Julia's sister, Honour, was sitting in the kitchen with toast and jam; she had brewed up coffee, proffering cups to the officers. She had merely been taken aback when they herded into the farmhouse at four-thirty that morning. Due to the size of the farm, there were double the officers handling the search, with co-operation from the local force. Damien Nolan had appeared more irritated than afraid. He had checked over the search warrants carefully and then, seemingly satisfied, returned them to Phil.

Fingerprints were being taken from obvious areas and the place was being turned over. Phil orchestrated a room-by-room inventory as they sifted through desk drawers, but found only mounds of old receipts, bank statements, income tax returns and used chequebooks, all bound casually with rubber bands.

Damien eventually joined his wife to eat breakfast. He asked how long the officers intended to be at the farm, as he was to leave later that morning to give a lecture. He was arrogant and dismissive; laughing when he saw them dismantle an old Hoover, saying it had never worked. He was only tetchy when they removed his computer, saying that he needed it for his work and that he wanted to know exactly why it was being taken. Honour tried to be equally dismissive, but didn't like the way they were searching through all her homemade jams in the pantry.

Phil was in the bedroom, checking over the duvet and the bedclothes, beneath the bed and behind the headboard under the mattress. He was not finding anything other than the dust that was making his eyes water. They checked every garment in the wardrobe, pocket flaps and trouser turn-ups. Honour's clothes were not fashionable, but hippyish in style: long skirts, embroidered blouses and brightly-coloured waistcoats. Her husband's suits were equally worn: tweedy, many with leather patches where they were threadbare. Riding jodhpurs, boots; nothing Phil looked at gave any hint that either were involved with their Mr Big.

The officers searching outside were faring no better. The barns were filthy and falling down; in one, they discovered a small kiln with broken bits of pottery on an old bookshelf. The kiln didn't appear to be in use. In the stable, the horse seemed about the only thing that wasn't crumbling with age. The roof and the stable walls were in need of repair, as were the barns and outhouses. The henhouse had fifteen hens in dire need of a new building; the hut was about to collapse. There was a small ladder leading up to it and a lock to keep out the foxes, just as Honour had described to Anna. The loft of the farm was filled to capacity with junk: old iron bedsteads and chairs, paintings, broken umbrellas, buckets, old kitchen equipment and, stacked against the walls, broken kitchen cabinets. They had to sift through every item, and they were all filthy.

Phil was very aware of the couple sitting in comfort at their big pine kitchen table. They chatted to each other, buttering their toast and pouring cup after cup of won-derful-smelling fresh coffee. He couldn't understand why they would want to live in this dump; apart from the kitchen, the whole house smelled of mildew. Damien had lit a fire, and he kept it blazing by throwing on logs. To Phil, the views and the stunning countryside surrounding the farm may have been picturesque, but the lane to the farm was a virtual bog; he reckoned that, in winter, they would be very isolated, and this isolation was abhorrent to him. The longer he searched, the more certain he became they were on the wrong track.

He walked into the library, a small room off the dank hallway, and sighed. It was filled with hundreds of books, some old and worn, others stacked in piles around the threadbare carpet like stalagmites. There were also stacks of newspapers – some brown with age, others quite recent. The thought of having to go through the room, leaving no book unturned, made him feel physically ill.

Anna was also not turning up anything she felt was useful. It was frustrating, to say the least. One of the officers asked if they were to search the au pair's bedroom. Anna hesitated, and said she'd like to look through the room. She didn't really know why at first but, as soon as she entered the small clean bedroom, she knew what she was looking for. Recalling that the girl had said how fond of Frank she was, and had gestured to the wedding photo-graphs, Anna hoped there might be one that Julia had not destroyed. She was disappointed; the room was devoid of anything connected to Julia or her family.

Clean sweaters were stacked neatly in her wardrobe alongside dresses, shoes and coats. There were some letters from Mai Ling's family, but in Chinese, so Anna put them aside. She opened a bedside drawer; there was a Bible and some beads, but nothing else. She sat on the bed, looking over the room, and then picked up Mai Ling's handbag, which had been left on her bed. She found a wallet with a driving licence, some receipts and three five-pound notes. She then took out a mobile phone and skimmed through the few numbers – home, Julia's mobile, dentist, doctor – and was about to replace it, when she clicked onto the icon for photographs.

There were over fifty pictures: many of the two children, some of Mai Ling with her friends and, lastly, wedding pictures. Anna scrolled through all the photographs: more of the children; one of Frank, cleaning Julia's car; another of Julia; one of Mai Ling holding a bouquet and smiling; more were possibly from the wedding, but showed no bride or groom. One Anna looked at closely was rather blurred: a man, aged around fifty to sixty, with long grey hair in a ponytail, was partly hidden by a large willow tree, but was leaning towards the two children with an ice cream cornet. It was an innocent, almost sweet photograph; Anna was unsure where it had been taken, possibly at the wedding?

Anna scrolled on to the next: it was of the two children, one holding an ice cream. The man was standing beside them. All that was in shot were his jeans and his shoes. Anna stared at the photograph, trying to calculate how tall the man must have been; the eldest child didn't even come up to his hips. The next picture was black, with a hand across the lens, as if someone had not wanted their photograph taken. Anna scrolled on to the end, finding more shots of the children, the Wimbledon house, and Mai Ling's bedroom, but no other shots of the grey-haired man with the ponytail.

She went down the stairs and looked into the drawing room. Julia was sitting, facing the window; the two children sat by a coffee table eating their cereal. She asked for Mai Ling to join her in the kitchen.

Anna explained that she was not in any trouble: all she wanted was for her to say who was in the photographs. She eased the nervous girl into describing where and when the earlier photographs had been taken, lastly showing the tall man with the ponytail handing an ice cream to the children.

'Oh, that was taken long time ago. I never printed any of them.'

'Who is he?'

'Mrs Brandon's partner.'

'This is Anthony Collingwood?'

'I did not know him; I did not speak with him.'

'But he is handing one of the children an ice cream.'

'Yes, he gave it to her, but I did not speak with him.'

'Thank you. I will need to retain your phone, but it will be returned to you.'

'Thank you.'

Anna then asked the dates of the photographs featuring the man with the ponytail. None were recorded on the phone. Mai Ling thought that they had been taken before they had moved to Wimbledon.

'That would be, what, about eight or nine months ago?'

'Yes.'

'And this man just came up to the children and offered them an ice cream? Didn't that seem odd?'

'No, Mrs Brandon was with him.'

'Ah, thank you. Again, you have been most helpful.'

'He did not like me to take a picture; he told me not to do so.'

'And you are sure this man has never been to this house?'

'Not when I have been here.'

There was the sound of loud voices in the hallway. Simon Fagan had arrived, and was being very abusive to the officer at the front door. 'What the hell is going on? I cannot believe, after what I have discussed with you—'

Anna excused Mai Ling and walked back into the hall. 'Mr Fagan, as I mentioned to you before, we are investigating the murder of Mrs Brandon's husband—'

'I am aware of that, for Christ's sake, but why all this? What on earth are you looking for?'

'Evidence. If you wish to see the warrant?'

'I don't, but I am going to make a formal complaint. You have persistently harassed Mrs Brandon without, as far as I can ascertain, a shred of evidence that implicates her in the unfortunate and tragic events surrounding her husband's death.' He was so pompous, and his voice so loud, that everyone could hear.

Anna asked him to join her in the kitchen to continue their conversation. Fagan refused to sit, but paced around the room. She quietly informed him that her enquiry not only focused on Brandon's death, but on three others they believed to be connected.

'What? And you think my client has something to do with them?'

'Please sit down, Mr Fagan.'

He leaned against the table and glared at Anna. 'My client has requested the release of her husband's body numerous times; this has been refused. She wishes to bury him, and try to forget this horrendous situation.

Now, please, what exactly are you suggesting? What other deaths are you trying to implicate my client in, because I am losing my patience?'

'I suggest you try to hold onto it! Or perhaps it is Mrs Brandon you wish to hold onto? It appears to me that you are being overly-protective—'

Anna was interrupted as he banged down a chair. 'How dare you! How bloody dare you make insinuations that I have anything but a professional relationship with my client?'

'Please sit down.'

Fagan still refused. Eventually Anna stood up and showed him the photograph on Mai Ling's mobile. 'Do you know this man?'

Fagan huffed and snorted, leaning forwards; he glanced at the picture then shook his head. 'No, I do not.'

Anna said that she would present him and his client with a list of items they would be removing from the house. If he wished, he could join Mrs Brandon in the drawing room but, until her officers were satisfied, the family would remain in there. Fagan stormed out, his face red with anger. Anna knew she should not have implied that he had more than a lawyer/client relationship with Julia.

Phil could feel the grainy dust clinging to his hands. He had been working through the so-called library for hours, and found nothing. He was sure his allergies would kick in; he had already started sneezing. Having cleared the bookcases, he started sifting through the old newspapers. Caught between two copies of the *Sunday Times* was a torn scrap of paper. It listed times of a flight arriving at Heathrow Airport. It gave a flight number from Miami, British Airways; no date, just arrival time, written as if in haste, with a felt-tipped pen. It was the scrawled writing that interested him: the number seven had a European line midway across it.

Phil was certain the writing matched the note found in the Mitsubishi giving directions to the farmhouse. He looked over to a stack of exam papers on a low coffee-table. There was a memo on top, the writing very similar. A thin spidery scrawl; Phil presumed it had to be Damien Nolan who had written it. The memo, dated eighteen months ago, had coffee-cup stains over it. Phil removed the page and added it to the note referring to the Heathrow flight times, placing them both in a plastic evidence bag.

Anna joined the officers upstairs, still dusting for prints and checking for anything that would give them a clue as to whether or not Alexander Fitzpatrick had ever been present, as she was beginning to doubt that he had. They had run a check on Julia's previous home; it had changed hands twice even in this short period, and was in the process of being converted into flats, so it was doubtful that, if Fitzpatrick had hidden there, at this late stage they would find anything.

As Anna made her way down the stairs, she paused, as she could hear raised voices. Julia Brandon was angrily asking Mai Ling about her phone and what photographs she had retained on it. Anna could not hear her reply, but as she got closer to the drawing room, she thought the girl was crying.

'You have no idea what you have done!'

'Now, now, Julia – calm down.' That was Fagan.

'Calm down? This stupid girl! After I have gone to so

much trouble, this idiot could have jeopardised everything. She has no idea what lengths I have gone to, to protect us!'

'Why don't you tell me why you are so upset?' Fagan continued, asking in a low quiet voice if there was anything he should know.

'I just want these police out of here. I have to bury Frank. You said you were going to arrange it, and now this! I have to have his death certificate, Simon.'

'If it's the life insurance you are worried about, that will automatically be paid to you,' Fagan said.

'You don't understand!'

'I am trying, Julia, but sometimes I really start to believe that you have not told me everything. I mean, who is this man that's making you get so hysterical?'

'You don't understand,' Julia repeated.

By this time, Anna was directly outside the door. It was not the argumentative Julia, but the fear in her voice that alerted Anna. It felt like a good opportunity to walk in.

'Mrs Brandon,' she said, 'could I please speak with you in private?'

'I have nothing to say. I just want to be left alone.'

'If you wish for Mr Fagan to be with you, that is your choice, but I do need to speak to you.'

Julia was twisting a tissue round and round in her hands. She suddenly seemed to deflate, slumping forwards in her chair, as if exhausted. Her two children were becoming upset, and went to her side; she clasped the girls to her.

Anna suggested that Mai Ling took the children into the kitchen. Julia remained in the chair, ripping at the tissue, her hands shaking.

'Do you recognise this man?' Anna asked, showing the photograph.

Julia nodded, and then sniffed, tossing her head back. 'Yes.'

'Could you please give me his name?'

'His name is Anthony Collingwood. He was my partner. You've asked me about him, and I have told you all I know.'

'We have been unable to trace him,' Anna said, sitting down opposite.

'Well, that's not my problem, is it?' Julia said churlishly.

'What *is* your problem, Mrs Brandon?'

'I don't understand what you mean.'

'Well, you seem very upset and angry that we have obtained this photograph. Can you tell me why?'

Julia closed her eyes. Simon Fagan leaned forward. 'Julia, do you want to talk to me in private?' he asked.

'No. Just go away and leave me alone! You haven't been any help to me at all.'

Fagan was nonplussed; he looked to Anna and back to Julia. 'Should I stay? Julia, do you want me to stay?'

'I don't fucking care any more!' She started to sob uncontrollably, hunching forwards in her seat, her arms wrapped around herself. Fagan hesitated, and then walked out.

Anna closed the door behind him. She went to the woman's side and sat on the arm of her chair. 'What is it, Julia?'

'I'm so scared. I think he will kill me, kill the children because I won't let him have it, and now it's such a mess.'

'Who will kill you?'

'Anthony.'

'Why would he want to hurt you and the children?'

'Money,' she wept.

Bit by bit, between long pauses and bouts of crying, Julia started to explain the complicated transactions she had done to protect her wealth.

Anna took notes as the jigsaw began to take shape. The more Julia talked, the more relieved she appeared to become, as if, by at last admitting the truth, she would be safe. She was scared that Collingwood would threaten her or take the children; she had already handed him the four million, but he was not satisfied. At no point did she admit that Collingwood and Fitzpatrick were one and the same; she continued to deny ever knowing anyone called Alexander Fitzpatrick.

Phil and his team were still searching the farmhouse and outbuildings, but were coming up empty-handed. They would not know for some time if the computer they had taken would give them any evidence or connection to Fitzpatrick. Honour had sat in the kitchen for hours, but Damien had insisted he go to college for his lecture. Phil had let him leave.

Every time Phil had passed Honour, she had asked the same thing: 'What are you looking for?' He said only that they were searching for evidence connected to a murder enquiry. She had proffered tea and coffee to the officers, and then asked if she could do some baking.

Phil was seriously doubting that Fitzpatrick had ever hidden out at the farm. If he had, there was not as yet any incriminating evidence. They had evidence that the Mitsubishi had been driven into the farm's courtyard, but were still merely surmising that Julius D'Anton had inadvertently come across Fitzpatrick at the farm, drove the Mitsubishi back to London, and then was murdered.

Phil headed up the stairs to join the three officers who were searching over the couple's bedroom and small box room. They gave Phil the thumbs down. He checked his watch; they had been there nine hours, and all he had to show for it was two scraps of paper.

He turned to walk out, then paused, looking up. 'You done the loft?' There was a pull rope attached to an old brass hook, very high up. He stood on tiptoe to release it and jerked it hard. The trapdoor to the loft opened and a ladder unfolded, but then got stuck; he had to reach up and pull it down the last few feet. It didn't look as if anyone had used it for years, but he nevertheless climbed up slowly, step by step. He crawled into the loft on his hands and knees, stopped and asked for assistance.

The far side of the loft had a camp bed, blankets and pillows. There was an overpowering musty smell, the dust was thick, with cobwebs trailing from every corner. But the area where the camp bed was situated was clean. There were fingerprints in the dust and, beside the camp bed, a jug with a glass, shaving equipment and a wash bag. When he gingerly eased back the sheet, there were some bloodstains. 'I think we might have just got lucky,' Phil said quietly.

The incident room was buzzing. The search of Julia Brandon's home was over; the search at Honey Farm was still active, and would be continued the following day. Cunningham gathered everyone together for an update. By now, it was half-six in the evening.

Anna was first up, to disclose her findings from the Wimbledon property. There was a murmur of disappointment when she said that, after an extensive search, they had found no evidence that proved Alexander Fitz-patrick was ever there – but she was certain that, using the name Anthony Collingwood, Fitzpatrick had been a very big feature in Julia Brandon's life.

She then opened her notebook and gave a look around at the expectant faces. 'This is quite complicated but, I think, a major step in sorting out the Frank Brandon connection.'

She went to the board and began writing up the details.

'A young and impressionable Julia Kendal, living in Oxford, meets up with the charismatic Alexander Fitzpatrick, using the alias Anthony Collingwood. This was fifteen years ago. He was in the UK, sorting out business transactions and money laundering; he had a lot of cash. He and Julia began a relationship and moved to London, where he bought a large property in St John's Wood. He then spent considerable time abroad – some-times taking her, sometimes not – and began to shift his cash around, using Julia as the innocent; laundering it via bank accounts in her name.'

Anna stopped and smiled. 'Just how innocent, I couldn't say, but she ends up with accounts worth twenty odd million, according to her. This he uses when he requires it, and she maintains the front: nice wife, nice house. He even arranges for her to have IVF treatment to produce two kids, since he has fertility problems, and shifts more money into accounts for them. He acquires many offshore accounts and various businesses. By this time Fitzpatrick was wanted by the FBI and the US DEA, so it became more difficult to move around. He lost millions when the BCCI bank crashed, and this is where it all starts to get unpleasant.'

Anna continued to explain how Fitzpatrick had

poured his liquid assets into a German bank that went big with the remortgage of properties in the US, but started to go belly up two years ago. At the same time, the FBI and the US DEA were closing in on Fitzpatrick, and he lost properties in Florida, Bahamas and Los Angeles. He also sold his yacht at the same time.

'Julia saw the high life going downhill fast. Fitzpatrick made visits to the UK as Anthony Collingwood. Each time, he wanted more and more money, and Julia started to freak out that she would end up with nothing. Even more so, when he became abusive towards her. At some point, she found out he had another woman. He said that, if she didn't do what he wanted, he would take the children. She felt betrayed and very angry; she repeated over and over that she had really loved him.

'Around this time, Julia used, as a chauffeur, Donny Petrozzo. He introduced her to Frank Brandon. Julia put into motion the salvaging of what she thought of as *her* fortune. She sold the house in St John's Wood and bought the Wimbledon property outright. At the same time, with the assistance of her financial adviser, she began moving the money around so that Fitzpatrick could not get his hands on it.

'We have to bring in David Rushton again,' Anna insisted. 'He has been lying through his teeth. Rushton was paid a fortune to protect the bulk of her cash, and make sure that Fitzpatrick cannot get his hands on it. Now we're coming to the point where Julia hires Frank Brandon to take care of her. She's terrified that, if Collingwood/Fitzpatrick finds out, he might do something terrible to her and to her children.'

Anna could feel the team getting restless; it was a lot to take in, but she pushed on regardless. 'Julia maintains that she was never aware of any kind of drug dealing. She believed that her so-called partner was only into property scams; she threatened him that, if he did put pressure on her, she would tip off the Inland Revenue.'

There was a general moan, and Anna laughed. 'I am just repeating what she told me: she wanted to make sure that Collingwood couldn't touch a cent, so this is where poor Frank comes into it. She now starts to switch accounts into his name, promising to pay him a big sum of money if he agrees to marry her, so they can use that as a cover. No sooner has she got it all organised, with Rushton working his butt off to lock the money down, than Fitzpatrick shows up. Julia claims he did not visit the house, but called her. He had told her he was broke – and not only broke, but pissed off because he couldn't get to his own money! He puts pressure on her to release four million in cash; then disappears, but returns, wanting more. When she refuses, he threatens her and the children. Again, she was adamant that he did not visit the house in Wimbledon, but phoned her.'

Anna closed her notebook. 'That, she swears, was the last time she heard from him. The next thing that she says happened was the police arriving to say that Frank had been found murdered. She gets her solicitor, Simon Fagan, to hire bodyguards to protect her; she is very frightened, but not enough to run into hiding, because she has to have the death certificate – not only to get Frank's life insurance policy but, as his widow, get her money returned from the accounts in his name. As I said, it's all very complicated – but that's it!'

She got a round of applause before she gave them the most important breakthrough: their prime suspect had been photographed on the au pair's mobile phone. The pictures had already been processed and she was able to display the two photographs of the man they were now certain was Fitzpatrick, handing his daughter an ice cream. It was not until she had sat down that she noticed Langton had joined them, and was sitting unobtrusively at the back of the room. She glanced towards him, and he gave her a small nod in acknowledgement.

Next up was Phil, who described how, after hours searching the farmhouse, they had discovered the possible hideout used by Fitzpatrick in the loft. They had already sent to forensics the sheets and pillowcases, plus the blankets from the cot bed: there had been a bloodstain, which might prove useful, and many fingerprints from the loft. The two notes he had found were being checked by an expert to see if the handwriting on the note from the Mitsubishi, and on the exam paper, did indeed belong to the same person.

This brought Damien and Honour Nolan into the picture. Honour had seen them checking out the loft, but had said nothing, and did not seem agitated in any way. When Damien had returned, he joked that no one had used the loft for months, apart from a young student. Phil, however, had kept two officers at the farm as security, and requested that neither Honour nor her husband leave the country.

Cunningham, after listening to the reports, said that she wanted to bring in both Honour and Damien for questioning. She also wanted David Rushton, the so-called financial adviser, brought in to clarify exactly what Julia Brandon had hired him to do. Lastly, Julia was to be brought in for further questioning and to make a statement regarding her complex financial transactions.

Cunningham said all this with her usual folded-arm

stance. She, more than anyone else, had felt the pressure of the silent Langton. She looked at him, to see if he wanted to say anything, but he shook his head for her to continue.

'We are getting a lot of action, but we still do not have the series of events that brought about the murder of four men. We know the Drug Squad is still holding our two dealers. They need to be re-questioned, especially with the Glock pistol situation: one of them may have killed the car dealer, Stanley Leymore. They might have also shot Frank Brandon, as we have only their word that the shooter was Donny Petrozzo.'

Cunningham paused. 'Last, but not least, where is Alexander Fitzpatrick now? If he did have a plan to begin using some of the stash of Fentanyl, where is it? We need to find out if he was at that drug squat and if he did use Frank Brandon. He was, as Travis has said, working for Julia – so why did he accompany Fitzpatrick to the squat?' Cunningham turned back to the incident board; with all the links, it looked like Spaghetti Junction.

Anna raised her hand. 'We do have confirmation that whoever drove the Mitsubishi left bloodstains inside it, which we have matched with prints to Fitzpatrick. We also know that he could have been wounded, as the blood matches that on the bullet from the Glock pistol. If the blood also matches the stains on the sheets taken from the Oxfordshire farm, then we know Fitzpatrick was in the UK, and was the man standing behind Frank Brandon when he got shot.'

Cunningham frowned in irritation. 'I am aware of that, Travis, but can someone bring in the bloody timing of events? We have four dead men and we are still unsure who died when; we know where, but we do not have a clear A=B=C=D, and we need it to clarify who the hell did what. This has to be a priority. Tomorrow, we concentrate on that but, for now, we leave Damien Nolan and his wife loose until we have completed the search of the farm, and forensic give us details on the items removed.'

The briefing over, it was after ten-thirty in the evening. Everyone was tired out, having been on duty since three in the morning. Then Langton eased his way to the front of them all. Those who had half-risen to leave sat back down again.

'I think DCI Cunningham has outlined pretty much everything we need to be concentrating on. We have made progress but we cannot sit back for a second. I am very concerned by the couple at the farmhouse; I think they appear too confident. As yet, we do not have enough to arrest them, but they should be brought in for questioning – see if we can put some pressure on them. My main concern is that we might have lost our prime suspect and he has gone to ground. If he hasn't, we have a very dangerous man on the loose. It is looking as if he has systematically wiped out anyone who could identify him, but he never guessed we'd get lucky – first with his fingerprint, and secondly with this.' Langton jabbed at the photograph taken from Mai Ling's phone. 'Get this to both Silas Roach and Delroy Planter; see if they can give us confirmation that he was the man with Frank Brandon at the drug squat.'

Langton had his back to the team as he glanced over the board; in his usual dramatic way, he paused, as he turned and stared at the team. 'If this bastard is here in the UK, I think our body count is going to go up. He's broke and he may have a stash of very dangerous drugs, so find him – before he kills again. That's it; go and recharge your batteries.'

The team broke up. Anna was heading towards her office when Langton asked her to join him. 'It was good work with Julia Brandon,' he said. 'Up to a point.'

'I'm sorry?'

'As soon as she started to open up, you should have brought her into the station. As it stands, we are going to have to go over all that ground again. Even though it was informative, we need dates, and we need that financial guy to collaborate everything she told you.'

'I was supervising the search of her property.'

'Don't make excuses. We can't afford to waste any more time. Like I said, Fitzpatrick may still be in the UK, but he could also have done another disappearing act – which is why those two at the farm are so confident.'

'Maybe they won't be if we get a result from forensics.'

Langton sighed with irritation. 'Which gives us what? They had a visitor. They were old friends. We've got nothing, Anna.'

'I disagree. If we can prove that Damien Nolan wrote the note with directions to the farm found inside the Mitsubishi with Donny Petrozzo's body, we know the same vehicle was driven by Julius D'Anton, and we know it was at some point at their farm – we've got quite a lot against them.'

'Bullshit. Until we know how that fucking jeep came to be driven first by Frank Brandon, then – you say – by Julius D'Anton, it's all supposition as to who did what. They can say that they never even saw Julius D'Anton! He could have driven there; he could have started up a Morris dancing team. We do not have any kind of order of events, and I asked you to make it a priority.'

'Yes, I know, but I didn't have that much time.'

'Then find it – because if we don't have it, this case will flatline. I want that photograph off Mai Ling's mobile taken to see if the lab can enhance it with one of the pictures of him off his website, as we have only a partial single fingerprint, and I want to be certain.'

Anna bit her lip. 'So, is it just me that you want to have a go at?'

'What?'

'Well, I am not the only officer on this case, but you seem to be insinuating that I am not doing my job.'

'I am not insinuating anything, just stating the facts, so don't start with the excuses.'

Anna said nothing, waiting for him to have another go at her.

He then moved close, close enough to touch her, and whispered, 'I love it when you get angry. It reminds me—'

She stepped away from him. 'Don't play games with me,' she said fiercely.

He cocked his head to one side. 'You're right. I'm sorry. Good night.' He walked past her.

Anna remained standing, not turning to look after him; instead, she stared at the photograph of the man in the ponytail. If she were Fitzpatrick, where would she move next? He wouldn't know that they had that finger-print, or even that they had this photograph . . . Her eyes focused on the lists of names and one stood out: *David Rushton*.

Anna sat at her desk, checking over the address and contact numbers for Rushton. She called his home; his wife said that he was working late, but that she had expected him back at nine. It was now almost eleven.

Anna called his office and the answerphone clicked on. She rang his mobile, but it was off. Jermyn Street was not on her way home, but she couldn't resist driving past Rushton's office.

She parked easily outside, as it was so late. She could see the lights were on and she went to the entrance. The glass doors were locked, but a night-watchman sat inside, reading a newspaper. She tapped on the door; he turned, and she showed him her ID through the glass. Accompanied by the night-watchman, she went up in the lift to Rushton's floor. The lights were on in the reception. The night-watchman keyed in the code and the doors glided back. She said he could wait in the reception, and she headed down the corridor. Rushton's office door was ajar and the lights were on; she called out, but got no reply. She pushed the door wide open, and saw the floor was covered in papers. As she stepped further into the room, David Rushton's dead eyes stared towards her.

He was sitting at his desk, leaning back slightly on the leather swivel chair. Anna moved cautiously around the desk, stepping over the strewn papers; she felt for a pulse, knowing there was not going to be one. His wrist felt cold; rigor mortis had already set in. She could not see any sign of violence; his immaculate shirt and tie were in place and his suit jacket had no bloodstains or tears. Anna looked beneath the desk: his well-pressed trousers were still immaculate, both legs bent at the knee, his shoes polished.

Anna eased her way back to the door. Moving around the opposite side of the desk, she paused: Rushton had a small bruise on the vein in his neck and a tiny trickle of blood. She remained standing for a few moments, unsure what she should do, then took out her mobile and dialled. 'It's me.'

'I know. Listen, I'm sorry if I sounded off at you—'

'You said he would kill again.'

'What?'

'He has; it's David Rushton.'

'How do you know?'

'Because I am looking at him.'

'Jesus Christ, are you there alone?'

'Yes.'

'I'll be with you in half an hour.'

'Should I call it in?'

'No. Wait for me, and for Christ's sake, don't touch anything.'

Anna couldn't resist sliding open the dead man's desk drawer. She took out a tissue, then removed a leather-bound diary and carefully flicked over the pages, until she came to today's date. Written in fountain pen, in a neat hand, was Julia Brandon's name.

Langton had the night-watchman in the palm of his hand; the man even offered to make them a cup of tea! Anna stood back, watching him, and was as impressed as ever at how fast he took control of the situation. He was pulling on rubber gloves as he walked into Rushton's office and, like Anna, he gingerly stepped over the fallen documents to examine the body. He checked Rushton over and said quietly that it looked like he had been dead only a few hours. He then crossed to a shredder and looked at the mounds of shredded paper in the compartment below. By the smell of the shredded strips, it had been put into action not that long ago. He then walked out of the office and returned moments later.

'Good, he's got CCTV cameras. See, just by the door? There's more in the reception area.'

Like Anna, he opened Rushton's desk drawer; when he got to the larger one, he gave a soft laugh. 'Look at this: it's for taping clients – unawares, I'd say. Let's see if there's a microphone.'

Anna pointed to the edge of the desk. By an in-tray was a small clip-on mike.

'It'd be too much to hope this recorded anything of use.'

'The recording light is still on,' Anna said.

'Yeah,' he said, and looked at the dead man. 'Well, we'd better do the right thing and get him removed.' With his gloved hand, he looked at the bruise on Rushton's neck, and then glanced over to a large TV screen. 'Let's see what's recorded on the security camera.'

Langton asked the night-watchman, George, for the tapes and to open another office for him to use, rather than remain in Rushton's. He carefully removed the cassette from the recorder and, hardly paying any attention to Anna, walked out.

George, when questioned about who he had seen entering the building, was adamant that there was no one else in the building when he came on duty at seven that evening. Mr Rushton had said he would be working late and so to leave his office lights on; he would turn them off when he left. George gave them details of his nightly routine: he was employed to oversee all the offices, so there would have been some considerable gaps when he was not in the front office, but touring the various floors. He would have liked to remain with Langton and Anna, but they asked him to return to the main reception to let everyone else in.

Langton sipped his tea and, still wearing his rubber gloves, inserted the tape from Rushton's desk. He pressed play and sat back, Anna beside him.

The tape began with Rushton detailing client interviews, with dates and times; they were from three days prior. Langton listened and fast-forwarded, only occasionally stopping.

'In his diary, he writes Julia Brandon—'

'Shhhh – is this her?' Anna leaned forwards.

'I had to try and explain everything to this detective; I had no option.'

'Why didn't you call me?'

'Because it happened whilst she was at the house. I was so hysterical, to be honest, I just felt sort of relieved.'

'Was Fagan with you?'

'He was, but not at that point.'

'Christ, Julia, why didn't you use him?'

'I just didn't!'

'All right, all right, calm down. Without any witnesses, what you said won't mean anything.'

'I told her everything.'

'Well, start from the top; what exactly did you tell her?'

Julia began, between sniffs and sobs, to say that she had come to him because she knew she needed help.

'You bloody got it, but I warned you about keeping quiet. I don't want any repercussions. I have a very legitimate business.'

'I know that.'

'I have done nothing illegal, Julia!'

'Yes, but you've also been paid a lot of money.'

'I charge all my clients for working out transactions with their finances, Julia, love. Yours was just that bit more complicated.'

'What is going to happen?'

Rushton sighed, and went into a lengthy diatribe

about how she would require her husband's death certificate for him to be able to revert monies back into her name.

'I keep asking to bury him but they won't release the body.'

'I've told you, they will in time; you are going to have to wait it out.'

'I'm scared.'

'Listen to me: nobody can touch your money. Right now, it's as safe as houses.'

'I'm not scared about that; it's what he'll do to me. He knows what we've done, he knows and it'll make him mad.'

'He can get mad, sweetheart, but he still can't release a cent; that's what I spent months working on. What you have to do is stay calm. As soon as they release Frank Brandon's body for burial, you will automatically get the death certificate and, once I have that, it'll all come back to you. In the meantime, I've left you a substantial amount of cash in your current account to cover any costs you have.'

'I want to get out, take the kids, and just leave.'

Rushton sighed, and then there was the tapping sound of a pen against the desk.

'Julia, stay put. This will all be ironed out in a few weeks, but if you run off to God knows where, it's going to look suspicious.'

'You don't know what he's like.'

'No, I don't, but I can't see what he can do. We worked this entire scenario out so he can't get his hands on your money. You already paid out four million.'

Julia was crying. *'I'm just so scared,'* she repeated.

The tap-tap of the pen on the desk started again. *'Yes, but Fagan got you bodyguards, what can he do? Plus you've had police all over you like a rash; you think he doesn't know that?'*

'I'm scared he'll take the children.'

'So pack them off somewhere.'

There was then a long conversation about where she could send the girls for their safety. She said she did not have any family, apart from her sister. At this point, Langton and Anna leaned forwards, as Julia said she couldn't leave her children with Honour; she would be the last person Julia could trust. Rushton suggested she send them with Mai Ling to Disneyworld for a week or so. Whatever he suggested put Julia in an even more panicky mode. She wouldn't be parted from them and when Rushton said he was sure 'he' wouldn't hurt his own children, this made Julia really angry.

'They are not his, for Christ's sake! You don't understand; he just wanted kids to open fucking bank accounts in their names. He used them like he has used me.'

Rushton sighed. They were going round in circles. He then asked if he had threatened her at the house.

'He's not likely to show himself there, is he? He just calls me.'

'Where is he?'

Again, Langton and Anna leaned forwards.

'Do you know where he is?'

'No, of course I fucking don't!' she screamed at him.

Rushton tried to calm her, and said he would call a taxi to take her home. She became abusive, saying she was with her bodyguards who were waiting downstairs. They then exchanged a few remarks and Rushton was heard walking her to the door. There was the sound of it opening and closing; next, they heard Rushton give a long sigh and swear under his breath.

Drawers were banged open and shut; then he used his intercom to call a secretary, but there was no reply. He swore again. They heard the door opening, as he called out for Serina. There was silence, then he slammed the door shut.

'*Fucking bitch. I said I was working late,*' he muttered.

A pause and there was the sound of the door being opened again. '*I was wondering where you . . .*' Rushton stopped mid-sentence. The door closed. '*Who are you? How did you get in?*'

The voice was deep, upper-class, with a heavy smoker's gravel tone. '*You mind if I sit down?*'

Langton glanced at Anna: this was more than they could have bargained for.

'*Yes, I do mind. I want to know how you got into my office.*'

'*I wouldn't do that if I were you. Put the phone down. Now, Mr Rushton, you have some explaining to do. You have been playing games with my business. You know who I am, Mr Rushton, and I want my money.*'

'*Jesus Christ, listen to me – I had no knowledge that your wife's finances were not—*'

'*She's not my wife.*'

'*I acted in good faith at all times. I can explain everything, every single transaction; in fact, I've got the files in front of me, and you are—*'

The tape whirred and then ground to a halt. Langton closed his eyes with frustration. 'I don't fucking believe this.'

As if on cue, George, the night-watchman, returned with the video recordings off the security cameras. He said they might not be good quality as they re-used the tapes. 'These are real old tapes; been used for about six months.'

'Never mind,' Langton said, eager to get George out of the office.

'There's a doctor and police officers in reception.'

'Show them into Mr Rushton's office, please, George. Anna, go and talk to them.'

Anna wanted to see what was on the video tape, but Langton waved his hand impatiently. As she left she saw him crouch down in front of the TV set to insert the tape.

She introduced herself to the team of SOCOs and the doctor called to check over Rushton. They had to have him pronounced dead at the site before his body could be taken to the mortuary. By the time Anna had led them into Rushton's office, Langton was waiting.

'There's no sound, but the guy walked in about two seconds after Julia Brandon left the building. He slid in after her before the main door closed. We lose him for a few minutes, then he appears on the stairs outside Rushton's office, chatting to a blonde woman.'

'The receptionist.'

'He then goes out of shot, heading down the corridor to Rushton's office.'

'Let me see him.' Anna could feel her heart racing as she sat beside Langton.

He was as tall as they knew Fitzpatrick to be, at least six feet four – and slender, with quite broad shoulders, but there was no ponytail. What they could see of his hair was dark brown, but he wore a cap pulled quite low over his face. He was wearing a long Harris tweed coat, jeans and cowboy boots. His hands were stuffed into his pockets as he headed for the lift.

The next sighting was on the stairwell outside Rushton's office. Again, they had no clear shot of his face; he was looking towards the receptionist and appeared very relaxed, shaking her hand, as she turned to direct him through the reception doors into Rushton's office complex.

The next footage was of the same man entering Rushton's office. Though they had only his back, they could see him talking and gesturing. They could also see the fear in Rushton's face. Both Anna and Langton knew what was being said because they had listened to the tape; watching it in mute was fascinating. He was so tall, he almost blocked out the whole picture; then he started to unbutton his coat. Still talking, he casually eased the tweed coat off; beneath it was a black polo-neck sweater. He held the coat in his right hand and then half-turned; he walked away from the desk to toss the coat aside, but even full face to camera, with the baseball cap pulled down so low they couldn't see all of it.

'Is it him?' Langton asked softly.

'I don't know, his nose doesn't look the same, nor his mouth.' His cheekbones were sculptured, and he had a dimple in the crevice of his chin.

'Shit, it has to be him,' Langton said. They still had no clear picture of their suspect.

Anna nodded, watching the man as he caught sight of the security camera. He was so tall, he could reach up to it; he didn't wrench it from the wall, but turned it away from being focused on Rushton's desk. The screen went blank.

'That's it,' Langton said.

Anna rewound the tape to look again at the head shot. 'We could get photo analysis to check this against the ones on the website and the one from Mai Ling. It would prove it definitely is him.'

'It's him, Anna. Now you see what I mean about this guy being fucking dangerous. He just walked in there,

off the bloody streets, dressed like some old Harrovian
gent, mixed with old groover. That is a man wanted
right across the States, and wanted in this country for
thirty odd years.'

'Do you think he got what he came for?'

'Who knows?' Langton yawned suddenly, and looked
at his watch. 'It's three o'clock. I'm going home.'

They left the building together. Langton pulled up
his collar as he turned to look back at Anna. 'You did it
again, didn't you? It's hard for me to reprimand you, but
you have got to stop this. You cannot skive off to do
your own fucking investigation, Anna. You'll get into
deep water, not just with me; one of these days, if you
don't straighten out, you'll get more than you bargained
for, and you won't have anyone to help you. This man is
very dangerous. How many times do I have to underline
that, eh?'

'I sometimes find it hard to take your lectures, knowing what I know about you.'

He swung round. 'Don't go there. Not now, not
ever.'

'So it's all right for you, but not—'

His face was taut with anger. 'You're not me, sweetheart. You don't have my experience or my ability to
take care of myself.'

'Oh, I know that. It wasn't me who almost died, but it
was me who had to pick up the pieces.' She was so close
to him. The anger in his eyes would at one time have
made her weak at the knees, but she wouldn't look away.

He seemed taken aback by her refusal to retreat, and
stepped away. 'I'd better watch my back, hadn't I?'

'I would never disclose to anyone what I know about
you, but sometimes you make me angry. I don't think

you give me credit where it is due. I've grown up, James. I'm aware that I should protect myself. It won't happen again. I apologise for acting without taking precaution.'

He turned away from her and hitched the collar of his coat higher, almost hiding his face. 'I loved you as much as I could, Anna.'

'Good night, sir.'

She turned and walked away from him, even though she was heading in the wrong direction. She needed to put as much distance between them as possible.

She had loved him too, but, at last, she really felt that it was history on her part too. In the past, she would never have been able to stand up to him as she had just done. She also knew that she had to buckle down and not act impulsively; it was going to be hard but if she put a foot out of line again, Langton would make sure it went on record, and he could really damage her career.

Chapter Eighteen

The murder of David Rushton gave Cunningham more headaches. As the information filtered into the incident room, the fact that their prime suspect was without doubt in the UK made the pressure go up a few notches. The shot of Fitzpatrick's face from the CCTV footage was now pinned at the centre of the board. Anna had pored over the blurred photo and tried to match it with the ones off the website. The man appeared to look much younger than she had thought. Perhaps he had undergone extensive plastic surgery around the lips and mouth, and it would have helped if they had got a clear picture of his eyes and nose. Until she could get the lab to confirm by matching old and latest pictures, she couldn't be 100 per cent certain.

It was imperative they get a detailed account of each murder. She had the case files lined up on her desk: Donny Petrozzo, Stanley Leymore, Julius D'Anton and Frank Brandon. She would need to spend time with the pathologist who had done the post mortem on each man. At the same time, now armed with the latest photograph of Fitzpatrick, she would need to reinterview Silas Roach and his friend Delroy Planter. Their statement that Donny Petrozzo was Frank Brandon's killer could be a lie.

Anna chewed the end of her pencil so hard, she had fine wood splinters in her mouth and spat them out. If they were to arrest Fitzpatrick, the evidence was still sketchy; they suspected he was involved in the murder of Frank Brandon, Julius D'Anton and, obviously, David Rushton, but whether or not he killed Donny Petrozzo and Stanley Leymore was questionable. As Anna chewed another pencil, she began to tap her foot against the side of her desk. What they did know was that Donny Petrozzo, Julius D'Anton and now possibly Rushton had all been killed with an overdose of Fentanyl.

Anna wrote down the word *Fentanyl* and underlined it. They still had no firm evidence that Fitzpatrick was shipping it into England; even if Delroy and Silas identified him, they would be dependent on the statements of two drug dealers. They had found no trace of it in the farmhouse, nor in the property at Wimbledon.

She sat back in her chair. Having only had a few hours' sleep the previous night, she felt worn out. She rubbed at her head and tossed her chewed pencil into the waste-bin. They had been running around like scalded rabbits, as one victim turned up after another. Unless they got something out of the two drug dealers, they could lose the case into one of the warrens they had created. She returned to the murder of Frank Brandon, and this time underlined the Mitsubishi. They had to establish the date Brandon came into possession of it. They knew it had been parked in the rented garage at Wimbledon; they also knew it had been stolen, and then passed on by Stanley Leymore.

Anna went to speak to Cunningham, but Phil was

just coming out of her office. 'She's not in until twelve; personal problems.'

'Shit!'

'Yeah, well, we just plough on. We are bringing in Julia Brandon, as she requested.'

'What about Honour and Damien Nolan? Are they being brought in?'

Phil shrugged. 'It'd be more convenient if we went and questioned them at their nearest station, as there's still an ongoing search.'

'I'll do it.'

Phil looked at her. 'I'm waiting on the forensic team to give me a result on the bedlinen we took from the farm. If it's Fitzpatrick's, we can arrest them. If it isn't, we just question them.'

'Phil, I really think you need to question the two drug dealers again – this time, with the photograph of Fitzpatrick.'

'I'm off there now. Sam Power kicked up about the expense of taking them out of the cells – transport to here, security, and then wheeling them back again.'

Anna nodded. 'One thing we need to know is if Stanley Leymore was shot before Frank Brandon. It's the gun – same weapon used.'

'Yeah, I know, the Glock,' he said tetchily.

'Maybe they just put Donny Petrozzo in the squat and lied about him being the shooter? We've still only got their word for it – and his prints.'

'Right.' Phil looked at her. 'Anything else?'

'Nope. I am trying to get a through-line on the dates and times of the deaths. We're all over the place.'

'Good – because that's exactly what we are. You know, this case expands every bloody day. Shipping in

more officers hasn't helped much.' He indicated
Cunningham's office with his head. 'And *she's* fucking
useless.'

Anna wouldn't be drawn. 'Well, let's get this show on
the road. We work it between us, Phil.'

He gave a half-smile; she knew he didn't like it that
she used 'we', but he stomached it. 'We should do just
that, Travis.'

Anna went into the incident room to talk to DC Pamela
Meadows, who was running the investigation on the
Stanley Leymore murder. The incident room was
becoming cramped. With filing cabinets and trolleys
overflowing with mounds of files, and the extra officers
allocated to the case, space was short. Desks buttressed
onto each other; it was a headache for the duty manager
to control.

Pamela pointed over to a desk in the far corner of
the room, where two detectives were sitting beside a
stack of grubby, dog-eared files. They had traced the
original owner of the Mitsubishi; the files were Stanley
Leymore's sales ledgers, dating back years.

'What I want from you,' Anna instructed, 'is the exact
date that Mitsubishi left Leymore's garage. I want all the
details on when Leymore was last seen alive, plus the
time of death.'

She joined the duty manager and gave him a list: Julius
D'Anton's wife was to be reinterviewed, to clarify the
exact dates of his last sighting, and reconfirm the dates
of the antique fair he was known to visit, plus his visit
to the antique shop, and the date his van was towed into
the repair garage in Shipston on Stour. Some of the dates
she was able to provide, but she wanted all the dates up

on the board. She also wanted Donny Petrozzo's time of death and last sighting printed up, and the last sighting of Frank Brandon next to the date of the shooting in the Chalk Farm squat. As yet, no post mortem had been done on David Rushton, but she also wanted his name alongside the other four victims.

Anna then instructed Gordon to make up a time-table of the yacht *Dare Devil*: when it had been chartered, and when it had been sold. As she went back to her office, she saw two plain whiteboards being set up, with *Timetable* in large letters. She felt that she had started to make progress, albeit as if she was using the incident room as a classroom; instead of the blackboard, they had the incident board, and felt-tipped pens instead of chalk.

The body of David Rushton was at the morgue. Ewan Fielding would begin the autopsy some time that morning. DC Pamela Meadows had been given the unpleasant task of informing his wife that her husband had been murdered. She was accompanied by another officer from the team. They would also have a warrant to remove any items from his home that they felt could be connected to the investigation.

Langton had made sure that, to date, there had been little press coverage; they were hoping to keep the case under wraps. What Langton did not want was a leak that they were hunting Alexander Fitzpatrick. This could create pressure from the US, and Langton didn't want their interference. None of the team were aware that DCI Langton was now going to be present full-time. As the case had mushroomed out of control, he had taken the decision that Cunningham needed help.

Phil Markham was the first to have his collar felt, as

Langton put a rocket under him. He would accompany Phil to interview the two drug dealers. As they now had the photograph of the man he was certain was Alexander Fitzpatrick, one or both of the dealers had to recognise him. It was crucial they work closely with the Drug Squad: Langton didn't want their noses put out of joint. If there was a possible deal to be made, then they should, with Sam Power's assistance, put the pressure on for the dealers to talk. They were being charged with possession and dealing in narcotics. If the charges were upped to murder, they would be looking at a very long stretch in prison.

Phil had never worked alongside Langton before, and he found him unnerving. He sat beside him in the patrol car; at first Langton used his BlackBerry, firing off messages, his fingers moving over the tiny keys like lightning. He then opened a window and lit a cigarette. Phil watched as he drew three or four heavy drags, then tossed it out. He opened his briefcase and took out the copies of the two dealers' statements. Then he replaced them, muttering to himself. 'We go for Silas Roach first,' he said quietly.

Phil nodded; he noticed that Langton kept rubbing his right knee as if it pained him badly.

'So how do we work it?' Phil asked.

Langton shook his head with a sarcastic smile as he repeated what Phil had just said, then turned to face him. 'You watch, listen and learn, son. You've had these two pieces of shit in and let them walk away.'

Phil sat back, smarting. 'You know, many of our problems have come from the long wait for the toxicology reports. I mean, in Donny Petrozzo's case, we didn't know what had killed him, then the same with

D'Anton. This Fentanyl stuff – I'd never even heard of it.'

Langton leaned back against the headrest. 'Fentanyl is used mostly in hospitals for fast-acting pain relief. It's an opiate, like morphine but nearly a hundred times more potent, faster acting and out of the system more quickly – a high of five or ten minutes. Mix it with OxyContin, or Acopolamine painkillers and maybe a dash of heroin, and you have a God Almighty high better than cocaine, and some poor suckers want this as a way of life.'

'Oh.'

'Yeah – *oh*. In case you don't know, we've already got a few problems in our NHS hospitals. Instead of chucking out the residue not needed in operations, it's being nicked, and there's been a few doctors shooting themselves up with it.'

'Wow.'

Langton just shook his head, before returning to check his messages.

'Where do you think Fitzpatrick is hiding out?' Phil asked.

'No idea, but the murder of David Rushton last night makes it pretty obvious our man is still close at hand. Whatever happened between them would be about money. Whether or not our kingpin actually got it, we'll hopefully find out. He must need a lot – it's expensive staying on the run, and it costs to build a network of shippers and dealers you can trust.' Langton gave a rueful laugh. 'I'd say that's where it went pearshaped; he chose the wrong ones, so he had to get rid of them!'

'You think that he hid out at the farm?'

'Maybe. We'll know soon enough. What concerns me is that the Nolans didn't seem too worried about the loft discovery.'

'So we charge Honour and her husband with harbouring a wanted felon?'

'I think there's a lot more to get out of that couple. They can just say they were forced to hide him out and were too scared not to.'

'But if Damien Nolan wrote the directions for Fitzpatrick to the farm, then it's not looking as if he was forced into doing it.'

'Correct.'

'So are we bringing them in?'

Langton sighed. Phil's constant questions were starting to annoy him. 'Not yet. They may be the only people that Fitzpatrick trusts; if they are, he may contact them.'

'Not when it's swarming with us.'

'The search should be over some time today, and we can get everyone cleared out. Most important is the go-ahead to put a tap on their phones and retain covert surveillance. If they make a move, we will know about it.'

Phil leaned back. He stared out of the window, as they hit a nose-to-tail traffic jam. Langton tapped the driver to put the siren on and get them moving; he was impatient to interview the two dealers. As he turned back to say something to Phil, he suddenly winced in pain. He gritted his teeth, then hunched over to grip his knee; it felt as if it was on fire. No matter how much pressure he applied, it continued to be excruciating.

By the time they drove into the Drug Squad's car park, Langton was ashen, with a film of sweat that made his face look even more pallid. He needed Phil to help him out of the patrol car, and he closed his eyes with the pain as he slowly straightened up. It took a few moments before he was able to walk into the building, stopping at a water fountain to take some painkillers.

Phil felt helpless, not knowing what to do, but eventually the colour came back into Langton's face, just as Sam Power approached. 'You're late,' he said. 'We got the pair of them ready for you.'

'Good. Sorry – we got into a God-awful traffic pile-up,' Langton said, shaking Sam's hand.

Phil was amazed at his recovery; it was as if nothing had happened. However, it had. Langton could still feel nightmare pain at every step. Thankfully, this time, his leg had not seized up. They had said he would suffer from housemaid's knee when he had been in rehabilitation. He hadn't really taken it seriously but, over the past months, he had upped his painkillers, as it had begun to hurt more frequently; the pain was very debilitating.

The aftermath of the nightmare attack, two years previously, the horror of almost being sliced in two, had taken its toll. He continued to have spasmodic pains in his chest, sometimes feeling very short of breath, and he suffered violent headaches and depression. The notion that he should take it easy was anathema to him. Langton's obsession about never allowing it to be known just how much he was physically affected by the attack, was his way of dealing with it. The thought of retiring, and possibly ending up in a wheelchair, was unbearable. Without the pressure of work, keeping his adrenalin pumping, he knew he would not survive the black depression.

Phil and Langton went into the interview room. Silas Roach was sitting with his solicitor, Margery Patterson. He seemed nervous: his head twitched, as he sat threading and rethreading his fingers. He repeated what had taken place on the night of Frank Brandon's murder. Langton let him talk, looking over his statement. Silas ended up swearing on his mother's life that it was the truth.

Langton spoke quietly. 'So, let me just get this straight: you have admitted to dealing drugs from the squat on the Chalk Farm estate, but the gun – the Glock automatic – you say did not belong to you, but Delroy Planter.'

'Yeah, but he didn't use it – he just had it for show, you know what I mean?'

'On this night,' Langton continued, in the same quiet voice, 'you have stated that Donny Petrozzo was there and that he was very agitated. You said he was high.'

'Yeah, well – he was actin' crazy like.'

Langton nodded, as if agreeing. He held the statement up in front of him. 'Describe the door to me, would you, Silas?'

'What door? The front door?'

'No, the door to the room you say you were using inside the squat.'

'Oh yeah, I understand. Well, it was a special door the lads fixed up. It had bolts across and we'd made a sort of grille in the middle of it; well, not the middle – up a bit.'

'Like in the old speakeasies.'

Silas was not sure what he meant but explained that, sometimes when the dealers were passing gear over, the junkies could make a grab, or try and throw a punch, so the door was for the dealers' protection, not just from them, but also from their rival dealers, or from the police.

Langton smiled, nodding his head. 'So there you are, working the deals, and you get a rap on the door. You say that Donny Petrozzo opened the grille, looked out, and then grabbed the Glock and opened fire.'

'Yeah.'

'Because he had seen someone he knew? Someone he was scared of? And he picks up Delroy's Glock, and fires at this person outside – he fires three rounds?'

'Yeah, that is exactly what he done; I think he said the guy was a cop.'

Langton nodded, placing the statement down in front of him, touching the sides as if to make the three pages neat and tidy. 'You say that Donny Petrozzo next opens the door, steps out and fires another three shots into the man who was lying on the ground.'

'Yeah.'

'So, Donny Petrozzo has the Glock pistol in his hands. You say he then ran from the building – in fact, you say you all got out of there as fast as possible.'

'Yeah, right, because I mean, what went down was crazy, understand me? Like, it was fucking bad, man.'

Langton nodded. 'You know Donny Petrozzo has been found murdered?'

'Yeah.'

'How well did you know him?'

'Donny? Well, he was a good buyer, you know? He used to score from us all the time; always paid up, no trouble. Not heavy stuff; he was mostly dealing a few grams of cocaine to the blokes he drove around, some spliff, but never the hard stuff, mostly coke and some ecstasy tabs, I think. Delroy knew him better'n me. Del always trusted him.'

Langton placed down the photograph of Alexander Fitzpatrick. 'What about this man?'

Silas shook his head.

Langton put the photograph back in the file. 'You escaped via the back window?'

'Yeah.'

'So you never went out the main door; never saw the dead man's face?'

'No, I just got the hell out.'

Langton sniffed, took out his handkerchief and blew his nose, then folded it to place it back in his pocket. He stared at Silas for at least fifteen seconds before he said, so quietly that Phil could hardly hear, 'You are fucking lying, son. Let me tell you something: Donny Petrozzo wouldn't worry about recognising the man at the door, because he was working for him. He also knew he was an ex-cop, so he would have no reason to open fire.'

Silas, having been gradually relaxed by Langton so that even his twitch had stopped, was now very tense and started to twist his neck.

Langton still kept his voice very soft. 'I think what happened is *you* recognised Frank Brandon. You had been busted by him: he was on the Drug Squad when you were arrested and now here he was again. You were the one to go crazy – *you*; you panicked and you opened fire.'

'No, that's not true, I didn't, I never shot him!'

'Silas, you are going to go down for murder. You'll not get a few years for dealing this time. You shot a man in cold blood, fired into his face three times. An ex-cop, it's eighteen years at the very least.'

'No, I swear before God, it wasn't me!'

'Who was it then, Silas? Give it up, because we have your pal's statement that you, and you alone, used that Glock pistol; that you were high on crack cocaine. Donny Petrozzo wasn't even fucking there, was he? *Was he?*'

'It wasn't me! Jesus Christ! It wasn't me that done him!'

Langton sipped from a beaker of water. 'Next, I need to ask you about a secondhand car dealer: this man, his name is Stanley Leymore.' Langton put down a photo of him. 'You see, the reason I know you have been bullshitting me, is because the same gun used to kill Frank Brandon,' Langton slapped down the photograph of Frank from his police ID, 'also killed Stanley Leymore. Look at him.'

'I never done that, I never done it.'

Langton laughed. 'Don't be dumb, Silas, you had the fucking gun when you were arrested! In your statement, you said that Donny Petrozzo went out of the room, then fired three more shots into this man as he lay on the floor. So did Donny hand the gun back to you whilst you were escaping out of the window? "Here, Silas, you take the gun"? Or did he, as you say, run off with it? If he ran off with it, how did it get back to you? Unless you also killed Donny Petrozzo? You see how this is building, Silas? You understand what we are going to charge you with?'

Silas kept on shaking his head. Langton placed down the photograph of Donny Petrozzo's body, bound in the plastic bin liners. 'Donny Petrozzo.' Next, he placed down the photograph of Stanley Leymore sitting on the toilet, dead, the bullet through his temple. 'Stanley Leymore; same weapon, Silas.'

Silas's eyes were wide, almost popping out of his head.

Lastly, Langton laid out the picture of Frank Brandon's dead body, face down in a pool of blood in the squat.

Silas started to whimper, sniffing. As the snot trickled down his nostril, he wiped it away with the back of his hand. 'Honest to God, I never done them.'

'Honest to God, Silas, you are going to go down for

403

all three. Your pal has given it up: you had the Glock. Out of your skull, you just went crazy and opened fire.'

'It wasn't me, it wasn't me!' Silas slumped forward, his head on his arms, as he started crying.

Langton looked at the tape recorder and gathered up his papers.

'You can have a five-minute break to talk to your solicitor, Mr Roach, but when I come back, I suggest you start telling me the truth, because I'm losing patience.' Just as Langton pushed back his chair, Silas grabbed at the photograph in front of him.

'I never done it – not to him or the other blokes, I never done it,' he choked.

Langton gave a wide, open-handed gesture. 'So tell me the truth. What did happen?'

Silas covered his face with his hands. 'Ah shit, shit! It wasn't fucking me!'

It took half an hour for Silas to make a second state-ment. He and Delroy Planter were working the squat, and had been there for a few hours. Delroy had told him that Donny Petrozzo had been by earlier, and wanted to talk about a big deal. A friend of his had some very high quality gear, and a lot of it; not heroin or cocaine, but a new drug, much more powerful, and one that Petrozzo knew they could get a lot of money for, from the kind of people that he scored for. Mixed with heroin, it was nicknamed 'Polo' in the States. Neither of them had ever heard of it, and Delroy said that, until he knew what it was, he wasn't going to mess with it. He also said that the kind of money Petrozzo was talking about was out of his league; he couldn't buy in, but he might be able to distribute, as he had a lot of guys he could bring in.

Petrozzo brought a vial of the drugs round for Delroy to test; he told them that he was getting a bit scared and he needed some cash. Silas was unsure how much money had changed hands, but was told that Stanley Leymore had the drugs at his garage. Both Silas and Delroy used Stanley to get their wheels. On the night Frank was murdered, Delroy had expected Donny to turn up; when he didn't, he became very agitated, as he was doing a lot of crack. When they got the knock on the door, Delroy recognised Frank Brandon as a cop and shot him. When he opened the door, he got scared because there was another man there. He ran back into the room, put the silencer on the gun, and reopened the door, but the man had gone – so he fired three more shots into Frank Brandon. The two of them went out the back window, and drove to Stanley Leymore's garage. Delroy was crazy, and threatened to kill Stanley if he didn't give him the drugs that Petrozzo said he was holding. Stanley refused, so Delroy shot him and, after searching the garage, gave up. They tried to contact Petrozzo, but his mobile was dead and his wife didn't know where he was. The next thing they knew, the pair of them were busted and arrested.

Langton remained in the small interview room as Silas was led away to the cells and Margery Patterson left. 'One down, one to go,' he said quietly to Phil, who had not said one word during the entire interrogation. 'Strange, isn't it? You first think we have this kingpin serial killer, wiping out everything and everyone in his way, and then it turns out to be two punks on a dirty crumbling estate, high on the stuff they're dealing to more part-crazed kids. Then they get gun happy and kill. Poor old Frank Brandon was a good guy; we still don't have the reason why he was at that shithole with Fitzpatrick – if that's who he was with.'

'Maybe they were looking for Petrozzo?'

'Maybe,' nodded Langton. 'Question is, who killed Petrozzo?'

Sam Power popped his head round the door. 'I got some fresh coffee for you. We're bringing up Delroy Planter from the cells. Might be a few minutes; his solicitor's not turned up yet.'

'Thanks.'

'You get a result?'

'Yep – and coffee sounds good.' Langton had to grit his teeth to stand; he held onto the back of the chair for a few moments.

'You want it in here or in the incident room upstairs?'

'Need to stretch my legs and take a leak, but back in here's fine.'

Phil watched Langton walk out. He was impressed, and somewhat self-conscious at how he had conducted his earlier interviews with Silas and Delroy. Langton was giving him a master-class.

Langton returned to the interview room to wait for Delroy Planter. He stood, leaning against the wall, using his BlackBerry. 'Mrs Julia Brandon has just turned up to be re-questioned,' he announced. 'Should be interesting.'

Phil looked up, as the handcuffed Delroy Planter was pushed into the room. Langton gestured to the seat and then proceeded to read him his rights, as his solicitor sat, opening his briefcase. The tape was switched on and Langton pointed to the video recorder. He then poured a beaker of water for Delroy and filled his own, placing the water bottle down beside him. Phil passed him the files; then they all waited as Langton slowly read Delroy's previous statement. Then he put it to one side and stared hard at Delroy. He didn't look away; his eyes were dark and angry.

'We have a statement from your friend, Silas Roach.'

'Yeah, an' you got one from me an' all.' Delroy leaned back and grinned; a gold tooth glinted on the front row of his teeth.

Langton sipped his water, placing the plastic beaker down carefully. Still, it left a small wet ring. 'You are being charged with—'

He was interrupted. 'Yeah man, I know what I bein' charged with, and I put me hand up. I said it all when we was first brung in.'

'You are now to be charged with the murder of Frank Brandon, and also with the murder of Stanley Leymore.'

Delroy sprang to his feet, shouting that it was bullshit. His solicitor asked him to sit down, but he jumped up and down on the spot, accusing Langton of framing him. 'Listen man, I never done nothing!'

A uniformed officer waiting outside came in, and pushed Delroy back into his seat. 'Where you think I'm fucking going with these on?' He held up his handcuffed wrists.

'You'll be going down for eighteen, that's where you'll be going.'

Delroy shook his head as Langton read sections from Silas Roach's statement. 'He's a fucking dead man.'

'So let me hear your side of it, Delroy. We know you lied about Donny Petrozzo being at the squat on the night of the shooting.'

Eventually, Delroy began to talk. They gained more information about Petrozzo trying to make a deal, having been a regular buyer, scoring from Delroy for a number of years. As Silas had said, Delroy claimed it was mostly small amounts of cocaine and hash, sometimes some tabs, but he was a good customer and always paid upfront.

Petrozzo had approached Delroy, asking if he could do some really big business with him; he knew someone who had a big stash of gear that he wanted to offload and, between them, they could make a lot of money. 'But I said to him, what gear was he talking about? You know I run a tight business; I keep on the move, right? There are gangs of bastards trying to squeeze in and I got to be careful. Just keeping my team together is fucking hard, so I wasn't sure about getting too big. I mean, I don't have the facilities to stash big loads of hash or grass, know what I mean? Anyways, he says this stuff fits into a real small box, no bigger than this.'

Delroy mimed with his hands the size: about eighteen inches by ten. 'I says to him, what the fuck is in that? He says it's a drug called Formalyn. I never heard of it, but he says it's worth millions. I says, how the fuck did he think I could lay my hands on that cash? Said he was off his rocker. He then says if we do a deal, me to use my runners, we can split the profits; says he's got the gear. I didn't believe him – he was a bullshitter – but then he says he's gonna bring us some stuff to test it out.' He started to laugh.

Petrozzo brought him two vials of the stuff and said they could either inject it, or take it liquid. 'I mean, I honestly didn't know what this fucking stuff was, so I ask around a few contacts, an' I start to get some interest, so next time he appears, I says to him, we can maybe do some business. He wants ten grand; I says I need to think about it – I mean, ten grand is big money – so I give him five in cash.'

'Do you mean Fentanyl? Is that the drug on offer?'

'Yeah, yeah – that's the word.'

'Did you do the deal?'

'Nah, 'cos he never showed up – and we got a problem, because one of the kids that took some of this stuff snuffed it. Next thing, we get a rap on the door, and there's this cop . . .'

Delroy implied that it was an accident; that nobody intended to shoot, but it was all panic. He denied that he was the shooter, and placed the blame on Silas. He said that they ran from the squat. Their first port of call was to Stanley Leymore, as they knew he was friends with Petrozzo, and they got their vehicles from him. Delroy explained that Leymore denied knowing anything; he swore he hadn't seen Petrozzo for months, and told them to leave.

While Stanley went to the toilet, they searched around and found some cash hidden under some tyres. 'That money was mine. That old bastard lied to me. That motherfucker was always trying to rip us off. He was screeching that it was his money and nothing to do with Donny fucking Petrozzo; he said he'd got it from sellin' a jeep and he could prove it. He started to get up, really screaming his head off, his pants round his ankles . . .'

'You killed him?'

'No, not me – Silas, he done it. He was crazy; he'd been coked up all night since we had that cop round at the squat. He'd been smokin' crack all morning; his nose was streamin' like a tap.'

Langton poured more water for himself and asked Delroy to make a new statement. He was not that interested in who had pulled the trigger; that would be down to further interrogations and the eventual trial. What he was interested in was trying to assimilate the actual series of events. Langton took out the photograph of Alexander Fitzpatrick, as Delroy leaned his head on his hands, his elbows on the table. 'Do you recognise this man?'

Delroy glanced at the photograph, then shook his head.

'He could have been with the man you believed was a police officer – this man.' Langton showed the picture of Frank Brandon's body.

'He was a fuckin' Drug Squad shit. I recognised *him*.'

Next, Langton laid down the photograph of Alexander Fitzpatrick again.

Delroy shrugged, unable to recall seeing Fitzpatrick. 'I mean, if he was outside the room – you know, in the outer room – I wouldn't have seen him. I got out the window.'

'You stood over Frank Brandon's body and you fired three shots; you had to have seen this man – he was standing directly behind him.'

Delroy sucked in his breath, and made kissing noises with his lips. 'Prove I shot him, 'cos I am not saying that I fuckin' did, no way. I'm just sayin' I recognised him, 'cos he pulled me in years ago. I never seen that other bloke, but the geezer on the floor, I knew; he arrested me ten years ago, mean son of a bitch. He gimme a real pasting when he nabbed me, and he fuckin' held up his ID. It was obvious we was gonna be busted, and I didn't wanna go down for a long stretch.'

Langton stood up. 'You are going down for one now – a very long one.'

Delroy gave a nonchalant shrug. Langton would have liked to smash his fist into his pugnacious, gloating, gold-toothed mouth. Instead, he walked out without a backward glance. It had not been successful, bar collecting up a few more pieces of the jigsaw. Still missing was the central piece: Alexander Fitzpatrick.

Julia Brandon was hunched over in her seat at Chalk Farm Police Station as if she had stomach pains. Her solicitor, Simon Fagan, glanced towards her; he had placed a hand on her arm, as if to comfort her, but she had brusquely shaken him away. He now sat tight-lipped, staring at some point on the wall above Anna's head.

Julia had been questioned for over half an hour. She had told them a rambling story about how she had first met her ex-partner when she was young and impressionable. He had a lot of money and he treated her with respect, like an adult, showering her with gifts and money and clothes. She had left Oxford to move into a flat in Kensington; she started sobbing as she explained that he had told her he was a property developer for wealthy clients. 'I didn't know anything about this business.' Julia rocked in her chair.

Anna sat listening quietly. Cunningham had instigated most of the questions, taking an interest in the relationship between Julia and the man she called Anthony; she had flatly refused to identify him as also being Alexander Fitzpatrick. 'I never heard anyone call him that; I never met anyone with him who didn't call him Anthony.'

Cunningham had sighed. 'All right. So you began this relationship with him – did you never at any time query where he got these vast sums of money?'

'Why should I? He was almost as old as my father; when he told me he was in property and got paid huge amounts, I believed him.'

'So the trips abroad?'

The interview was becoming tedious, with Julia trying to recall where they had been on various trips and how many properties he had, from the Bahamas to St Lucia to Mallorca, the yachts, the private planes; all the while, with her rocking and sniffing, as she cried and wiped her eyes, and started to make hiccup sounds. She said that she had spent many weeks, often months, alone in the house in St John's Wood while he was away.

'What about your sister?' Anna said softly.

Julia looked up, almost in surprise. 'Yes, well, I had Honour, but she hated to come to London and I wasn't welcome at her place; she used to have a flat in Oxford. When she did see me, we just argued because she didn't approve of me living with Anthony.'

'So she met him?'

'No, she just knew I lived with a rich guy. She said I was an idiot to waste my time on an old man like him, who was just using me for sex, which wasn't true. I really liked him – I loved him – but I got lonely all by myself.'

'So when did your partner begin to open accounts for you?'

'Well, early on. It wasn't ever that much, but I had a credit card and could basically buy what I wanted.'

Anna crossed her legs; her knee hit the underside of the table, but she said nothing. This was Cunningham's interview and she didn't want to antagonise her.

'So how old were you at this time?'

Julia sat up straighter. 'Early twenties.'

'When did the relationship change?'

'What do you mean?'

'When did you stop feeling as if you had a Svengali manipulating you?'

Julia shook her head. 'I never felt that; I really loved him. The fact that I got so lonely, and sometimes felt trapped, didn't mean that I stopped caring about Anthony or enjoying living with him, because I did. I had a fantastic life: trips abroad, skiing whenever I wanted. Like I said, I had carte blanche with my credit card.' Julia had stopped her rocking and even her tears, but she was still tense; she twisted one ankle around, as if doing an exercise, and then tapped her toe forwards, her expensive stilettoes flattering her slim ankles and perfect legs.

Cunningham turned a page in her notebook. 'So this relationship became on what – equal terms?'

'No, never that.'

'But you have a considerable amount of money, Mrs Brandon.'

'Yes, and I had a lot more: it was to save on the Government making him pay taxes or something. Well, that's what he told me. It was investments and stuff like that. To be honest, I never really understood how it moved from one account and country, in and out. I never paid any attention to how many accounts he had drawn up in my name. I mean, I didn't have the chequebooks.'

'What other countries?'

'Well, there was Switzerland – Geneva – Germany and Florida; I had money there for when I was in the United States.'

Anna was fascinated. The more Julia talked about the life she had lived, the more arrogant she became. She twisted her diamond rings and diamond earrings, often seeming more interested in her nail polish than the flow of questions from Cunningham. Anna wondered if this was a ploy by her superior; the more queries were posed about her lifestyle, the more Julia gained in what

413

appeared to be confidence. Doubtless certain that the two women opposite had never lived the luxurious life that she had, Julia started to behave as if she was almost enjoying herself.

'And you never had any indication that this lifestyle you are describing was funded by drug deals?'

Julia shook her blonde hair away from her neck. 'No. I never even had an indication that what I was being told was anything but the truth.'

'Did you ever take drugs yourself?'

'No.'

'What about your partner?'

She wafted her hand. 'He used to smoke dope, for relaxation, but nothing else; he was quite a fitness fanatic and always worked out. We even had a gymnasium on the yacht. I think sometimes he felt that, being so much older than me, he had to keep up.' She laughed.

Cunningham nodded, and tapped the table with the tip of her pencil. 'So, take me through the period when you were still living at the St John's Wood property. If I am correct, there was a substantial change in your lifestyle.'

'What?'

'You became pregnant, isn't that right? In fact, you had two children in quite quick succession.'

'I wasn't living at the St John's Wood house then.'

'Where were you living?'

'I moved into a mews house just behind the Albert Hall. I think we rented it; we were having an extension built or something at the big house. I can't really remember.'

'Where was your partner?'

'I can't remember; he had been abroad a lot.'

'He arranged this move?'

'Oh yes.'

'Do you have the address?'

Julia sucked in her breath and sighed; she said it was Albert Hall Mews, but she had only lived there a few months before she moved into a rented flat in Harley Street. Cunningham scribbled on her notepad, asking for the exact address. Julia couldn't recall if it was forty or forty-two; again, the property was rented. She crossed her legs and, like Anna had done, knocked her knee beneath the table. She muttered and examined the tiny snag in her stocking.

'So you moved from one rented place to another, for how long?'

'Well, it would be about two years.'

'During this time were you together, or alone?'

'A bit of both.'

'Who else lived with you?'

'I had a girl come in and clean, but I was on my own really. I had a car, so I could drive. I'd failed my test a few times, and then when I passed I got a Porsche, a birthday present.'

'And the two children?'

Julia pursed her lips. 'I had treatment at the Chelsea Fertility clinic.'

'The father of your two children is not named on their birth certificates.'

'No.'

'Is the father of your children the man you knew as Anthony Collingwood?'

'No. He was, as they say, firing blanks. I used a donor.'

'Do you have a name?'

415

'No. It was a donor provided by the clinic.'

'The same donor for both children?'

'Yes.'

'Was your partner happy about this situation?'

'Yes, he organised it.'

'Was he a good father?'

'Not really. He didn't have much time for the girls; they were just babies.' Julia frowned and chewed at her lips. 'Sometimes I wondered if he was so insistent, you know, so it would keep me tied to him.'

'Did it?'

'Pardon?'

'Were you able to have the same lifestyle or, with two small children, was it less free?'

'We still travelled a lot.'

'He travelled with you and the children?'

'No, I would bring the children to see him.'

'Where?'

'Well, wherever he was.' Julia listed Florida, Germany, France, India, Switzerland and Scotland among the places she had taken her children to visit him. She was obviously becoming bored; she tilted her head back and closed her eyes. 'You can check all this out with passport control. Both children have separate passports. A few times they went with a nanny he hired, but mostly I travelled with them.'

'Can you give me a list of the hotels you stayed at during this period?'

'What, all of them? I can't remember all of them.'

'I'd like you to try. Why don't you start off with Scotland? Where did you stay there?'

'Skibo Castle; we often went there, but we never stayed in the Castle, always in one of the cottages. You can send over to the restaurant and they deliver food, whatever you want. You could play golf – well, not me, I don't play, but we would ride . . .' She continued discussing the other activities she had enjoyed, as Cunningham jotted down a note to Anna for the photograph of Alexander Fitzpatrick to be sent for identification to the hotel.

When Anna returned to the interview room, Julia was still trying to recall the various hotels where she had taken her children to stay. By now, she was leaning her chin on her hands, elbows propped on the table. The extraordinary thing was that Simon Fagan had not said one word since Julia had recoiled from him; he had remained sitting stiffly, almost as if determined to keep his distance. He had a leatherbound notebook in which he wrote odd notes with a Cartier fountain pen, unscrewing and rescrewing the top. Then he would stare down at the page, or back to the wall, as Julia talked on, and on, and on.

Cunningham spoke into the tape recorder that DI Travis had returned to the interview room. Anna slipped her a note to say they were checking into the Scotland connection; she then inched her legs under the table and picked up her pencil, straightened her notebook and waited, but Cunningham remained silent. It was a little unnerving. Julia looked to Fagan, but he didn't pay any attention to her. Instead, he coughed and straightened his immaculate tie.

'When did it all go wrong?' Cunningham asked suddenly.

Julia sat back as if she didn't understand the question.

'You moved into a property in Wimbledon and you married Frank Brandon. Then, it appears from our previous interviews, you were coerced into handing over a considerable amount of money: four million. Your financial adviser apparently persuaded you not to release any further monies. He then ends up dead, as does your new husband. So I am asking you, Mrs Brandon, when did it all go wrong?'

'I never had anything to do with their deaths. I can prove where I was at all times. I wasn't involved in any way at all.' Her voice had become shrill.

'I never said that you were involved, but it is rather a coincidence, isn't it? So, what I am asking you to explain to me is, when did this wonderful relationship – with a man you knew only as Anthony Collingwood – *when did it go wrong?* Was he aware of your marriage? Perhaps he even arranged it? He seems to have arranged everything else about your life.'

'I haven't seen him for a long time, I swear I haven't.'

'But why not? If, as you have taken pains to describe to me, you had a very special and very luxurious life together, what happened for you to marry someone else?'

Anna tapped Cunningham's arm and she leaned close; they whispered together, and then Anna took out her report of when Julia had broken down at her home when Anna had interviewed her very early in the investigation. Julia began to twist her ankle round again, then tapped her foot as Cunningham read Anna's report.

'I am waiting for you to answer, Mrs Brandon. I need to know exactly when you last saw Mr Collingwood.'

'He had another woman.'

'I'm sorry?'

'I said, he had another woman. She'd moved into the house in St John's Wood.'

Cunningham sighed and glanced to Anna. 'When was this, Julia?'

'Years ago, whilst I was living in the Mews. He told me he was abroad, but I think he had been living at the house all the time. I couldn't tell you how long, but he had this woman, and I knew she had been living there.'

'Did you find out who it was?'

Julia was now leaning forwards, wrapping her arms around herself. 'I couldn't believe it, but when I confronted him about it, he admitted it. We had this terrible argument.'

'Was this before you conceived your children?'

'Yes! I threatened to leave him and, to make up for betraying me, he said he had put a lot of money into my account. He said that he had been very stressed because of some business transactions, that he needed me even more to divert funds. He said the house in St John's Wood was mine, but I was very upset and angry. Then he said he wanted me to have children. I said before, that it was probably to keep me bound to him. I went along with it, but things were never the same between us. I was so hurt.'

'Did he continue seeing this other woman?'

Julia wouldn't look up. 'He disappeared again – said he had suffered huge losses. Some bank had collapsed.'

'Would that be BCCI?'

'I can't remember. I had my hands full with the first baby. I suffered from terrible post-natal depression. And I was obviously suspicious of him.'

'Because of this other woman?'

'Yes!'

'And you never discovered who she was?'

Julia's lips tightened, and she began rocking again. 'I knew, I knew, but I wouldn't face it.'

'So you did know who she was?'

'Yes! I'm not dumb, I put two and two together; it was a painting.'

Cunningham leaned back in her chair as if this was going nowhere, but now Anna spoke up. 'Was it a painting of a yacht?'

Julia looked in surprise at Anna, but made no reply. There was a long pause and, at last, Fagan seemed to feel he should interject.

'What painting are you referring to, Julia?'

'I was feeling so wretched, you know, with a new baby, and I had never asked her for anything, ever. She'd got married and had moved with her husband to this farmhouse, so I packed a case and drove to Oxfordshire. The place was hideous, falling down, damp, and the spare bedroom was so small I couldn't breathe. I hated it, and I was very obviously not welcome. I was no sooner there than I wanted to leave, and then I saw the painting.'

'At the farmhouse,' Anna said quietly.

'Yes. As soon as I saw it, I put two and two together, and I knew.'

Anna continued. 'So you discovered that the other woman, the woman who had been living at your house in St John's Wood, and in fact driven you away, was your sister?'

Cunningham glanced at Anna; she hadn't put it together.

'Yes,' Julia hissed.

'Did you confront her?'

'No. I fucked her husband and left. I lied to you about the IVF. I only had it the once; my second baby is her husband's. I didn't even think I was pregnant. If I'd known about it earlier, I wouldn't have had it, but it was too late for an abortion. I told Anthony that it was IVF again, and he accepted it.'

'Did you ever tell your sister?'

'No, I don't speak to her. It was after I had the baby I decided that I had taken enough, all his lies, and that's when I sold the house.' Julia sighed, really tired now. She had been interviewed for a long time, but it wasn't over. She asked for some water, and was handed a beaker and a plastic water bottle; she unscrewed the cap and drank from the bottle.

'I contacted David Rushton; it was luck, really. I had no idea who to turn to and it was my hairdresser who told me she'd had problems with tax, or something, and had this wonderful accountant. So I went to see him. He handled the sale of the house.'

'For how much?'

'Eight million. He arranged a deposit account, and then organised the Wimbledon property.'

'And the other accounts?'

'Well, when he knew I had access to so much, he started to say I had to really protect it – you know, start to make it earn more money for me. So he opened all these offshore accounts, and arranged various invest-ments, making sure that I lived off an allowance. I needed a lot of money to refurbish the Wimbledon property and furnish it.'

'Did Mr Rushton have any indication that the money was not actually yours but Anthony Collingwood's?'

'No. I told him I had inherited some, and the rest had been given to me by my partner. I wanted him to make sure that no one could get their hands on it.'

'Wasn't he suspicious?'

'No – well, if he was, he didn't mention it. He was very, very clever, and always tried to explain everything to me, but to be honest, I was never really sure exactly what he was doing – just that he had invested the bulk sums.'

'Which were what?'

'Around twelve or thirteen million, to begin with.'

They were reaching the point where Julia moved into the house in Wimbledon with her children, and employed the Chinese au pair, and Frank Brandon. It was now that Fagan insisted that his client have a bathroom break. Anna needed one herself. Just as she was washing her hands, Julia walked out from one of the cubicles.

'All right?' Anna asked pleasantly.

'Yes, thank you, but I want to have a few words with my lawyer before I continue.'

'I'll arrange that,' Anna said, but knowing that Cunningham wouldn't like it.

Julia remained by the wash basins, until the remaining engaged cubicle was vacated by a uniformed female officer. As soon as the door closed, she went back into a cubicle and opened her powder compact. She lifted a gauze from the compact; pressed flat was the cocaine.

She took out a small silver spoon and used two scoops, snorting the fine-cut coke. She then rubbed her gums, sniffed and, unlocking the door, went back to the wash basins. She checked her nostrils for any residue, reapplied her lipstick and took a damp tissue to rub beneath her eyes, where her mascara had left black smudges from crying. She ran a comb through her hair and then shook her head so her hair fell in loose, silky strands onto her shoulders. She gave herself a look of approval, biting at her lip as the cocaine had numbed her gums slightly; by the time she walked out, the coke had kicked in.

Langton had already been into the incident room with his update on his interviews with Delroy and Silas, and the team were able to see how the jigsaw was slowly building, piece by piece. Phil turned to Anna, asking how it was going with Julia, and Anna pulled a face.

Phil gave her a rueful look. 'Well, we're not getting much from her financial adviser's murder. We have the CCTV footage and we have every indication that Alexander Fitzpatrick was the last man to see David Rushton alive. What we don't have, obviously, is where in God's name he is! We've also got more bloody paperwork; it's been a real argy-bargy getting the Julia Brandon files from Rushton's partners but, from what we've ascertained so far, there are about four files missing.'

'But you have some idea of what he was doing for her?'

'Yeah, but it's a maze of companies and investment banks and fucking hedge funds; we've got three guys on it. We might find out Rushton was feathering his own pockets big time.'

Phil sighed, and they both looked back at the board. They now knew that Delroy and Silas were blaming each other for the shooting of Frank, but Langton was certain it was Delroy who also shot, with the same gun, the garage-owner Stanley Leymore.

Phil called over to Gordon, who joined them. His desk was stacked with papers from the garage. They were still trying to unearth the date that Leymore received the Mitsubishi. They had the date and time it had been stolen in Brighton, but by whom they didn't know.

What they were trying to piece together was when the jeep was taken over by Frank Brandon, driven to the farm in Oxfordshire and how Donny Petrozzo's body came to be in the back of it. They still had no timeframe for when it came into Julius D'Anton's possession.

Phil moved along the incident board. 'The start date would be when whoever bought it from Leymore. Gordon here's been checking over the garage's farcical receipts and invoices. The turnover wasn't bad, considering it was such a shithole.'

Gordon pointed to the area on the board that he was writing up. 'I'm going back two years, because I've found a Mercedes listed by Leymore: its reg plates were found in a stack at the back of the garage. They match a vehicle stolen from Kingston in Surrey. This Merc, a silver four-door saloon, was the one driven by Donny Petrozzo; we've got a match on the engine number. The car Petrozzo used for his wife and her niece to drive around was on Leymore's legit books. I've also traced the BMW driven by our drug dealer from the squat back to Leymore's garage; this was stolen almost a year ago. This could be the reason Leymore's prints were found in the squat; they could have been left there before the murder went down: prints minus fingertip, right? I've got another vehicle Leymore also sold to—'

'Enough already, Gordon! We'll concentrate on the start date of whoever bought the stolen jeep from Leymore. You got anything on the Mitsubishi?' Phil asked.

'Not yet. For the hot vehicles, he had a whole lot of legitimate documents for vehicles bought from car auctions; there's a load of equipment for respraying, et cetera. I've also got a stash of receipts for paints and electrical spare parts. They were stuffed into a black bin liner.'

'What about his personal bank account?'

'We've got two accounts, a savings and a current; there is really not that much in either, but . . .' Anna and Phil waited expectantly . . . 'he's got a timeshare on the Costa del Sol. I'm waiting for a bloke there to get back to me with more details, but Leymore has had it for years; he could plough his cash into the villa and carry it out in a suitcase.'

'So when he wasn't up to his elbows in grease, he was sunning himself in Spain?' Phil said, swearing under his breath.

'Hang on, Gordon,' Anna said suddenly, 'the Mitsubishi that was stolen: had it had a respray?'

'No, but it's only got thirty-five thousand miles on the clock.'

'So whoever got it from Leymore might have done so almost as soon as it was stolen?'

'Could be.'

By now, both Anna and Phil were standing beside Gordon's desk. The grubby papers were stacked in piles, dated, and clipped together; there were still hundreds more in black bin liners to sort through.

'You've got your work cut out for you,' Anna said, smiling.

'You can say that again!' Gordon held up his hands; some of the grease from the stained papers had rubbed off onto his fingers.

Anna turned as Cunningham signalled for her to return to the interview room: Mrs Brandon's bathroom break was up.

As they left the incident room, Gordon got the call in

from the property company in Spain. They confirmed that Stanley Leymore had bought from them a timeshare apartment on the Costa Del Sol for £150,000; with inflation, it was now valued at over £200,000. He had paid the previous owner in cash.

As Gordon took down the details, he accidentally knocked over a stash of papers he had not yet checked. When he finished the call and picked them up, he noticed a receipt for a Mitsubishi tail-light from the main dealers of the jeep. When Gordon checked with them, they were able to give him more details: the tail-light was for a 2008 Mitsubishi jeep. The date was one week after the vehicle had been reported stolen in Brighton: 15 March 2008. It was highly probable that Stanley Leymore had the jeep in his garage by that time.

Julia was sitting with her back pressed into the chair, her legs crossed. Fagan's arms were folded, his leatherbound notebook closed on the table.

'Can we now return to the date you say you moved into your home in Wimbledon?' Cunningham asked.

Julia sighed. 'It'd be early March. I owned the house before that, maybe five weeks before, but it needed furnishing and redecorating.'

'You were with your children and their au pair?'

'Yes, I'd got the girls into a local nursery. Mai Ling came from an agency; she had a place of her own, so she would just come in for the day and evening, then go home. She didn't move in full-time until March.'

Cunningham interjected. 'I would like to know the date that you first employed Frank Brandon.'

Julia looked to the ceiling. 'It'd be about a month after I'd moved in.'

'You say you put an advert in the local paper?'

'Yes. I needed someone for the garden, and someone to drive for me.'

'A chauffeur?'

'Call it what you like. Frank contacted me and came round, and we discussed wages.'

'When I spoke to you originally, Mrs Brandon, you said you actually wanted a bodyguard as well as a driver.'

'Yes, well, you know I am a woman alone. I have some very valuable jewellery, so I thought it would be best to hire someone with experience.'

'So you knew he had been a police officer?'

'Yes, he told me. He said he could maintain my car, do whatever I wanted. Mostly, he was driving the children to school and back, because I was always scared, you know – in case someone found out I had money. I felt protected having him around, and he got on well with the children.'

'So this was in late March?'

'Yes.'

'So when did the relationship become more personal?'

Julia sniffed, and smiled. 'Well, if having sex is personal, then it was a few days later.'

'When did you ask him to move into the house?'

'Maybe in May? I can't really remember the exact date; it just happened.'

'But Mr Brandon was also working as a driver for someone else.'

'Oh, that. Well, it wasn't as if it was an everyday thing. This man would call him and ask him to do odd pick-ups when he was too busy.'

'Did Frank work for Donny Petrozzo?'

Julia shrugged. 'I never knew his name, I never met him. He would call Frank on his mobile and Frank would say yes or no. Often he would drive to wherever and pick up a car to do the chauffeuring, mostly to the airports.'

'Frank had his own car, a VW?'

'Yes. Just like I said, he would go in his own car to wherever this man lived and then he would use a Merc, I think it was.' Julia sniffed and began tapping her foot against the leg of the table. She kept on glancing at Fagan as if he should say something. He remained silent.

'So when did you see Mr Brandon in possession of the black Mitsubishi jeep?'

'I never saw it.'

Cunningham slapped the table with the flat of her hand. 'Stop lying, Mrs Brandon! You knew that Frank Brandon drove this vehicle; you also knew where it was parked – you gave Detective Inspector Travis directions on how to get to the garage he used to park it in.'

'Of course I knew about the garage – I paid the rent on it. I had my two cars so we needed another garage.'

Fagan leaned forwards. 'I think Mrs Brandon has answered your question. She did not know Mr Brandon had this jeep; she has clearly just said that she never saw it.'

'Thank you,' Julia said curtly.

'Let's go to the date you were married.'

'I am getting sick and tired of this. I have told you about the wedding.' She jerked her head towards Anna.

'I just need to know when you and Mr Brandon agreed to be married.'

'Why? What business is it of yours?'

'Please answer the question.' Cunningham was starting to sound irritated now.

'It was sometime in May.'

'He had worked for you for two months?'

'My goodness, how clever of you, yes! After two months we realised we wanted to be married; we loved each other, and we went to the Isle of Man and got a special licence and we got fucking married.'

Fagan whipped round on her. 'Julia, that was not necessary.'

'Of course it is! They keep asking me these ridiculous questions that have nothing to do with anything.'

'The life insurance policy your financial adviser arranged for Mr Brandon?' Cunningham persisted.

'Yes, you've bloody asked me about that. I was looking out for him, that is all.'

'But it was payable only if he died.'

'That is not the point! If he had a life insurance policy, he could get mortgages and things like that.'

'Why would he want a mortgage when you owned your house outright?'

'Maybe he wanted to show me he had a pair of balls rather than live off me!' she shouted. Fagan again warned her to be quiet and behave. She sniffed and then rubbed at her nose. 'I just want to go home to my children,' she said, in a whine.

'Were you afraid? Was someone threatening you?'

'No.'

'Can you tell me about the four million you took out recently?'

'It's my money. I have already told you, I paid for the house and I had a lot of things to buy.'

'We will need the receipts.'

'Oh, for Christ's sake, this is just harassment.' She turned to Fagan and pushed at his arm. 'Do something, for God's sake! This is driving me crazy.'

'Just answer the questions, Julia.'

'What the fuck do you think I *have* been doing?'

'Mrs Brandon, your husband was murdered.'

'Well, I didn't fucking do it!' She pushed her chair back so abruptly that the table rocked, and Cunningham's bottle of water spilled into her lap and over the table. She stood up trying to salvage her dripping notebook and soaked skirt. The incident made Cunningham so angry she ordered another ten-minute break.

Cunningham was in her office, using tissues to dab at her skirt. 'That bloody woman! She makes me so mad I want to slap her face.'

Anna nodded her agreement. She mentioned that the team were pretty certain that the Mitsubishi jeep, that was so important to their enquiry, had been in Leymore's possession a week after it was stolen. This helped with their still-incomplete timeframe, because Eddie Court had seen the jeep being driven by Frank Brandon on the night of his murder. Phil was pressing the team to track back, to see if there was anything that would indicate whether Frank had bought the jeep, or was just using it via Donny Petrozzo.

Just as Anna and Cunningham were returning to question Julia Brandon, a further piece of the jigsaw came from the officer rechecking Donny Petrozzo's diary and work ledgers. There was, in one of his bank statements, two withdrawals of sums of money: one for ten thousand pounds cash, and another, from a different account, for five thousand. The date was 17 March; in his diary, he had written the initials SL and the time.

The following day there was another cryptic note: *Paid SL, but did not collect faulty light.* This tied in with the receipt for the tail-light found at Stanley Leymore's garage. So they now knew that Donny Petrozzo had been the buyer. Four days on, there was another one of his odd memos: *Cash × 25. Nice 1.* Donny's bank account showed that he had deposited twenty-five thousand pounds into his current account on that date; did he sell on the Mitsubishi for this amount? If he had done, they did not have the name or even an initial of the buyer.

Cunningham listened as they updated the incident board, and said: 'Take a look into Julia Brandon's accounts and see if she was out by twenty-five grand.' She waved her hand towards Anna to join her and returned to the interview room.

No sooner had Anna sat down than there was a tap on the door; Phil gestured for Anna to come out into the corridor. Cunningham started to record her absence for the tape, but Anna returned almost immediately, placing a note on to the table. Cunningham glanced at it. Julia Brandon had signed a cheque for twenty-five thousand pounds, made out to her husband. The cheque had been paid into Frank Brandon's account, and he had withdrawn the same amount in cash on 20 March.

When this was pointed out to her, Julia simply shrugged and said it was Frank's wages.

'But he withdrew this exact amount in cash.'

'That was his business.'

'So you have no notion what this amount of money was for?'

'Why should I know? He had a life before he started to work for me.'

Cunningham sighed: the woman had answers for everything. Cunningham decided not to pursue the cheque but pressed on, asking about the dates Julia and Frank married. Julia was trying hard to concentrate; her nose was running and she kept sniffing, and twice got out a handkerchief. She was becoming abusive and quite argumentative as she snapped that they had fallen in love, had sex, and more sex, and then decided to marry.

'There were photographs of the wedding,' Anna interjected.

'And I told you that I had torn them up, because he was dead and I didn't want any memories. I had to take them down because the kids were asking me about him and it was making me want to cry all the time.'

'You didn't keep any of these wedding photographs?'

'No. They weren't done by a professional – they were just snapshots from his camera and my mobile.'

'Who was the older man in one shot standing behind Frank?'

'The fucking vicar. This is getting ridiculous.' She turned and glared at Fagan, who leaned back.

'I have to say my client has a point; we have been here for a very long time, and we appear to have come full circle.'

Cunningham closed her notebook.

Anna flicked a page in hers. 'Why did you recently hire not one but two bodyguards?'

'Christ! My husband had been murdered! Simon here suggested that I should replace him; he was concerned for me so he arranged for me to meet them. It wasn't my doing, it was my lawyer's.'

Fagan frowned.

'He got them from an agency, he took me to meet them – I had nothing to do with it. Go on, ask him! Give me a break!'

'So you were that concerned for your client, Mr Fagan?'

'Yes, I was concerned, especially as I had received a call from Mrs Brandon's au pair. She was frightened, and I can understand why, obviously. She said that Mrs Brandon was deeply distressed, and without anyone looking after her. I then received a call from her business adviser who also stressed his concerns; it was on his advice that I contacted—'

He was interrupted by Julia, grabbing at his arm. 'I never told David to contact you! *You* called *me* and told me that I had to take care!'

'Yes, I did say that to you, Julia, but only after I was contacted by David Rushton. As I said, your au pair also phoned—'

He was interrupted again. Julia's voice had become shrill. 'Since when has my au pair had anything to do with my personal life?'

Fagan was very uncomfortable. 'Julia, she was simply concerned.'

'But it had nothing to do with her!' Julia was becoming very agitated.

Cunningham interrupted their conversation. 'Mr Fagan, could we just clarify that, after you were called by David Rushton, and by Mrs Brandon's au pair, you brought in—'

'I was given the number of this company that employ security guards – bodyguards, whatever – with good qualifications and experience, and obviously with references.' Fagan was becoming uneasy and loosened his tie.

Anna leaned forward across the table; something was not right. 'Who exactly gave you the contact for this company?'

Fagan hesitated. 'I think it was David Rushton; he also mentioned that Mrs Brandon's au pair had spoken to him.'

'Why would *she* call David?' Julia's voice was high-pitched.

'I really don't know, Julia; you should ask her. All I am saying is that the reason I suggested to you that you hire these two men to look after your safety, was because I was advised by David Rushton to do so.'

'Where are these security men now?' Anna asked quietly. 'You see, we have been unable to trace the company these men work for. The Range Rover they have been using is registered to a—' She was interrupted by Julia.

'Simon picked me up and brought me here, so I didn't need them; they're at the house.'

'With your au pair?' Anna asked.

'Yes.'

'And the children?'

Julia stood up. She was finding it difficult to breathe; her chest heaved as she gasped. 'Oh my God, oh my God.'

'Mrs Brandon, sit down, please.'

Julia backed away from the table, her chair overturned. She looked as if she was about to faint. 'What have I done? You don't understand, you don't understand!' She turned as if to run to the door, her arms flailing. 'I have to get home, I have to get to my children.'

Anna moved quickly from the table to approach Julia. She could see the fear in her eyes, as she repeated, 'What have I done?'

Fagan was also now on his feet, concerned. 'Julia, calm down. We don't understand what you are saying.'

Her voice was rasping; she still seemed unable to catch her breath as she hissed out, 'You fucking idiot! He will have taken my babies!'

Chapter Nineteen

Julia sat hunched forward in the passenger seat of the squad car, demanding that they use the siren to get to Wimbledon as fast as possible. As Anna and Julia travelled across London, Cunningham continued to question Fagan about the two men he had hired for Julia's protection, while Phil ran checks on the company, but they still only could come up with box numbers and dead telephone lines. Next, they tried to trace the Chinese au pair's references from the papers removed from Julia's property. They were all false: the families she had supposedly worked for had never heard of her.

Anna received confirmation of this just as the car drew up outside the house. Julia ran from the car almost before it had stopped, Anna following, as she fumbled with her keys and rang the doorbell, shouting out for Mai Ling to open the door. Anna took the keys and opened the door. Julia pushed her aside, racing into the house. She ran first into the kitchen and then up the stairs, screaming out for Emily and Kathy. The house was ominously quiet.

To calm Julia, Anna said that perhaps they were at nursery, but when she followed her into their bedroom,

437

it was obvious they were not. Julia was opening drawers and the children's wardrobe, to find rows of empty hangers. Her face was chalk white.

Anna sat back on her heels in front of the distressed woman. 'Julia, look at me. *Look at me!*'

The tears streamed down Julia's cheeks, and all the fight in her evaporated, but she wouldn't look at Anna.

'We have found out that both the bodyguards and your au pair may not be who they say they are.'

'*He's* taken them.' The woman's voice was leaden.

'Who, Julia? For God's sake, start to help me find out what is going on. Who do you think has taken your children?'

Julia flopped back onto one of the beds and lay there, as Anna got to her feet.

'Listen to me. If you think someone has taken the girls, if they could be in danger, then for heaven's sake, talk to me.'

'He won't hurt them. It's me, it's all my fault.'

Anna could have shaken her. She repeated their concerns about the au pair and about the bodyguards, in the hope that it would jolt Julia into explaining what had happened.

To her surprise, Julia straightened out, getting up from the bed and heading out of the room. 'I need a drink.'

She never ceased to amaze Anna; from hysteria over the possibility that her children had been taken, she now appeared resigned to the fact. She went into the drawing room, opened a bottle of brandy, poured a heavy measure into a tumbler and drank it like water. Anna tried to stop her, but the woman shrugged her arm away. 'You want me to talk, then fucking let me have a drink, all right?' She didn't drink it all, but went and sat on the sofa, kicking off her shoes. 'When I found out he was using me, using the kids – that he had lied to me about everything – I decided that I'd pay him back.'

'Anthony Collingwood?' Anna asked.

'Who the fuck else do you think I am talking about? You tell me it wasn't his name, but that's the only name I knew him by: Anthony fucking Collingwood, the bastard.' She sipped the brandy and then leaned forwards, holding the glass loosely in her hands. 'He used me. I was foolish enough to go along with it, or maybe greedy. You can say whatever you like about me, but the trappings were all part of it. I'd never had such a life and I truly believed he loved me. If you knew him, you'd understand why I stood by him for so long.'

Anna remained silent, not wanting to stop Julia talking.

'I was always afraid of him, you know. I'd have done anything he asked, until I found out; it sort of both happened together, his affair with my bloody sister, and then the phone call.' She sipped some more brandy. 'He said that he was in trouble financially, and would be coming to England as he needed money. Something in the US had gone wrong, and this bank in Germany . . . I never really knew exactly what he was talking about, but I decided that he wasn't going to use me any more. So I took the children and moved out of the house, and kept on moving so he couldn't track me down until I had done it. I switched every account so he couldn't touch it; couldn't access a single cent! I had used this driver – not Frank, as I didn't know him then – to chauffeur me and the kids around. I was scared, you know, really frightened that Anthony would find me, so I asked him about anyone he knew who would be a good bodyguard.'

Anna leaned forwards. 'What was the name of the driver?'

Julia shrugged. 'Can't remember.'

Anna passed over a mug shot taken of Donny Petrozzo. 'This man?'

Julia peered at the photograph. 'You know, it's weird, but sitting in the back with him in front, you only really see the back of their head.'

'But this one you recognise?'

She sighed. 'Yes.'

'Sure you don't recall his name?'

'No, sorry.'

'Does Donny Petrozzo sound familiar?'

Julia nodded. 'Yeah, that sounds like it.'

'And this man, Donny Petrozzo: you asked him if he knew anyone who would be a good bodyguard/ driver?'

'I'd put an advert in the local paper and this awful little man applied, so I was asking around . . .' Julia at least had the temerity to look a trifle ashamed.

'Frank Brandon,' Anna said quietly.

'Yes, poor Frank. Even though I had covered my tracks, I was still scared Anthony would find me; it was then I talked to Frank about marrying me. I'd have another name, he would live in the house; then, when Rushton had finished working on all the accounts, I planned to leave the country – you know, go somewhere he'd never find me. It was stupid, I was stupid, I *am* stupid – I'd never really done anything on my own but, whilst I was planning it, I felt stronger than I had ever felt. As if I was, for the first time, in charge of my own life, not treated like some object that could be kept quiet with presents and flash cars.' Julia drained the glass of brandy and hurled it against the wall. It splintered and fell soundlessly on the thick pile carpet.

'Julia, listen to me. If this man has taken your children—'

'Emily and Kathy are *his* children — his money provided for them,' she said dully. 'He will have got passports — by now they'll be on a plane somewhere.'

'This man is wanted in the United States as well as here.'

Julia gave a strange, hard laugh. 'He's been wanted for how many years? You told me that! You say he is this Alexander Fitzpatrick — well, how long have you been trying to find him? Twenty years? Thirty? He is out of your reach, and out of mine. At least he's left me alive. I even believed him when he said that, if I gave him four million, he would disappear; he had no intention of walking away from the rest of the money. He forced Rushton to reverse all the accounts we'd worked on hiding, back into his hands.'

'We wish to question him about the murder of David Rushton.'

Julia gave a hollow laugh. 'Question him? You'll have to find him first! He was in England from the moment I moved into this house, laughing because nobody could ever touch him; somehow he got to Frank as well. You know what is sick? All I'll be left with is Frank's insurance money! Still, it's something out of all this mess; I deserve that much at least. So, now you know it all.'

Anna stared as Julia's egotistical side emerged. She loathed the sight of her, but she wasn't finished. She now had to find out exactly what Julia meant by saying that she knew the man they were hunting had not only been in England, but had obviously contacted her numerous times. 'When did you first know he was here in London?'

'He turned up at the wedding! He thought it was all very amusing; he said that it would be very useful to have another name! He had a virtual card deck of passports; he planned to do some business here and then go back to Florida.'

'This business, did you have any idea what it would be?'

Julia shook her head, smiling. 'You tell me! All I know is, Frank was just like everyone else who ever came into contact with him: won over totally, and then got screwed – in his case, shot dead.'

Anna stood in front of the team, repeating all this new information. Langton was leaning against the far wall of the incident room. He raised his hand. 'Do we now have the connection between Donny Petrozzo and Frank Brandon clarified? Not that he was hired as a driver, but how Petrozzo's body was found inside the Mitsubishi?'

Anna turned to the board. 'Julia recalled Frank saying he was going out to do business; this was on the night of the murder. She did not see him with Fitzpatrick, but she knew they had met on numerous occasions, and it was possible Fitzpatrick had negotiated some big pay-off.'

Langton threaded his way to the front. 'Did you get from her where Fitzpatrick was hiding out?'

Anna shook her head, saying that she had repeatedly asked this question. Julia had said that he would not hide out anywhere, but more than likely stay at the Ritz or Claridges.

'What about Honey Farm?'

'I obviously asked about that. She said she doubted it, as it was not his style.'

'But her sister was?'

'Again, she was not able to tell me if Honour was still in contact with him. She felt that he was more than likely using Honour, as he had used Julia herself. She was very scathing about Honour, as she was part of the reason Julia had attempted to hide Fitzpatrick's money. The sisters are not even on speaking terms.'

'So what are you saying? That he might have been staying in luxury hotels, or could have been in Oxfordshire?'

Anna said that they had, so far, no evidence that Fitzpatrick had been in the farmhouse; tests on the cot bed in the loft had proved inconclusive. The blood stains did not match the smear on the bullet, and according to Honour might have been left by a student at some time in the past. She said that no-one had stayed there for months. Langton paced up and down along the now sprawling incident-room board. The number of names and statements listed was awesome.

He jabbed his finger at the board. 'Okay. We now have the timeframe for when Donny Petrozzo was killed; next, Stanley Leymore. Still outstanding is Julius D'Anton's murder. Even though we have the fucking bastard on CCTV footage from David Rushton's office, we still do not have any evidence that Fitzpatrick was the killer. We do have the drug Fentanyl that connects Donny Petrozzo's death, David Rushton's death . . .'

Phil stood up with his notebook open. 'We've got confirmation that the handwriting in the glove compartment of the stolen Mitsubishi probably belonged to the same person who wrote the notes on Damien Nolan's examination papers.'

'Probably?' snapped Langton.

'Yeah. They won't confirm it one hundred per cent.'

'Shit. Is the surveillance of the farmhouse still in place?'

Phil confirmed that it was, but that there had been no suspicious movements or visitors. Langton swore again; the investigation was way over budget and seemingly still gathering moss. He hitched up his trousers and again turned to the board. 'Bring that bitch Julia Brandon back in and re-question her. Have we anything from customs or ports?'

Gordon said that they had no report of anyone using Fitzpatrick's known aliases, or the name Brandon, and no report of anyone with two young children leaving the UK who fitted his description.

He could be on a private plane or boat, Langton muttered; in fact, their wanted man could be anywhere. 'The key is, we trace him via the money he regained from Rushton. It has been moved, right? Find out where!'

'What about the couple at the farmhouse?' Phil asked.

'Leave them there. We bring them in when I'm ready. We need some more details on this fucking Mitsubishi, like who drove it to Oxford, and how come Julius D'Anton was wheeling around in it and then ended up in the Thames. We are putting a massive load on this man being superhuman: he's killing one guy after another, kidnapping two kids. I don't buy it – he's got to have help.'

Anna interjected that he had the two bodyguards, and maybe the Chinese au pair! If they also took on board Julia's claim that Fitzpatrick – or Collingwood, as she knew him – had been in the UK since May, the time she moved into the Wimbledon property, he could have done a lot of planning: it was now October.

The sheer length of time they had all been working the case hit home and Langton, especially, became angry at the lack of developments. He returned to the information on the board, detailing the murder of Frank Brandon. 'We know he went to the drug squat; we know there was someone else with him; we have a possible – and it's only a possible – ID from this junkie, disco rapper Eddie Court, but we still have no real evidence on the man who accompanied him. We are pretty certain that this man sustained a bullet slash or graze wound and, we suppose, that this same man was in the Mitsubishi. Now, what we *don't* know is whether or not Donny Petrozzo was already dead in the back of it. Everyone with me?'

There was a low murmur of agreement. Langton moved on to the photograph of Julius D'Anton. 'Right: our Thames floater was seen by the antique dealer in Shipston on Stour driving the Mitsubishi. His van was located, dumped in a local garage for repair. His body was discovered, two days after Frank Brandon's murder. Forensic have come up with nothing, but lab reports say that he was possibly drowned around four days before Brandon's murder.' Langton sighed with irritation as he continued, ruffling his hair until it stood up on end. 'I have been asking for a fucking timeframe for two weeks, because from what I can see, that jeep was at the farm *before* the murder of Frank Brandon. That puts our unknown man, our prime suspect, driving it from London to Oxfordshire, maybe hiding out there, then allowing it to be used by Julius D'Anton.'

Langton clapped his hands and stared around the room. 'Any bright ideas? Did this bastard accompany D'Anton back to London, kill him, and then arrange with Frank Brandon to visit the drug squat?' He shook his head, returning to the board. 'I still think we are heaping a hell of a lot on this motherfucker's shoulders. We are presuming he escaped, because Frank Brandon took the bullets: does he then drive to meet Donny, kill him, dump the jeep and take off to we don't know where, having already knocked off D'Anton? Everyone still with me?'

Again, there was a murmur of agreement from the team.

'Now, we have a new load of evidence against him from Julia Brandon. She maintains that he was actually in London for months, possibly staying at Claridges or some other five-star hotel. Have we anything on that?' There was, to date, no one at any of the top hotels who recognised the photograph they had of Alexander Fitzpatrick, but enquiries were still ongoing.

Langton continued. For his part in diverting funds, to make them inaccessible to Fitzpatrick, Julia's financial adviser was also killed. This had given them Fitzpatrick's picture, caught on the security cameras at Rushton's office; their hunted man had audaciously looked into the camera and turned it to face the wall. 'He bloody knew he was on camera! He could have ripped it out of the wall, but he didn't. So, we have yet another death down to him. At least we know he didn't shoot Stanley Leymore, the bloke who owned the garage and who, we think, sold the Mitsubishi on to Frank Brandon through Donny; it's pretty conclusive because of the movement of money into Frank's account and then out again in cash.'

Langton drew up a chair and sat; he bowed his head as if he was having a real headache, wincing and clenching his teeth. 'Something does not add up.'

Anna stood up, and he looked at her gratefully. 'We know from your interviews with Delroy and Silas that Donny Petrozzo was trying to offload this Fentanyl, but it wasn't working because they had no idea what the drug was, or how powerful.' She stopped.

'Go on, Travis.'

'I think a possible scenario is that Donny Petrozzo had recognised Fitzpatrick: we know it's a possibility, from an old trial years ago. He was constantly doing pick-ups and drops at Heathrow Airport. He might have seen him and approached him; he might even have been driving him to Julia Brandon's.'

Langton nodded and sighed, as if bored. 'So get the bitch back in and re-question her. She's lied from day one; maybe she's also lied about not knowing about the drug trafficking her lover boy made his fortune from.'

Anna nodded. 'I sort of believed her but, by all means, we should re-question her – maybe put the frighteners on her, charge her with perverting the course of justice. But I am telling you, she is a very hard nut to crack.'

Langton looked at Anna. 'So what are you suggesting?'

'She might be more useful if she thinks we are no longer interested in her.'

Langton gave a rueful shrug. 'Thing is, our man is now with two kids, two bodyguards and a Chinese au pair; I doubt if he can move as easily as we've suspected. He'd need a bloody camper van.' Langton looked to Phil, to ask about the paper trail of money; they were still waiting to hear back from the various banks that Rushton had used. Langton raised his hands in frustration. 'How bloody long do we have to wait, for Christ's sakes? We need to know if this bastard is moving around with millions or waiting like we fucking are! Get onto it now!'

Cunningham now joined everyone. She was very agitated. 'Julia Brandon left her house ten minutes ago, carrying an overnight bag.'

'They let her just drive past them?' Langton snapped.

'They're right on her tail. I'll bring in the box so we can hear the progress, but she was heading towards the A3.'

Langton clenched his teeth; he was so angry, it was obviously hard for him to keep control and not explode. 'Okay, let her run. The A3? It isn't as if she is heading towards Oxfordshire, is it?'

Cunningham brought up the street map. She indicated that it was possible for Julia to branch off the A3 and pick up the M40 to head towards Heathrow. She got a scathing response from Langton, who pointed out that she could also be driving towards Southampton; even more likely, Gatwick Airport. Cunningham became agitated by his rudeness in front of the team and said, curtly, that they were holding Julia Brandon's passport. Langton turned on her, saying that, as Alexander Fitzpatrick appeared to be able to print off Christ knows how many for himself, with so many aliases, it was possible she would be using a forged passport.

He then addressed the team. 'This woman is something else. After hours of interrogation, screaming that her babies have been kidnapped, she's now heading down the A3 to Christ knows where. Travis, you were the last person from here to talk to her.'

Anna stood up. 'She was very distressed, and drinking. In all honesty, I found her to be telling me the truth. If she was lying, and knew where her children were, then she deserves an Oscar.'

'Thank you for that insight! Think over what she said

to you; was there any time you suspected an ulterior motive?'

'You mean her panic about the children being taken?'

'Christ, yes! It got her out of the station and back home, didn't it? Was she also giving, as you say, an Oscar-winning performance in the interview room?'

Anna shrugged. 'It's hard to tell. At one point she seemed very hyper, as if she'd taken something. When she learned, via her lawyer, that it was David Rushton who had suggested the bodyguards, she went haywire. The only time I did feel she was not behaving like a woman whose children had been taken was after she was certain they had gone.'

Langton closed his eyes, shaking his head. 'Go on?'

'Well, it was then she disclosed how she had lied about never seeing the man she called Anthony Collingwood. I was with her for over an hour.'

'Could she have been stalling for time?'

'I don't understand.'

Langton had a go at her. '*Think:* have her kids been kidnapped? Or did she know they wouldn't be at home?'

By now, Cunningham had set up the connection with the surveillance team. She had organised a back-up vehicle, to help keep track of Julia. The radio crackled, as they reported that Julia had turned off the M25. Via the surveillance team, they put in a request for any patrol cars in the vicinity not to pull her over; she was driving at over 90 miles per hour and they didn't want her journey halted for a speeding ticket.

Langton returned to discussing the case. He under-lined Julius D'Anton's name. This was one death he couldn't quite fathom out. They knew that Julius went to Shipston on Stour for an antique fair; they knew he wanted to buy a table from the antique dealer Michael Sudmore, but Honour, Julia's sister, working in the shop that day, had refused until he made a cash payment. D'Anton had called on the woman who owned the cottage close to the farm, as he reckoned that, if the table came from her cottage, she might have something else to sell. Did he, at some point, have contact with Alexander Fitzpatrick? And, therefore, become a real risk? Because the next sighting they had was D'Anton driving the Mitsubishi, trying to fit the table into the back; so, since the time of the fair and his failed attempt to get the table with a deposit and a rubber cheque, he had come by a fistful of cash and a jeep.

All the while Langton talked, the radio continued to report the whereabouts of Julia Brandon. Still driving way over the speed limit, she was cutting across the M25 to head onto the slip road for the M40. The next four radio contacts silenced the incident room.

Julia's Mercedes had driven at eighty miles an hour off the motorway, careering and skidding along the slip road, and hurtling at an even higher speed onto the hard shoulder of the M40; she had created a near-collision as she got onto the motorway. They listened as the two surveillance teams reported, in pitched voices, that the Mercedes had jack-knifed across the slow and middle lanes. In an attempt to steady the skidding car, she appeared to turn the wheel to her right to avoid heading back into the traffic, only to do an almost ninety-degree spin, and crash through the barrier, directly into the path of a juggernaut.

The incident room could even hear the colossal bang and squeal of brakes, then a terrible sound of crunching metal and splintering glass, followed by an almighty boom as the massive juggernaut tipped onto its side and caught fire.

By the time Anna and Langton arrived at the crash site, traffic cops had laid out cones to direct oncoming cars to use a single lane. Cranes were hauling the juggernaut out of the motorway. Already moved was the crushed and blackened Mercedes, the roof completely caved in, the driver's side covered in blood. An ambulance was at the scene, but there was no hope of anyone getting out of the car alive. Langton and Anna walked over to the ambulance.

The driver of the juggernaut was being attended to; he appeared to have no severe injuries, just deep cuts and bruises. They were waiting for a second ambulance to take him to hospital. Langton spoke quietly to the ambulance attendant. He was told that the victim had virtually been sliced in two, and decapitated. Langton then looked from the open back door into the interior. He turned to Anna and said he was sorry to put her through it, but they needed to know for certain.

Anna stepped inside and placed a mask over her face and put on rubber gloves. It was hideous; the body was so severely mangled. She gave a nod that she was ready for the attendant to pull back the cloth from Julia's decapitated head. The blonde hair was matted with blood, but Anna recognised the diamond earrings. She couldn't really look into the face at first, but she had to; she bent down, moving some hair away from the cheeks. It was definitely the once-beautiful Julia Brandon.

Langton was standing with the police around Julia's wrecked Mercedes, as they prised open the boot. He removed the overnight bag, and was handed a handbag in a plastic container. The contents were crushed almost flat: a pair of sunglasses shattered, likewise a perfume bottle. To avoid getting shards of glass on his hand, he wrapped a handkerchief around it, then brought out a smashed mobile phone. He closed the bag and said they would examine it later. There was no passport.

By the time Anna returned with Langton to the station, it was late. She felt drained, but he was still energised and eager to discuss what the car crash meant to the investigation. Julia's belongings had been sent to the lab, but nothing would be done until the morning. Anna was told by Cunningham to take off and return early. She looked towards Langton for his confirmation that she could go home. He wafted his hand and turned back to talk to Phil.

'Get the wrecked car checked over and put the pressure on,' Langton told him. 'The surveillance guys said that she was driving that fast down the slip road, and onto the motorway, like someone hellbent on suicide.' Phil, who also was tired out, having worked from eight that morning, nevertheless went off to arrange it.

Cunningham looked at her watch, then at Langton. 'Maybe you should take a break.'

'Was she going to her sister's?' he muttered, ignoring her suggestion.

'That's what we all thought.'

'Not Gatwick, not Heathrow, and not Southampton, so that excludes boats and planes. Do we have anything from her landline?'

'No calls,' Cunningham said, trying to hide a yawn.

Langton removed from his pocket the crushed mobile, still wrapped in his handkerchief. 'Get this checked over; see if we can find out who called. She had to have made contact with someone to do a runner, right?' He frowned. 'Unless it was already planned.'

Cunningham said nothing, but looked at her watch again, eager to get home. 'When are you going to pick up the sister and her husband?'

'When I'm ready. As long as we know they are holed up at that farm, they can stay there. One move out of it that looks suspicious, we pick them both up and bring them in, but I'm not quite ready for them.'

Again, Cunningham said nothing; nor did she remark that it now appeared, to all intents and purposes, that James Langton had taken over the case.

Anna hadn't realised how tired she was until she got home. It had been strange to work alongside Langton. He never showed her the slightest familiarity – in fact, quite the reverse – but it was not as difficult to work beside him as she had thought.

Like Cunningham, she knew that he had taken over the case. She had to admit that, with him at the helm, they were regrouping, as if he had picked them all up and shaken them. She also wondered, just like Cunningham, why he had not yet brought in Honour and Damien; she was as certain as everyone else of their involvement. Her eyes started to droop as she lay back on her pillow; the last image before she fell asleep was the dead Julia's face, and the glinting diamond earrings.

Chapter Twenty

Laid out on a trestle table covered in white paper were the items removed from Julia Brandon's handbag. The shards of glass had been swept to one side in a small heap. The wallet contained three hundred pounds in crisp new notes. There were sunglasses, now with a twisted frame, and two photographs of the children in a small leather case. There were some dry cleaning receipts and old car parking tickets, paid for at a machine. A silver powder compact was open, with the lid caved in as if someone had stamped on it. Everything had a strong smell of Julia's perfume, from the broken bottle of Chanel No. 5. The diamond earrings were in a small plastic bag, with a Rolex watch, a gold chain with a large dewdrop diamond, and a small daisy chain diamond bracelet.

Anna stood, staring down at the items – then jumped with fright as someone came up behind her.

'Long time no see.'

'Pete!' She turned. She couldn't resist telling him that she had dropped by his house after her drinks with Langton. 'But just as I was drawing up,' she concluded, 'I saw your friend Daniella paying a taxi, so I headed home.'

'Oh right – yeah, she did come by. You should have joined us.'

Anna laughed. 'I'm sure.'

'You two seemed very familiar.'

'I'm sorry?'

'You and Langton.'

'Well, we've worked together a few times,' Anna said defensively.

Pete said casually, 'I suppose you must have got a shock, seeing me there.'

'No – it is your local, isn't it?' Anna was surprised at how readily the lie came. 'I was concerned you might feel I'd said one thing to you and then done another.' She apologised for not calling him and explained that they had been run ragged with the case.

'So I hear. In fact, I was beginning to wonder when you lot would bring in another body!'

'Well, you've got one – or her possessions, at least.'

'Yeah, I hear she was pretty mashed.' Pete looked over the table. 'Okay . . . most interesting – and please do not ask me how I can be so certain – is the powder compact.'

'Yes?'

'Pure, very high quality cocaine.'

They walked further along the table to the overnight bag and its contents which were laid out, item by item: a satin nightdress with matching dressing-gown; a small pair of silk slippers; a lace brassière and matching panties; two new packs of seven-denier stockings and a suspender belt; some make-up in a velvet bag. There were also two cashmere sweaters, a pair of Yves Saint Laurent black trousers and a pair of soft leather, high-heeled boots.

Anna could smell Julia's perfume; to touch the luxurious and very expensive clothes made her skin crawl.

'She must have been a very sexy woman,' Pete said, folding his arms; then he said there was one other item that had been locked up – the dead woman's jewellery case. 'We didn't put the other jewellery in, as it has traces of blood on, so will need to be tested.' He unlocked a small safe, signed a book by the side of it, and took out a square black leather jewel bag. It unfolded like a large envelope; if Anna had been impressed by the size of Julia's diamond earrings, she now looked on in amazement.

'Don't quote me, because I don't really know, but the emeralds look magnificent. Each item is, in my estimation, exceptional quality. What do you think?'

Anna agreed. As she had never owned an emerald, she wouldn't know, but the colour of the stones in the large necklace was beautiful. Amongst the items were rings and spectacular drop earrings of ruby and pearl; the pearls were large, and glowed on the black velvet lining.

'Nice booty; maybe why she couldn't stand to be broke,' Langton said, making both Anna and Pete turn.

'Not broke if you sell this lot,' Pete replied.

'Ah, but she reckoned she'd earned these. You know what they say about a woman scorned? She wasn't going to sell this lot; she wanted it all. Like she said, "What have I done?" Well, what she did was get very greedy, and underestimate what Lover Boy would do.'

'Have you seen the items taken from her handbag?' Pete asked.

Langton walked back along the trestle table as Pete returned the jewels to the safe. He paused for a moment by the silk nightdress, and then gently lifted a part of the hem to smell it. 'Nice. Some women know what's a turn-on in the bedroom, and I'd say this lady was hot to trot. No wonder he kept her for all those years.'

457

'You can tell all that from her nightdress, can you?'
Anna wished she'd kept her mouth shut. 'Pete said there's
cocaine in the powder compact,' she added quickly.

'And old Pete would know!' Langton said softly. His
mobile rang, and he moved off slightly to take the call.

Pete returned. 'Shall we meet up tonight?'

'Why not? It'll be down to what time we're through.
I didn't get back until after eleven last night.'

'Well, call me. I can come to you, or you can come to
me, or we can go Italian or Indian.'

'Travis!' Langton was already banging through the
door into the corridor. As Anna scurried after him down
the stone stairs, he told her they had come up with
something in the mechanical forensic section in the yard.

They left the building and headed into a cordoned-off
yard with large hangars. Inside, a team of four forensic
experts were checking over the appalling wreckage of
Julia Brandon's Mercedes. It was cut into sections so as
to prise apart the crushed metal. Langton went up to the
men and conferred with them; then they walked him
round to show him sections laid out on a big workbench.
Anna felt like a spare part as she moved around the
wreckage, standing back as a metal cutter was used on a
section of dashboard.

The engine had shifted into the front seats and a
section of the bonnet had already been cut away. Now
cleared, the mangled dashboard was visible and they
could get access to the buckled glove compartment. They
used a crowbar to prise it open. The contents – like those
of Julia's handbag, which must have been on the front
seat – were flattened and soaking wet, as there had been a
bottle of water inside. They slowly began to withdraw,
with large steel tweezers, the crushed plastic bottle, then

a leather-covered road map, an AA book and the Mercedes' manual. Each item removed was placed into plastic evidence bags.

Langton joined Anna. He watched for a few moments, and then said quietly that Julia hadn't stood a hope in hell of getting out of the car alive; what surprised him was that it hadn't happened sooner. 'The brakes were tampered with, virtually severed in two.' He then took off, shouting out his thanks to the workers, and headed back towards the car park. 'Fucking surveillance.'

Anna chased after him. 'If the car was parked in her garage, there were the two so-called bodyguards inside the house, plus the children, plus the so-called au pair! There's a connecting door from the kitchen into the garage; they would have had plenty of time to cut her brakes without being seen.'

Langton glared. 'Somebody, either the two beefed-up bodyguards, or some unknown bastard, took her kids and drove fucking out, right under our noses.'

'Their routine was to be taken to nursery school.'

'Jesus Christ!'

Anna persisted: after the surveillance team saw the children go into the school, they returned to the property.

'Letting them just walk out of the school!'

'The officers were *told* to return to the house, as Julia was by then in a patrol car, with me, heading back there!'

'Fine, fine. Make excuses for total incompetence!' He got into the front passenger seat beside the driver and slammed the car door so hard it rocked.

Anna refused to rise to the bait. She got into the back of the patrol car and sat, tight-lipped.

He calmed down as they drove out of the yard.

'Unless that is exactly what she intended to happen: lead them off, then come into the station and have a screaming fit.'

'I think she was a liar, and a very good one, but I honestly don't think she had any prior knowledge that the children were going to be taken.'

'Well, thank you for that insight, Travis,' Langton muttered. He turned to face her, leaning his arm along the back of the seat. 'What if she did have? You said you thought it strange the way she went from hysteria into giving you a eulogy; even admitting that Collingwood had been to the house.'

Anna shrugged, not believing it. 'What she didn't know was that her brakes would be liable to give way.'

He turned back to face the front, as they continued the journey across London towards Chalk Farm and the station. 'The clothes, the overnight bag; that doesn't look like someone who didn't know where she was going. The suitcase should have sent alarm bells ringing, albeit to two dozy fuckers on surveillance.'

'They were on her tail the moment she left the house.'

'Yeah, I know, but where was she going? M40 to Oxford? Unless she was doing a drive-around to lose the tail? They said she was doing over ninety most of the time – so *was* she leading them on a runaround? Or was she heading for the farmhouse and her sister?'

'Well, it's going to be hard to question her!'

'Very adroit, Travis.'

She asked why he had delayed on bringing in Honour and Damien Nolan.

'I'm not positive I've done the right thing, if the surveillance team on them is as fucking useless as the one on Julia Brandon.'

'But surely they're both implicated?' They knew the Mitsubishi had been there; they knew Damien probably wrote the directions, too.

Langton slapped the seat with the flat of his hand. 'You presume! We can't presume anything!' He took a deep breath, exhaling slowly as if to control his temper. 'They are involved in this up to their necks but, until we have something to really pull the carpet from under their feet, we stay off them. We watch and we wait.'

'For what?'

Langton remained silent, then murmured, almost to himself, 'He is going to surface.'

'You presume,' Anna said, equally softly.

He suddenly laughed, tilting his head back. *'Touché.'*

They continued in silence, getting into heavy traffic in the West End. Langton stared out of the window, sighing. He then instructed the driver to put the flashing lights on and move. 'Not that we've anything to hurry back for,' he muttered. After a while he leaned forwards, rubbing his head. 'You know, if anything had happened to Tommy . . .'

'Your stepson?' Anna asked.

He gave a soft laugh. 'My *son*. If anyone had taken him – harmed him in any way – I wouldn't have sat there, giving you a lengthy rundown of who did what to whom.'

'She didn't have much option.'

'But wouldn't she have been screaming to go and find her kids, get a search going or something – like a caring mother would? Unless she knew who had taken them and, like I said, possibly even set it up.' Langton paused for a moment. 'Didn't she tell you that the father of her second daughter Kathy was Damien Nolan?'

461

'If the children were taken to Honey Farm, we'd know.'

'Maybe they weren't taken there, but somewhere that Julia Brandon knew about – which could mean that the couple might be getting ready to do a runner. We've assumed that, because she was heading for the M40, that's where she was going. Maybe, for once, we're right.' Langton clicked on his mobile and gave instructions to the team to get more surveillance standing by, and bring in the local Oxfordshire police, to make sure the Nolans were surrounded at the farmhouse and unable to make a move without a trace on them. Anna then saw him physically tense, listening. He swore and said that he would be there in ten minutes. As he cut off the call, he punched at the dashboard with his fist.

'What's happened?'

She didn't get an answer as they drove into the Chalk Farm Station car park. Langton was out before the patrol car had stopped and, bad knee or not, he ran into the station. Tapping in the code at the back door, he was already halfway down the corridor as Anna entered the station after him.

The incident room was busy, phones ringing, as Phil hurried to join Langton. 'He's in with Cunningham. She's giving him all the information we've got so far.'

Langton had thrown his coat off and was heading towards Cunningham's office.

Anna still had no idea what was going down. 'What's happening, Phil?'

'Fraud Squad. DCI John Marlow is in with her.'

'*Travis!*' Langton bellowed, waving one arm for her to follow him.

Langton opened Cunningham's office door, Anna on

his heels. She froze on seeing the man who stood up to greet Langton.

The face blocking the CCTV security camera in David Rushton's office was printed indelibly on her mind. They had unsuccessfully attempted to match it with the old photographs of Alexander Fitzpatrick taken from the Internet: it was blurred, with only three-quarters of his face showing due to the baseball cap. It was this image that had been used to confirm whether or not he had been a guest at the top London hotels. They had got nowhere, and this was obviously why: the man on the CCTV footage was DCI John Marlow.

The small office felt claustrophobic. Marlow was a big man, at least six feet three, with broad shoulders. He had dark brown collar-length hair combed back; it looked as if it was gelled, as it was so stiff. Both Anna and Langton drew up chairs, as Marlow gave them details of a fraud his team had been investigating for two years. A client of David Rushton's had got in touch with them, about missing funds. They had begun an undercover investigation, quietly contacting other clients as the fraud began to unravel. Rushton had been misappropriating clients' money in a complicated paper-trail of fictional companies, whilst moving millions into his own offshore accounts. They had not, as yet, begun to delve into the accounts of Julia Brandon, but were about to start.

Marlow said that he had already approached Rushton, acting as a potential client. He had a deep resonant voice, and calmly continued, 'I had an appointment with Rushton in his office at around six-thirty. I had implied that the funds I had to be taken care of were proceeds from something illegal. He wasn't fazed, quite the reverse. He said he would not ask questions, but what he could do was outline the options for securing a safe way of moving the money out of the UK without any problems from the Inland Revenue.'

Langton leaned forwards, rubbing at his knee. Anna could hardly breathe, she was so taken aback. In the flesh, Marlow was rather handsome with very good, white teeth. Why she was even thinking about his teeth, she could not imagine, but she found it hard to concentrate on what he was saying.

'I was there for no more than a few minutes. When his phone rang, he apologised and said that he had to rearrange our meeting as he had a client desperate to see him.' He shrugged. 'To be honest, I believe he may have sussed what was going down – he may even have been tipped off by the caller – but he couldn't wait to get me out. To make a show of my possible criminal activities, I got up and remarked about the security camera; he said it wasn't turned on, but he was very nervous, really agitated, which again led me to believe he was on to me. I turned the camera to face the wall and said I didn't like being messed around. He said we could meet in a few days, but it was necessary he saw this client immediately. We made another appointment and I left.'

'Did you get to see this client?'

'No, but whoever it was must have come in directly after I left.'

Cunningham showed him a photograph of Julia Brandon. Marlow didn't recognise her. He had not left via the main reception, as Rushton had told him that the main door would be locked, but used a service exit at the rear of the building, the same way he had entered, which was why he had not been caught on the reception

CCTV camera. Cunningham had already given him details of what they had so far been able to uncover about Rushton, but had only just passed him Julia Brandon's documents. Marlow spent some time glancing over them, and asked if he could retain a copy for his file.

They watched the replay of the reception area footage showing Julia Brandon entering and moving towards the lifts. Marlow shook his head. 'He must have buzzed her in almost as I left, because I went back into Jermyn Street to wait and see if I recognised who this client was. I sat in the car for about half an hour, and then walked back to the service door to see if anyone entered that way. I was there for at least another half-hour, then called it quits and left.'

'Play the audio tape,' Langton said.

Marlow looked surprised. 'You've got one?'

Cunningham set up the tape, explaining, to Langton's irritation, that Rushton had had a hidden tape deck, but that, except for the section with Julia, the security camera footage had no sound.

'Well, if it's of any use to me, I'd like to hear it.'

Marlow leaned forward to listen. Anna watched him intently, but he gave no reaction apart from shrugging his shoulders when the tape ended.

'Pity it cut out, and because I turned the camera around you didn't get a shot of the killer. Still, I'd like a copy of the tape for my files.'

Langton was sitting in sullen silence. Gordon tapped and entered. He had photocopied the documents showing the money transfers made by Rushton for Julia Brandon. Marlow thanked him.

'We continued our investigation and, as we had no suspicious contact from Rushton, we were planning for

465

me to keep the new appointment; that was when we found out about his murder.'

'Bloody marvellous,' muttered Langton.

'Why I'm here,' Marlow added, with a shrug.

Langton seemed tired out. He stood up and asked for access, if it was possible, to the Fraud Squad's findings and their list of clients. Marlow asked if they believed one of them killed Rushton.

Langton shook his head. 'I doubt it, unless you've got one dealing in Fentanyl.'

'What's that?'

'The way Rushton was killed: injection, big overdose of this lethal drug.'

'Shit. Well, that's two years down the fucking drain. I'll talk to our guys and get the files over to you.'

Marlow was thanked for coming in and left. When he had gone, Langton was cursing. 'We've been acting like bloody fools, going after the wrong man.'

He stalked out to have a smoke outside, to try and calm his fury.

The team looked to Cunningham, who was sitting, arms folded, by the incident board. She stood up and nodded to Anna. 'You almost missed Marlow; he was about to leave before you two came back. I'll need the update from the labs, but I suggest we all take a break from the case for tonight; pick up tomorrow.'

There was an overall feeling of dejection. Anna asked for someone to get in touch with their computer boffins to see if they could access any of the calls from Julia Brandon's mobile.

Langton made them jump, the doors banged so hard as he walked into the room. 'Get onto the Fraud Squad,

Phil,' he rapped out. 'Get me the details of Marlow.'

Phil looked surprised. 'You have a problem with him?'

'Yeah I do, a big one. Just do it!' Langton had to sit down. He asked someone to get him a beaker of water. He was so tense that Anna was worried.

She crossed to his side. 'You okay?'

'Could use some of that Fentanyl; my knee's killing me.' He gulped at the water. She could see his hand was shaking, as he fumbled in his pocket to take out a foil wrapper of tablets. He pressed out two, taking them both with a mouthful of water, then tossed the beaker into a trash can. 'I think we have all just been fucked over.' He said it so quietly, it was hardly audible.

Phil was holding on, waiting for a connection. 'Looks like they've gone home. You know those guys – work a nine to five.' Then he was through.

Langton couldn't contain himself. He got up and snatched the phone. 'This is DCS James Langton, Murder Squad; it's imperative we speak to one of your officers, a DCI John Marlow.' There was a pause. 'In connection with the ongoing investigation into a fraud involving a David Rushton.' Langton listened; he was so tense, Anna could see the muscles in his neck twitching. 'Thank you – must be some screw-up our end.' He put the phone down. 'There *is* no DCI John Marlow working with the Fraud Squad, and no ongoing investigation involving David Rushton.'

The room fell silent. Anna couldn't quite take it in.

When Langton eventually continued, his voice was like gravel. 'I think we just had a visit from Alexander Fitzpatrick. The bastard had the cheek to walk in – walk in! – and we all fell for it!'

Cunningham had to clear her throat before she could

speak. 'But he had ID – he showed it to me. Why would he take such a risk?'

'He carried it out with him, the information about what Rushton has done with Julia Brandon's cash; he also now has every single piece of information we've got involving him. Maybe he just wanted to see how close we are to catching him!' Langton gave a short bark of a laugh. 'Answer is, we're so off the mark that the two-faced bastard had the audacity to walk in off the street with fake ID.'

What had made Langton suspicious? Anna wanted to ask. No one else had questioned Marlow's authenticity. On the contrary, they had passed over a copy of the file he requested and even thanked him for coming in.

'Well, at least we know he's here in London. I said that, didn't I?' He looked to Anna. 'I said he would surface. Well, he did, and he's made the lot of us look like total arseholes. At least we know one important thing: Alexander Fitzpatrick is broke and hurting for cash so much that he risked walking in here. Rushton did us a favour; now we concentrate on that money he stashed away for Julia Brandon, because Fitzpatrick is after it, and we are going to get him. Right now, he must think he's so clever he's out of reach, but he's not.' He made a gesture with his right hand as if catching a fly; then he clapped, as if killing it between his hands.

Langton's speech seemed to inject energy into the team. He picked up his coat, saying he would be with them first thing in the morning. He needed to get home, suggesting that a break would probably do all of them good. He didn't say anything more to Anna; not that she was expecting him to.

It had sounded strange to her that he had said he

needed to get home. Langton had never appeared to be, in all the time she had known him, a man who needed a home life; quite the reverse. It was yet another sign of how far apart they had grown. The thought that he now had a domestic life that he wanted to get back to made her envious, because she didn't have one.

She felt the need for company, at the very least – which was why she called Pete, and arranged to drive over to his house. He was, as ever, pleased to hear from her, and said they could order in a pizza.

'I'd like that,' Anna said. She replaced the receiver, and collected her briefcase and coat.

As she went out to her car, she felt better. She decided she would stop off to buy a good bottle of wine. To have someone waiting, eager to see her, was exactly what she needed.

Chapter Twenty-one

Pete and Anna had drunk half the bottle before the pizza arrived. The fire was lit and they ate in front of it, leaning their backs against the sofa; the bottle empty, they opened another. Pete sat back on his heels. 'I know you don't approve, but I'm going to have a joint.'

Anna, rather tipsy, said she didn't care. She started to tell Pete about the man they had suspected to be Alexander Fitzpatrick posing as a Fraud Squad officer. Pete handed her the joint and she took a couple of deep drags, as she went on to explain how they had all been totally taken in by his fake ID.

Pete was having a hard time following the gist of what she was saying. 'You are telling me he just walked in?'

'Yes, and everyone was taken in by him.'

Pete started to laugh; it was so preposterous and so audacious, he couldn't stop laughing.

Anna, at first, wasn't that amused, but the more he laughed, the less serious it all sounded, until she too was helpless with giggles. 'He hoodwinked us all,' she said and then broke up, rolling about laughing.

It took a while before they both calmed down. Anna crawled over to her briefcase and took out the folder with Fitzpatrick's photograph. Pete, although bleary-eyed, took a long look at it; then Anna showed him some of the website pictures from years before. Pete fetched a large magnifying glass, and held it over the image taken from Rushton's CCTV camera. Then he looked at the younger man's pictures. 'He's had a lot of work; you see the way his earlobes are sort of stretched? That's a telltale sign of a full face-lift. Jawline is firm, and his neck – and what were his eyes like? I mean, how old is he?'

'The guy calling himself Marlow didn't have any bags or lines, looked a lot younger than Fitzpatrick's age, early sixties.'

'Doesn't look it. His nose has been reshaped, and I'd say he's had implants in his cheekbones, plus, judging by the texture of his skin, he's maybe had a face peel; there's hardly a line on him. You see this early photo off the website and the one with the ponytail and the two kids?'

Anna leaned closer.

'On both he's got a mole on his right cheek. But not on the one with the baseball cap. Did you catch it?'

'No – no, I didn't. Shit, I didn't even think about it.'

Anna held the magnifying glass and peered at the face of Fitzpatrick. 'No one thought it was odd he was attached to the Fraud Squad; if he had been, he would have retired years ago. He's well over six feet, and he didn't look as if he was carrying any excess weight.'

Pete yawned. 'Liposuction.'

Anna felt as tired.

'You going to stay overnight?' he asked, as she closed her eyes.

'There is no way I could drive home.'

Pete gave a soft laugh. 'Well, that's really encouraging – not so much as a peck on the cheek! I meant, are you going to stay with me – *in bed*, with me?'

'Yes.'

He reached over and took her hand, and hauled her to her feet. 'Come on, let's go upstairs. It's after three.'

He had to steer her up the narrow staircase; she was so out of it, he had to help her undress. By the time she was down to her underwear, she was half-asleep; he flipped back the duvet for her to crawl inside.

'Oh, this feels so nice,' she said sleepily.

Pete looked at her, curled up like a child, her hands cupped beneath her chin. By the time he had undressed and got in beside her, she was dead to the world. He didn't wake her, but turned off the light to lie next to her and smoke his bedtime joint.

He couldn't fathom her out: why she had called him, why she had come round. He wasn't sure if it was just loneliness, or whether she had really wanted to see him. Her red curly hair was just visible above the big duvet as he took a couple of deep drags, inhaling the grass deeply. Sex had been on his mind – was, to some extent, on it even now – but after a while, his eyes drooped, and he stubbed out the roach and snuggled down beside her. She turned, in her sleep, onto her side and he curled up around her, resting one arm across her waist. There was an innocence to their sleeping which belied both their professions.

Langton had taken a load of medication to ease the never-ceasing pain that affected his knee. Sometimes, at night, his chest felt as if it was on fire where he had been sliced by the machete; the scar burned and was often inflamed. Only when he lay naked, his chest bared, did he feel it cool. To embrace sleep, he drank heavily to block out the constant pain, but most nights were restless and tormented. Often, while he was sinking into limbo before he slept, he would go over the case – or now, in his position, various cases – but tonight, all he could turn his mind to was Alexander Fitzpatrick. He couldn't help but have some admiration for his risk-taking, even though he knew that, if it were to get out, it would make not only himself but the entire murder team a laughing stock. As he lay half-asleep, the pain finally easing, he wondered if he had been correct about it just being the money Fitzpatrick was after. With his senses lulled, he came to the conclusion it had to be something else, but what, he was unable to grasp, as at last he went into a deep sleep.

Anna woke up with a start; then had to flop back against the pillow, her head throbbing.

Pete was already showered and dressed; he carried a mug of steaming black coffee to the bedside. 'I've already been called. My guys are at the station dusting down every surface our superhero may have touched for prints. I'm going to have to make an appearance, so I suggest you get this coffee down you. I'll cook us some scrambled eggs and we can drive in together.'

'What time is it?'

'Eight-thirty.'

'Oh God!' Anna showered and dressed and, with a raging headache, went downstairs. 'I don't think I could eat anything.'

'Try – you'll feel better; then we should get a move on.'

Anna perched on a stool as he dished up breakfast.

He hooked an arm around her and nuzzled her neck. 'You slept like a baby.'

'I don't remember getting into bed.'

'Well, I didn't have any physical contact with you! I think we were both out of it.'

'I'm sorry.' She dipped her fork into the eggs.

It was nine-thirty when Anna hurried into her office, and the incident room was hopping. Thankfully, there was no sign of Langton. No sooner had she put her briefcase down than Cunningham marched in.

'This is an almighty fuck-up. We've got them dusting for prints all over my office and on the file we handed to the piece of shit, but so far . . .' She shrugged.

Anna wasn't sure how to respond.

Cunningham didn't appear to want her to; she just leaned against the wall. 'Christ Almighty. I couldn't sleep last night, just thinking about it. The fucking civilian on the desk ushered him in and he walked straight up to the incident room – talk about over-confident! It just beggars belief. We've had financial experts in since the crack of dawn trying to assimilate Rushton's accountancy expertise. The room looks like it's spewing out the bloody phone directory: we've faxes that cover the length of the entire floor, and some accounting machine that they keep clicking that's knocking out what looks like the National Lottery numbers.'

'I'm sorry I was a bit late.'

'Well, Langton's not in yet. We're all sort of on tenterhooks trying to be one jump ahead of him. I've given up trying.' Cunningham looked at Anna. 'Did you have so much as a hint who he really was?'

'To be honest, I was so taken aback when I saw him, it took a while to sink in. I noticed his teeth though, how white they were – probably implants or caps, but very good ones.'

'I didn't, to be honest, and I'm not ashamed to admit it.'

'I think he's had a lot of facework, so it's no wonder we didn't recognise him.'

'That's not really the point, is it? Not only did not one of us suss out who he was, we bent over backwards thanking him for coming in!'

Gordon appeared, rather flushed in the face, his red hair standing on end. 'Excuse me, Ma'am, but Pete Jenkins wants to see you.' Cunningham walked out. Gordon glanced at Anna. 'You seen the incident room? Looks like a snowstorm!'

'I'll be right there.'

'What a joke, eh? Bloody walked in off the street!'

Anna sighed. 'Yes, Gordon, I think we are all aware of that.'

Cunningham looked glum, as Pete gestured to the edge of the desk she had been certain Fitzpatrick had touched. 'We've got smudges, plenty of them, but no clear prints, and we've none off the document you handed to him.'

'That's impossible.'

'Not if he covered his fingertips with a coat of clear nail varnish. I'm not saying that is what he did, but you can see in the dust the marks on your desk where, if he hadn't used something, we would have prints.'

'Christ, he thought of everything, didn't he?'

''Fraid so, Ma'am. I'll go back to the lab, shall I?'

'Yeah. We are still waiting, you know, on that blood swipe off the sheets at the farmhouse.'

'I know that, Ma'am. We have ascertained that it did not match the small residue taken from the Mitsubishi, nor the sample taken from the bullet DI Travis found at

476

the drug squat. As we don't have a sample of your suspect's blood, I can't—'

Cunningham interrupted him. 'Yes, you do. We had a sample brought in from the Oxfordshire police. They had it from the time Fitzpatrick was picked up for drink driving.'

'I am aware of that. I did send a memo to say that it was proving impossible to make a match with the bullet and the swipe mark as, not only due to the age, but—'

'Why is that?'

'Well, as I said, it's coming up for forty years old. It had been opened, and possibly left open, so could have been contaminated. For DNA extraction, we need—'

'I know what you need!' she said irritably. At that moment, Langton appeared at the end of the corridor and signalled for Cunningham to join him.

The team were all gathered as Langton took the floor, holding up an Internet print-out. It described how the Metropolitan Police were introducing a new warrant card to deter forgers. Langton shook his head, as he read how these warrant cards would have the name, rank, number and a clear digital photograph. 'As you can see, they also supply, on the same webpage, a clear picture of the Met Badge. It doesn't take much brainpower to see just how Fitzpatrick was able to show the civilian downstairs a fake ID, and for him to bring him up to the incident room.' There was a sort of embarrassed murmur around the team. Langton asked the guys working on the financial paper trail to stop clicking their machines for a few minutes, as they were giving him a headache.

Next, he looked around the team and asked, one by one, for them to repeat the exact interaction they had had with Fitzpatrick.

'I hold my hand up,' said Phil.

'What's that supposed to mean?' Langton said moodily.

'Well, when he was brought in, I was the one that had the most conversation with him.'

'Okay, what exactly was that?'

Phil explained how Fitzpatrick had said their case crossed over with his supposed fraud investigation. He had asked about the suspects and then about the progress to date.

'When he was asking about the suspects, did he focus on anyone particularly?'

'No, not really. He walked up and down, and made a joke about how we were collecting bodies like acorns.'

Langton asked him to think again: was there anyone out of the dead men that he spent more time on? Phil shook his head.

It was Gordon who interrupted. He said that, whilst Phil went to fetch Cunningham, Fitzpatrick had spent a while longer looking over the board. Langton looked at Gordon, asking him what he felt Fitzpatrick was looking at when Phil left the room.

'Well, sir, he just sort of did a slow walk, looking at all the photographs; he then got a chair and sat down.'

'Where did he sit?'

Gordon took a chair and turned it to face the incident board. 'Here.'

Langton sat in the chair. It was positioned directly in front of the photograph of Julius D'Anton. He remained silent for a while, thinking, staring at the dead man's face. He then gave a signal for the financial experts to continue working. Their machines spurted back into life, spewing out more pages.

Anna went into her office and spread out all the

different photographs they had of Fitzpatrick. She was so focused that she physically jumped when Langton walked in. 'Morning!' she said, flustered. 'I've been looking over . . .'

'Yes, yes – I can see that.'

'He's had extensive plastic surgery. Whether or not it was a wig he was wearing, I couldn't say, but if so, it was a good one. This is the picture of the man seen at the supposed wedding of Julia and Frank, but his grey hair is thinning and worn in a ponytail. Also, in this picture and in all the others we have off his website, he had a mole on his right cheek which could have been removed.'

Langton tapped the photograph of Fitzpatrick with the two little girls.

'This was taken six months ago, maybe more?'

'Yes, but I am sure it is him; he's put his hand up to stop the au pair taking any more pictures.'

'And what do you think that gives us?'

'Well, not a lot – but if he had all this plastic surgery, he must have left England and then returned with the new face. We might get lucky with immigration.'

'Yeah yeah yeah.' Langton sat down and rubbed at his knee.

'What gave it away to you?' she asked.

Langton looked at his worn suede shoes. 'His shoes.'

'His shoes?'

'Yeah. He sat like this in Cunningham's office.' He crossed his legs, resting his right leg across his left knee, and tapped his shoe. 'I had a clear look at his shoe; since when have you known any Met officer to wear handmade Lobb shoes?'

'Lobb?' She'd never heard of them.

'They're a very prestigious shoemakers in Regent

Street. They make a mould of the feet that'll cost you about two grand; they retain it and you order your new shoes, whenever required, and they deliver them.'

'They delivered them to him?'

Langton nodded. Due to the quality, they were not something reordered every six months. The last delivery of dark tan, lace-up shoes with hand-stitched soles was over two years ago. The address they had been delivered to was a substantial property in St John's Wood.

Anna leaned back, shaking her head. Again, the audacity of Fitzpatrick was beyond belief. This was the property that he and Julia Brandon had lived in, so openly he was even ordering handmade shoes to be delivered there. 'The shoe-prints we found at the drug site . . .' she said.

Langton shrugged. 'Well, I don't have laser eyes, but I'd say what he was wearing fits the description. When we find him – haw, haw – we can see if they match.'

Cunningham tapped and entered. 'Need you in the incident room, James.'

'Great. This is what I've been waiting for.'

The financial experts stood with their faxes and adding-machine rolls and began to list on a large sheet of paper the different countries where they had, so far, tracked the transfers of bulk sums of money. They had a list of names of the holders of the accounts: Julia Brandon, Julia Collingwood, Julia Nolan, Julia Henson. They pinned up a vast map of the world and, using a red marker pen, showed the movement of the money between London, Geneva, the Cayman Islands, Florida, Germany and Argentina. Next, they listed the sums of money, showing how there had been a virtual circle of transferrals. The second list of names was suspicious, because they were aliases of David Rushton; on each transfer for Julia, in all her various names, he cut a slice for himself and fed it back to an account in New York.

'So he was dipping his fingers in the honey pot?' Langton said.

Their FT expert was a dome-headed man in a pin-striped suit. 'Yes, he siphoned off around four million.'

The next list of names none of them recognised. With another red marker, they showed on the map that, as money was transferred into Julia's accounts, it was diverted into bank accounts held by these unknown names in the Bahamas, Miami, the Philippines and, lastly, India. Like a landslide, all the monies were gradually being poured into the last three accounts.

'How much?' Langton asked.

'Well, with the missing amount taken by David Rushton, I'd say there's about eight million in English pounds. Remember, each transfer is affected by the ex-change rate; with the dollar, it gained, but then dropped back when it was withdrawn from the Caymans.' He turned over a clean white sheet. 'The account in the Bahamas was emptied two days ago and the Miami account was transferred to this one in the Philippines.'

'So all the money you say is now in the Philippines?'

'Correct, but I couldn't tell you how long for; they were the least co-operative.'

Langton asked how fast this had all taken place, and was told most of it had been moving within the last forty-eight hours; therefore, as they spoke, it could be on the move again. Whilst the financial people packed up, with instructions to monitor the Philippines account, the team were quiet, waiting for Langton's response.

'I was wrong,' he told them all. 'Fitzpatrick has to

think he's got the dough; in fact, when he came here he knew it – so why *did* he come here?'

Langton still sat in Fitzpatrick's chair. He asked himself, was it the act of a desperate man? Or one with such an ego, he just wished to make them a laughing stock? He dismissed the latter as being too far-fetched; there had to be something he needed. He stood up and, with his back to the team, paced along the incident-room board past the victims' photographs: Frank Brandon, Donny Petrozzo, Stanley Leymore, David Rushton. Julia Brandon's picture was not, as yet, up.

He stood in front of Julius D'Anton's picture. 'Right, if our man visits Rushton and gets him to rework the money transfers – say, back to him in the Philippines – he's served his purpose, so he kills him.' Langton's voice was quite hard to hear; he spoke quietly, as he thought it through. 'Julia Brandon had already attempted to cheat him, using Rushton; she had become a thorn in his side. So he gets rid of her.' Langton sat down again in the same chair, staring at Julius D'Anton's picture. 'We know somewhere he has two children, two henchmen and the au pair, but we have no trace on them – nothing coming in from any port – so they could all still be hiding out in the UK.' Langton repeated twice, almost to himself: 'Why take the risk of coming into the incident room. He had the money, why didn't he just get out?'

'Maybe he already has,' Phil said.

'No, no. Eight million, or whatever he thinks he's got his hands on, isn't enough. Remember, a man on the run needs a hell of a wedge to keep him safe. It's payout time every bloody minute; to cover his tracks will cost. So *what* did he come here for?'

Langton turned to Anna and asked her to run by him the entire scenario that involved Julius D'Anton.

Anna opened her notebook. She detailed the sighting of Julius D'Anton driving the Mitsubishi, trying to collect the antique table with a wad of cash; his broken-down van, traced to the garage in Shipston on Stour; the discovery of his body, floating in the Thames; the post mortem, detailing that death was due to an overdose of Fentanyl. 'As with Donny Petrozzo.'

Langton stopped her. 'Forget Donny Petrozzo; just focus on D'Anton.'

'Well, he had been at Balliol at the same time as Fitzpatrick, so we thought that, when he crashed his van, he might have walked up to the farmhouse, seen Fitz-patrick there and recognised him; that's how he got access to the Mitsubishi, and enough money to go back to buy the table.'

'Go on.' Langton wafted his hand.

'His widow at first said that he hadn't returned that weekend, but she later retracted her statement, saying she had not actually been at home, so it was possible that he had returned. She said that she was having an affair with the builder, and was away the entire weekend with him.'

'What about the property?'

'Well, the D'Antons had only just bought it and were renovating it. They made their living doing up property to sell, though D'Anton continued to deal in antiques. His widow also admitted that he was still using drugs; he spent time in rehab but was, invariably, clean for only a short while before he started using again.'

'Where was his body found?' Langton asked, rubbing his head.

'Just by the weir in Teddington. It was estimated that

he had been in the water for at least two or three days, but death was down to an overdose of Fentanyl, as with Donny Petrozzo.'

'Just keep off fucking Petrozzo, I said, and stick to D'Anton!'

'That's about it.'

Langton pursed his lips, and said that it was all supposition.

'We do know the Mitsubishi was at the farmhouse,' Anna said quietly. 'We have had soil and horse-manure samples tested.'

He sat in brooding silence; nobody liked to interrupt. After a few moments, he stood up and tapped D'Anton's picture. 'He, I think, is the key. He and his wife buy houses, sell up, move on. Hard to find an address, right?'

No one could fathom out where Langton was going with his queries; he seemed unsure himself. 'There are no coincidences! All that "he maybe recognised Fitzpatrick" – well, not one of us did, did we! So take that out of the equation. Look at his character: D'Anton, junkie, did time for drug dealing, wife stands by him, in and out of rehab – a real loser. There he is, with an eye for antiques, and a table that the dealer himself said he had wrongly underpriced – everyone with me so far?'

Anna sat on the edge of her chair, tense, listening; finding her old admiration for him flooding back. You could almost see the wheels turning in his brain as he attempted to knit together a scenario that made sense. He gave long pauses, rubbing at his temple, and then he smiled. 'So much for clapping my hands and catching at a fly,' he said. Then he stood up and tapped D'Anton's photograph. 'Okay, try this for size. Our junkie antique guy can't get the table because he's been turned down, but he learns that the table came from a cottage. Like a good cheap creep dealer, he pays a visit. He discovers that the old lady has already sold up anything of value, so he asks about any other properties close by. Right so far, Travis?'

'Yes, we interviewed the old lady in question. She remembered directing D'Anton to Honey Farm.'

'D'Anton drives his van into a ditch, and can't reverse out, so he walks to the farmhouse. He needs to get someone to haul him out.' Langton turned over the sheets of paper the financial team had used. He drew the farmhouse and the narrow lane leading to it in childish and rather inept strokes. 'According to our surveillance team, the couple stay very much at home. They don't use the front entrance, but the rear – correct, Travis?'

'Yes, the bell doesn't work.'

Langton nodded. 'Julius D'Anton – no money, pissed off; no deal with the table, pissed off – gets to the farmhouse. No answer. What if, parked in their yard, is the Mitsubishi? Not only parked but, maybe with the keys in the ignition?' He looked at everyone.

Anna coughed. If her theory was supposition, this was surely just as much so.

'D'Anton opens it, looks inside. What if there are drugs or a stash of money in the glove compartment? I'm not talking big money, maybe a couple of grand; could have been in a wallet, whatever. He needs something to go back and sort his van out. Nobody around, so he just gets in and drives off. D'Anton gets to the village; tries to buy the table, pays over money, but it won't fit in the back of the jeep. He drives on; even arranges for his van to be shifted by the locals. Guess what? Honour is serving in the shop! Honour, who fucking knows that jeep, but does not know D'Anton. I am assuming Fitzpatrick was the one who drove it to the farmhouse. Did she call, to ask Fitzpatrick if he had let this creep drive it?'

Langton patted his pockets, really needing a smoke, but then controlled himself; instead, he began to twist the pen round and round. He asked Travis to give details of the vehicles known to have been used at the farm: there was only the old Range Rover. If the Range Rover had been used to follow the Mitsubishi on the motorway, it would have had a hard time keeping up. There was now a time gap, he believed, due to the fact that whoever was following D'Anton lost him. 'Hard man to track down, if he moved addresses. This time gap is vital.'

On the board, he marked up:

1) *Donny Petrozzo knew D'Anton*

2) *Donny Petrozzo was involved with Frank Brandon*

3) *Frank Brandon had come into contact with Alexander Fitzpatrick, but knew him only as Anthony Collingwood; Frank had been offered a deal that it was hard to walk away from: a lot of money, enough to marry and buy a house*

Langton drew links between each man, and circled D'Anton's name.

'We now have this junkie wheeling around in a stolen jeep. He's found a stash of money in the glove compartment – remember, this was the same jeep that Frank

Brandon drove to the squat.' He drew another link over to where he then wrote *drug squat*, underlined it, and tossed the marker pen aside. Langton then continued, covering the night Frank Brandon was shot dead, and the fact that whoever was with him was wounded but escaped and drove to Honey Farm.

'Now, what if – and it's a big if – what if Julius D'Anton did contact Petrozzo, because he had something big to sell?' Langton looked around the room. 'The box of Fentanyl was still in the back of the Mitsubishi. I don't think he knew what the hell he'd got.'

There was a unanimous gasp; suddenly everything started to make sense.

'Julius D'Anton may not have been murdered; he could have tested the stuff out and killed himself. We all know it's fucking lethal. If he was dead as a dodo in the jeep, Donny could have tossed him into the river, driven the Mitsubishi back to the garage in Wimbledon – and bingo, walks straight into the hypodermic needle, courtesy of Fitzpatrick.' It was not a curtain down, but it felt like it. Anna wanted to applaud him because, as theories went, it was a bloody good one.

They were all given their day's investigation by the duty manager, working alongside Cunningham. She said to Anna, 'You are with Langton; he wants to reinterview D'Anton's wife.'

She looked confused.

'Langton didn't quite finish his oration this morning. James thinks that the reason Fitzpatrick brazened it out here is because the drugs are still missing.'

'Shit!' Anna said. 'So that's what he's after. Does he think they're at D'Anton's house?'

'Maybe. They haven't surfaced anywhere else. That's for you to find out.'

By the time Anna got into the patrol car alongside Langton, he was resting his head back on the headrest. 'You didn't give us your punchline,' she said, smiling.

'I need to stop off at a chemist; pick up my prescription,' was all he said in reply. He closed his eyes, as if all his speech-making had exhausted him.

Chapter Twenty-two

Anna was surprised at how much work had been completed on D'Anton's house since she had last been there. The roof was finished, and the tarpaulin removed, though there was still a lot of evidence that work was in progress: a stack of wood in the small front garden, wheelbarrows, cement bags and two big crates of tiles. The front door was open, with sheets of plastic leading along the hallway and into the kitchen. The noise of some kind of drill was deafening; there was no point in ringing the doorbell.

'Mrs D'Anton? Mrs D'Anton!' Anna called out loudly.

There was no reply, so they headed into the kitchen. Again, Anna was impressed at how much had been done: new kitchen cabinets, a new cooker, and the floor tiled in black and white. A fitted breakfast area replaced the old fireplace that had been there on her last visit. Anna passed Langton to look up the stairs, calling out again. Eventually, the sound of drilling stopped, and there was a heavy footfall on the bare wooden stairs.

'Is Mrs D'Anton at home?' Anna enquired. It was the same builder she had seen on her last visit.

'Hang on,' he said. She heard him crossing the landing

above her on the wooden floorboards. 'Sandra? Sandra!' he bellowed.

Anna began a slow move upwards, as there was no reply. He shouted for Sandra again and then looked down to Anna who was by now midway up the stairs. 'She's not up here – isn't she down there?'

'No.'

'Well, I don't know where she bloody is. *Sandra?*'

'When did you last see her?' Anna got closer.

'She said she wouldn't be long. Are you from the council? We've not been working late since the last time we had a complaint, but as it's just the two of us, we need to work all the hours we can.'

'We're not from the council,' said Langton, and showed his ID. 'You had any other visitors this morning?'

'Bloody hell. You're not back again, are you?'

'I am Chief Superintendent James Langton and this is Detective Inspector Anna Travis.'

'Shit – now what is it about?'

'Can we come up and talk to you?'

'Sure – mind the stairs, they're a bit dodgy. I dunno what's going on. Sandra said she would just go with them.'

Langton had an uneasy feeling in the pit of his stomach. 'Go with whom, where?' he asked quietly.

'The cops that were here earlier. They searched the entire bloody house. I dunno what they was looking for; Sandra was dealing with them.'

It was about ten minutes before Langton got the description of the three officers who had arrived at eight that morning: two heavily built, and one very tall and well-spoken, who did all the talking. Sandra was told it was in connection with her husband's death. They had searched every room and then asked if there was anywhere else that her husband might have kept items; she had said that they had a storage bay for their own furniture and some antiques that Julius had been trying to offload. The three men were polite and totally believable, as they asked if Sandra could accompany them to the storage facility. When shown the photograph of Alexander Fitzpatrick, the builder identified him, without hesitation, as being the well-spoken officer.

Langton got the address of the storage facility and walked out to their patrol car. He was silent as they headed towards New Malden. Anna sat in the rear passenger seat; she hardly said a word, because she knew as well as Langton what they might find at the warehouse.

'Looking for the drugs,' Langton suddenly said, hardly audible. He lapsed into a brooding silence as they headed from Chiswick down into Kew; then he told the driver to cut through Richmond Park, go across Kingston Hill, then straight down Queens Road, turning left past Kingston Hospital.

Leaving the patrol car in the car park, they headed towards Brick House Storage Company. There was a security guard in a small hut beside the double doors into the storage facility. Langton showed his ID; he and Anna were led towards two huge doors, similar to a garage but three times the size.

'The one you want is over to the right; I'll take you through.'

Langton thanked him, but said they would find it. He asked if anyone had recently been to open the storage and was told that it was possible, as the man had only come on duty at eleven; there was another security guard who handled the late shift, from seven in the evening until mid-morning.

KT2 was, as he had indicated, along a lane of storage compartments; the last in the row. Langton had the key but, when he twisted the handle, the door was already open. 'Doesn't bode well,' he said softly.

As the gate swung up, all they could see were sofas, chairs and tables stacked on top of each other, with many boxes piled in a neat, orderly fashion. They were each labelled – *kitchen equipment, crockery,* etc – and only the plastic strips strewn around showed they had recently been opened. There were also some antiques and other furniture piled high: lamps and coffee-tables, kitchen stools and beds. They had to squeeze down between the piles of stored items to see more and more straw, and bubble wrap, tossed to one side. Some boxes were open, left on their side.

'She's not here,' Langton said, as he kicked aside the mass of old newspapers that must have wrapped china or glassware. He took out his mobile and called Sandra's house, as Anna walked back to the entrance and made her way down the first aisle again. Branching off it, not seen at first, was another area, which looked different: there were visible spaces, as if something had been stored and removed. There were scrapings, where a crate could have been moved aside.

'She's not arrived home yet,' he said, calling to Anna from the end of the aisle.

'Something was stored here and taken out,' she said, indicating the spaces. She spotted a hairslide and turned, holding it up for Langton to see, but he was standing by a large cardboard crate. He squatted, resting back on his heels. Taking a pen from his pocket, he inched out a torn, folded piece of white paper from between the two crates.

Anna continued searching but, finding nothing, she turned and edged around the other side. Her foot crunched on something and she quickly lifted it. It was a single earring; not a clip-on, but a beaded drop. Anna held the earring in the palm of her hand and moved further around the crates; then she stopped. Wedged between the crates was a body. Sandra was literally rammed in between them, her body almost crushed.

'I've found her,' she said.

Langton appeared behind her, and said not to touch anything; then he turned away to make a call on his mobile. Anna joined him as he ordered an ambulance.

'She's dead,' Anna said quietly.

'Get out to that security guy. We need to talk to the other man who was on duty before him.'

Anna left him making more calls to the station, asking for the necessary back-up. By the time he joined her outside, she had already made contact with Harry Framer, the night security guard. Langton handed her the scrap of paper. It was a cargo invoice for supplies of medical drugs destined for delivery, but to where, she couldn't tell, as it had been torn off. There was a part-stamp from Gatwick Airport customs, dated six months ago, but the signature of who had taken the order was missing.

'That's how he must have been shipping his supplies in; we can run a check on it at the airport,' Langton said, then turned to look back at the massive warehouse.

Mrs D'Anton had a broken neck, and substantial bruises to her face and throat. Two of her nails were broken; it looked as if she had put up a fight. By the time her body was being eased out and checked over, both

Anna and Langton had talked to Harry Framer. He was badly shaken, seeing the uniformed officers cordoning off the entrance to the warehouse. He said that, around nine, just as he was about to get some breakfast, a Range Rover had pulled up. He described the two thick-set men who approached him; they were accompanied by Mrs D'Anton, who did not, as far as he could remember, appear nervous in any way, but chatted to him as he opened the main doors of the hangar. He couldn't recall if he had even heard the two men speak. The third man had remained inside the Range Rover until the doors were opened; when he got out, he went straight to the hangar. He was tall, well over six feet, and wore a long draped coat. When shown the photograph of Alexander Fitzpatrick, Framer said it was the same man.

'So take me through exactly what happened.'

'Well, they went inside. Mrs D'Anton had her keys. Like I said, it was around breakfast-time, so I went to the café up the road, got a coffee and a bacon sandwich, and came back. I said to the tall man that he couldn't stay parked up outside; he said that they were just leaving. The two guys came out; one was carrying a box, and stashed it in the back of the Range Rover. The tall man was already sitting inside.'

'So Mrs D'Anton wasn't with them?'

'I didn't see her, but I reckoned maybe she'd left. I watched them drive out, then went into the security office and ate my breakfast.' Framer was sweating with nerves and kept on repeating that he didn't see anything suspicious.

'This box, how big was it?'

Framer said it was maybe two feet by two, miming the size with his hands; not big, and it didn't look too heavy.

He didn't know if there were other boxes already stashed in the Range Rover. Langton asked when he had last seen Julius D'Anton. Framer said he had never actually met him, just his wife. The other security guard, when asked the same question, said that, as far as he could recall, although D'Anton used to pay regular visits, he hadn't seen him for about five or six months.

Langton gestured for Anna to follow as he headed back to their car. 'You know what's not making sense? The way she's been beaten up: neck broken, face in bad shape. If you match this killing with the others we're lining up against Fitzpatrick, it's not got the same MO. If they were picking up just one box, that I suspect to be Fentanyl, then why not kill her in the same way as Rushton, as Donny Petrozzo? She put up a fight, but there were three of them; they could have held her down and injected her.'

'Well, you just said it – there were three of them. Maybe this kill was down to the two heavies.'

Langton nodded. He was now feeling very uneasy about the two missing children. Both men, he and Anna knew, were involved in taking the sisters to and from the nursery school.

'I think we should move in on Honour and Damien Nolan. If they don't know where the children are, then like you, I'm really concerned,' Anna said.

They drove in silence for a while, then Langton muttered, 'He bloody did it again – showed up at D'Anton's, fake ID, and fucking searched the house before he came here. They said when he was in the incident room, the only person he seemed interested in was D'Anton; placed a chair directly in front of his data.'

'That's how he got the address,' Anna said flatly.

'I keep thinking back on that last case we did together. The children, the baby we found buried in the pigsty.'

'So why are we waiting to pick them up?'

Langton stared out of the side window as they headed down the motorway towards Gatwick; she could see his drawn face reflected in the wing mirror. 'They can't make a move without us knowing. I'm not ready for them yet.'

Anna said nothing. Finding the body of Julius D'Anton's wife had really affected her. Langton had not had any interaction with her, so the missing shipment of 'medical supplies' preoccupied him more than anything else.

Gatwick customs were very edgy about their enquiry. They produced documents that were all, as far as they were concerned, totally legitimate. The shipment of Fentanyl had been sent via a well-known pharmaceutical company that had shipped many times before to the UK. The documents were checked over and stamped at the customs warehouse; they were subsequently collected by an official, with counter-documentation, to ensure delivery was made to the various hospitals across London.

Langton retained his composure, requesting copies of every single paper concerning the shipment. He sat in the patrol car, flicking through them; then passed the papers to Anna. 'I would put my life savings on these being very good forgeries; those clowns wouldn't know shit from a shovel.' Anna read over the vast folder of shipment agreements and collections. To her, they did look authentic, even down to the cases being opened and double-checked. Even the collection papers were seemingly very orderly; yet, like Langton, she had to assume they were forged.

'He sends this stuff right out in the open and not one person questioned it. Oh – the collection was made by a white van with a medical supplier's logo! Big fucking deal; somebody did their bloody research.' He shook his head. 'That somebody had to be in the UK for a long time to get this organised. We'll have to check back to the US side, but I doubt it'll be much help, as this end was so tight.'

'What do you think it's worth?' Anna asked.

Langton shrugged. 'Street value, I'd say we're looking at millions. Thing is . . .' he tapped the dashboard with his finger '. . . he would have to have a big network of dealers over here prepared to buy it. I don't for a second think it was those no-hopers we've arrested from the Chalk Farm squat.' He sighed, and then turned to face her, swivelling round in the front seat. 'You know what I think?'

Anna smiled, and shook her head. 'There was a major cock-up somewhere?'

'You can say that again.' He turned back to face the windscreen. 'How many boxes do you reckon were stored at the warehouse?'

'I don't know. The security guy saw just the one being carried out, but there could have been more in the Range Rover.'

Langton made the same gesture with his hands as Framer the security guard had done. 'Two foot by two foot; easily placed into the back of the Range Rover, right?'

'Yes, from what he said.'

Langton grunted, then went into one of his silences.

Not until they were in front of the team, giving their update, did he add that they would have to work backwards. 'Fitzpatrick, we know, was short of cash. He put the pressure on Julia Brandon to get four million out from Rushton; he also killed him, because he wanted access to every cent she had squirrelled away. We know he has now started to funnel it into various accounts. I surmise that he is not in this deal alone. We've gone with the assumption that these two heavies were used by Julia Brandon to act as bodyguards.' He paused. 'What if they were something more? What if this shipment was also theirs? Fitzpatrick had done some kind of deal to ship it in, and they would control the dealers. As far as I can tell, Fitzpatrick has been out of the game too long to have these contacts in the UK; it could be he was paid to organise the paperwork, for a cut of the profits.'

Everyone was attentive, as Langton appeared to be thinking out loud; he clicked his fingers, as if he couldn't quite get to the conclusion of his theory. He paced up and down along the incident-room board, and then stopped. He jabbed his finger at Julius D'Anton's photograph.

Gordon came forward. Via CCTV footage they had traced the white van from Gatwick. It was hired from a 'Rent a Van' company a week prior to the collection. The medical logo could easily have been made up and stuck over the sides. Gordon said the hire of the van was done via the Internet; the company was paid in cash, by a Mr Rodney Fuller, on collection. He had the van for three days before it was returned to their yard, the keys left in their overnight letterbox. Langton doubted they would discover any new evidence, as the van had been hired out twelve times since. However, Fuller was described as being very tall, and well-spoken . . . Gordon was sent to the hire company to see if they had any more information.

Anna had the unpleasant job of returning to Sandra D'Anton's house with Phil to give the builder the bad news. They would also ask for more details about the men who came and searched, and ask whether Sandra had said anything else that would help their enquiry. Meanwhile the team, along with Langton, had begun the marathon task of working backwards through the entire data collected for the case. Still Langton held off from picking up Honour and Damien Nolan. The surveillance team were still present and had reported nothing unusual or suspicious.

By the time Anna returned, there was hardly a desk or office not brimming with statements and files. Langton was in her small office, files piled either side of him.

'We didn't get anything from D'Anton's house; her boyfriend was in a state of shock, so it was impossible to question him for a while. Outcome was, Sandra had said nothing that he could recall that made him concerned. She said the men were searching for a painting on which her husband had put a down payment, which was why she agreed to take them to the warehouse. It appeared that D'Anton had a habit of putting down payments on antiques, and not paying off the debt, but reselling the items.'

Langton looked glum as he pressed a pencil into Anna's desk, making small dents with the point. 'I don't know which way to move,' he said.

Anna still could not understand why Langton hadn't brought the Nolans in. 'Any sighting of the children?'

499

'Nope, nor our two goons. They could be anywhere, right?'

'With two children plus an au pair, somebody has got to have seen them.'

'Or know where they are,' he said flatly. He swivelled in her chair, then picked up the last file he was studying. He sighed and then began to jab with the pencil again.

Phil knocked on the door. 'Boss, I've got something that's not quite kosher; it's connected to the Mitsubishi.'

'What?'

'Well, we know it was reported stolen, before it was taken to Stanley Leymore's. Next we know that Frank Brandon was driving it with, as far as we know, Alexander Fitzpatrick on board. Then, we get it sighted in Oxfordshire, this time with Julius D'Anton driving it . . .'

Langton sprang to his feet. 'No, no! Julius D'Anton was driving it *before* Frank visited the drug squat – then we discovered the body of Donny Petrozzo in the back – right, Anna?'

'Yes.'

'Shit!' Both Phil and Anna looked to Langton, who was bending forwards, rubbing his knee; jumping up out of the chair had made it throb with pain. He hobbled to the door and walked out. 'I never got to give him the nitty gritty,' Phil complained.

'Which is what?' Anna demanded.

'There's no trace of the guy who reported it missing. We have an address, right, but we're getting a dead phone signal. We've contacted the local police to see if they can help us.'

Anna hurried into the incident room. The Mitsubishi had been reported stolen by a man called Adrian

Summers; his address was one of the elegant houses in Hove with direct views of the pebbled beach. The house had been rented on a short lease and, as far as the locals could ascertain, the renter had not been in residence for months.

Adrian Summers, aged twenty-two, worked as an odd-job man for holiday rentals. The Mitsubishi was registered in his name, and he had reported it stolen. It had been parked on the forecourt of the property. It didn't help that there had been a spate of car thefts over the past year; although the Mitsubishi had been reported stolen, the police had had no success in tracking it down.

Langton fired off orders for a team to get over to the house. He wanted it dusted from top to bottom for prints, and for them to remove anything that gave them a clue as to who had rented it. The owners were contacted in the Bahamas; they gave an address and name of the management company. The rental contract didn't help: it had been taken out in Adrian Summers's name, and the rent paid in cash for six months; they had also been left a substantial deposit, which remained unclaimed.

Whilst the team set about tracing Summers and visiting the property, Langton sat in front of the board. Dates, dates – how many times had he asked for the chronological order of events from Travis? It all hinged on this bloody jeep; was it stolen to order by Stanley Leymore? Did he have a string of kids stealing for him, driving the vehicles to his garage and respraying, repairing, replacing the plates? It was doubtful he would be stealing cars for himself; they knew he had sold Donny Petrozzo his Mercedes, so the cars would have been upmarket vehicles that he knew he could move. Brighton police confirmed a spate of upmarket vehicle thefts a while back, but nothing recently.

Somehow the Mitsubishi was moved from Brighton to Leymore's garage. Langton began a list of names: he marked only those who had a direct link to the jeep. First up was this boy Adrian Summers, who had bought the jeep, new, from a Brighton dealer; paid cash. It was next reported stolen, and surfaced:

1) At the drug squat with Alexander Fitzpatrick aboard, plus Frank Brandon

2) At the farmhouse, driven by Julius D'Anton

3) With Donny Petrozzo's body in the back, in the garage at Wimbledon

Langton began shifting the dates around. At the same time, he had the team double-checking the times of death for Petrozzo and for D'Anton. Due to the latter being some time in the water, they were not able to give the exact date. Donny Petrozzo's body was also very well-wrapped and preserved. The timeframe in which they both had died was therefore, loosely, a three-week period.

Langton then drew an arrow to link each man. Donny Petrozzo knew Frank Brandon; he also knew Stanley Leymore, the car dealer. Did Frank arrange with him to take the Mitsubishi? They had no record of exactly how long he had been driving it; the insurance certificates they had taken from Julia Brandon's, along with other papers, were for her car and his only. Lastly, he underlined the now infamous name: Alexander Fitzpatrick.

Just as he had half-completed his arrow-making, there was contact from Brighton.

It appeared someone had made a fast getaway. Food was still in the fridge, beds were unmade and, though they were removing trash from the waste-baskets, the main garbage had last been collected weeks ago. When shown the picture of Alexander Fitzpatrick, neighbours either side of the property were certain that he had been in residence. The sheets were bundled up to be tested for DNA at the lab, but it looked as if whoever left in a hurry also did a clean-up job: rubber gloves were found along with disinfectant and window-cleaning sprays.

There was still no sighting of Adrian Summers, but the neighbours had said he was a familiar sight around all their houses; he did part-time gardening, window cleaning and car washing. He appeared to be a pleasant young man, who was studying part-time at the local college for a master's degree in graphic art. They would have to check out if Adrian Summers had made up the insignia for the hired white van.

His parents had been contacted; they lived locally in Hove, but they had not seen him for seven or eight months. They were not too concerned, as it was usual for their son to go off without contacting them, but they changed their minds when told he had not been at college for the same period of time.

They now had photographs of the young man. Sussex police had agreed to begin trying to locate him. Langton glanced uneasily at the fair-haired boy, as he pinned his picture up along with everyone else's.

Langton had been moving arrows and dates around the board, as if he was playing chess. His theory that there were no coincidences was being proved with a vengeance; the more he had tried to calculate the time-frames, the more bizarre were the coincidences that must have occurred.

'As you know, from early on I have been requesting some kind of timeframe; we are still surmising that this or that happened, so I am coming up with something else. Let's go back to the report of the missing Mitsubishi.'

In his opinion, for Alexander Fitzpatrick – even via Adrian Summers – to report a vehicle stolen would be a huge risk. He was still trying to fathom out the pick-up of the drug haul from Gatwick. Going by the dates on the customs certificates, this occurred before the theft of the jeep. But they still had no idea where the drugs were taken afterwards.

'Now,' Langton continued, 'it is my belief that, when the jeep was stolen, on board was maybe one box of the drugs. Stanley Leymore now has this box of drugs; he's unsure what they are. As soon as Fitzpatrick sees Frank Brandon with his fucking jeep, he has to want to know where he got it from. So, that leads him back to Leymore. What if – and I am grasping at straws here – but what if Leymore contacted Donny Petrozzo, a known small-time drug dealer? He takes the drugs, and tries to do a deal with our two punks at the Chalk Farm squat, but being cautious only gives maybe a few vials of it.'

The team all had quizzical expressions, trying to follow Langton as he walked up and down in front of the board.

'Frank drives Fitzpatrick to the drug squat,' Langton went on, 'and there all hell breaks loose, as Frank is recognised by the two dealers, and the shootout goes down. The dealers had paid Leymore for the drugs; we know they have admitted killing him, and there is a time gap between them making a run for it from the squat and killing Leymore. In that time gap, I think D'Anton got hold of the drugs – not the motherlode, but a box containing some of the Fentanyl. Is everyone with me?'

There was a low murmur, and a few jokes that they were trying to keep up. Anna sat quietly, watching Langton at work. He was, as he always had been, an extraordinary man; his mind ticking over so fast, he spoke in short sharp sentences as he tried to work out his theory. She knew he was treading water, though, as so much depended on the very thing he always detested: coincidences.

'Now!' Langton paused. He explained that Fitzpatrick had possibly been injured in the shooting. He couldn't return to his rented house in Brighton and, with Frank Brandon's murder, he couldn't stay at Julia's, so he needed a place to hide out.

Langton printed in large letters: FARMHOUSE. He then stepped back and gave a soft laugh. 'Okay, I am hoofing it now but, around the same time – remember, this is all taking place within twenty-four hours of the murder of Frank Brandon ...' Langton brought up the note found in the glove compartment of the Mitsubishi, with directions to the farmhouse. Did Fitzpatrick call and ask how to get there? Did he drive to the farmhouse? And did he stash the box of drugs in the Mitsubishi? He jotted down the dates of the antique fair; again, this crossed their timeframe. 'Julius D'Anton: junkie, loser, desperate for money, rams his own rundown van into the ditch, no more than a mile from the farmhouse. Coincidentally,' he said, looking to Anna with a grin, 'Julius D'Anton walks along the footpath. We know from Travis that the couple never use their front door, but what if Julius does try the doorbell first. It doesn't work – right, Travis?'

'Yes.'

'Okay. What if D'Anton takes a look at the Mitsubishi, left parked; he sees the keys in the ignition – remember, we are just surmising all this, or I am!' He laughed, then stared at the floor, and shrugged. 'D'Anton opens the glove compartment, and there's a stash of cash. Remember the two drug dealers said they'd paid five grand to Petrozzo? Maybe it was that cash, maybe not; either way, for D'Anton, it's like fucking Christmas.' Langton sat down, rubbing his head; he finished by saying that D'Anton had to have got a wad of money from somewhere, as he returned to the antique shop and tried to take the table, but he couldn't fit it into the back of the jeep.

Langton asked for some water as he pointed to the board. 'Julius D'Anton drove home. To make sense of the theory, he discovers the drugs, takes them to his storage warehouse and stashes them there.' Langton sipped at the beaker of water handed to him. He stood up. 'The one person that connects to almost everyone is Donny Petrozzo. D'Anton scored from him: did he contact him? They arrange to meet, and here I am really out on a limb. D'Anton OD'd on the stuff, he's a junkie, maybe killed himself trying to fathom out what it was, Donny simply tips him into the Thames, and drives the Mitsubishi to Frank's garage, like a fucking homing pigeon.' There was a long pause, and eventually Langton looked at the team. 'So what do you think?'

Anna waited for someone else to take the lead, but no one did.

'Yes, Travis?'

'I think if any part of your theory is correct, we have to arrest Damien Nolan and his wife. We also have to focus on tracing the two missing children. They should be our priority.'

There was a hubbub of everyone talking at once.

Anna held her ground. 'We now have yet another missing person, Adrian Summers; it's quite likely he was just a pawn in the entire thing. There is also the au pair. If we are to take on board everything DCS Langton has suggested, our prime suspect is still on the loose, and missing is a substantial load of drugs, which looks to be the reason he is still in the UK.'

Langton turned to Cunningham, who had not said one word throughout. Now she coughed, clearing her throat. 'I personally need time to digest everything. I buy some of it, but not all; we need to really start ripping it all apart and get that timeframe set, so we can dismiss or agree this scenario. I also feel that we should now arrest both Damien Nolan and his wife.'

Langton looked as if he was going to jab his finger in her chest. 'No! We hold off until I am ready. In the meantime, I want a full press release. I want them at Scotland Yard: every pen pusher possible, from every crime page. We break the news on the search for the two children and the au pair – they are to be the priority – and we name our suspect, Alexander Fitzpatrick! Let them Google him, and see what they come up with!'

Cunningham had two pink spots on her cheeks as she controlled her anger. She asked politely if Langton would join her in her office before she walked out. They broke for the night; it was after nine.

Anna went into her office and collected her briefcase.

She could still see the strange jabbing pencil dents in her desk made by Langton. She ran her finger over them, and realised the indentations were her own initials, A.T.

Chapter Twenty-three

Pete was appalled that, since he had last been at Anna's, the flat was still in the same state, as if she had only just moved in. Anna opened a bottle of wine and they ate fish and chips, sitting on kitchen stools. When Pete asked how the case was going, Anna went into an edited version of what Langton thought went down.

Wafting his fork around, Pete mimicked Langton, launching into the various coincidences, especially the Most Wanted man in the UK and the USA leaving his drugs to be stolen from the jeep, not once but twice! 'You know what I think?' he ended up.

Anna scooped up some chips in her fingers, dipping them in ketchup. 'Surprise me.'

'I think you've lost him. All this surmising about who did what and where, is crap: the reality is that Alexander Fitzpatrick is way out of your reach.'

'I don't agree.'

'Agree or not, you are still facing the fact that he walked into the station, hoodwinked the lot of you, walked out armed with the address of whatsit, D'Anton, picked up his wife, collected what you presume to be his missing drugs and oh, I almost forgot, strangled her to death!'

Anna pushed her half-eaten meal away. He was starting to annoy her.

'Why this delay in bringing in the only suspects other than Fitzpatrick: Julia Brandon's sister, and her husband?' Pete demanded.

'The surveillance reports are giving us a day-to-day rundown; the couple can't make a move without us knowing.'

'If the surveillance guys are as obvious as they usually are . . .'

She snapped at him. 'They are not! We've got a crew digging up a part of a field for, supposedly, BT, and another crew laying down cables . . .'

'Very inventive!' he said sarcastically.

'Yes – and costly. I shouldn't even be telling you all this.'

'Why not? Who the hell do you think I am going to repeat it to?'

Anna sighed and sipped her wine; she was tired and getting a headache, so she fetched a bottle of aspirin. Pete watched her, then picked up the dirty dishes and crossed to the sink.

'I'm going to take a shower,' Anna said wearily.

'Terrific. Is that an invitation for me to join you, or should I go home? Sometimes you get me feeling like I should have a bike with *Takeaway, Deliveries* printed on it!'

'I'm sorry.'

'You've got a headache?'

'One coming; I can feel it tight round the back of my head.'

'Ah, so that's the excuse tonight, is it? You've got a headache! Well, fine. You go and shower; I'll clean up and get my coat.' Anna didn't answer; she walked out, leaving him stacking the dishwasher. As she was about to step into the shower, she heard the front door slam shut. She had no sooner showered, and got into her pyjamas, than the doorbell rang.

He stood on the doorstep, glowering. 'I can't get my car out. The gates won't open without the remote and I don't know the code.'

Anna wrapped her arms around him and said she was sorry. She was about to pass him the code, when he kicked the door shut behind him. 'Let's go to bed.'

She didn't feel she could reject him. By the time he had showered and joined her in bed, she could hardly keep her eyes open. He kissed her lovingly and she knew they would have sex. She didn't want that, but went through the motions, hoping it would be over as quickly as possible. It was a strange feeling; her mind was so distant from her actions. It was Pete who fell asleep first, lying next to her, one arm resting across her chest protectively. She gently stroked his hair, almost as if he was a child, feeling his warm breath against her neck, and a little guilty that she had not wanted him to make love to her. That was what really played on her mind: not the case, thankfully, but the fact that her relationship with Pete was for her just as friends. She didn't even think of Langton; instead, as she closed her eyes, it felt like she was floating above herself, detached from Pete, looking down at her nakedness entwined with his and feeling nothing.

She woke with a jolt when his wristwatch started buzzing. It was after eight and she went into panic mode. The team were to organise the big press gathering and she wanted to be present. By the time she had dressed and gulped down a cup of black coffee, they were both ready to leave. As they entered the car park, he kissed her and said he would call her later; maybe if she had time, they could take in a movie.

Anna wasn't really listening as she threw her briefcase into the Mini and switched on the engine. She reckoned if she put her foot down, she'd just make it for nine. Wrong.

The garage doors refused to budge. Other tenants eager to leave for work were in the same predicament, and there were heated rows with Mr Burk, the security manager, who was attempting to open the gates manually; he could only manage to get them open a few inches before they clanged shut again.

James Fullford kicked at the closed gates. 'I should get a fucking boat! This is the third time in less than a month this has happened!' He turned to Anna and Pete. 'I could fucking anchor it on the river by the time this idiot gets these working; even if he does open them, there is no way I can make my meeting in time. I'm going to lose a fortune.' He stomped around, as more tenants appeared and stood helplessly, watching Burk as he tried to operate the doors, but they held firm.

By the time Anna was able to get a taxi to the press conference, it had already disbanded, so she caught a tube up to Chalk Farm. She knew she would be in the firing line; making an excuse about the garage doors would not be acceptable. Thankfully, Langton was not at the station – but Cunningham was, and she was furious. Anna was about to apologise when the photograph of the missing Adrian Summers caught her eye. Anna's mind started ticking. She could feel it down to the balls of her

feet, jigsaw pieces tumbling, and she had to catch her
breath to steady herself. She snatched down the photograph and almost ran to her office. 'Gordon, get in here,
now!'

She didn't even realise she had done a familiar gesture:
the Langton hand-waft, which had always irritated her.
'You recognise him?' She held up the photograph.

Gordon hurried in after her. 'No.'

'Nor did I, until I looked at it from a distance. Take a
good look, Gordon.'

He stared at the photograph as she moved around her
desk, holding it at chest height. 'Go back to when we
went to the farmhouse, Gordon.'

He still looked nonplussed. She was exasperated, wanting him to get the same recognition. 'The boy we saw
when we were there, remember? The one who walked
into the yard. Is it him?'

'Christ, yes. Yes, I think it is!' Gordon picked up the
photograph as she tossed it onto the desk.

'I'm bloody sure it is,' she said, as she heaved files onto
her desk from where they were stacked on the floor.
'Okay, now we go back to the painting in the farmhouse:
the boat.'

'Yes, it was there and then not – I remember!' Gordon
could feel her energy; it made him nervous.

'Okay, you tell me why would anyone remove it?
It was of an old boat belonging to Alexander Fitzpatrick,
right?'

'Yes, *Dare Devil*, but we had confirmation that it had
been sold,' Gordon said.

'That's not my point.' She began to give out orders.
She wanted the marina in Brighton checked out; she
wanted to know of every boat anchored there for the

past six months and any boat coming and going; she wanted owners' names – and fast. 'Come on, Gordon, get thinking. Alexander Fitzpatrick's rented house was in Brighton. What if he also had a boat anchored there at the marina as well? We've not been able to trace him staying at any hotels, but we know he's been in London – so get onto it.'

Anna didn't even put forward their findings to Cunningham, but instead left the station a little later and, in a patrol car, went over to Scotland Yard. After checking in at the reception, she took the lift up to Langton's office.

She could hardly contain herself as she approached him. 'I think we've got him cornered,' she said.

She had never been to his office before and was surprised at the size of it; his desk and comfortable sitting area were impressive. There were numerous family photographs of his ex-wife and the two children, Kitty and Tommy. That took her aback, as it was so unexpected: the domesticity of his life of which she now knew so little.

'Come on, let's hear it.' Langton sat in a large leather swivel chair behind his desk, but Anna couldn't sit, she was so eager to give him the update.

Langton listened as she described the sighting at the farmhouse of Adrian Summers, certain she was correct. She gave details of how, after two hours, Gordon had traced a large boat called *Maiden* to Brighton Marina. The boat had to give the harbourmaster details of ownership: the name was one of Alexander Fitzpatrick's aliases. The same boat was now anchored in Chelsea Harbour. According to the harbourmaster, it had been registered there for only one month.

'I went along with your theory, but now I've come up with a slightly different one.' Anna's chest heaved because she was talking so fast; Langton had to gesture for her to slow down. Anna dragged out papers from her briefcase. One of the things that had bothered her was the scrap of paper with directions to the farm – written, they believed, by Damien Nolan. How had that paper got into the Mitsubishi's glove compartment? If, as they believed, Fitzpatrick knew the location, why would there be directions? Unless . . .

'The white van hired to collect the drugs: what if that van was driven by Adrian Summers to Honey Farm? We've so far not found any trace of the drugs: what if they were taken there, straight from Gatwick, and the directions were for *him* to find it? The van is then emptied and driven back to London by Summers. By this time, the stuff from that glove compartment has been put into the Mitsubishi: this includes the directions, money, and maybe one box of drugs – for sales purposes, you know? Fentanyl is not a common street-trader's drug, right?' Anna fumbled with her array of papers. 'This would place Fitzpatrick at the farmhouse when Julius D'Anton is sniffing around the cottage, trying to find some antiques. He takes advantage of the jeep sitting there and nicks it. On board he has, as you suggested, the box of drugs.'

The desk phone rang. Langton picked it up, then switched it to speakerphone. Phil, who had been sent to Chelsea Harbour with two other officers from the team, was now able to verify that the boat was occupied by a young blond guy, identified as Adrian Summers. There was no sign of Fitzpatrick, or the children, but the harbourmaster said he had seen two small boys on deck two days ago. As the call continued, with Phil obviously somewhere he could monitor the boat, he swore. Walking along the harbour was the au pair, carrying two bags of groceries.

Langton gave out the order to maintain surveillance, and not to approach the boat. He was silent for a few moments before asking Anna to take him through exactly what had happened on her first visit to the farm. She described how they had been lost, so had stopped at the small cottage and spoken to the elderly woman who had directed them to the farm. They had found Honour round the back of the house, tending to the henhouse. Anna went on to explain about the painting of the boat that was subsequently removed.

She took out a map and indicated the route Julia Brandon had taken on her last journey, from Wimbledon out to the A3 and then a loop, as if going back to the M40. 'What if she knew she was being followed and tried to throw off the surveillance vehicle? They kept on saying she was driving at a reckless speed; what if she was trying to head towards Brighton, and the boat?'

Langton stood up. They had enough supposition, he said; now they had to act on the possibility that they had their man cornered. If he attempted to withdraw any of the money that he had forced Rushton to transfer for him, they could track him. So far there had been no withdrawals, and still no sighting of him, so where was he?

As they went down in the lift together, he smiled at her, and touched the nape of her neck. 'Good work, little one. You are working on the adrenalin rush. I know just what it feels like.' The touch of his fingers to her neck sent shockwaves through her, but she said nothing. He was right, she was buzzing.

She turned to him. 'They searched the farm, right? Found nothing. If Honour was tipped off by my visit, enough to remove the painting, then she would also know enough to be wary about the drugs. I think they were stashed in the henhouse.'

They were heading towards the patrol car, when Anna stopped in her tracks. 'She was very relaxed when the search went down – *because she knew we'd find nothing.*' She looked up at him. 'We never searched the cottage, did we! The old lady said it had been refurbished, with all mod cons. She could be connected – I mean, she could have tipped Honour off about me making enquiries, which was why she was locking up the henhouse.'

Anna was rubbing her head so that her hair stood up on end, as the sirens screamed and they sped across London. Langton turned round in the front seat and touched her knee. 'Just relax. I agree with you. I think we've got Fitzpatrick cornered. Now we bring in Honour and Damien Nolan.'

The station was on full alert as Langton arranged for a helicopter to get to Oxfordshire fast. The local constabulary were on standby to assist in the arrests, and to instigate the search of the cottage. Via their surveillance officers, they were told that both Damien and Honour were still at home. Langton had said he wanted to go in very softly, no sirens blazing. He spent considerable time orchestrating the hit. In the meantime, the surveillance on the *Maiden* in Chelsea Harbour was stepped up and they ran a check on the cottage, specifically the old lady.

By the time the helicopter had landed in a field over a mile from the farmhouse, Anna's stomach was in a tight knot. At the Chelsea Marina, there was still no sighting of Fitzpatrick, so the surveillance officers were instructed to stay back and wait. Langton was using his mobile, listening to a call; when he shut it off, he gave one of his strange short laughs. 'She's his fucking mother! Mrs Doris Eatwell – previously married to Alistair Fitzpatrick – and she's owned that cottage for forty years.'

The patrol cars were lined up at the end of the lane, leading into the dirt track to the farmhouse. It was a clear sunny day. As everyone waited for orders, it was the sound of birds twittering that Anna found extraordinary; on the surface, it was all so peaceful. Langton was concerned that somehow Adrian Summers might have been contacted, so decided that they should move in to the boat at the same time. The two sisters were dressed as boys, so he made certain that Phil had photographs to prove their identity, though he was sure that they were Julia Brandon's children.

It was now 4.15 p.m. Langton and Anna, in the lead patrol car, drove past the cottage and stopped. Behind them came two more patrol cars and a van, with four locals to begin the search of the cottage and outhouses. Anna watched them heading up the flower-bordered pathway. Before they reached the front door, Mrs Eatwell opened it. She appeared frightened, as they showed their warrants; then they were inside. At the same time, two more uniformed officers with sniffer dogs approached the garage. Snapping off the padlock, they heaved open the old wooden door which swung upwards and back into the small garage. Two more uniformed officers went over to the tumbledown greenhouse and lean-to sheds. The search began.

It didn't last long. The officer who had entered the garage walked out and signalled to Langton. They had

found the 'motherlode', protected by only a cheap padlock and covered by a tarpaulin. 'Crates up to the ceiling,
about thirty of them.'

Langton clapped his hands and gave the go-ahead to
the driver to continue up the lane. Anna looked from
the rear window to see Mrs Eatwell being led to a patrol
car and helped inside. She appeared to be crying.

It took no more than five minutes to drive up the
narrow lane and reach the open gate. The car behind
Langton drove round to the rear of the farmhouse.
Hemmed in, with more officers still in their surveillance
positions, Langton and Anna walked round the side of
the house. Honour was baking bread, her hands covered
in flour. Damien was sitting at the kitchen table, marking
up papers from his lectures. Langton leaned on the
half-open stable door and showed his warrant card.

Anna was fascinated by Honour's reaction. On hearing
she was being arrested, she asked if she could wash her
hands. Damien screwed back the top of the fountain pen
he had been using and carefully placed it down on top of
the papers. They were separated and led to two different
patrol cars, and driven past the cottage that now looked
as if it was under siege, with so many uniformed officers
around. Honour showed no reaction when she was told
that Mrs Eatwell had also been arrested. Damien sat with
his head bowed, hands held loosely together; he glanced
at the action around the cottage but then, like his wife,
chose to say nothing.

At the local station, they were read their rights and
the charges against them, and told that they would be
driven to London to answer questions. Neither said a
word; they did not appear resigned or scared about their
situation, but quietly confident. Damien had written

down names of two solicitors he wished to represent him and his wife.

Phil had gone on board the *Maiden* at exactly four-fifteen. The two children were watching a DVD on a small TV in the main cabin. Adrian Summers was lounging on a bunk bed, reading some maps. Mai Ling was cooking their tea; she started screaming hysterically when they showed their warrants. The little girls had short, boyish haircuts, but were well and, although initially frightened by the appearance of so many officers, were excited to be driven in a patrol car with the siren wailing, their au pair seated between them. Adrian Summers acted the innocent, but then grew quiet as he too was led out to a patrol car.

By the time arrangements had been made for the children to be placed in care with a family liaison officer, Adrian Summers had been read his rights, and the charges of drug trafficking and perverting the course of justice. He had become very agitated, and was placed in a holding cell.

When Langton and Anna questioned Mrs Eatwell, she became very distressed and a doctor was called to examine her. She said she didn't know what was in the boxes and had agreed to allow them to stay there because her son had asked her to help him. She recalled that she had only seen him a few times in the past eight months and had had little or no contact with him for twenty years. She had only met her grandchildren once, when they had stayed with their mother at the cottage. She had no idea where her son was and insisted he was not a bad person.

As Langton stood up to leave the room, he had leaned close to Mrs Eatwell. 'I don't think you ever knew your son because, believe me, he is a very bad man. And with or without your help, we will find him.'

At the same time, Damien and Honour were being driven to London. It was almost 9 p.m. when they were placed in cells beside Adrian. Meanwhile, Langton and the team had a major briefing session. From his initial elation, Langton now seemed moody and tired. They had plenty of ammunition to fire, but no trace of Alexander Fitzpatrick himself. The boat was impounded and a search was in progress. They also had the motherlode of drugs, and their suspect's very own mother. Due to her age, she had been returned to stay at her cottage, along with a female officer.

To give them time to orchestrate the interviews, and arrange for solicitors to be present, Langton decided that they would wait until first thing in the morning to interview Damien and Honour, but would see what they could get out of Adrian Summers that evening. In the meantime, he wanted the search for Fitzpatrick to continue; by now, the evening papers were plastering his photograph on every front page. The TV news and morning papers were told that arrests in connection with the enquiry had been made. Langton also asked that they give good coverage to the fact that they had discovered drugs to the value of ten to twelve million pounds.

Adrian Summers was represented by a solicitor from the station's lists. She was young and a tad inexperienced but, at such short notice, was the only one available. Summers had no police record and by the time he had spoken to his solicitor, he was very scared. Knowing what heavy charges were levelled at him, he gave them more than they could have expected.

Via Adrian, the jigsaw puzzle with so many of its pieces still missing finally took shape. At long last, Langton got what he had wanted from day one: a timeline.

First, they got from Adrian that he did not know Alexander Fitzpatrick's real name. He knew him as Anthony Collingwood; however, Langton suggested they now use 'Fitzpatrick' for clarity. Adrian was asked about the theft of the Mitsubishi jeep. Although it had been bought in Adrian's name prior to the theft, it had been paid for by Fitzpatrick. Adrian said that, whilst Fitzpatrick maintained the rented house in Hove, he was aboard his boat in Spain, preparing to bring it to the Brighton Marina.

Adrian was getting into debt repaying his student loan, when he met Julius D'Anton in Brighton. D'Anton was quite a familiar figure to the students, and had at one time run a shop in The Lanes. Though he went bankrupt and sold up, it was well-known that he could always get a stash of dope to sell onto the students. He still kept up the odd visit to The Lanes, rummaging around for antiques, and it was there that he got into conversation with Adrian.

Over coffee, Adrian told D'Anton how broke he was. D'Anton, seeing the jeep, suggested he should sell it. Adrian explained that he didn't own it, it belonged to the guy he worked for. However, it was registered and insured in his name. D'Anton said he could pull a bit of a scam. He knew someone – Stanley Leymore – who would take the jeep and give it new plates. Adrian could report it stolen, claim the insurance money and get the same jeep back and split the insurance cash. Taken with the idea, Adrian let him drive off with the jeep.

Langton asked if Fitzpatrick had been aware of the scam at any time. All he knew, Adrian said, was that the insurance had paid out. D'Anton took a few hundred from the insurance money, and Leymore even more. Leymore had fixed the engine numbers and new plates, but had no time to do anything else because Fitzpatrick had arrived back in Brighton sooner than expected.

Adrian remembered that, around this time, Fitzpatrick had said he was having problems with his ex-partner – and he was very short of funds. 'It was about the only time I ever saw him really angry. He told me that he had a major deal going down so he had to raise money and fast.' He swore that he had no idea who Fitzpatrick was, nor that the 'major deal' was drugs. He had been hired by him eighteen months prior, when he had knocked on the door at the rented house in Hove to ask if he needed any odd jobs done. He had done some sweeping up of leaves and window cleaning in the area. Fitzpatrick offered to buy and insure him a vehicle, the Mitsubishi, so he could act as his driver when he needed to make trips back and forth to London.

'So he came and went?'

'Yeah. I knew he was organising the boat. Like I said, he left Brighton to go to Spain to bring it into the Marina.' Adrian became increasingly nervous when they moved on to the hire of the white van. He admitted that he had made up the plastic stick-on logo, and also that he had helped Fitzpatrick load up the crates. Adrian then clarified another detail: he had indeed driven the white van with the drugs to Oxfordshire, to leave at Honey Farm. Honour had helped to unload the crates, and they had stashed them in the henhouse.

'Where was Fitzpatrick at this point?'

Adrian puffed out his cheeks, trying to remember the exact order of events. Eventually he said that, as far as he could recall, Fitzpatrick was in the Isle of Man – didn't know why. His job was to ship out the crates to the farm. He returned to London, deposited the keys of the van back at the rental, and burned the logos. Then he got a phone call from Fitzpatrick, worried about how safe the crates were, wanting them moved; he also wanted one box to be retained and brought back to the house in Brighton.

Adrian then drove the jeep back to Honey Farm and moved the crates, having split open one and removed one box. He was driving back down the dirt track when he saw Julius D'Anton, whose van had driven into a ditch. Adrian gave him a lift into the village, to arrange for the local garage to haul the van out and repair it. At this point, D'Anton asked if he could borrow some money, as he had a good deal on a table in the local antique store. He would split the profits with Adrian. When the table wouldn't fit inside the Mitsubishi, the deal was off.

Adrian, with D'Anton as passenger, drove them both back to London. During the journey, D'Anton said he needed to sleep – he was having the sweats – and he curled up on the back passenger seat. He then saw the box and wanted to know what it was, but Adrian was very cagey and refused to tell him. 'I should have just said it was cleaning fluid, you know, anything; D'Anton was a real nosey sod. By me not coming clean, he sussed there was something inside the box and wouldn't stop going on and on about it.'

At this point, Adrian's solicitor leaned close and

whispered to him; he bowed his head, listening. It was obvious that she was advising him to keep quiet. Langton swung back in his chair, and urged Adrian to tell the truth. If he assisted them and was totally honest, it would prove beneficial. He soft-soaped about how their main priority was the capture of Fitzpatrick. Adrian was nervous and sweating, but went on.

D'Anton had opened the box and, never having seen the vials of Fentanyl before, asked Adrian what the stuff was. All Adrian knew about them was that Fitzpatrick had taken crates of the same stuff from Gatwick customs. Via his mobile phone, D'Anton had gone onto the Internet to find out exactly what it was. He told Adrian that it was worth a fortune and that he had a friend who could offload the stuff. Adrian had become very anxious about the whole thing.

'Did he give you the name of this friend?' Langton asked.

Adrian sipped at a beaker of water, unable to remember the name; just that he thought it was Italian.

'Donny something,' he recalled after a moment. 'That's all I can remember.'

Langton wrote down the name Donny Petrozzo, but did not repeat it to Adrian; he just began to tap the table with his pen. 'Go on, Adrian. You're in the jeep with D'Anton; what happened next?'

They waited as Adrian squeezed his hands together; sweat hung in small drops from his hair.

'Let me help you.' Langton opened his folder and put down the photographs of the dead Julius D'Anton. 'You have anything to do with this?'

'No, no, I swear before God.'

Langton pushed the photographs further towards the

now shaking boy. 'So, if you didn't have anything to do with this, keep talking. We are treating his death as murder, Adrian.'

Adrian spent a few moments whispering to his solicitor. She asked for a bathroom break to confer with her client. Langton agreed to ten minutes. They left a uniformed officer in the room.

When Langton and Anna returned to the interview room, Adrian seemed calmer. He spoke quietly, picking up from where he had left off.

He said that D'Anton kept on and on at him, saying that he could help deal the drugs. He even wanted Adrian to contact Fitzpatrick, which he refused to do. By this time, Adrian had come off the motorway at a roundabout, as he wanted to head back to Brighton. At some point – he couldn't exactly remember where, but they were stuck at traffic-lights – D'Anton snatched up the box and got out of the car; he spilled a whole load of the vials over the back seat. 'I couldn't do anything; he was running and I was stuck in the traffic. I couldn't overtake. I saw him get into a taxi up ahead.'

Langton leaned forwards. 'Keep going.'

'I got back to Brighton, and I was in a real state because of what had happened. I called Fitzpatrick, told him everything. He said I had to sort it out, but I didn't know where D'Anton lived – all I had was his mobile number. I kept on calling him, but just got his answerphone. Then Fitzpatrick came back. I expected him to go ballistic, but he just made me repeat it all over again to him, and then I gave him the number.'

Langton looked to Anna, shaking his head. 'Try that one more time, Adrian, because I don't believe you.'

'It's the truth!'

'You expect me to believe that Fitzpatrick loses drugs worth thousands and he just accepts it?'

'I told you, he was just really kind of calm. In a way, I'd have felt better if he'd punched me out, but he didn't.'

'So he made contact with D'Anton?'

'Yeah – well, I heard him talking to D'Anton; he said he'd like to meet this dealer. I heard him asking about customers. He repeated "City types?", and he laughed. After he finished the call, he told me to give the house a thorough clean. He went out in the jeep about an hour later. He took the packages that had fallen out of the box and put them in a plastic carrier bag. I spent two days cleaning up, wiping all the surfaces as he had instructed me, then I went onto the boat. He didn't come back for about three days, and then he said he had to go back to the Isle of Man.'

'With you on board?'

'No. He gave me a few hundred quid, and said he would be in touch if and when he needed me. That time, he was more angry. He said that if I wanted to make a lot of money, and if I wanted to stay working for him, it was vital I keep my mouth shut.'

'Did he threaten you?'

Adrian nodded. 'He said that he would always be able to find me, and if I fouled up again, he'd kill me. I went back to college and didn't hear from Fitzpatrick for a few months. Then his boat came back to the Brighton Marina.'

'So during the time you were cleaning up the rented house in Brighton, he was using the jeep?'

'Yes.'

Langton opened the file and placed Julia Brandon's photograph down in front of Adrian. 'Do you know this woman?'

'No.' Nor did he recognise the property in Wimbledon or the picture of Frank Brandon. Lastly, they showed him the photograph of Donny Petrozzo. Again, he had never seen him. Langton stacked the photographs and replaced them.

Adrian explained that the next time he had been contacted by Fitzpatrick was to join him on the boat moored in Chelsea Harbour. He was hired to clean and get groceries; during that period, he did not drive the Mitsubishi. When he learned that Fitzpatrick's two daughters were coming on board with their au pair, Adrian prepared bunks for them.

The interview was concluded but, when told he would not be released, Adrian burst into tears. Langton ended their tape recording and walked to the door; there, he glanced back at the snivelling boy and said, 'It's not over, Mr Summers.'

Anna didn't feel like breaking for the night, even though it was after eleven. It was hard to come down from the excitement of the day. Pete was still at the lab, so she went over to see him.

Like Langton, Pete was organising his team, listing in order of priority the items he wanted checked out. He gave Anna a perfunctory kiss on the cheek, then led her to a table with some of the forensic evidence examined that morning. 'Right, the lady found strangled in the storage warehouse: we've got some hairs and the root is attached, so we can get strong DNA.'

Anna leaned close to him as he placed a slide under the microscope.

'I think she snatched at her killer's hair, because we've quite a few samples. It's very, very dark – and some kind of hair oil had been used. Not African – maybe Portuguese or South American.' He moved aside for Anna to look. 'We've also got fibres – wool, a distinctive colour and not from the victim's clothes.'

Anna noticed that the pockets of his white coat were covered in blue pen stains; he looked tired. 'We maybe can get a clear print off her neck: right thumb. It was pressed so hard on her larynx, it left a dark bruise. We'll be lifting off using the Superglue technique.'

'Are you hungry – I can order a pizza?' she asked, and he shook his head.

'Nope. I am going to carry on here for about another half-hour, then I will need to crash out.'

Anna looked at her watch and said that she should probably do the same. She was more miffed at his rejection of a late-night pizza than she realised; even more so when he smiled at her and said, 'Shoe on the other foot for a change!'

She laughed it off and said she would talk to him in the morning. He muttered a reply, but she didn't hear it. She turned to look back at him as she reached the door, and he was already peering at something else under the microscope, his body arched. She was impressed. He seemed totally consumed by his work. She hadn't really realised before how much his work meant to him.

It was after one in the morning when she finally turned in. She didn't fix anything to eat, but had a large glass of wine from a bottle left open in the fridge. Sleep didn't come easily, and she lay in the darkness, staring up at the ceiling.

Now certain that Fitzpatrick had met up with Donny Petrozzo, she wondered if he had also met up with D'Anton. What she did know from the timeframe was that the deaths of both men came almost together. Turning on her bedside lamp, Anna got up and fetched her briefcase. She climbed back into bed and took another look at the copies of the post-mortem report on Julius D'Anton. The quantity of Fentanyl in D'Anton's body was very high. He was a heroin user; she wondered if he had tried out the Fentanyl, unaware of its potency – eighty times stronger than morphine.

Donny Petrozzo had died from an overdose but, from the way his body had been found wrapped up, it was obvious that he had been murdered. The Mitsubishi was parked, with his body inside it, at the garage used by Frank Brandon. Anna was certain that Petrozzo's death occurred after Frank had been shot. She was so restless, trying to figure out what might have occurred. She thumped at her pillow, trying to get more comfortable but she still couldn't sleep – this time returning to the date she and Gordon had visited the farmhouse, and had seen Adrian Summers there by the gates.

Adrian had to have lied about only going to the farmhouse to deposit and then move the crates of drugs, as the timeframe didn't add up. Did he also drive the injured Fitzpatrick back to the cottage? The blood trace on the bullet she had found, they had always believed came from the man standing behind Frank Brandon – and it matched the swipe taken from the jeep.

She was certain Adrian knew a lot more than he had admitted to, and she was glad that Langton had not released him. Tomorrow, they would have the interrogation of Damien and Honour, but first, she wanted to have another session with Adrian Summers.

Chapter Twenty-four

Before any interviews took place, the team were given an update by Cunningham. The boat anchored at Chelsea Harbour had been dusted for prints; they were confident that, this time, they would find concrete evidence of Fitzpatrick. They had also recovered two hundred thousand pounds in cash, plus – and this was very important – a charter map of the boat's journeys and prearranged moorings. This would help their timeframe. They had also found documentation of ownership: Fitzpatrick had used an alias to make a substantial deposit on the boat, and payments were still outstanding.

Even more importantly, they had found two passports in different names, but with Fitzpatrick's photograph and two more passports in the names of the children. Added to this was a jewel case containing diamonds and emeralds worth a substantial amount belonging to Julia Brandon. It was a massive haul of fresh evidence. They had virtually stripped Fitzpatrick of every means to survive on the run. The question was: where could he be?

The distressed au pair had been questioned through an interpreter the previous evening and allowed to remain with the children. Eventually, she had admitted that the man she knew as Anthony Collingwood was the man in the photograph of Alexander Fitzpatrick. She also gave another insight into the way Fitzpatrick had organised his time in London.

Fitzpatrick had instigated her approach to Julia, as au pair. She was instructed to care for the children and report back using her mobile phone, details of what was happening in the house in Wimbledon. He had paid her for this on top of her wages; he had also arranged for her to take the children to the boat in Chelsea Harbour. She was adamant that she knew nothing about who he really was, or his drug trafficking. He was a good man, she insisted; a man who cared for his children, contrary to what Julia had implied. She also maintained that she did not know the final destination of the boat; her job was simply to care for the children. She said that Julia was a difficult woman to deal with, and could be very unpleasant; she was certain she had used Frank Brandon to cheat on Fitzpatrick.

Mai Ling could not elaborate on what she meant by 'cheat'; she was just aware that something was obviously very wrong, even when the marriage was taking place. They now had confirmation that Fitzpatrick had turned up and there had been a confrontation between him and Julia on the Isle of Man. When asked if Fitzpatrick met Frank Brandon, Mai Ling said that he had; the three of them had been talking for many hours. She was not aware what the outcome was, just that Julia was in a terrible state and, on the supposed wedding night, had not slept with Frank Brandon but Anthony Collingwood. She described the two 'heavies' that had been hired by Julia as being very unpleasant men; one did not speak English very well.

Asked if it was possible that Fitzpatrick had been the

one to arrange for these two so-called bodyguards, she had shaken her head. She said that they wanted payment, but for what, she couldn't say. She described overhearing them talking on a mobile phone; they were threatening Mr Collingwood. At the end of her interview, she said that, no matter what Julia had said, she was still in love with Collingwood.

Anna had taken notes throughout; some of it made total sense, some not. But the facts were that Julia, via David Rushton, had attempted to block all the money she had from Fitzpatrick. The four million she had withdrawn must have been passed to Fitzpatrick, perhaps to pay for the boat. Anna also wondered if the two heavies could be connected to the drugs? She put in a call to Fagan, who reconfirmed that Mai Ling had called him about her concerns for Julia, as had David Rushton, who had passed on the contact information for the men. He had, as he had already explained, then instigated their meeting with Julia. He was able to confirm that one man did not speak English well; the other, he said, was American.

Adrian Summers looked very crumpled that morning and in need of a shave. Langton put him at ease, assuring him that they would probably be releasing him shortly, but needed to clarify a few things. He looked to Anna to begin.

She opened her notebook. 'You stated that you only ever visited the farm in Oxfordshire to deposit and then move the drugs.'

'Yes.'

'We have two witnesses who saw you on the eighteenth of March at the farmhouse. This would have

535

been one month after you stated that you drove there and met Julius D'Anton. You've been lying, Mr Summers. Now's the time to start telling the truth.'

Adrian swallowed, and asked for some water. Anna passed him a small bottle; his hands were shaking as he unscrewed the cap.

'You stated that you did not know this man.' Langton put Donny Petrozzo's photograph in front of him.

Adrian's chest heaved, as if he was short of breath.

'You see, Adrian, since last night, we've been able to really look at the charges levelled against you. You are in very serious trouble.'

'I didn't do anything!'

'Then you should be in the clear – but right now, I am about to up the ante, and charge you with murder.'

'No, that's not right!'

'Isn't it? Then try explaining to us why you lied. Is it connected to this man?'

Adrian took a deep breath; then, after a moment, he touched the photograph of Donny Petrozzo.

'Take a look at how we found his body, Adrian.' Langton slapped down the pictures of the body in the back of the Mitsubishi.

'Oh shit. This isn't right. I swear before God, I didn't have anything to do with that man.'

'But you did meet him?'

Again, Adrian hesitated and sipped more water. 'I was on the boat and I got a call. He said he was injured and needed me to help him out.'

Langton started to write, then looked up. 'Who called you?'

'*Him* the man you keep saying is Alexander Fitz-patrick. He says to me, he needs me to come to this

536

garage in Wimbledon, as he needs my help – and to bring some tape and bandages and disinfectant.'

Adrian went on to describe how it had taken him some time to get there, as he didn't have a car; he'd hailed a taxi from Chelsea Wharf. When he arrived at the garage, the doors were shut, but he could hear a big argument going on. He had waited for a while and then knocked. He pointed to Donny Petrozzo's photograph. 'He opened up and let me in. Mr Collingwood was sitting in the front seat of the Mitsubishi with a wad of torn shirt held against his shoulder. He told me to pass him something clean to put on it, so I folded him a piece of lint. All the time, this Donny was going on and on, saying that he wanted to get cut in on the deal, that Julius D'Anton had told him all about it and that, if Mr Collingwood didn't like it, he would tip off the cops as to who he really was.'

Adrian closed his eyes. 'I saw Collingwood break open one of the ampoules. He poured it over the lint; next minute he's got hold of him.' He pushed forward the photograph of Donny Petrozzo. 'He covered his mouth. They struggled for a bit, then the Petrozzo guy just went limp; he slumped down on the garage floor.'

Langton put up his hand and asked Adrian to repeat what he had said about the ampoule. Adrian said he didn't know what it was. It was dark, and he was scared; it had happened so fast.

Anna passed Langton a note. Donny Petrozzo had been injected beneath his tongue; the pathologist had found a hypodermic needlepoint.

Langton nodded, and folded the scrap of paper, running his fingernail along the crease. 'You say Fitz-patrick simply covered Donny Petrozzo's mouth with a pad onto which he had broken an ampoule of Fentanyl?'

'Yes, I saw him do it.'

'What else did you see, Adrian? Because we don't believe you.'

'It's the truth, I swear – I saw him do it; the guy just fell to the floor.'

'Did you leave Fitzpatrick alone for any time with the body?'

Adrian frowned. 'Yeah, but only for a few minutes. I went to get some cleaning fluid from off a shelf in the garage. When I came back he was leaning over the man, saying he was dead.'

'Did you see him administer anything else?'

Adrian looked confused, but said that Fitzpatrick had been holding the man's face in his hands. He demonstrated by gripping his own cheeks. Langton looked to Anna: this could have been Fitzpatrick making 100 per cent sure that Donny Petrozzo was dead, by giving him an injection beneath his tongue.

Adrian continued to describe how he had cleaned up the wound to Fitzpatrick's shoulder. He was ordered to wrap Petrozzo's body in the black plastic bin liners stored in the garage. They wrapped the tape around the body and stuffed it into the back of the jeep. Together, they cleaned up the car, wiping the steering wheel down and the door handles. Adrian was told he had to get rid of the body by taking the jeep to a crusher.

'You just went along with it?'

Adrian hung his head and said that he didn't know what else to do. He took Petrozzo's car keys and drove Fitzpatrick to the cottage. 'I returned the car, his Mercedes; I left it near his home. I then went to drive the Mitsubishi out, to get it into a crusher, but I saw all the cops around, so I did nothing. I just went back to the boat.'

'Were you offered money to do all this?'

'Yes, ten thousand.'

'Did Fitzpatrick contact you again?'

'Yeah, I told him what had happened and that I wasn't able to move the jeep. He said to lie low on the boat, and contact no one. He'd be in touch; there was more money for me.'

The interview with Adrian was concluded by ten-fifteen. He was taken to the magistrates' court to face charges of drug trafficking, accessory to murder and perverting the course of justice. Langton asked that bail not be granted, concerned that Alexander Fitzpatrick might try to contact him and pressing home the lethal potency of the drug.

Mrs Eatwell was a feisty old lady. Even though she was in her late eighties, she hovered round the officers, demanding to be shown each item that was removed. The forensic teams working at the cottage had found more prints, and a pillowcase with bloodstains, which were being matched with the blood from the bullet taken from the squat.

They matched. However, there had still been no sign of Fitzpatrick. Although there had been numerous calls from the public after all the press releases, having sifted through the timewasters, it was clear that there had been no real sighting of their man. Pete Jenkins was still working on the print taken from the neck of Mrs D'Anton but had, as yet, had no confirmation it was Fitzpatrick's.

As the teams broke for lunch, and took a breather before the big interrogations, there came further information from the crates retrieved from Mrs Eatwell's garage. The amount of Fentanyl was staggering. Separate, small supply boxes were numbered and packed inside larger ones; these had been stored in protective wooden crates. There were thousands of ampoules that they believed were originally destined for hospitals in the United States. The Drug Squad began to contact the US drug units.

Chicago had reported not only a massive theft from a pharmaceutical company, but an alarming rise in the Fentanyl problem; increases in opiate overdoses had prompted tests, which had revealed its presence. Reported overdoses were also coming in from a variety of other states, including Detroit, St Louis, Philadelphia and Pittsburgh. The potency of illegally manufactured forms of Fentanyl was underlined as deadly: combined with heroin, the street names for it were 'Drop Dead', 'Flatlines' and 'Suicide', as well as 'Polo'. The amount removed from Mrs Eatwell's garage was a terrifying sign that the UK was about to be flooded with this lethal drug.

Langton was deeply angry on hearing just how potentially dangerous this consignment was, had Fitzpatrick distributed it as planned. He was now certain that Julius D'Anton, having been tipped off about the drugs, but not really aware of what they were exactly, had used Donny Petrozzo to test the waters with his dealers. They knew the junkie D'Anton had not drowned, although his body was fished out of the Thames; they were pretty certain that D'Anton had administered the fatal Fentanyl to himself.

D'Anton's death meant that the whereabouts of the box he had stolen out of the Mitsubishi would have been unknown to Fitzpatrick. Petrozzo had been in touch with his dealers in the Chalk Farm drug squat about the Fentanyl; it must have been at some point thereafter, that he contacted Fitzpatrick. Did Petrozzo know where the box was stashed? Was that why Fitzpatrick paid that disastrous visit to the squat? Anna agreed it was possible, but still found it strange that Frank Brandon would have become involved. Langton was more sanguine.

'I don't, sadly. You could say that about Adrian Summers. It all boils down to money. Frank, we know, had said to his girlfriend that he was coming into a big wedge of cash. What I am pretty sure about is none of them really knew just what a massive shipment Fitzpatrick had unloaded into his old lady's garage.'

'You think those two henchmen – Julia's bodyguards – are in his pay?'

'Unsure. More likely, they are in for the deal, and were putting the pressure on Fitzpatrick for payment.' As Langton finished talking, the investigation took another turn. Pete Jenkins had lifted off the print from the neck of Mrs D'Anton. It did not match Fitzpatrick's.

Pete had sent the print to the FBI lab in the United States. It had come back with an ID of a known felon, Horatio Gonzalez, a man who had ties with the Columbian cartels, and who had already served two prison sentences for drug dealing. They now had the US Drug Enforcement Agency putting pressure on them for more details. Langton became tetchy, insisting his team hold on to the reins and ordering that any evidence Pete was uncovering should be run by them first. He then asked that Damien Nolan be brought up from the cells for questioning.

As Anna and Langton were preparing for the

interview, files and photographs stacked in front of them, Langton gave a strange half-laugh. 'You know, if Frank Brandon hadn't been recognised at that drug squat, and those punks hadn't put two and two together to come up with a hell of a lot more and shot him, all this would never have gone down.'

'And we'd have a potentially lethal street drug killing hundreds, as it has already in the States,' Anna replied.

'It'll still come in some day, in the not too distant future. There's always a Fitzpatrick who doesn't give a shit and just wants to make millions.'

It was left unsaid that, even with the mass of new evidence, the man they had been hunting for what seemed an interminable time was still at large. The good news was they had his shipment of drugs; they had blocked his access to what was left of his fortune; they had his boat, his fake passports, his children. They even had his mother.

Anna observed once more what an attractive and handsome man Damien Nolan was. Even after a night in the cells, he appeared to be freshly shaved. His belt had been removed, as had the shoelaces from his brown suede shoes. On his left pinkie finger, he wore a heavy gold signet ring; his hands were very expressive, with long tapering fingers. Anna also noticed this time that, like Fitzpatrick, Damien had a very good set of teeth. She reckoned they were capped, but they were very white. His tawny brown hair, although thinning slightly, was combed back from his brow; he had a high forehead, and his eyes were dark brown.

Anna wondered about his affair with Julia. She could understand the attraction, not so the fact that his wife,

Honour, had also had a relationship with Fitzpatrick. She shook her head, wanting to concentrate on the inter- action between Langton and Damien. By comparison, Langton appeared rather seedy, not helped as he sniffed and cleared his throat, as he opened file one.

Damien's solicitor was elderly, white-haired and rather flamboyantly dressed, in a dark navy shirt and pinstriped suit, with a loud pink lining and matching pink satin tie. John Pinter had a leatherbound notebook, larger than most solicitors'; inside was a gold pen, and many scrawled notes. He turned the pages until he found an empty one, and pressed it down with the flat of his hands.

Langton, for the benefit of the tape, went through the charges, from aiding and abetting a drug trafficker to per- verting the course of justice. Not until he was satisfied that all was in order did he begin, by asking Damien to give his name and address.

Damien spoke in a low cultured voice; he then crossed his long legs. He was about six feet tall and looked healthy and fit, in contrast to Langton.

'Would you please describe your profession?'

Damien said that he was a Professor of Chemistry at Oxford University. These were the only words they got out of him, before his solicitor raised his hand. 'My client is fully aware of the charges levelled against him, and wishes it to be made clear that he has no connection to any drug offences. Nor has he, in any way, perverted the course of justice, or maintained any kind of relationship with the said Alexander Fitzpatrick.'

Langton ignored the pompous Pinter, concentrating on Damien. 'We know about your relationship with Julia Brandon, and that she admitted—'

543

Pinter tapped the desk. 'Detective Langton, Julia Brandon is now deceased, therefore anything she might have alluded to is hearsay.'

'Is this your handwriting, Mr Nolan?'

Damien glanced at the plastic-covered note discovered in the Mitsubishi and shrugged. Pinter sighed and said that the note could have been written by his client but, as to when, he could not recall.

Langton placed down the pictures of Donny Petrozzo's body. 'This man's body was found inside a Mitsubishi jeep, along with that note in the glove compartment, which gives directions to your farmhouse.'

Again, Damien did not answer. His solicitor became impatient, claiming that, as he had just stated, the note may have been written by his client but, as he could not recall when, or to whom he had given it, he could not see how Mr Nolan could be connected to the dead man.

'So you admit that you knew Mr Petrozzo?'

Damien shook his head. 'I do not know the man you say is Mr Petrozzo.'

Langton then displayed Adrian Summers's photograph. Again, Damien denied knowing him; he said it was possible he could have been at the farmhouse but, as he spent most days at college, he could not say for sure. It was frustrating, as Pinter jumped in at every opportunity to protect his client although, at no point, did Nolan appear to be in any way concerned by the barrage of questions put to him by Langton.

As the questioning got closer to the discovery of the drugs, Damien shook his head, smiling. 'As far as I am aware, the drugs were not found at the farmhouse I rent – not own, by the way – but in another property. So how you can assume I had anything to do with them, or have any connection to assisting to store them, is yet again supposition on your part, without any evidence of my culpability or connection.'

'So it was your wife?'

'No comment.'

'Your wife visited the cottage owned by Mrs Doris Eatwell and arranged for the drugs to be stored there?'

'No comment.'

'Was your wife also having a sexual relationship with Alexander Fitzpatrick?'

'No comment.'

'Were you aware of this relationship?'

'No comment.'

'Do you admit to knowing Alexander Fitzpatrick?'

'No comment.'

It continued for another twenty minutes; at no point did Damien Nolan answer a question with anything but either a 'no comment', or a rather droll response.

Even when Langton said that he must be aware of who Fitzpatrick was, Damien just sighed. 'I am aware of who he is, mostly due to the amount of publicity he has garnered, but I do not know him.'

'But your wife does?'

'No comment.'

'You also knew Julia Brandon well; we have confirmation that her youngest child was fathered by you.'

At this, Damien shook his head as if bewildered. 'No comment.'

'We can very easily verify this by DNA tests.'

They received a nonchalant shrug by way of reply. Pinter asked why they were even questioning his client with regard to whether or not he had fathered a child by his sister-in-law, when the charge was assisting a known drug trafficker to avoid detection. He had denied ever having anything to do with Fitzpatrick, or his drug connections, so how they could level perverting the course of justice at his client was really beyond his comprehension.

Langton was getting very rattled; he snapped out that perhaps Mr Nolan only knew Fitzpatrick by his alias, Anthony Collingwood.

'No comment.'

Langton gritted his teeth. 'Mr Nolan, I find it very hard to believe that you were totally unaware, as you claim to be, of the wanted criminal Alexander Fitzpatrick: you live close to his mother.'

Damien laughed. 'I know a Mrs Doris Eatwell but, as to her relationship to this man, I am at a loss; she was simply a neighbour.'

'One your wife spent considerable time with.'

'Quite possibly; my wife is a very caring woman.'

'Caring enough to look after Fitzpatrick who was injured and staying with his mother?'

'No comment.'

When shown the photograph of Julius D'Anton, they got the same response: Damien had never met him.

'Do you know about a drug called Fentanyl?'

'It is a very potent opiate that creates respiratory depression if over-prescribed; because of its low costs, it is now favoured in medical practice. It was first used in the sixties as an intravenous anaesthetic called Sublimaze; subsequently, other short-acting agents were introduced – one called Aifentanil, another Sufentanil – up to ten times more potent than Fentanyl, used in heart surgery. There are now manufactured transdermal patches called Duragensci, for chronic pain management. Another form

of Fentanyl is a citrate called Acted; this can be administered in the form of a lollipop to children. It is a major
breakthrough for pain relief in cancer patients.' He raised
his hand. 'Would you like me to continue?'

'You are obviously aware of the dangers of this drug.'

'Obviously. You have to understand that, as a low-
cost drug, it is favoured by hospital administrations.
Its use has been correlated with a certain amount of concern over second-hand inhalation of the vapours. This
can create brain damage, and also makes abuse depend-
ence and behavioural disorders more likely.' He smiled.
'You would be surprised how many anaesthetists and
surgeons have become addicts due to their exposure to
the drug.'

'So, with this awareness, Mr Nolan – and, I must say,
you have been very helpful with regard to explaining
the potency of Fentanyl – how did you feel about being
involved with the mass of crates containing Fentanyl,
stored first at your farmhouse, then at Mrs Eatwell's
cottage?'

Damien said steadily, 'Because of my work, I am
obviously aware of any new drug, be it natural or chemically produced. That does not in any way demonstrate
that I was aware of, or played any part in, the shipment
you appear so determined to prove I knew something
about. If you wish to go to my college rooms, you will
find untold information with regard to chemically produced opiates; in fact, it goes back to about 2003 when
three epidemiological reports were published.'

'Did your wife also have this knowledge, and was
therefore aware of the dangers of the drugs that she
assisted in storing?'

'No comment.'

Pinter now requested that, if they had any further evidence that involved his client in their accusations against him, he should be made privy to it without delay. If they did not, he felt that his client had exonerated himself and should therefore be released.

Langton ended the interview on a sour note, saying that, until he was satisfied, Mr Nolan would remain in custody.

'You have had my client here since yesterday evening. Please be mindful of the amount of time you are allowed to detain him without charges.'

'I am aware of that,' Langton snapped, as he ended the interview tape.

Damien smiled at Anna as he stood up; she had a strange *déjà vu* feeling about him.

'Are you related to Alexander Fitzpatrick?' she asked suddenly.

It was the first time there had been a glimmer of concern behind the affable mask. 'I'm sorry?'

'It's just you have a very familiar look.'

'Really?'

'Yes. So are you?'

'Am I what?'

'Related to the man you may call Anthony Collingwood, whose real name is Alexander Fitzpatrick?'

'How very intuitive of you, Detective Travis.'

The fact that he knew her name was a surprise, but more so was his subsequent reluctance to answer her question. Langton glanced at Anna and back to Damien Nolan. 'We can find out easily enough. Let's not waste any more time. Until we are satisfied with our enquiry, Mr Nolan will remain here.'

A uniformed officer led out Damien and his solicitor,

as Langton stacked up his files. 'That came out of left field.'

'I know. It's his looks – don't you think they are similar?'

'Slightly. I'm not sure what it gives us, even if we prove it.'

'That it is also his mother down the lane, not only Fitzpatrick's? If the whole clan is so entwined, without doubt he is part of the set-up.'

Langton rubbed at his head, and told Anna to see what she could find out. She went into the incident room to ask Gordon to check births, deaths and marriages.

The place was bubbling, as they were coming up with more information regarding the drug haul, the crates having been filled with different varieties of the drug, from ampoules to vials.

Phil was sweating. 'Jesus Christ, this was some haul; the biological effects of this stuff are similar to heroin, except that Fentanyl can be a hundred times stronger. It can be smoked or snorted, but is usually taken intravenously, so if it was to be released onto the streets, it could create havoc, because there is no way of knowing its potency and it can kill within seconds ...' Phil was hard to interrupt in full flow but, as Anna already knew pretty much everything he said, she was more eager to find Gordon and see if she was correct about the siblings.

Unable to track him down, she returned to her office to call Mrs Eatwell. As she searched for the contact number, she couldn't help but go over parts of the interview with Damien Nolan. Langton, she felt, had been way below par, and had allowed the solicitor far too much say; it was very unlike him, not to have put more pressure on. She wondered if he was saving firing on all guns until Honour was brought up from the cells.

A female liaison officer answered Mrs Eatwell's phone. Anna was told that all calls were being monitored in case her son tried to make contact; so far, he had not.

Anna waited for quite a while before Mrs Eatwell came onto the phone. 'Mrs Eatwell, this is Detective Inspector Travis.'

'Good afternoon,' came the brusque, upper-class voice.

'Thank you for agreeing to speak with me.'

'I don't really have any option. I have a policewoman with me all the time; they even do the grocery shopping. Is Honour coming home?'

'Mrs Eatwell, I need to ask you about Damien.'

'What about him?'

'Is he related to you?'

There was a pause, then Mrs Eatwell repeated her question about Honour returning home.

'I am unsure when Honour will be allowed home.' Anna asked again if Damien Nolan was related to Mrs Eatwell.

'He is a wonderful man. I won't have a word said against him. Damien has nothing to do with my son, and whether or not he is related to me, is none of your business.'

Anna tried again; this time, she said that she could make enquiries to check out Damien's background, but it would be far simpler if Mrs Eatwell just answered her query.

'It's not your business; I refuse to be drawn into implicating Damien in any of this. Leave him alone.'

Anna gave up and ended the call. Even if she did

discover that Damien was related to Alexander Fitz-patrick, she was unsure what it would mean, bar the fact it would implicate him more deeply; however, as yet, they had no evidence of his involvement whatsoever. It was the note that still irritated her: the torn scrap of paper with directions to the farmhouse. It would make sense if Damien had been in London, and written them for Adrian Summers to use to drive the drugs to Honey Farm. But he had denied being in London, and denied having any knowledge of the shipment.

Anna made a note to re-question Adrian Summers regarding Damien. She then returned to the incident room, where Phil collared her again. 'We're getting quite a lot of feedback on known thefts of Fentanyl. One has just come in from York: a guy working as a radiologist has been arrested up there. They found a large quantity of empty vials wrapped up in hospital surgical supplies and hidden in a ceiling tile. Apparently, the guy was stealing them by entering operating rooms after pro-cedures had been performed and taking what was left over from the medical waste containers.'

'Phil, I can't really spend time on this. I don't see the connection with our case.'

'I'm only doing what Langton told me to do!' he said, tight-lipped.

'Where is he?'

'I dunno; I thought he was interviewing Damien Nolan.'

'He was, but then he left. We still haven't questioned Honour Nolan.' Anna looked around the incident room, and then headed towards Cunningham's office. It was empty. Frustrated, Anna approached her own office but, when she tried to open the door, she found it locked. 'Is somebody in here?' She pressed her face to the window, trying to see inside. Then the door was unlocked, and she had to catch her breath.

Langton looked terrible. His face was pale, and it had a sheen of sweat, making it appear almost grey. His shirt-sleeves were rolled up, and he had no shoes on.

'James?' she said, closing the door quickly behind her. She saw his jacket on the ground, his shoes beside it.

'I needed to have a break,' he said, slumping into her chair.

'Have you got a temperature?' She felt his brow; it was cold, and he shivered. Anna picked up his jacket and slipped it around his shoulders. 'You want a cup of tea?'

'Just some water,' he said quietly.

Anna opened one of the desk drawers and took out a bottle of water, unscrewing the cap and passing it to him.

He took a few sips and then closed his eyes. 'Sorry,' he muttered.

'Do you want me to take you home?'

'No, I just need a few minutes.'

'I think you should see a doctor.'

'I'm fine; just couldn't get my breath. If I sit tight for a while, it all eases up. There's no need for you to stay with me.'

Anna sat on the edge of her desk. 'How often does it happen?'

'It happens,' he whispered, leaning forwards.

Langton had suffered from a collapsed lung after his attack; he had almost died and the scars on his chest were proof of his appalling injuries. He seemed very frail and his hand shook, as he continued to take sips of water.

'I've just been listening to Phil collecting information regarding numerous thefts of Fentanyl.'

'Yeah, the medical profession has got to pull out their fingers and get some kind of tamperproof mode of Fentanyl administration. What we've got coming in is widespread theft from various institutions – could create a fucking epidemic.'

'I think we should concentrate on our case,' Anna said. 'We haven't even questioned Honour Nolan yet.'

Langton pushed back the chair, and got unsteadily to his feet. 'I am aware of that!' He started to redo his tie. She bent down and placed his shoes in front of him; he slipped them on. 'Thing is, Travis, we've only just touched on what that bastard intended dealing. In my position, I have to look at the whole perspective. If Fitzpatrick was able to ship this amount of Fentanyl into the UK, it's only the beginning.'

'It would be good to get him locked away.'

'Quite, but my gut feeling is he's long gone.'

Anna shrugged, annoyed by the suggestion that they had lost Fitzpatrick. 'You fit to question Honour now? Or do you want to wait until after lunch?'

Langton slowly pulled on his jacket and yanked the collar down; she could see that the colour was coming back into his face. 'Let's go in ten minutes.' He walked to the door and unlocked it.

'What about Damien Nolan?' she asked.

'What about him?'

'His solicitor's getting very tetchy.'

'We hold him until we're finished with Honour.' They walked out of her office.

Anna asked if he felt Damien had just been drawn into the edges of the Fitzpatrick scenario, but played no part in it. Langton gave a soft laugh. 'He's a player, Travis, and a clever one, because we don't have anything to pin on him, bar the fact he lived at the farmhouse, is married to Julia Brandon's sister, supposedly had an affair with Julia and, according to her, fathered her child! For someone on the periphery, he certainly got into heavy relationships.'

'I didn't find out if he was related to Alexander Fitzpatrick. I spoke to Mrs Eatwell; she said it was none of my business and that Damien was a wonderful person.'

'Maybe he is just that.' Langton opened the interview-room door.

Already sitting, waiting with her solicitor, was Honour Nolan. She gave a nervous smile to Anna, and nodded to Langton, as he took his seat opposite her. She was wearing the same dress she had been arrested in: it was hippy-styled, caught under the bust with a row of hand-embroidered strawberries, and fell in loose folds of soft fabric over her motherly figure. She wore numerous heavy silver bangles and rings, and silver hoop earrings. She wore no make-up but her skin looked fresh, none the worse for a night in the cells. Her long dark hair was wound around her head, the two braids long enough to cross over the top and coil around again, rather like the Mexican artist, Frida Kahlo.

Langton took a while, selecting his files and placing them in order. Anna took her notebook and pens out, and her own file. She glanced at him; he showed no ill-effects from the episode she had just witnessed.

Langton started the tape, explaining that they would also be recorded on video. He repeated the charges against Honour: she was being questioned with regard to drug trafficking, harbouring a known felon and perverting the course of justice. He added that this alone was a very serious offence and, if charged, she could be given ten to twelve years, as the authorities took a very serious view of anyone tampering with the law. Honour had her hands folded across each other on top of the table, heavy silver rings on almost every finger, even one on her right thumb.

'Very well, Honour, let's go from the top, shall we? Please give your name and address.' Langton kept his voice low, almost encouraging, as Honour cleared her throat and answered his seemingly innocuous questions about how long she had lived at the farm, how long she had been married to Damien Nolan, when she had worked at the antique store, and her relationship with Mrs Doris Eatwell. Her answers were concise and to the point.

Seated beside Honour was her solicitor, a grey-faced man, with extremely bad halitosis. Matthew Webb used a stubby pencil to jot down notes in what looked like a child's exercise book. His solid square face gave no hint of expression, his watery eyes unblinking, as his client continued.

Langton paused before he asked Honour to detail her relationship with Alexander Fitzpatrick.

Webb looked up. 'My client will refuse to answer that question, on the grounds that it could—'

'Your client, Mr Webb, has already admitted to knowing Mr Fitzpatrick and, according to her sister, had an ongoing sexual relationship with him.'

'That is a lie,' she said.

'I'm sorry; do you want to explain why you say it is a lie?'

'My sister did not tell you the truth. I have never had a sexual relationship with him.'

'When was the last time you saw him?'

Again, Webb interjected that his client would not answer, on the grounds that it might implicate her.

'Your client, Mr Webb,' said Langton, 'was fully aware that Fitzpatrick was a man wanted on both sides of the Atlantic. Your client aided Mr Fitzpatrick to store a sizeable amount of medical drugs, first at Honey Farm, and then subsequently in Mrs Doris Eatwell's garage.'

'I did not.'

'Were you aware that your husband fathered a child by your sister?'

'That is preposterous! If my sister claimed that this happened, then she lied to you. Julia was incapable of ever telling the truth.'

'Could you please explain why this has been brought up?' Webb tapped the notebook with his stubby little pencil.

'We are simply trying to establish the relationships that enabled Alexander Fitzpatrick to avoid detection for such a considerable time. His mother, Doris Eatwell, was a close friend to you, Mrs Nolan; you assisted in moving the drugs to her garage with the help of Adrian Summers.'

'That is not the truth.'

'Do you admit to knowing Mr Adrian Summers?'

'I have never met him.'

'But we have a witness who saw him at your farm-house,' Langton persisted. 'He also submitted a statement, claiming that you helped store the crates containing the drugs in the henhouse at your farm.'

'I did not.'

'Then, at a later date, when it became known that the police were making their presence felt, possibly about to orchestrate a search of the farmhouse, you moved the crates to Mrs Eatwell's garage for safekeeping.'

'That is not true.'

'At this time, you assisted the injured Mr Fitzpatrick; you tended to, I believe, a flesh wound to his right shoulder.'

'That is not true.'

Langton glanced at Anna, and took out a photograph of Julius D'Anton. 'Do you recognise this man, Mrs Nolan?'

Honour hesitated, then admitted that she did recall seeing him, when he tried to buy a table from the antique shop where she worked. She was shown the photograph of D'Anton, taken when his body was dragged out of the water. She gave a strange lift of her eyebrows, but said no more.

Anna sat patiently, as Langton began to bring out the photographs of all the victims: David Rushton, Donny Petrozzo, Frank Brandon, Julius D'Anton's wife, Sandra. Lastly, he laid out the pictures of Julia Brandon's mangled car, and the mortuary shots of her body. He kept up a fast delivery, slapping down the pictures, not giving Honour time to query, or her lawyer time to interject. He spread the photographs out like a fan across the table and stared at Honour.

'Why are you showing me all these terrible photographs?' Her voice was now starting to sound strained.

Langton laid down numerous photographs of Alexander Fitzpatrick, taken from Rushton's security CCTV footage. 'This is Alexander Fitzpatrick, correct?'

Honour chewed her lips.

'Or maybe you still refer to him as Anthony Collingwood? Which name do you call him by?'

'I don't know him.'

'All these people – *including your sister* – died because of him!'

'That is not true!'

'Yes, it is. She had the brakes of her car sliced in two, Honour. Now, for God's sake, why are you protecting him?'

'I'm not! This is all supposition; you have no proof of any of these accusations.'

Langton leaned forwards. 'What makes someone like you willing to put their own life on hold? Because you will go to prison, Honour. You have consistently lied to cover the truth, and now you maintain this farcical front that you never even knew Fitzpatrick.'

Webb rapped the table with his pencil. 'Detective Chief Superintendent, you are trying to goad my client into answering these accusations. I advise her not to make any reply, on the grounds that it may—'

'Are you maintaining that your client never knew what was going on right under her nose – that she never saw anything?'

'You have no evidence that Mrs Nolan ever, at any time, allowed her premises to be used for storing these drugs.'

'It doesn't matter how many people die; how many people this man, whom you are so desperate to protect, has killed? He even used his elderly mother! You think she'll be let off? Mrs Eatwell is going to stand trial just like you, and she will die in prison. So what is so great about her son – about this evil, twisted, sadistic monster, who even used his own children to launder money?'

Webb now banged the table in anger. 'If you have any further questions relating—'

'I haven't finished yet!' Langton snapped, then he pointed at Honour. 'He used you, Honour; you are just like everyone else who has ever come into contact with him. You should try and assist my enquiries, because I am going to charge you with accessory to murder.'

'Exactly who are you now referring to?' asked Webb.

'Take your pick.' Langton pushed forwards the array of photographs.

Honour began to remove the clips from her hair.

'Can you please stop that,' Langton said angrily.

'It's tight – I have a headache,' she said, as she loosened her two braids, uncoiling them to hang down around her shoulders.

'Right. Let's go from the beginning again, shall we?'

Anna could feel her own headache starting, never mind Honour's. She was surprised how exhausted she felt. She knew Langton must be as drained, but he didn't let up, this time trying a calmer approach. Still Honour maintained her composure, but kept on fiddling with the hair grips she had removed.

They were getting nowhere; even Webb began to show that he was tired of the repetition, as Langton continued to ask the same questions and again received the same replies. She knew nothing; she did not admit to knowing Alexander Fitzpatrick by that, or any other name; she was not aware that any illegal drugs had been stored at her farmhouse and subsequently moved to Mrs Eatwell's garage. It was preposterous: she claimed to be totally innocent of all charges.

Anna could sense Langton's frustration building to boiling point. It was at this moment that he leaned close and whispered that she should take over. Anna began by picking up the photographs and stacking them like a pack of cards. 'Could you tell me about your relationship with your sister?'

Honour gave a small shrug. 'We were not on good terms.'

'Why was that?'

Honour sighed. 'We were very different creatures. All Julia ever cared about was herself, and money – the more she had, the more she wanted.'

'So, when Julia was living at the house in St John's Wood, were you a frequent visitor?'

'No.'

'But you did visit the property? According to Julia, you moved in for some considerable time, as Alexander Fitzpatrick's mistress?'

'That is not true.'

'Why would she lie about it? According to Julia, you were in love with her partner. When she found out that the woman he had moved into her home was her own sister, she began to arrange her finances, to block his access to any of the monies he had arranged for her to live on. In a fit of jealousy, she also claimed that, although her first child was conceived by IVF treatment, the second child was in actual fact your husband's. She was adamant that the relationship was purely sexual.'

'That is a lie.'

'That Damien Nolan fathered her second child was the reason you and she were not on good terms. You found out. Not content with having a relationship with Fitzpatrick, you became very distressed to discover this liaison; partly out of jealousy but, Julia maintained, it was more to do with the fact that you were unable to have children of your own.'

Langton kept his head bowed; he knew what Anna was doing, leading in with a more personal motive to try and open Honour up. It was working.

There was a flash of anger as Honour shook her head. 'Julia was a liar; she couldn't tell the truth to save her life, especially if it didn't suit her. She was very manipulative.'

'And you are not? I would say that living with her lover, in her house was—'

'I did not live with him.'

'Who are you referring to?'

'You know who; you are trying to trap me into admitting something that is just a pack of lies. I love my husband.'

'Really? So it must have hurt you considerably to find out he fathered her child?'

'He did not.'

'We will be taking DNA tests to prove it, so it is immaterial whether you admit it or not. It must have been very hard for you: your sister was younger, beautiful and wealthy, living in great luxury, able to conceive two children and, at the same time, arrange a very complicated scheme to block her partner from gaining access to her fortune. You claimed that you were not aware she had married Frank Brandon—'

'I keep on telling you that I had very little contact with my sister. We did not get along; to be honest, I never liked her.'

'But you were jealous of her.'

'No, I was not; I had my own life.'

'In a rented, rather squalid farmhouse?'

'That is your opinion.'

'It's a fact. It must have been very tempting when Alexander Fitzpatrick surfaced – and he did, didn't he?

How did he first approach you after almost twenty years living abroad?' Anna placed down his photograph. 'He is still a very attractive man, isn't he? Did he cajole you into helping him? He must have dangled untold wealth to get you to take the risk, and allow him to store crates of drugs at your property; or maybe he threatened you? Put you under terrible pressure to assist him?'

Honour remained silent.

'We have a witness, Honour, who has given a statement that you were fully aware of the content of the crates, and that you assisted in moving them to Mrs Eatwell's garage.'

'No, I did not.'

'I'm sorry, what was that? You didn't know what the crates contained?'

Honour was twisting her braid round and round in her fingers. 'You are making me say things.'

Webb sighed. He tapped the table. 'My client has denied, over and over again, any knowledge of what was in these crates. She is fully aware that nothing was discovered at her farmhouse that connected her to the drugs haul—'

'Because she had already helped move them to a safer place! Mr Webb, we have a witness who assisted her; to persist in denying any knowledge of them is now ridiculous.'

'I didn't know what they contained.' At last, a breakthrough.

'You were totally unaware that these crates contained a class A drug, Fentanyl, in vast quantities?'

'I didn't know what was in them.'

'Who arranged with you to store them at the farmhouse?'

Honour was cracking. Her cheeks were flushed, and she licked at her lips nervously.

'Do you see his picture amongst these photographs? Yes or no?'

Honour shifted her weight in the chair. 'I got a call from Julia.'

'Your sister.'

'Yes. She said that she needed to store some things, as she was buying a new house in Wimbledon, and this young man . . .' she tapped Adrian Summers's photograph '. . . drove up and stored them in the old henhouse.'

'I see. So when you knew the police were making enquiries and returning with a search warrant, you agreed to move these items to Mrs Eatwell's garage?'

'Yes.'

'If they were just household items, why did you bother moving them?'

'Julia told me to; she said a few things were very valuable.'

Anna wrote in her notebook, before she gave a smile to Honour. 'Thank you. So this means that, contrary to what you said earlier, you were still on reasonable terms with Julia.'

'She was my sister.'

Anna took out the mortuary shots of Julia's injured body and passed them across the table. 'The brake wires of her Mercedes were sliced in two. She was driving at over ninety miles per hour when her car jack-knifed across the dual carriageway into the path of a truck. As you can see, she was decapitated.'

Honour turned away.

Next, Anna put down photographs of the boat anchored in Chelsea Harbour, with the two children on board. She kept up an easy conversation about the children being well cared for, and the fact that the boat had also been anchored previously in Brighton Marina; she showed pictures of the rented house in Hove. She could sense that Honour was unaware of the floating palace owned by Fitzpatrick. 'Did you ever pay a visit to this boat, or the property in Hove?'

'No.'

'So you were unaware of Fitzpatrick's lifestyle, and that he intended to take the two children out of the country? The Harbour was also, we believe, where Julia was heading the night she was killed.'

Honour was frowning, staring at the pictures. Webb interrupted, asking what these new pictures had to do with the charges against his client. He was ignored.

'Julia was going to join Fitzpatrick; she had some jewellery with her, and we discovered the rest of her valuables on board the boat.'

Again, Honour seemed perplexed, shaking her head.

'After attempting to cut out Fitzpatrick and keep his money for herself, the couple obviously came to some very amicable arrangement. As I have said before, Julia was very beautiful: he must have still wanted to be with her. He never used her to store his illegal drugs, did he? Just you. Did you know Fitzpatrick was even at her sham of a wedding? We believe he instigated it, as a means of moving out his money—'

'No, that is not true.'

'You know about the wedding; we discussed it, Honour. You said you were unaware she had even married Frank Brandon – I think you said he didn't appear to be her type! You were used by the pair of them, isn't that correct?'

Every time it looked as if Honour was going to open up, she recoiled in her seat. She was now very tense and sat hunched over the table.

Anna was basically 'hoofing' it, trying to dent Honour's confidence. She was certain that she was moving in the right direction, but unsure where she could go next.

Latching onto Anna's theme, Langton rocked back in his chair. 'Whatever lies you were fed to protect him, Honour, must now seem sickening. What did you believe? That you would replace Julia in his affections? That it would be you, living a life of luxury? You can salvage some self-respect by giving us information about where we can find him. It will also help your defence.'

Honour began to cry, covering her face with her hands. Her braids had come undone and her hair was hanging loose in waves. Anna could see there was a thick grey line in her parting; now, the hippy style made her look old-fashioned, almost frumpish. They let her cry, passing over a box of tissues. As she wiped her eyes and blew her nose, they waited; the floodgates were about to open.

Two hours later, Honour was led back to the cells, while Anna and Langton looked over the ten-page statement.

It had been painstakingly long and drawn out. Even though they now had more pieces of their jigsaw in place, there still remained one gaping hole: where was Alexander Fitzpatrick? Honour denied knowing where he was hiding out, but said she was waiting for him to contact her. According to her, over two years ago, Fitzpatrick had surfaced in Oxfordshire. He had turned up unexpectedly at the farmhouse and was staying at his mother's cottage. He explained that there had been some disastrous investments and he had lost most of his fortune. He had said that he was preparing to go back to work; neither Honour nor Damien queried what that would be. He had returned to the US after a few days, but began seeing Honour again when he returned. She did go with him to the house in St John's Wood, and lived with him on and off for a few months. She admitted that she was obsessed by him, but was concerned that Julia would find out.

Julia had discovered that he was having an affair; she did not know for some time that it was with her own sister. When she did find out, she travelled to Oxfordshire and confronted Damien, who didn't really care either way. Honour explained that she and her husband had an open marriage, Damien constantly having affairs with his young students.

As his investments went into a downward spiral, Fitzpatrick became worried that he could not get the finances for his latest drug deal. He had joined up with two Chicago mobsters, and they had agreed to part-finance the shipment; however, Fitzpatrick was then being screwed over by Julia, who was moving all his money into accounts that he couldn't access. She was eaten up by jealousy over the affair and wanted to pay him back. It was at this point he had forced her to give him the four million pounds to pay off the Chicago mobsters and to bring in the shipment to Gatwick. He was waiting to take possession of the drugs when it all started to fall apart.

Julia was scared, and so hired Frank Brandon to act as her bodyguard, but Fitzpatrick was onto it. He used Frank to help him transfer money, and promised him big dividends, enough to set him up for life. Having sorted out Julia, promising that they would leave England together, he then set about using Honour to store the drugs. He was still in debt to the gangsters, but believed he would be able to get away with it. His plan was to hide the drugs, but hold on to one box of samples; this was the box discovered by Julius D'Anton.

Honour could not recall the exact order of events. She knew that Adrian Summers was going to deliver the crates; she helped him store them. The piece of the jigsaw that had constantly bothered Anna was the hand-written note with directions to the farm. Honour explained that Damien had to visit London for a lecture; he had met Adrian and given him directions. She maintained that Damien had no knowledge of what was going down. She was deeply in love with Fitzpatrick and believed his promises of living a new life in the US, which is why she agreed to do everything he wanted. The crates were driven to the farm, and loaded into the henhouse. At this point, Anna and Gordon paid a visit; scared the police were onto him, Fitzpatrick had insisted they move the crates to his mother's garage. He said they would find a better place at a later date.

Honour corroborated Adrian's story about D'Anton turning up first at Mrs Eatwell's and putting the fear of God into them all, then driving to the antique shop to pick up the table in the Mitsubishi. Honour was unable to explain how Donny Petrozzo came on the scene, as she had never met him. She just knew that the last time she had seen D'Anton was when he came into the antique shop. Fitzpatrick was told what had happened by Adrian Summers.

'I don't know exactly what happened,' Honour said,

'but Alex was in a rage, and said that D'Anton had stolen something from him. I knew it had to be part of the shipment, but I never asked him about it. He didn't know where D'Anton lived; he was in a really unpleasant mood and very concerned.'

Langton looked to Anna. Concerned? They wondered if this was the moment that D'Anton contacted Donny Petrozzo. Did he then give him a sample to sell to the drug dealers? That would make sense, but they had no way of finding it out. The only solid facts were that the two drug dealers agreed to pay five thousand upfront and another five when they got more Fentanyl. Again, Honour could not give details of these transactions, as she didn't know about them; all she could give was her side of the events.

She recalled Fitzpatrick turning up at Honey Farm, wounded. It was not a bad wound; the bullet had cut clean through the tip of his shoulder blade, but it needed attention. Whilst it was healing, he stayed at his mother's cottage, having left a trail she knew nothing about: the bodies of Frank Brandon and Donny Petrozzo. With Frank dead, all the financial deals they had made with Rushton didn't make sense, so Fitzpatrick had to go and rearrange the transfers. Again Honour had no idea who Rushton was, or that he had been murdered. She maintained that, throughout all the 'problems' Fitzpatrick was going through, she just remained at the farmhouse.

'He stayed with Doris looking after him. He had a high fever, as the wound was infected, but we couldn't call a doctor. He then became very agitated, as he said he had two men looking for him; they were from America. He said that he had been able to string them along, and that they were looking after Julia until he could raise the money he owed them. I think it was a considerable amount; he was angry with Julia because of something she had done with his money in England. He said that they were threatening him, so he got up too soon, because he said he had to find Julius D'Anton.'

Again, Langton glanced at Anna: this matched up with his audacious visit to the station. He cannot have known D'Anton was dead.

Honour was adamant that Fitzpatrick did not have anything to do with Julia's death. She was unsure if he had arranged for the children to be taken, as she did not know about the boat. She said that she did have one call from Fitzpatrick: he was shocked by the news of Julia's accident and also desperate for news of his children. When Honour was asked if, at that time, she felt he was lying, she refused to answer.

'But surely you must have seen all the news coverage about the missing children, the au pair?'

'No, I didn't know. I hardly ever read newspapers.'

Anna and Langton stitched together their scenario. They reckoned that, to make sure Fitzpatrick didn't back out of the deal, the two thugs had threatened Julia. Their threats had proved to be very real: they cut her brakes and she died in the accident. Now Fitzpatrick was really up against it, because the police had tracked down all his money. If he withdrew any cash, they would be able to trace him.

A depressed and dejected Honour repeated over and over that she did not know where he could be. She had no energy left, her eyes were like dark-rimmed saucers. She asked if she could see her husband, but permission was refused. She yet again repeated that Damien was innocent and had known nothing about the drug deal.

She began crying again when she said that Fitzpatrick had promised to take her away and that they would bring up the little girls together.

'I have been a fool. He took me in, just as you have said he took everyone else in, but I loved him – I always had from the first time Julia brought him to meet me. She was young, and here was this handsome, charismatic man. I didn't believe all the things I read about him in the papers. Julia didn't even seem concerned. I have spent my whole life scrimping and saving, and living in rented places, while she has lived in the lap of luxury. If Alexander was a criminal, he never seemed to have to pay the price. He was always so glamorous, so generous and . . .' The tears rolled down her drained face. 'He made me feel special.'

Langton stood up, the interview over.

'If you think of anywhere he might have gone to ground, it will help your defence if you assist us. We have to find him, Honour.'

She made no reply, her head bowed. Her lawyer helped her stand, even picking up her hairpins for her, as she was led out and taken back to the cells, where she would remain until she was brought before a magistrate for the charges to be listed. As with Adrian Summers, Langton expressed concern over bail being granted: he was certain that Fitzpatrick would make contact with her.

Gathering up the photographs and paperwork, he sighed as he placed Fitzpatrick's photograph on top of the file. 'The longer he's free, the less likely we are to find him.'

'I know,' Anna said quietly. She too packed up her notes, placing them into her briefcase.

It was in many ways 'case closed', apart from the

capture of Fitzpatrick. Langton headed into the incident room to give an update, and Anna went into her own office.

Gordon tapped and entered. 'Well, that was very satisfactory,' he said.

'I felt sorry for her in the end. She's going to spend a lot of time in prison, all because she loved him.'

'But she doesn't know where he is?'

'No, and to be honest, we don't have the faintest idea either. He's had days to go Christ knows where.'

'But he's broke and we've got all his passports, so he might not have left the UK.'

'Maybe not, but the thing about Fitzpatrick is the way he always covers his back. He could have more fake passports stashed, he could even have access to cash – we just don't know.'

'Where would you go?'

'Me?'

'Yes.'

'Gordon, I have no idea.'

Gordon swung the door back and forth. 'Eurostar, St Pancras – that'd be the best place. Hop on the train, be in Brussels in just over an hour.'

'Well, we've pumped out his photograph, and we'll probably keep that going until we get something back.'

'What if we don't get any feedback?'

Anna rubbed her head. 'Then we've lost him,' she said flatly.

Gordon nodded and then leaned against the door-frame. 'Strange, isn't it? If it hadn't been for Honour Nolan covering for him, we'd probably have picked him up. If you think about it, we were spot on when we first went to her farmhouse.'

'Yes,' she said, wishing he would leave.

'You were – you had him in your sights from early on.'

'Yes.'

'Why do you think Honour took such a risk? She didn't seem the type, you know, to be infatuated. I mean, he's no spring chicken.'

'There's no reasoning with infatuations. She was taken in by him, fell in love with him. Mix that with envy and sibling rivalry, and don't forget the promises – he must have laid them on with a trowel.'

'But what about her husband?'

Anna shrugged, impatient with Gordon's hovering. 'Open marriage – he's younger than her, screws his students. She maintained that he was totally innocent.'

'Well, up to a point. He had to have met Fitzpatrick, so he knew who he was – he could have blown the whistle on him.'

Anna sighed. 'Gordon, can you hop it? I need to go over Honour Nolan's statements and type up the report.'

'He's just been released. No charges.'

Anna looked up as Gordon strolled out. 'Damien Nolan's been released?'

'Yeah, he was waiting for a taxi in reception.' The door closed behind Gordon.

Anna sat down again. She didn't want to, but she couldn't help thinking about what Gordon had said. In reality, Damien had to have known who Fitzpatrick was.

She got up and opened the door. 'Gordon!' she called, as he was just turning into the main corridor. 'I asked you to check on Damien Nolan's background, birth and marriage certificates.'

Gordon hesitated. 'Shit, yes – I'm sorry, I was going to get onto it but Phil wanted me to do something.'

'Do it now, Gordon. Thank you.'

She closed the door and rested against it for a moment. She then checked her watch; she knew by the time she had typed up her report and filed it, she wouldn't get out of the station until early evening.

Unlike any other case she had worked on, when coming to the conclusion had always been a high, this felt quite the contrary. Fitting all the jigsaw pieces together at long last should have been a very positive feeling, but the one vital piece was still missing. If Fitzpatrick wasn't captured, it would always remain incomplete.

Chapter Twenty-five

The following morning, as the team prepared the wrapping up of the case, Anna submitted her report from the previous evening. They still had a list of interviews to be completed, along with various charges but, to all intents and purposes, the case was closing. Obviously, the search for their prime suspect, Alexander Fitzpatrick, would be ongoing but, even without him in custody, the cases would go for trial.

Honour Nolan was taken before the magistrates; she was not granted bail, due to the gravity of the charges levelled against her, and was taken to Holloway Prison. Adrian Summers was to await trial at Brixton Prison. They were minor players in comparison to Fitzpatrick, but they would still have to pay the price of their association with him.

The incident board was testament to the complexity of the enquiry; just how many hours of police work had gone into the investigation was obvious. No matter that so many loose ends had been tied up, it was still an unsatisfactory end to a long investigation. Although they did have the drug haul, and they were able to knit together the events from the night Frank Brandon was murdered, charges against his killer were still in the pipeline.

The photographs of the victims were being taken down and boxed, ready for the trials:

Frank Brandon: shot by a lowlife drug dealer who mistakenly believed he had been at the Chalk Farm drug squat to make an arrest

Donny Petrozzo: murdered because of his attempt to force Fitzpatrick into cutting him in on the deal, with an overdose of Fentanyl

David Rushton: murdered, again by Fitzpatrick, because of his association with Julia Brandon and his movement of her funds, with an overdose of Fentanyl

Julia Brandon: murdered by persons unknown but possibly the men connected to Fitzpatrick's drug deals, her car brakes tampered with, resulting in a head-on collision

Julius D'Anton: possible death by his own drug addiction and use of Fentanyl, but also connected to Fitzpatrick

Sandra D'Anton: murdered by unknown assailants connected to Fitzpatrick; the suspects were still at large, but one of them had been identified from the thumbprint taken from her neck

Whether or not Fitzpatrick was still in the UK was doubtful, but the FBI were keen to continue their search for him, and placed him high up on their Most Wanted lists. The US side were also still searching for the two henchmen.

Anna and the team were to wind up the investigations by interviewing Doris Eatwell, to ascertain how much she was involved with protecting her son, Alexander Fitzpatrick, and allowing her premises to be used to hide the crates of Fentanyl. Due to her age, she was not to be held in custody, but she could face charges.

When Anna went to see Cunningham to sort out the interview, she found her sitting with her head in her hands, crying.

Cunningham took a tissue from a box on her desk and blew her nose. 'I've had some bad news. I won't be here for a few days.'

'I'm sorry.'

'My partner collapsed last night and is in hospital. They have found another tumour and ...' She had to wipe her eyes before she could continue. 'If you could hold the fort for me, until I have time to make other arrangements ... DCS Langton is still overseeing the final stages but, until the trials, we are obviously required to see what loose ends we can iron out.'

Anna felt that having not traced Fitzpatrick was more than just a loose end, but she didn't think it was the time to bring it up.

She returned to the incident room and joined Phil. 'I suppose you've heard: Cunningham is not going to be around for a few days.'

'Yeah, not that it's that much of a loss. She's been at half-mast since this enquiry started.'

'The duty manager's got the details. I'll take the trip to Oxfordshire to interview Mrs Eatwell; you keep on wrapping up here.' Anna also wanted to question Adrian Summers again to double-check a couple of things from his statement.

As Anna was returning to her office, Gordon approached. 'Damien Nolan: I don't have a birth certificate registered, but I've got a marriage licence – register office in Oxfordshire, dated 1984 to Honour – says his date of birth is eighteenth March nineteen fifty-eight, but there is nothing else. He has a passport—'

'Then you have to have a birth certificate, don't you?'

'Well, I've not traced one yet.'

'Never mind, we can have another attempt later. I want to get over to Brixton Prison and interview Adrian Summers; and then we'll drive to Shipston on Stour to see Mrs Eatwell.'

Adrian looked dreadful. Eyes red-rimmed, unshaven; his face already had a prison pallor, even though he'd only been inside a few days. 'My parents have been in to see me,' he said, almost in tears.

'I just need to ask you a few more questions,' Anna said.

'I don't know anything else, I swear to you.'

'It's just that I am unsure about one small thing: the note we found in the Mitsubishi.' Anna waited, but Adrian just looked at her. 'It had directions to the farm in Oxfordshire.'

'Yeah, well – I didn't know where it was.'

'Who gave you the directions?'

Adrian looked confused.

Anna sighed. 'We know you drove there; you have admitted taking the drugs to the farmhouse.'

'Yes, I said that I did.'

'So who gave you the directions?'

'I think it was the man you call Alexander Fitzpatrick. I swear I didn't know who he really was – I've said this.'

'My problem is, the note is not in his handwriting.'

'Then I dunno, I can't remember.'

Anna sighed. Gordon glanced at Anna; he couldn't fathom out what was so important about the note. Anna tapped her foot with impatience. 'Come on, Adrian! Did Fitzpatrick just hand this note to you?'

Adrian scratched at his head. 'Okay, I loaded up the jeep. As best as I can remember, Mr Collingwood—'

'You mean Fitzpatrick?'

'Yeah, he was shutting up the tailgate and he was telling me to drive carefully, as the last thing he wanted was me to be pulled over for speeding – well, it's obvious why. He gave me some money to fill up at a petrol station, which I did; it was the one midway down the M40.'

'So he just passed the directions to you?'

'No, he gave them to me before – he said the farm-house was hard to find. I was to follow the directions and not miss the small lane as it was badly lit around there.'

'So he had this note with the directions for you?'

'Yeah, that's right.'

'Did you see who gave the note to Fitzpatrick?'

'Mr Nolan wrote them out for him.'

'Damien Nolan?'

'Yes, he lives at the farmhouse with Honour, his wife.'

'So you saw Mr Nolan?'

'Not really. He drove up and they talked for a bit, then Mr Nolan scribbled the directions and handed them to—'

'Where did this take place?' she interrupted.

'It was on the boat. It was the day we drove to Gatwick, but in the morning, quite early. Like I said, he didn't come aboard, he just drove down the jetty and they met and he handed over the directions.'

'Thank you,' Anna said.

Gordon glanced at her; she was packing her notebook away. She then stood up and asked for the prison officer to open the interview room door.

'Is that it?' Adrian asked.

'Yes, Mr Summers, that is all I came here for.'

As Anna unlocked her Mini, she couldn't help but smile. She had known all along the note was of importance, even though Langton had dismissed it.

'Go on, Gordon, ask me,' she said, as she reversed out.

'Well, I can't quite fathom out the importance of whether or not Damien Nolan wrote the note. We know that he did, because it's his handwriting, right?'

'Because, Gordon, Mr Nolan has walked with no charges. He claims he knew nothing, saw nothing and heard nothing, like the proverbial monkeys – but he has lied. He claims not to know Alexander Fitzpatrick. He claims the note could have been written at any time; he also claimed that he couldn't even recall writing it! We now know he was not only in London, but also knew of the boat anchored at Chelsea Harbour. He passed the note on the day Fitzpatrick and Adrian Summers picked up the drugs from Gatwick Airport.' Anna glanced at Gordon. 'Do you understand now?'

Gordon looked blank.

Anna slapped the steering wheel with the flat of her hand. 'Mr Nolan is in this entire set-up, Gordon! Until now, we never had any proof of just how involved he was. He must have known exactly what was being picked up, and known that they were going to store the drugs at his farmhouse.'

'What are we going to do?'

Anna said nothing as she drove through Brixton towards the M40.

'Shouldn't we relay this back to the incident room?' Gordon asked.

Deadly Intent

'I'm not ready yet.'

Gordon made no reply; he found it hard to get a handle on what Anna was intending to do, and he also found her attitude egotistical, to say the least. But the conversation was halted, as she put on Radio 4, and continued to drive.

Anna parked in the small lay-by at the side of Mrs Eatwell's cottage in Oxfordshire. There was a Ford Fiesta parked up, with a police logo, and ribbons flapping around the garage from the scene of crime search. When Anna knocked, the door was opened by the family liaison officer assigned to Mrs Eatwell, who was under house arrest. Wendy Hall was a pleasant rotund officer, who immediately asked if they would like coffee, and ushered them into the kitchen.

'Where is Mrs Eatwell?'

'She's resting. She doesn't really come down but for her breakfast, and then stays up in her room, reading the papers.'

'How is she holding up?'

Wendy laughed. 'She's a feisty old lady, but half the time I don't really think she is aware of how serious her situation is. I've tried to explain to her that she will be charged with allowing her premises to store the drugs.'

Anna sat at the table as coffee brewed. 'She's also going to be charged with perverting the course of justice, and allowing her son to stay here, because she was obviously aware of exactly what he was up to.'

'She won't hear a word said against him,' Wendy said, as she fetched cups and opened a biscuit tin.

'Has Damien Nolan been here?'

'He came by last night, brought sausages and some

581

ham and vegetables. She adores him; gets all flirtatious when he's around her. I have to say, he is very charming and seems to genuinely care for her. He told her that Honour was in Holloway, but that he would be able to look out for her.'

Anna sipped the piping hot coffee – she really needed it – while Gordon tucked into the chocolate creams. Wendy sat down with them and, like Gordon, wolfed down biscuits. She told them how she was working on a shift with another officer, as Mrs Eatwell was not to be left alone. She said that most evenings they had supper together. Damien had joined them the previous evening; they had even opened a bottle of wine.

'She spends hours looking over her photo albums: she's had quite a life. Two marriages, both with very handsome men and both younger than she was. Her first husband divorced her over an affair with an Army officer, the second died about five years ago of cancer. As you can see, the cottage has been renovated within an inch of its life; all mod cons and central heating.'

Wendy chatted on as Anna finished her coffee, then asked if she could see some of the photo albums. Gordon helped himself to a fresh cup and more chocolate biscuits as Wendy brought in four leather-covered albums.

'Is Damien related to her, do you think?'

'Mr Nolan? She has never mentioned it if he is. She doesn't really talk much about recent events, or her son; she closes off if you bring up his name. She mostly talks about the past: she was a real beauty with flame-red hair, and quite a snazzy dresser. From what I've gathered, Honour took great care of her; she didn't appear to want for anything.'

Anna listened, turning over the pages of the album.

Mrs Eatwell had indeed been a very attractive young woman. There were shots of her by various cars and on holidays with a young boy, smiling and waving into the camera. A couple of pages were filled with photographs of a man whose face had been scratched out, and others of a good-looking man holding a tennis racket. Wendy said that it was her late husband, Henry Eatwell.

Anna began to flick through the pages until there were more recent photographs: Damien standing smiling with his arms around Mrs Eatwell, Damien in a Panama hat, drinking on a balcony somewhere; many of Damien and Honour together, some with a small white terrier, others with Mrs Eatwell in a group. There were also numerous photographs of Alexander Fitzpatrick as a young child and teenager; even one when he was wearing a mortarboard and gown. Like his mother, Alexander had been very good-looking in his youth; there were many photographs of him in various poses with cricket whites, tennis shorts, always smiling and laughing. There were a few of Julia Brandon, one with a baby in her arms and another with a toddler, but there seemed to be no recent pictures of Alexander.

Anna closed the album. 'I need to talk to Mrs Eatwell, Wendy, so if you could ask her to come in when she is ready.'

Wendy agreed and walked out. Anna sat, tapping the photo albums, as Gordon took their dirty cups to the sink.

He looked out of the window into the garden. It had a massive willow tree, taking up almost all of the lawn. As they were at the back of the house, they couldn't see the garage where the drugs had been stashed. The garden was reasonably well-maintained; there was a child's swing hooked over a branch of the tree and a few large plastic toys. 'Looks like her grandchildren might have visited.'

Anna texted the duty manager to see if they had gained a DNA result from the children. She wanted to know if Damien was the father of one of them, if not both.

Phil turned to Langton and said that he had tried to contact Anna, but received no reply. He was able to confirm that she and Gordon had visited Adrian Summers in Brixton Prison. Langton asked why the interview had taken place, but Phil couldn't confirm what the reason was; just that Anna had specifically asked for it to be arranged.

'She was going to interview Mrs Eatwell after seeing Adrian Summers, so maybe she's there by now and has turned off her mobile.'

Langton frowned and asked if they had the liaison officer's number; they should double-check if Anna was in Oxfordshire. He also wanted it confirmed that Damien Nolan was still in Oxfordshire.

'He was released,' Phil said as he dialled.

'Yes, I know. But that doesn't mean to say I've finished with him.'

Phil was put through to Wendy. He passed over the phone.

Langton had a quiet conversation with her, and asked her to make sure Anna called him when she was through. 'Yeah, she's with Mrs Eatwell,' he muttered, and then took himself off to use Cunningham's office.

Once inside, Langton took off his overcoat and chucked it over a chair, then he sat at the desk and opened the file with Alexander Fitzpatrick's name on the front. Inside was a record of all the data they had acquired on him. He proceeded to check all the various sightings and suppositions that had been accumulated. Anna Travis's name popped up over and over again: she had doggedly persisted with the possibility that he was their man from the earliest stages of the enquiry. Langton closed the first file, and began to read the second which dealt with Honour and Damien Nolan.

Someone rapped on the door and Phil put his head round. 'Gov, the results of the DNA test on Julia Brandon's children: the firstborn, can't get enough for a positive, but the second little girl *is* Damien Nolan's child.'

'Has Travis called in yet?'

'Nope, but I just texted her the results as she wanted it confirmed.'

'Thanks, Phil. Can you see if the Governor of Brixton will okay a phone call to Adrian Summers?'

'Sure. He's popular today.'

Langton grunted as he returned to reading the file. Yet again he noted just how often DI Travis's name cropped up; she was really hands-on throughout the enquiry. It was mainly down to her that they had forged ahead to the final conclusions. The fact that, after their extensive investigation, they still did not have Alexander Fitzpatrick banged up was a real bone of contention with Langton. It was like rubbing salt into a wound; the fact that he had been a witness to the man's audacity when he impersonated a Fraud Squad officer made Langton really smart.

He leaned back, closing his eyes, trying to place himself in Fitzpatrick's position. Did he by now have another false passport? Had he somehow arranged to get out of the UK? Or was he still hiding out? If he was, who could possibly give him shelter? The more Langton tried to think where Fitzpatrick could go, the more he came to a grinding halt.

Langton physically jumped as the desk phone rang, and he snatched it up. Phil had got Adrian Summers's permission to take the call and he was being brought to the phone. It was a matter of minutes before Langton spoke to him, querying what had been discussed with DI Travis. He replaced the receiver, now privy to the fact that, according to Summers, Damien Nolan had written the directions to the farmhouse. Langton buzzed into the interview room to ask Phil to bring him the statements from Damien Nolan. He then checked the time, and his face twisted with annoyance. Travis had received this information at nine-fifteen that morning; it was now after three. Once again, he felt that Travis was acting as she had done in the past – without team input – but, at that precise moment, he was not sure of the relevance. However, after rereading Damien Nolan's statements, Langton knew full well.

Nolan denied passing any note; his lawyer had said that the directions to the farmhouse could have been written at any time. Nolan had also denied being the father of Julia Brandon's youngest child. Nolan had implicated his wife as being part of the drug scam by his refusal to answer any question with regard to Honour; all he had responded was 'no comment'.

Langton rapped the edge of his desk with his knuckles; he then placed a call to his contact. The undercover officer was able to verify that the suspect was in residence, and showed no signs of moving out. Langton, without any confirmation to the team, had retained twenty-four-hour surveillance on Damien Nolan. He was now concerned that his plan of waiting might be jeopardised by Anna Travis. It never occurred to him that, like his protégée, he too had acted unprofessionally by not consulting the team. Like Anna, he had suspected Nolan of being implicated; unlike her, he had not placed the note as a priority.

Mrs Eatwell was wearing a pale oyster twin-set with a pearl necklace. She had a tweed skirt and velvet slippers and, for her age, was remarkably sprightly; only her hands were an indication, as they were very arthritic. She was sitting in a wing-backed chair close to the fire, and spoke to Wendy as if she was her personal maid, asking for a cup of green tea. Anna recalled the first time she had met her: how she had explained about the table and D'Anton's visit, and how she had given directions to the farmhouse further along the lane. Anna now suspected that she must have phoned Honour to expect visitors – the police. Just how much she knew, Anna was determined to find out.

'Thank you for agreeing to talk to me,' Anna began.

'I don't really have an option, do I?'

'Not really.'

'I don't see that I can be of any help. I really have nothing else to add to my previous statements. I have been questioned over and over again . . .'

'I know that, Mrs Eatwell, and you have denied being aware of the drugs discovered in your garage, but you have admitted caring for your son – so you were, at all times, fully aware that he was a wanted criminal.'

'He is my son: what was I supposed to do?'

'Do you know where he is now?'

'No, I do not.'

'When was the last time you saw him?'

Mrs Eatwell explained that Alex, as she called him, first visited her over eighteen months ago. She said that she had had no contact with him for many years, and was surprised when he called in to see her. She hardly recognised him, though he had provided for her since her husband died.

'So did your son arrange monies to be paid to you?'

'He opened an account, and I just withdrew any money when I was required to pay for work done. The cottage needed to be renovated, and I only have my pension.'

'What name is the account under?' Anna asked.

Mrs Eatwell became wary, and said that it was her personal account. Anna whispered to Gordon and he left the room. He went to talk to Wendy to ask about Mrs Eatwell's bank accounts and access to any statements. In the meantime, Anna pressed on, asking about the time her son came to stay, when he was injured. Mrs Eatwell said that he had turned up very late one night, and she had wanted him to go to hospital, as the wound to his shoulder was infected.

'Did he seek medical advice?'

'No. I bathed it with disinfectant, and replaced the bandages; it was a deep flesh wound, and he was in a great deal of pain.'

'How long was he here with you?'

'Just a few days. He slept in the spare bedroom; in fact, he slept most of the time. He hardly touched his food, then he showered and dressed and said he would be leaving.'

Anna flicked the pages in her notebook back and forth, as she worked out the timescale of when Alexander Fitzpatrick had stayed; she knew it had to be directly after the shooting of Frank Brandon. 'During the time he was here, did he have any visitors?'

Mrs Eatwell conceded that Honour had been to see him.

'What about Damien Nolan?'

'What about him?'

'Did he also visit your son?'

'No.'

'Was there anyone else?'

Mrs Eatwell pursed her lips, trying to think.

'What about the visit from the antique dealer?'

'Oh yes – *he* came. He wanted to know if I had any other furniture to sell. He asked about the table I had sold to the local antique shop.' She continued to explain that she had not been aware of the table's value; it was outside the kitchen door and she used it to stack firewood. When Sudmore had seen it, he paid her two hundred and fifty pounds for it. 'It was in a dreadful state. I couldn't believe that it would have had any value at all, so I agreed to sell it.'

'Did you know that it was Georgian?'

'Good heavens, no – then Julius D'Anton came to the cottage. He said he had seen the table at an antique fair and wondered if I had any other pieces. You see, there was quite a lot when I moved in here, but I didn't like it. A lot I gave away to the local charity shops, and I also burned some of it to make way for all this nice modern furniture.'

Anna let her continue talking, as she underlined in her notebook *Julius D'Anton*; the fact that Mrs Eatwell knew his name made her suspicious. 'This man, Julius D'Anton . . .'

'Yes? I've been asked about him before. As I just said, he came round.'

'Did you know him?'

'I didn't. Even when he told me who he was, it didn't mean anything, but he said that he remembered *me*.'

'Remembered you?' Anna repeated.

'Yes. He said that he had known Alex, and that he had met me numerous times when they were undergraduates together, but I didn't remember him. To be honest, I didn't really like him; he seemed rather seedy.'

Anna asked if Fitzpatrick had also seen him, as he was in the cottage recovering.

Mrs Eatwell shrugged. 'He could have seen him, I don't remember. When he came back, I wouldn't open the door. He said that his van had tipped into a ditch, so I gave him the number of the local garage.'

'And where was your son?'

'Upstairs, I told you: he was sleeping.'

Anna couldn't get any more details as to whether or not Fitzpatrick had confronted Julius D'Anton, as Mrs Eatwell maintained that he did not leave his room. However, she suspected that he had; he must have been very wary that D'Anton was sniffing around. She knew that D'Anton had got a lift from Adrian Summers in the Mitsubishi; that he had tried to buy the table and had cash enough to pay for it; then he was driven to London and, according to Adrian, had taken the drugs that were stashed in the back of the jeep.

Gordon returned and bent to whisper to Anna: all Mrs Eatwell's accounts had been checked. She had one for her pension to be paid into, which was also topped up by her late husband's pension; there was also a mortgage account, but they had found no other accounts or chequebooks.

'Mrs Eatwell, we have your pension account, but we do not seem to have any others. You said that your son opened an account for you: could you give me these particulars?'

Mrs Eatwell said that was all that she had, and Anna must have been mistaken.

Anna joined Wendy in the kitchen. The accounts were laid out on the kitchen table. Looking down the deposits and withdrawals, she could see no large sums of money. There was only eighty pounds in her pension account. The mortgage account had monthly withdrawals, and was virtually empty.

'She's got to have another account. We need to know how much she has, and if her son is also a signatory. Get onto the local branch and see what they can tell you.'

Anna returned to questioning Mrs Eatwell, eager to put more pressure on her. She was certain that Fitzpatrick had to have been unnerved by seeing Julius D'Anton, especially when D'Anton had recognised his mother. It was a coincidence that they had not even considered, but it made it more likely that Fitzpatrick had played a part in D'Anton's death.

Anna sat down as Gordon picked up Mrs Eatwell's empty teacup. 'Would you like a refill?' he asked.

'No, thank you.'

'Right, Mrs Eatwell, can I just go back to the time your son was staying with you?'

'I've told you all I know.'

'Maybe you have, but there are just a few things I need clarified.'

'I don't feel like answering any more questions. What I would like to know is when I can see my grand-children. As their mother is dead, I should be allowed to have access to them. They can come and live with me.'

'Your grandchildren? Are you aware that Damien Nolan is the father of the youngest child?'

She looked shocked but recovered remarkably quickly.

'We'd like to take a DNA test from you to determine if the first child is your son's, as we were informed that this child was conceived by IVF treatment.'

'You can take whatever tests you want; it doesn't alter the fact that they are my grandchildren.'

'I think it does, Mrs Eatwell, because Damien Nolan, as the child's biological father, will also have a claim – unless he is also related to you.'

Mrs Eatwell remained silent.

'*Is* Damien Nolan related to you?'

Again, there was no reply, but the old lady was now becoming very agitated. She began twisting her gnarled, bony hands in her lap, and she suddenly snapped out, 'That woman, that Julia, was a money-grabbing whore! I don't believe for a second that Damien would have had anything to do with her. She is a liar. I know it's not good to speak ill of the dead but she was a nasty, vicious little bitch.'

'We have it verified that Damien is the father, Mrs Eatwell, so it seems not only did your son Alexander have a relationship with her, but so did Mr Nolan.'

'I don't believe you; he wouldn't have done that to Honour.'

'Well, apparently he did. Honour was having a

relationship with Alexander. They were living together in Julia's house in St John's Wood.'

'No! She wouldn't do that – she wouldn't do that to Damien! She loves him.'

'She has said to me that she was in love with Alexander and that her marriage to Damien was a sham.'

'That is not true!' The old lady's voice was becoming shrill.

At this moment, Wendy tapped on the door and gestured for Anna to join her. The local NatWest had refused to give any details, bar the fact that there were other accounts with Mrs Eatwell's signature, along with that of a Mr Anthony Collingwood. Anna instructed Gordon to drive to the bank and show his ID to get more information; she then turned to Mrs Eatwell.

'I think, Mrs Eatwell, you should start telling me the truth: do you know where your son is?'

'No, I do not.'

Frustrated, Anna began to show Mrs Eatwell the photographs of the victims they knew to have been killed by Fitzpatrick. Last of all, she showed her Frank Brandon's photograph. 'This man was with your son the night he got injured and came here to you; he was shot dead. Your son left this man, Donny Petrozzo, dead in his jeep. This man was Julia's financial adviser, David Rushton; we know your son killed him. This woman was strangled—'

'Stop it! Don't do this to me!'

'Mrs Eatwell, I need some answers from you. I need to find your son.'

The old lady broke down and started crying, repeating that she didn't know, as she plucked a tissue from a box beside her. 'I swear to you, I don't know where he is. To be honest, even though he is my son, if I knew I would tell you. He has been nothing but trouble from the time he was a student. I have been through hell because of him.'

'But you took money from him?'

'Yes, because I didn't have any medical insurance for my husband. I was desperate. You cannot imagine what I felt when he just turned up, as if all the years between meant nothing.'

'Had he kept in touch with Damien and Honour?'

'No, no, he just topped up the account for me. We never mentioned him; it was too painful. I had the police morning, noon and night when he was first arrested all those years ago; they hounded me and I swear it was because of him that my husband got so ill. The strain of it all was terrible.'

'So when he came to the cottage, before he came here injured . . .'

'I didn't know what to do. I said I didn't want to see him after what had happened to my husband and he just laughed at me; said that I was living very comfortably for someone who didn't want anything to do with him. Sometimes it felt as if he hated me, blamed me for everything, and I had such guilt. You see, he was such a lovable little boy and he worshipped his father; having to bring him up on my own was difficult. It's strange, but the older he got, the more he became like his father; he could still turn on the charm, and he had this manner to him. He could draw people to him like a magnet but, underneath it all, he was very cruel.'

'But he knew Damien and Honour, didn't he?' Mrs Eatwell was now very distraught. Anna felt bad about continuing to put pressure on her, but she carried on nevertheless. 'Mrs Eatwell, your son kept in contact with them, didn't he?'

'He had to, because of the money. It was the only thing he ever cared about – money, and that nasty little bitch.'

'Julia?'

'Yes! She was the reason why he came back. She had done something with his accounts and he had lost all his money in America. You don't seem to understand that we were frightened of him.'

'I don't think Honour was frightened of him.'

'She was – we all were. Whatever she is saying now isn't the truth. I had to have him here. I had no option, because he was sick, and if you think I wasn't scared about what would happen if anyone found out, then you are wrong. Telling me all these terrible things about what he has done gives me even more reason to have been frightened.' She wiped her eyes, and blew her nose, slowly calming down. 'I did not know what was in those crates, but it wasn't hard for me to guess. I had no option but to let him store them in my garage, just as poor Honour had to let him put them at the farm; she was as frightened as I was.'

'Damien had to be aware of what they contained,' Anna said.

She refused to agree, repeating that only she and Honour knew, and that Damien was innocent. Anna's mobile rang and she moved into the hallway. It was Gordon calling from the bank.

Mrs Eatwell's account, under the joint signature of Anthony Collingwood, had been cleaned out of seven hundred thousand pounds. The money had been transferred to an account in Geneva and subsequently moved on from there; the transaction was done by Anthony Collingwood. When asked if he had been to the bank in person, they admitted that he had; it was the first time they had actually met him.

Anna cut off the call; this was really bad news. It meant that Fitzpatrick, far from being cornered and broke, was now fully financed. With that much money, he could be anywhere. It also meant that Mrs Eatwell had only her pension left.

When Anna told her, instead of being angry or even upset, the old lady said she felt nothing but relief. 'I told you that all he ever cared about was money. Well, now you can see he's taken everything – even from me, his mother.'

'I'm sorry.'

Perhaps it was the relief of knowing her son had taken the money and gone that made Doris begin to give Anna more details of her past. 'You know, he blamed me for everything – even blamed me for his obsession with wealth. You see, his father, my first husband, was a very well-off, aristocratic man. Never did a day's work in his life. We lived a life of luxury: beautiful house, chauffeurs and staff, holidays abroad. Alex went to an expensive prep school in Kensington; he was exceptionally clever. Even as young as six, he had such a charm, but he was very spoiled. He got whatever he wanted from his father.'

'You were divorced?'

'Yes, it was very unpleasant. Alex blamed me; he was too young to understand what had happened. We went from having everything to nothing. I had to take him out of Eton because I couldn't afford the fees. In those days, there was no real protection for divorcees and even though I was awarded alimony, it was never paid.'

Anna sat at the kitchen table as Mrs Eatwell made some toast, then spread a cheese slice on top and put it under the grill. She sliced up tomatoes and some ham, and then put the slices together, carefully cutting off the crusts. She got a plate and placed the sandwich onto it, and sat unfolding a napkin.

'I was pregnant,' she said quietly.

Anna said nothing. Then, after a long pause, while Mrs Eatwell stared at her sandwich and cut it into small neat pieces, she spoke. 'You were pregnant?'

Mrs Eatwell eventually whispered, 'Damien,' and pushed the plate aside. Anna had been right.

Damien Nolan had been adopted at birth, as Doris had been unable to care for him since she had to go out to work. She explained how, ten years ago, Damien had contacted her. He had become everything that Alexander was not. Honour had looked after her; without them, she doubted she would have been able to cope with the death of her husband. Her second marriage had been very loving, but Alexander had loathed his stepfather, who was the antithesis of Alexander's own father: a simple, quiet man who tried to care for his stepson, only to have to go through the public outcry when it became known he was an international drug dealer. With the press over the arrest of her son, her husband lost his job, then was diagnosed with throat cancer. She was once again financially insecure, until money started to come in from Alexander to pay for medical bills.

The sandwich remained untouched. She asked Anna if it was possible to keep Damien's relationship to Alexander secret as, if it was to get out, he would lose his job at the University. Her eyes brimmed with tears. 'I love him, and to have him back in my life meant so much. To have Alex back was a nightmare. Part of me hopes that you will find him, but the other part prays that you won't because, if you do, it'll start again; the press will hound us and I don't want Damien hurt.'

Anna said she would try, but couldn't make any promises. She did not mention that Mrs Eatwell would still be charged with perverting the course of justice, along with various other charges.

As Anna walked down the pathway of the cottage, Gordon was just pulling up. 'DCS Langton is on his way; he said we should meet up at a fish and chip restaurant in the village. He does not want you to interview Damien Nolan.'

'Bollocks to that,' she said, and started to walk up the lane. 'Tell him you just missed me. I'll be at the farmhouse.'

Gordon watched her for a moment before he reversed into the driveway of the cottage to turn and head back to the village.

It was further than Anna had remembered and, in some places, almost impassable, as there were deep muddy potholes. She hopped over a few and then sank into a deep one she hadn't noticed. Turning a bend in the lane, she saw two men digging a trench; they had reels of steel pipes and a trailer parked in a field. She watched them covertly for at least five minutes. They immediately reported the sighting of Anna, unaware of who she was.

Anna guessed that the two men were surveillance officers; at least they appeared to be hard at work. Langton had not mentioned that the farm was still under surveillance – typical of him, she thought – and at the same time realised that he too must have had suspicions about Damien Nolan.

Anna did not go towards the front door, but headed around the side of the farmhouse, as she had done previously. She could see the stable door to the kitchen was open at the top end, and there was a distinct smell of burning toast. As she approached, charred bread was hurled out and she could hear swearing.

'Hello,' she said, as she came closer.

Damien appeared with a mesh toasting-rack in his hand. 'I didn't hit you, did I?' he asked.

'No, just missed me.'

He waved the rack. 'I always forget how fast toast does on the Aga. You want to see me?'

'Yes.'

He opened the bottom of the stable door and wafted the rack like a tennis racket to indicate she should enter. 'Are you hungry?'

Anna stepped into the kitchen. There was a roaring fire in the grate and the lid of the hot oven open on the Aga.

'I can offer you cheese on toast, or scrambled eggs and bacon, or a BLT,' Damien said, as he went to the big pine table and began to cut two slices of bread from a fresh crusty loaf.

'I'd like a BLT,' Anna replied.

'Right, you keep an eye on the toast. The bacon should be ready any second.'

Like Doris, his mother, he sliced tomatoes, moving back and forth to a big, old American fridge to fetch some lettuce. He appeared to be totally at ease and in no way alarmed by Anna's presence.

She crossed to the Aga and checked on the slices heating in the toast rack; she had never used an Aga before and was amazed how fast it had toasted the bread.

She turned the rack over as Damien took out a tray of crisped bacon and then opened a jar of mayonnaise.

Anna removed the bread, joining him at the table. 'I've just come from your mother's.'

He spread the mayonnaise over the toast. 'Yes, she said you were there.'

Anna laughed; Mrs Eatwell must have sussed that Anna would be coming to see Damien, so had called him.

'Now then, would you like a nice glass of Merlot or a coffee?'

Anna asked for a cup of tea. He placed the big Aga kettle on the burner, uncorked an open bottle of wine and poured himself a glass. He moved quickly and decisively, very much at home, fetching plates, glasses and cutlery and placing them onto the table with napkins. Then he gestured for Anna to sit as he made her a cup of tea. 'Do you take sugar?'

'No, thank you.' Anna was itching to start eating, but waited until he sat down and handed over her tea; he then raised his wine glass.

'Cheers!' He sipped the wine and let it linger in his mouth. 'Mmm, bit rancid, but it'll do; I could open a fresh bottle if you changed your mind.'

'No, the tea is fine.'

He sat opposite her, and took a large bite of his sandwich. Anna tucked into hers, feeling in a quandary as to how she should begin questioning him.

'Will she have to go on trial?' he asked quietly.

'Probably. She seems able to deal with it. I doubt that she'll be badly treated, but she did lie about the whereabouts of her other son. Even though I don't believe she knew what the crates contained, she nevertheless knew they were there.'

'She's in her eighties, for God's sake!'

'I am aware of that, but allowing her son to hide out in her cottage is an offence. She obviously knew he was wanted by the police; then there is the fact that, by not being honest with us, her son has now gained access to a large sum of money.'

Damien took another bite of the sandwich. She noted that he gave no reaction to the fact that Fitzpatrick had withdrawn money.

'Seven hundred thousand,' Anna said, as she too continued eating, then licked her fingers as the mayonnaise had dribbled.

'Will she be taken into the station in London?' he asked, still not referring to the money.

'Possibly. We have an officer with her and she is aware she is under house arrest; at least she has not been uprooted from her home. Did you know about the account in Anthony Collingwood's name, with your mother as a signatory?'

'No.'

'So how did you think she was able to renovate the cottage over the years?'

'I presumed she had been left money by her husband.'

It felt like they were just making conversation but, by the time she had finished her BLT, she picked up her briefcase and took out her notebook. 'I'm here to confirm a few outstanding things. From your statement, you denied meeting Fitzpatrick.' She glanced up at him; he was scraping around his plate with the crusts from his toast. 'The handwritten note with directions to the farmhouse: we have verified that it is your handwriting—'

He interrupted her. 'This is stupid. My lawyer made it clear that, as evidence, it was rather pointless, as there is no proof of exactly when it was written. But I have actually given it a bit more thought.'

He got up, collected her dirty plate and his own, and crossed to the dishwasher. Anna waited as he stashed their dishes and then ran water over the oven tray he had used for the bacon. He was wearing jeans and a fawn cashmere sweater, with brown suede loafers and no socks. He was, she could tell, very fit; his lean stomach and long legs made him attractive physically, and he had an easygoing, unaffected manner. She had liked him from the first time she had met him.

She flushed at herself even thinking about his attractiveness. 'You said you'd been thinking about the note?'

'Yes. It had to have been about two or three years ago, maybe even more, but I wrote the directions for Julia. I mentioned she stayed once; well, she didn't actually stay at the farm – she hated it – and so moved into the cottage.'

'With your mother?'

She saw a small glimmer of a reaction. He smiled and returned to the table to pour himself more wine. 'I said you were very intuitive, didn't I?'

'Why didn't you admit it when I asked?'

'I didn't think it was any of your business. My mother has been very protective about her private life. It was a period when she regrets many of her decisions.'

'You were adopted?'

'Yes. I didn't even consider trying to trace my birth mother, as I had no real reason to: my adopted parents were a very caring couple. It wasn't until they passed away that I contemplated trying to find her. They never made any secret of my adoption. After they died, I found many letters. They had always kept in touch, so it was very simple for me to make contact.' He sat opposite Anna again. 'My mother had been through some very hard times, especially after my birth. I think Alex suffered from the divorce; one moment he had everything any child could want, and a father, then it was all taken away. It probably warped him for the rest of his life. He was in trouble with drugs from a very early age; not as an addict, but he discovered that it was a very easy way to make a lot of money. This was before I knew him, obviously. He made headlines when he escaped from court, but I had no reason to even think about our being related. I just always knew about him.'

'When did you contact your mother?'

He shrugged and ran his fingers through his hair. 'Be about fifteen years ago. Another reason was, Honour and I hoped to start a family, so it was understandable that I should want to know more about my background.'

Anna nodded; it was all so easily acceptable, everything he said. 'Did Honour know Mrs Eatwell before you discovered she was your mother?'

He nodded. 'I believe so.'

'So she also knew about Julia and Alexander Fitzpatrick?'

He became evasive, turning away. 'It's a very small world.'

'Did Honour suspect you were related?'

'Not really.'

'But she had to know her sister was being kept by him?'

'Obviously, but she had little to do with Julia.'

'We have verified that her second child is yours.'

'Really? Well, that's something I didn't know.'

Anna suspected he was lying, not that his manner had changed; he was still appearing very relaxed and at ease. 'According to Julia, at this time, Honour was living with Alexander, so you had to have been aware of who she was seeing – she was your wife.'

'Yes, I suppose I did.'

'So you knew who he was.'

'Yes, obviously.'

'Why didn't you contact the police? You must have known he was a wanted criminal?'

'Ah, well, it's slightly more complicated. By this time, I knew he was my brother. Something I haven't really told you was that Honour was Alex's girlfriend before I met her; he met Julia through her. Julia was, as you know, a lot younger – twelve years – and it was very painful for Honour when he took up with her sister.'

Anna jotted down notes. The complicated marital situation between the two brothers and sisters was like something out of a soap opera. She asked if he could repeat how Alexander had made contact. She was told that he simply just turned up; first at his mother's and then he came to the farmhouse.

'Did he know about you?'

'I suppose he did. As you saw, we do look similar – well, more so now since he's had so much plastic surgery. He's also taller and older.'

'And you knew he was a wanted criminal from the moment he surfaced?'

'Yes, as I just said, but it was impossible for me to shop him. I had to consider Honour.'

'Consider your wife?'

'Yes. Her sister was his mistress and had been for years; in fact, I think she was only sixteen or seventeen when he took up with her. I was not aware of how often he returned to London, nor what Julia's relationship with him entailed. All I knew was that Julia had a very luxurious lifestyle and, on the rare occasions she visited, it wasn't all that pleasant.' He gestured to the kitchen. 'We live a very simple life; Julia was jetting around the world and dripping in jewels.'

'But surely you knew how she came by this lifestyle?'

He shrugged.

'Alexander Fitzpatrick was an international drug dealer. He was on the US Most Wanted lists, yet you say he was often in London with Julia, and visited here?'

'No, that is not correct; he did not visit here. As I have said, I did not have any personal contact with him until about nine months ago. I was aware that he continued to see Julia, and that she joined him all around the world when he sent for her. As to whether or not he came in and out of the UK, I had no idea.'

'But Honour knew?'

'Possibly, but the sisters were not on good terms with each other. As I explained, Honour had been Alex's lover before Julia and he dropped her. I think it happened when he took them both on his yacht to the South of France.'

'The painting.'

'I'm sorry?'

Anna said that she had seen a painting of the boat, *Dare Devil*, but that it had been removed by the second time she had been to the farm.

'Well, that would have been Honour. It was while she and Julia were away with Alex that he took up with Julia, then it was years before they contacted each other again. By that time, Honour and I were married. We used to live in Oxford, and only moved here to be close to my mother.'

Anna flicked through her notebook. 'So Honour always knew about Alexander Fitzpatrick?'

He sighed, becoming irritated. 'Yes, I'd say it was pretty obvious, but she was not likely to tip off the police. Besides, he came and went for years on end, usually taking Julia with him. He lived in Florida for a time, and I think in the Bahamas and also in the Philippines, but I had no interest in him. My wife was not likely to tell me if she had seen him.'

'Did you like him?'

'Like him?' He shrugged. 'He was very charming. I never really got to know him – well, not until recently. He was rather desperate as he had got into financial trouble; he said he'd lost a fortune, all his investments.'

'So did he mention to you what his intentions were?'

'No.'

'He never brought up the subject of importing drugs?'

'No.'

'But Honour knew?'

'I doubt it.'

Anna tapped her notebook with her pen. 'So he turns up, desperate?'

Damien leaned forwards and patted the table with the flat of his hand. 'No, that isn't quite what I said. He may have been desperate for money, but he was not a desperate man. You have to try and understand the type of person he was. Alex had millions stashed all over the world; I doubt if he could recollect half the places he'd got hidden accounts. The bulk of his fortune was tied up in Germany and the US. The recent mortgage fiasco over there had closed the German bank, and all his investments went belly up on Wall Street. The amount of money he lost must have been staggering for him to take such risks, coming back here to do business. I only ever saw him really angry once, and that was when he tried to explain how Julia had done some kind of fraud against him. Apparently, she had switched over his accounts into offshore banks. Don't ask me how or what it entailed, because I don't have the slightest idea. All he said was that she had really screwed him over and he needed to release a lot of money to pay off some people in Miami.'

'So, the time you say he appeared angry, would have been before he picked up the drugs? Did he discuss that he had a shipment coming into Gatwick . . .'

Again, she was interrupted. 'No, he did not. I have answered this at the station. I was not privy to him turning up here with any drugs, nor did I see anyone else with him. I was at work. I had no idea that Honour had agreed to stash the crates in the henhouse. To be honest, if I had known, I would not have allowed it to happen. I was not here when she moved them to my mother's; I would not have allowed that either. All I did know was he turned up and was staying at my mother's because he was injured. I never saw him or spoke to him during that time.'

'And you never thought to contact the police?'

He said that he thought of it, but he couldn't, because of Honour and his mother.

'Even when you had seen the papers, the news broadcasts, the crime shows? You had to have known that he was wanted – and, not only that, but he was dangerous?'

Damien got up and stuffed his hands into his pockets, standing with his back to the fire. He became quite tense, his voice harsh. 'Why don't you try putting your-self in my position? My wife in love with him and now embroiled in his drug dealing, my mother unwittingly involved, and Julia terrified about what he would do to her. Then there are the children – my child! How in God's name could I do anything but behave like the proverbial ostrich? I did nothing. I am starting to get really irritated by your persistent attempts to make out that I was in any way involved.'

'I am only attempting to get to the truth,' Anna retorted sharply.

'The truth is exactly as I have described: he had us all caught like rabbits in the spotlight, afraid to make a move. You asked me if I liked him – *liked* him? I hated his guts. He was a vain, egotistical bastard; he would use anyone, and that included his kids and my wife.'

'Your wife claimed that you had an open marriage.'

He gave a short, mirthless laugh. Turning to put more logs on the fire, he kicked at the burned wood with the toe of his shoe. 'I don't know what she claimed. You could say it was open on her side; she never stopped loving him.'

'Did you have a sexual relationship with Julia to get back at her?'

'No, I did not. I had sex with her once.'

'To get back at him?'

He sighed, shaking his head. 'It was years ago. It wasn't connected to the drug deal. I had Julia calling me and crying about some woman who had moved into the house in St John's Wood. I didn't even know he was in the country, and I hadn't even met him. This was the time I gave Julia the directions to come here. As soon as she told me Alex had another woman, I knew it had to be Honour, because she was not at home; she'd made some excuse about a friend being ill. Julia turns up here and ...' He gave an open-handed gesture. Then he walked back to the table and sat, stretching his long legs in front of him. 'That's life, isn't it? Honour desperate for a child; I spend one night with Julia and she's pregnant.'

'How did your wife react to that?'

'Honour is a bit like a homing pigeon; settled back here and just accepted it. I am going to see her later today. She's called and asked me to take in some clothes. She's wearing the same ones she was arrested in.'

Anna closed her notebook and reached down for her briefcase. 'Have you any idea where he is?' She opened her case on the table and put in her notebook.

'I hope wherever he is, he rots in hell.'

Anna snapped the locks on her case. 'So no more brotherly love between you?'

'My wife is in prison because of him; my mother may even be subjected to a trial. He's taken every cent out of her account; she was hoping she'd get custody of Julia's children. He's hurt everyone he came into contact with.'

'He killed a lot of people, or they died because of him,' Anna said, standing.

'If he surfaced here, or even tried to contact me, I'd strangle him.'

She smiled. 'Well, that would be a mistake. I'll give you my card and contact numbers; if he does try to see you, call me.'

He flicked at the card, holding it between thumb and forefinger. 'Can I call you?'

'I'm sorry?'

'Maybe for dinner one night? I sometimes have to

lecture in London. I would enjoy your company when all this is over.'

'It won't be over, Mr Nolan, until we find him.'

'But I can call you?'

She smiled as she crossed to the back door. 'I don't think it would be very ethical, but thank you anyway. I appreciate the time you have given me, and the sandwich.'

He joined her at the stable door and reached over her head to open it, swinging the top part back. Langton stood there, framed by the half-open door. 'Good afternoon, Mr Nolan and Detective Travis.'

'I was just leaving,' she stuttered.

'Really? Well, I was just arriving. You mind if I come in?'

'Not at all,' Damien said pleasantly enough, 'but, dear God, don't tell me I have to go over everything again!'

Langton waited as the lower part of the stable door was open and he stepped inside. Anna could feel his contained anger as he passed her.

Rather nervously, Anna reported that she was satisfied that Mr Nolan had answered all her queries, and she had been about to leave and meet up with Langton.

Langton glared at her and then looked at Damien. 'Maybe I'd like some answers.'

Damien gestured to the table. 'Sit down.'

'I'll stay standing, if you don't mind.'

'Please yourself.' Damien sat.

Anna hovered, unsure whether to remain by the door or sit back at the table.

'Where's your brother, Mr Nolan?'

'I have absolutely no idea.' Damien turned to Anna. 'I have explained to Miss Travis that, quite honestly, if

I did know where he was, I'd probably be arrested for trying to strangle him.'

'Really? Could I see your passport, please?'

Damien walked to a sideboard and opened a drawer; he searched around inside it, and then opened another. 'That's odd. I always kept it in here. Perhaps my wife has put it somewhere else.'

'I suggest you gave it to your brother, Mr Nolan.'

'I did not.'

'Really. Can you look at this, please?' Langton passed over a search warrant.

Damien glanced at it. 'I wouldn't have thought it necessary to get another one. The farm was thoroughly searched when it was presumed there were drugs hidden here.'

'Well, I am going to do another. You can join me or remain here with Detective Travis.'

Damien smiled, and drew out a chair to sit down. 'Carry on.'

Langton gave Anna a cold look and took off his coat. He tossed it over a chair and went to the sideboard. He began to search through the drawers and the cupboards below them. Satisfied he had found nothing of importance, he looked towards the small office room located off the main kitchen. This was the room where Gordon had taken the photographs of the boat, the *Dare Devil*. Langton left the door ajar; he could be seen checking over the desk, opening more drawers, working quickly and methodically.

Anna stayed sitting at the table. Damien was opposite her, twisting round and round the large signet ring he wore on his left pinkie finger.

Gordon then appeared at the open door; he rapped on

the frame with his knuckles and Langton walked out. He went to Gordon's side and they had a whispered conversation. Langton then continued his search of the office. Gordon remained standing outside.

Anna joined Gordon to find out what was going on. Gordon glanced back into the kitchen and moved away a fraction. 'We reckon Fitzpatrick has escaped using Damien Nolan's passport. We're checking all ports now.'

Anna kept her voice low. 'So Fitzpatrick made it back here, took his passport and cleaned out his mother's bank account? He couldn't have been given it by Damien – he was at the station being questioned.'

Langton asked for Damien to join him in the office. He had lifted a loose floorboard from beneath a rug. It had, by the look of it, been checked out before: there was no dust. 'Mr Nolan, I want you to see this.' Langton held up a plastic-wrapped bundle of fifty pound notes; they matched a large amount more, neatly stored beneath the floorboards.

Damien got slowly to his feet.

'We can get these serial numbers checked out, but why don't you tell me about how they come to be here?'

'I have never seen them before. I certainly had no idea there was this much money hidden in here. I mean, the farmhouse was almost stripped bare the last time your officers searched.'

Langton continued to lift out bundle after bundle; all had clear plastic bags wrapped around them, with a paper wrapper giving the amounts of each bundle. Langton was hardly audible as he counted: ten thousand, twenty, thirty, forty . . . And still he kept on stacking the bundles.

The money was taken from the office and carefully

put on the kitchen table. Damien looked on with a puzzled expression; as the amount grew, he kept on shaking his head.

'I make it close to two and a half million,' Langton said, to no one in particular.

'I have absolutely nothing to do with this. I had no idea it was hidden in the house, but I am nevertheless interested: that is a lot of money. I'll be very keen to know whether, as you found it here, if no one claims it, it will automatically be returned to the property-owner.'

'Don't get cheeky, Mr Nolan. You are in a lot of trouble.'

'I didn't know it was there!' he exclaimed.

'Just like you didn't know your passport was missing?'

'I had absolutely no idea.'

'I am arresting you on suspicion of aiding a wanted criminal to escape justice.'

Gordon took Damien to the station in a patrol car while Anna travelled back to London in her Mini, Langton beside her, his anger palpable.

'Can I just say something?' she asked.

'By all means. I can't wait to hear what you've got to say for yourself.'

'I honestly do not think Damien is involved. I really questioned him—'

'I'm sure you did – over a BLT, wasn't it? Very chatty and comfortable – so much so, he was asking for a bloody date when I turned up.'

'Then you must have also heard that I turned his request down! You have had surveillance on the farm: if Fitzpatrick returned there and took Damien's passport, then they must have seen him.'

Langton snapped that they were not in place until Nolan was released from custody. It would have given Fitzpatrick time to go back to the farmhouse, stash his money and then get a plane ticket out from the UK to anywhere.

'Can we check if the money was the payout from Julia? We know Rushton handed over close to four million in cash,' Anna said.

Langton said nothing, sitting in moody silence. Anna continued to drive; she could not think of anything to say that would ease the tension between them.

By the time they approached the station, Langton was in a contained fury. He got out of the car, slamming the door hard as he walked off.

Anna got out and was about to shut her door, when he returned and leaned his elbows on the roof. 'You are in trouble, Travis. I don't like it, but I am putting you on report. I gave instructions that you were not to interview Damien Nolan, and you ignored me.'

She went right back at him. 'For goodness' sake, I was there! Why not interview him? And, excuse me if I am repeating myself but I do not think Damien Nolan is involved.'

'Because you fancy him?'

'For Christ's sake, that has nothing to do with it. My concern is we are wasting time; right now, Fitzpatrick has got his brother's passport and if the cash at the farmhouse wasn't from his local bank account, then he's got money.'

'Well, sweetheart, I bet you any money he's out of our reach. We've lost him!' And he turned and walked into the station, leaving Anna seething.

★

Langton paced up and down the incident room as they waited for a hoped-for sighting. All ports had been warned to look out for Fitzpatrick; his description, and details of the missing passport, had been forwarded, with photographs, to customs, ferries, trains and Eurostar stations. They had also contacted heliports, private airstrips and private plane charters. The *Evening Standard* had front-page coverage, and the morning papers all had been given details and photographs.

They knew that there had been two days and nights when there was no surveillance at the farmhouse. If he had taken the passport and hidden the money, it had to have been done inside that timeframe. Langton had questioned the SOCO officers who had instigated the search of the farmhouse; the office room had been very thoroughly searched and they were certain that no money had been beneath the floorboards. The money removed from the farmhouse was held in the property lock-up as they tried to verify by the note numbers if it was recently withdrawn.

It was 6.15 p.m. when Anna handed in her report, keeping a good distance from Langton. She had checked and double-checked her notes, making it clear that she had agreed to eat with Damien, as she had wanted him very much at ease, and so had been able to gain a considerable amount of background information. The threat of being put on report really infuriated her; considering the amount of work she had done to move the case forwards, she felt Langton had been unnecessarily vindictive.

Damien's solicitor had agreed to come in, so that they could interview his client first thing in the morning. The charges were withholding evidence and assisting a known criminal to escape arrest. Damien had remained calm, almost resigned to being banged up for yet another night in the cells. He had asked the uniformed officers who brought him from the farmhouse to the Chalk Farm Station if they could take the clothes he had packed for his wife to Holloway jail.

The overnight bag was still at the station, and no one appeared interested in delivering it. 'Is anyone taking this to Holloway?' Anna asked, as she was leaving. The desk sergeant just shrugged, so Anna said she would take it. She carried it out to her car and placed it on the passenger seat. She drove from Chalk Farm over to Camden Town, heading towards Holloway Prison.

Parking in the spaces allocated for prison staff, Anna picked up the case and then unzipped it. She took out the contents: a bar of soap, moisturiser and hand cream in a small satin vanity bag; two pairs of new tights, a navy cashmere sweater, a dress and three pairs of panties and brassières; combs and a hairbrush. Rather sadly, she saw that Damien had also included a box of dark chestnut-brown hair-dye and shampoo.

As she replaced them, she felt down the sides and under the base of the bag, but there was nothing else. She zipped up the bag, and then unzipped a small pocket at the side: it contained a folded slip of paper. In faint pencil handwriting was the list of items she had just checked over and, beside each one, a tick in red pen. There was nothing else. She felt, as Honour probably would, disappointment that there was no other message. There was finality about the ticks, like a schoolteacher's appraisal. She returned the note to the pocket and carried the bag to the prison reception.

Anna was not allowed to see Honour, as it was after

visiting hours and the inmates were locked up for the night. She signed over the bag and wrote that the contents were on a list in the pocket. 'Has anyone been to see her?'

The receptionist reached for the visitors' book, and flicked over until she came to Honour's name. 'Yes, her husband was here this afternoon.'

Anna's nerves jangled. 'Her husband?'

'Yes, Mr Damien Nolan came in at two-thirty.'

'Did he show any identification?'

'Yes, his passport. She had a visit from her solicitor; that was in the morning, but no one else.'

Anna hurtled into the incident room. There were only skeleton staff on duty, so she asked if Langton was around. She was told he was in Cunningham's office. She barged in, gasping, 'He was still in London at two-thirty this afternoon!'

Langton sprang up from behind the desk. 'What?'

She tried to get her breath. 'He visited Honour Nolan in Holloway; he bloody gave Damien Nolan's passport for identification!'

'Jesus Christ! Did you talk to her?'

'No, I came straight back here as soon as I was told! This narrows down where he might have gone to next, so we can step up the search for him . . .'

Langton was already out and yelling for everyone to get onto the airports; then, gesturing for Anna to join him, he said he would telephone the prison. 'They won't let you see her,' she responded.

He turned on her, and snapped that they would drag her out by her hair if needs be.

Chapter Twenty-six

Anna again made the journey across London, this time in a patrol car, with sirens blasting. By the time they had been checked through the prison reception, and led along various corridors to wait in a small anteroom, it was after 10 p.m. Langton had a terse conversation with the prison governor who, as Anna had said, did not approve of a visit at this time of night. They had to wait another fifteen minutes before Honour was brought in.

She was wearing a prison-issue nightdress; for a dressing-gown, she wore her coat. Her hair was in two braids, the grey parting even more prominent.

'Sit down, Honour,' Langton instructed. 'I'll get straight to the reason why we're here. You had a visitor this afternoon. Don't waste our time pretending it was your husband, because we know it wasn't. It was Alexander Fitzpatrick, wasn't it?'

'Yes,' she said, hardly audible.

'Okay, Honour, it will really help your defence if you now tell us where he is.'

'I don't know.'

'You must have talked about where he was going?'

'No.' She had tears in her eyes and chewed at her lips.

'So, tell me – what you did talk about?'

Anna leaned forwards and touched Honour's hand, going for a softer approach. 'Your husband has been arrested again.'

'Oh God.' She bowed her head.

'We know Fitzpatrick has Damien's passport, Honour. We also found a large sum of money hidden under the floorboards at the farmhouse.'

She shook her head, trying not to cry.

'Did Damien know about this money?'

'No, no, he didn't. It was for me, for my lawyers, and to help his mother. He said he'd used her savings – had them transferred – so he was concerned about who would look after her.'

'So Damien didn't know he'd hidden the money,' Anna said again, and glanced at Langton.

'No. I knew he was using Damien's passport; he said he'd taken it out of a drawer in the kitchen. I'm not sure where the money came from.'

'So he told you all this, Honour, and yet didn't tell you where he was going?'

'No. I swear to you I have no idea. This is probably why he didn't tell me. I have never known where he was; it was always that way.' She started to cry, and searched in her coat pocket for a tissue. 'He said the money was not stolen, that it belonged to him, that Julia had given it to him. It's all been *her* fault.'

'She's dead, Honour, your sister was murdered. The brakes of her car slashed!'

'He had nothing to do with that. I know he would not have done that. You keep on making him out to be this monster but he isn't, I know he isn't; she made it impossible for him.'

Langton slapped the table with the flat of his hand, his

patience running out. 'You mean impossible to pay for shipping in a fucking cargo of lethal drugs? You need to get yourself straightened out, Mrs Nolan. You are going to have a lot of time behind bars to come to terms with the fact that you were used.'

'I was not!' she said angrily.

'Alexander Fitzpatrick used everyone he came into contact with; either that, or he killed them. You have protected him and you seem prepared to let your husband take responsibility. He'll be charged—'

'No, please, he was never involved, I swear to you!'

'So, you care for him, do you?'

'Yes, of course I do.'

'But you are prepared to let him take the punishment? He's in the cells right now, Honour. If you say he's innocent, prove it – *tell us where Fitzpatrick is.*'

'I don't know, but I do know that Damien was not involved, you have to believe me.'

'Give me one good reason,' Langton said, leaning forwards.

She cried and twisted the sodden tissue round and round. 'You just have to believe me. Alex didn't even want to get me involved, but then that man Julia had got working for her got shot, and Alex was injured . . .'

Langton snapped bitterly, '"That man" was an ex-police officer, Honour, a decent hardworking guy who was about to get married; but between you, and that sister of yours, he got drawn into your lover's dirty business.'

'I'm sorry about him, I am really, but after that happened, it just all spiralled out of control. I only agreed to hide the drugs because he had no one else he could trust.'

'So whose idea was it to move them to Mrs Eatwell's?' Anna asked quietly, trying not to get Honour too upset – unlike Langton, whose patience was exhausted.

'Mine. She called to say the police had been round asking about him. All the time he was there at the cottage, he had told her they had to be moved quickly. He didn't believe that anyone would make the connection. So that's why I did it.' She blew her nose and wiped her eyes, then looked up. 'You have to understand something: I have loved Alex for many years. I still love him and, you may find it hard to believe, but he loves me.'

Anna patted her hand again. 'I am sure he does, to take such a risk, coming here to see you.'

'To make sure I will be all right, and his children, and his mother; he's not a bad person.'

Langton banged back his chair and stood up. 'Not a bad person! Tell that to David Rushton's relatives, to Donny Petrozzo's wife, to that boy in Brixton Prison, Adrian Summers – even your sister! Those kids are going to grow up and find out their father killed her. Whatever excuses you give, you are just as despicable as he is. And, I've not even brought up how many people would have died if that Fentanyl had got to be sold on the streets.'

Langton walked to the door and rapped hard with his knuckles; a female officer was waiting outside. 'We're through. Take her back to her cell. She's going to have to get used to sleeping in one.'

'As long as he is free, I don't care where I am,' Honour said defiantly.

Langton turned back and pointed. 'You think he's out of reach? Think again, Honour. I will get him – then

watch the two-faced bastard turn into a sniffling wreck.'
He stalked out.

Anna sat for a moment longer and then she stood
up too. Honour gave her a sad look, and then looked
down at the damp tissue in her hands. 'You don't choose
who you love; it's fate. I married Damien because he
reminded me of Alex, only to find out just how close he
was – his brother. That's fate, isn't it?'

'I'm sure it is. Is it also fate that your own sister
became his mistress? Or was that just to keep it in the
family?' She could see the hurt flash across Honour's
face. Anna leaned across the table. 'If you care anything
for Damien, then for God's sake, tell me if you know
where Fitzpatrick is.'

'You know something? I think I would, if I did know,
because Damien is a really wonderful person and doesn't
deserve this, but I truthfully don't. Alex wouldn't have
told me anyway; you see, he lives on secrets. It's what
makes him always so unobtainable. I was foolish enough
to be satisfied with scraps, until this time; we were going
to be together.'

'But it wasn't going to be you, Honour. Julia was
driving to meet him with the children. She was going to
meet up with him on the boat.'

'That's not true! That is not the truth!'

Anna turned and walked out towards the waiting
prison officer. She left Honour sobbing, but she didn't
feel any compassion for her; quite the reverse.

Langton was standing by the patrol car, smoking; he
turned as she approached. 'You get anything from her?'

'Nope. I don't think she does know.'

'She made out that Damien was in the clear,' he said,
stubbing out his cigarette on the ground.

'Yes, well, I told you that.'

Langton gave instructions to drive back to the station; again he constantly used his phone to answer and send messages. 'Still no sighting, and we've no way of tracing where all that cash came from, as Rushton's dead along with Julia. If it came from her we'll never know,' he muttered.

Anna remained silent, going over the entire interview with Honour, then she leaned forwards and tapped Langton's shoulder. 'Where are the children?'

'Safe house, still with the same au pair and a family liaison officer, plus security. In fact, we're going to have to sort them out, as it's costing the budget. Why do you ask?'

'Wherever Fitzpatrick is going, I doubt if he'll ever make it back here to the UK.'

'So?'

'Well, he sorts out money for his mother, tells Honour it's for his kids and for her to get a decent lawyer; he takes a big risk going to the prison . . .'

'He thrives on risks! Look at the way he came into the station. I think he's kind of crazy . . .'

'Yes, maybe, but it also shows the other side of the monster we rate him as. Do you think it's possible he might try to see his children?'

Langton began texting to the station for them to check out the safe house. By the time they were back in the incident room, Phil had already contacted the safe house. There had been no phone calls; the children were well cared for; the Chinese au pair was still in residence. The family liaison officer was still there and a second uniformed officer had been posted; the only contact they had had was a query from the au pair about her wages.

Langton suddenly flagged, tired out, and suggested

that Anna take off home as well. In the meantime, the night-duty staff would be on call if there was any sighting of Fitzpatrick. They were instructed to contact Langton if they received any news.

Anna had poured herself a very tepid, stale cup of coffee, and was sitting on the edge of a desk talking to Phil, when the place lit up.

In a flurry of calls, they had three separate sightings of a man fitting the description of Alexander Fitzpatrick. A man had been seen at Paddington Station heading for the Heathrow Express. The train moved out four minutes later. A man had also been seen boarding the Eurostar train at St Pancras. A third man was being held by Gatwick security guards; he admitted that he was Alexander Fitzpatrick.

The latter they were able to dismiss quickly, as he was only five foot four. The second proved to also be a mistake, but they had not, as yet, got any further details on the Heathrow Express sighting. However, the airport security guards were waiting.

Phil was red-eyed from tiredness. Anna offered to stay on, but he said he would keep going and suggested that she went home, so at least one of them would be fresh for the next day.

As she walked through the station, Anna hesitated, passing the stairs that led down to the cells; she told herself to keep on walking out but something made her turn back and head down.

There were four old-fashioned holding cells; only two of which were occupied, one by a very drunk and morose teenager, the other by Damien Nolan.

The night-duty officer looked surprised to see her; he was sitting at his post, reading the evening paper.

'Everything okay?' Anna asked.

'Yeah, well, the drunk kid is a pain in the arse, cleaning up after him puking; he's made the place stink.'

'And Mr Nolan?'

'He was reading – I let him have a book from the ones we get left lying around. Seems a very nice bloke.'

'Has he eaten?'

'Yes, sausage and chips and a cup of tea.'

Anna looked at the closed cell door and then asked for it to be opened.

Damien was lying on the bunk bed reading, even though there was only a dim ceiling light on. He put the book aside and smiled. 'I would never have believed it – Barbara Cartland!'

Anna laughed, although she felt very uncomfortable, even more so when he stood up and put his hand out to shake hers. She told him to sit down. 'I went to see Honour this evening, to take the holdall with her clothes and washbag.'

'Thank you. Is she all right?'

'Yes, she's fine.'

'Do you think you could get me some writing paper and a pen? I'd like to get a letter to her.'

'Sorry – but your solicitor will be here first thing.'

He sat further back on the bunk bed, his long legs stretched out in front of him. He was wearing the same clothes she had last seen him in.

'Did she know where Alex had run off to?'

'No.'

'Well, I hope you find him. It's about time he paid for all the trouble he has caused.'

'Bit more than trouble,' she said, hovering at the door, wanting to go but wanting to say more.

'Thank you for coming to see me. I take it, I hope correctly, that you believe me about the money and passport.'

'Yes, I believe you.'

'Good.'

She changed the subject. 'Do you think your brother cares for the children?'

'I don't know,' he said, shaking his head, bemused.

'Maybe he never really cared for anyone,' she said quietly.

'He did, but circumstances were always hard for him. I know he loved Honour, as much as he could love anyone.'

'What about Julia?'

'Same applies – but neither woman could ever be more important than number one.'

Anna wondered if she should tell him that Fitzpatrick had visited Honour, but she decided against it. 'Good night.'

'I meant what I said to you at the farmhouse,' Damien told her. 'When this is all over, I'd really like to see you. Would you mind if I called you?'

She flushed and turned away from him. 'Good night,' she repeated, and left.

Anna felt uneasy as she walked to her car. She knew she should not have visited Damien, but she found him a very attractive man. It wasn't like her friendship with Pete, or even Langton; in fact, Langton had already become part of her past. This was something else: an unexplained emotion that she was not able to deal with, but it still sat inside her. She wanted to know him better, but realised it was not only unethical, but also unprofessional.

She drove home and, without any hitches with her garage door, without any food in her fridge, without really wanting to be at home alone, went to bed. It was just after four in the morning when she was woken by her phone ringing.

She was disorientated for a moment, as she had been so deeply asleep. It was Langton: they had a firm sighting of Alexander Fitzpatrick, following through on the Heathrow Express sighting. The security forces at the airport had been put on alert, monitoring everyone alighting from the trains. When he was not recognised, they were about to call it off, but had then spotted a man fitting his description caught on CCTV cameras, heading from the short-stay car park into the airport at Terminal 3. They had alerted all terminals to check for anyone using the name Damien Nolan; as yet, he had not been traced, but could have already got a ticket via an online booking, so they were upping the security checks made at the various gates.

By the time Anna joined Langton at Heathrow, three hours had passed. He was depressed and annoyed that they still did not have him. Anna asked to see the CCTV footage; although it was not in good condition, and very fuzzy, she agreed that the man seen heading from the car park amongst a group of backpackers was Fitzpatrick. Two of the backpackers had been tracked down and, when shown the photograph, said that the man could have been him – but were not 100 per cent sure.

It was frustrating, and not helped by Langton's irritation. 'He's in the fucking airport!' he kept on muttering.

Anna, along with two security guards, sat in the office,

surveying the screens covering all the terminals, the baggage claim and the entry gates to the flights. There were so many passengers milling around, and they still had no verification as to which flight he could be taking. All they could do was wait as the checks continued.

'He's bloody hard to miss, at six feet four. It doesn't make sense; if he was coming here to get on a flight, he has to have a ticket or they won't let him through the barrier.'

Anna accepted some coffee, still watching the CCTV footage, and then she exclaimed, 'There he is – camera four! He's by the escalator. It's him!'

Langton leaned forwards, as the security guards used radio contact to warn the officers on the floor.

'He's heading down the escalator,' she said, standing up.

'Where does it go?' snapped Langton.

'Out to the tube station, and level one; he could also take the lift down to the car park.'

'Let's go!'

By the time they reached the escalator there were uniformed officers and airport security everywhere; they had already checked the floor below, but had no luck. They were now spreading out back inside the car park at levels one and two; they were even heading back up the escalator, in case he had turned around.

Langton was getting into a real temper. Fitzpatrick could, he said, have bought a ticket online at any one of the booths. Anna disagreed: he would have to have a credit card in the name of the passport-holder, Damien Nolan – he would not be allowed on the plane with different names on his passport and ticket.

'Of course he could! If I wanted to buy a ticket for you, I could pay on my credit card or in cash and give your name as the passenger.'

'Then the computers will give us the details. If he's on any flight leaving, they'll pick him up.'

But they had no verification of any passenger using a passport in the name of Damien Nolan. By the time they had hurried from one end of the airport to the other, used the escalators, and even checked out the short-stay car park, the pair of them were not only exhausted, but beginning to think they had lost him. Anna had even listed the entire catalogue of aliases known to have been used by Fitzpatrick, but they had not come up on any computer.

They eventually made their way back to the security section, and stood in the darkened room, glancing from one screen to another.

'You're sure it was him?' Langton said quietly.

'Well, I can't be one hundred per cent sure. It looked like him – the right height; draped coat . . .'

'Christ, you're now saying you're not sure?'

'Yes! All I said was I *thought* it was him – but why would he be going down the escalator, back to his car?'

Anna moved away from Langton and asked for one of the officers to replay the section again. She waited for him to get the right tape and scroll it through. It had now been over an hour, and no result.

'Stop there – back a fraction.' She watched the man she had said was Fitzpatrick; her heart was beating rapidly as she stared at the screen. Slowly walking into frame, but with his back to camera was the man: he carried one small holdall and, under his left arm, what looked like a folder. 'Freeze it there.'

Anna leaned closer, asking if they could enlarge the section with the folder. It seemed to take forever, but it was only a few seconds, as gradually the area she wanted to see was magnified. His arm mostly covered the folder.

'Can you make out anything?'

The officer stared at the screen; both he and Anna had their heads bent sideways to try and read the few words visible.

'It's a navigation file. I can see the logo: air traffic control,' the officer said.

Anna, trying to keep her voice steady, asked if the private sector had an office within the terminal.

'They have to get permission from this terminal if they are using a private plane, but that airstrip is on the other side of the main runways. We can contact them to halt any plane leaving.'

Anna told him to get onto it straight away, and grabbed Langton's arm. 'He's heading for the private airstrip. He'd need a car to drive there.'

Within seconds, they had confirmation that an Anthony Collingwood had been given permission to fly out from the airstrip where the private planes were housed in hangars. They were driven in one of the airport's passenger cars, used for transporting the elderly or disabled to the gates. It was frustrating that it could only go at five miles per hour, but they had a blue light flashing to clear their way to the main exit.

The patrol car was already in position and, with sirens blasting, they headed out to the private sector. They could see in the distance the small planes lined up; one was already taxiing down the airstrip, as the fuel tanker moved away.

Langton was beside himself, shouting at the driver to

go faster, but they had to manoeuvre around the lines of traffic pulling up to drop passengers off at departures and arrivals. Anna hung on in the back seat as the patrol car swerved and, with tyres screeching, drove out of the main exit gates from Terminal 3. They made up some time by using a road blocked off for repairs and smacked through a barrier to get onto the slip road leading to the hangars.

Langton was using the radio microphone to instruct the air traffic controllers to halt the plane that they could see moving slowly down the airstrip, and turning into position, ready to head onto the runway. The sound was very distorted by the roar of overhead flights and their car siren. Langton was shouting instructions, asking if they had information on the plane and pilot. He was so stressed out, Anna thought he would have a heart attack. It was reported back that there was no passenger fitting the description.

'He's fucking flying the thing himself! Did anyone, anyone, get information that the bastard had a pilot's licence? Jesus wept!'

By the time they entered the airfield, there were numerous security officials running round like headless chickens but they could only watch helplessly as the plane continued to taxi towards the runway, ready for take-off. Anna was trying to listen to an official on her mobile, but again it was hardly audible.

'Keep driving – get onto the airfield!' Langton instructed and the driver, with his accelerator foot pressed to the floor, sirens screaming, chased the twin-engine Piper plane.

The patrol car was catching up as the plane completed its curved journey onto the straight airstrip ready for take-off.

'Keep going! Try and cut across him!' Langton shouted. He still had the car radio and it crackled as the distorted voice fed details of the flight's destination: Spain.

Anna couldn't make out what they were saying to her, and kept on asking them to speak up, but they now had the plane literally within a hundred yards ahead of them and they could hear the engines revving up. Langton again said to drive across the nose of the plane to force it to stop, when Anna eventually heard what they were telling her from the control tower: there were two young children on board.

'No, no! Don't cut across the plane, he's got the children on board!'

They were so close they could see the small faces at the window. Their patrol car driver slammed on the brakes; Langton shouted for him to keep going. Anna screamed that it was too much of a risk and instructed the driver to stop the car. He did so with a hideous protest from the brakes. Then it was all over: the plane roared down the runway and lifted off.

They sat in stunned silence, apart from the sound of the disappearing plane, and the security trucks screeching up behind them. It was too late.

Anna watched Langton get out and stand, staring upwards to the plane, his coat flapping in the tail wind. He shaded his eyes, still staring skyward as the sun broke through clouds and bathed them in the early morning glow. When he eventually turned back to their patrol car, his face was white and his jaw set in a rigid line. He got back into the car, slamming the door hard.

Anna swallowed, her nerves ragged, and she was shaking as Langton, in an icy-cold voice, gave the driver instructions to head to the safe house where Emily and Kathy had been staying. He radioed for back-up to be there waiting for them.

They found the female liaison officer, thankfully alive, but bound with torn sheets. The uniformed officer was shut inside a cupboard; he had a deep bruise to his cheek and a bleeding cut over his temple. Fitzpatrick had done it again; he had shown a fake ID to the duty officer, who had allowed him entry to the house. The family liaison officer had been in bed in the room next to the two children. Mai Ling had given the game away. As she had been woken by Kathy crying, on seeing Fitzpatrick she had started to scream. Fitzpatrick had slapped her into silence, and then grabbed the liaison officer. Mai Ling had been forced to help him tie her up. When the uniformed officer walked in, as he had heard the screaming, he was hit over the head by Fitzpatrick. Although he tried to fend him off, Fitzpatrick had punched him in the face and dragged him into the cupboard. It had taken only fifteen minutes.

Mai Ling had run – whether or not he had given her money, no one knew – but he had calmly packed the children's toys and clothes and walked out. He was using a hire car, and had driven to the airport. He had not, as they had suspected, used the Heathrow Express. The sighting there was a mistake.

The family liaison officer was very distressed; she kept on repeating that it wasn't her fault. Anna tried to comfort her, but Langton was bitterly angry and almost abusive. They waited for back-up to take over and get their statements of the abduction.

Driving back to the station, it was by now ten o'clock

in the morning. Langton remained so angry he was unapproachable. Although they had confirmation of the route and destination of Fitzpatrick's plane, they knew it would be difficult to get him picked up, as they doubted he would stick to landing in Spain. They did, however, contact the Spanish authorities, with orders to arrest the pilot and retain the children. They had no confirmation that the plane had landed.

The incident room was full of the entire team. They were quiet, aware of the morning's débâcle. Langton gave them a curt briefing about what had taken place. He said he was still hopeful they would get details of where Fitzpatrick was landing. He also said that it was a very wretched situation that no one had discovered that, not only did Fitzpatrick own a private plane, but was also a qualified pilot: in other words, the man had covered all possibilities, from the boat to the plane, for yet another escape. They would all look like incompetent, unprofessional idiots. Langton looked directly at Anna when he said it, and she flushed.

As the team prepared to continue packing up the case ready for the trials, Langton, with Phil, reinterviewed Damien Nolan. The latter was released from custody without any charges. Anna did not see him, as she was writing up the report from the airport.

Gordon tapped on her door, and peered in.

'We're not going to get much information from all this money,' he said. 'It may have come from Julia, but without Rushton, it's impossible to trace its source. The Fraud Squad have taken over investigating it so it's out of our hands.'

Anna made no reply. She nodded her head, eager for him to leave.

'Did you see him?'

She looked up.

'Fitzpatrick,' Gordon prompted.

'For a brief second, yes.'

'What was he like?'

'I don't know, Gordon. I never spoke to him.'

He nodded and then grinned, saying, 'I'd have liked to have seen him. He's something else, isn't he? I mean, I know there's a slew of dead bodies down to him, but at the same time you can't help admiring his bottle.'

'Maybe, but I have no admiration for a man whose sole intent was releasing millions of pounds' worth of lethal drugs to live in luxury . . .'

'I know that, and I didn't mean I admired what he was doing, but you have to admit he was bloody audacious.'

'Yes, Gordon, he was. Now, will you excuse me?'

'Oh, right . . . yes. I've really enjoyed working with you, Anna. I've learned a lot from you, and I hope we work on another case together.'

She gave a brittle smile. 'Yes, Gordon. Thank you.'

He closed the door.

She physically jumped with nerves when Langton walked into her office a few seconds later.

He stared at her. 'We could have stopped the plane,' he said quietly.

'But the risk, and with two children on board . . .'

'If he went to that much trouble to take them, he wouldn't have endangered their lives. It's another side to him, Travis; he wanted his kids, and he took them, and we had to bloody watch him go!'

'I'm sorry. I didn't know if you'd seen their faces at the window.'

'Yes, I fucking saw them!' he snapped.

Anna didn't know what to say. She sat with her head bowed.

'I've warned you, Anna. You are already on report; now I'm going to really make you sit up and learn a lesson. I am going to have you back doing traffic.'

'I never did traffic.'

'Then it's about time you did! You are unprofessional and headstrong; you have to buckle down or give in your notice.'

She wanted to cry, but she refused to allow herself to show even an indication to him of what she felt.

'You got anything to say?'

'No. I believe I acted with caution.'

'You overrode my instructions and gave the driver orders to stop the patrol car. You have constantly disobeyed instructions and worked solo throughout this investigation. This is not something I am treating lightly – for the simple reason I believe you do have a future, and you are an exceptionally intuitive and clever officer – but policing is working with a team, and you need to understand that, because this is not the first time since I have worked with you that you have trodden a very dangerous line.'

'Yes, sir.'

'That's all.' He stood looking at her for a brief moment, and then walked out. He didn't slam the door this time, but closed it softly.

She couldn't control herself. Her face puckered like a child's and she wept.

Anna would not be joining the team for a drink; she couldn't. Instead, she packed up her office and handed in her report. She felt that everyone knew she was in trouble, as they gave her furtive looks.

Phil obviously knew, as he put his arm around her shoulders. It made her feel worse. 'Sorry if things look a bit bleak right now.'

'Yes, well, somebody had to take the flak for all the screw-ups; I guess it's me.'

'Come and have a drink.'

'No, thank you. I'm not in that great a mood.'

'Pete's coming.'

She said nothing, wanting to get out as fast as possible.

As she got to her Mini, Pete was just parking his Morgan. He called over to her. 'Hello, stranger! You coming for a wind-down drink?'

She shook her head, as she felt the tears welling up again. 'Nope, I'm heading home. I've been up since four this morning.'

He laughed and ruffled her hair. She always hated it when men did that and she turned her head away.

'Hey, come on, ease up. Have a drink, you'll feel better. Mind you, if I was in your shoes, I'd be wanting to tie a real load on.'

'What do you mean by that?' she said angrily.

'Well, I hear you lost him – flew over your heads!' Again he laughed.

She wished she could also find some humour in the whole mess, but she couldn't. She turned back to open the car door.

'Anna.' He moved close, putting his hand on her arm. 'You know he'll get copped some day. They may even get him wherever he lands so, come on – have a drink and then you and I can go back to my place.'

'No, Pete.'

'Come on, I know how you must feel.'

She looked into his friendly face, and stood on tiptoe to kiss his cheek. 'No, you don't. I think we should keep some space, maybe I'll call you some time.'

He stepped back, hurt. 'Some time? Well, that's a slap in the face. I've really tried with you, Anna, but forget some time. I'm losing patience, so don't bother calling me at all.'

He walked away. She knew she should have gone after him, but she didn't have the energy. The truth was, she didn't want to take their relationship any further. It was over, probably before it had really begun.

Anna felt really low when she walked into her still half-furnished flat. Her bed was as unmade as she had left it, and she sat on the edge, feeling depressed and scared. She knew Langton would go through with his threats, and she was unsure how she would be able to deal with it. She flopped back, closing her eyes. She wondered what her beloved father would think of it all, and that made her tearful again.

Then her old fighting spirit woke up, and she forced herself to get up, undress and take a shower. If Langton threw the book at her, she'd throw it back – she had more secret weapons than anyone else. She would defend her decision at the airport, because it was a risk to have attempted to stop the plane; not just a risk but a very dangerous one. They could all have been killed; she felt that her decision was the correct one.

The more she thought about how she would approach the situation, the better she felt. If it came down to it, she would bring up what she knew about Langton. If anyone's career should be in jeopardy, then it was his.

She was not going to take the flak for everyone else's fuck-ups, and there had been many in this case. In fact, *she* had instigated the connection from day one to Alexander Fitzpatrick. She began to feel more positive, knowing just how much of the case had been directed by her.

Showered, and wearing just a towel wrapped around her, she opened a bottle of wine. All the time her brain was working through exactly how she had joined the dots, how she had pieced the jigsaw together. She was not going down without a fight. She felt a whole lot better after two glasses; she also felt hungry, as she hadn't eaten all day. She really fancied a BLT but she had no bacon, no bread, no lettuce and no mayo; just thinking of it made her mouth water. Then her phone rang.

She hesitated to answer it. If it was Langton she wasn't ready to talk to him, and if it was Pete she didn't want to speak to him. She let it ring.

It clicked onto her answerphone.

'Hello, Anna, this is Damien. I suppose you know I was released today and I was hoping I'd get to speak to you.'

She sipped her wine, staring down at the answer-machine.

'I was just wondering . . . I didn't go back to the farm and . . . well, as you are not home, there's no point – but I just would have liked to have seen you.'

Anna knew she shouldn't, but she couldn't resist it. She picked up the phone. 'I am at home and I would like to see you, and also want to know how you got my home number.'

'Ah! Don't think of me as some crazed stalker, but an ex-student of mine lives in the same block of flats. James

Fullford drives a very expensive car, lives in flat two B, do you believe in coincidences?'

'Not really . . .'

She loved the sound of his voice and the way he gave a soft laugh when she asked if he could stop by a grocery store, as she wanted him to make her a BLT. He said he could take her out to dinner, but she said that was what she really fancied. She had about an hour in which to wash her hair, make up her face and get dressed. Damien Nolan was deeply involved in the investigation; he was also married to the woman who would be standing trial for assisting Alexander Fitzpatrick to store drugs, and who might even have helped his escape. But there had been something about Damien she had sensed from the first moment she had seen him. She was being both unethical and unprofessional, but it made her feel good.

Anna Travis was growing up. Whether or not she would learn from her mistakes, only time would tell. All she did know was, at long last, James Langton had no hold over her. On the contrary, they would, she knew, have to face each other out, and she intended to do that, but she also needed someone in her life. If it were to be Damien Nolan, she would take the risk; if it proved an unwise decision, then so be it.